SCREAM QUEEN

By Wray Cotterill

POWERHOUSE
PUBLISHING

wkcotterill@comcast.net

Cover and interior design by
Toby Cowan, Performance Design Group
Sebastopol, CA 95472

Cover images by Shutterstock

Print ISBN# 978-0-578-96947-3
eBook ISBN 978-0-578-96950-3

Table of Contents

Cast of Characters

Vera Horowitz .... Scream Queen
Jake L'Hommedieu .... Director
Rhonda Roundhouse .... Pro Women's Wrestler
Zissell Horowitz (Bubbe) .... Vera's Grandmother
(Zaydeh) Horowitz .... Vera's Grandfather
Naomi Nivens .... Aging Scream Queen
Serena Miles .... Aging Scream Queen
Shelley Arcongioli .... Gossipy Receptionist
Felix Short .... 1st Assistant Director
Andy Faull .... 2nd Assistant Director
Barry Whitscomb .... Owner Of Falchion Films
Alex Boxwell .... Barry Whitscomb's Nephew
Lola Grubb .... Ugliest Woman in the World
Brian .... Handsome Director of Lighting
Jacqueline L'Hommedieu .... Jake's Mother
Benny Edwards .... Cruel Acting Coach
Thelma Gladstone .... Therapist
Levi .... Good Cop
Ira .... Bad Cop
Aaron Finklestein .... Worst Cop
Dark Snout .... Rugged Super Spy
Helena Gutierrez .... Niece of Dr. Alvarez
Dr. Alvarez .... Tijuana Plastic Surgeon
Ken Adams .... Paramedic
H.P.S. .... High-Fidelity Human-Patient Simulator
Otto .... Surfer
Sammy .... Surfer
Pete .... Surfer, Bartender
Scott Brinker .... Head Paramedic

Chapter 1
Scream Queen

It was a hot and sunny day in West L.A. as Vera Horowitz ran from the restaurant in tears.

"Get out!" the owner yelled after her, "You're the worst waitress ever!"

Curious pedestrians made room on the sidewalk as the distressed young woman, with short black hair, tried to find her footing. Jake L'Hommedieu, clad in a retro pinstriped suit, found himself at the front of the crowd. He stepped back as Vera's slender frame bumped him, graceful even as she stumbled backwards into traffic. Startled by bright lights and the hyper-real image of a tractor-trailer upon her, Vera faced the rush of death, fingers splayed. She locked her neck and shrieked with all she had.

The three second blast of the semi's air horn ended—but Vera's scream continued. It was beautiful and bursting with primal outrage at her life's ending at just twenty-three. The scream split the air—floating to a higher octave. Pedestrians covered their ears, and stared—all neck and arm hairs bristled to rigid attention. The tires that skidded and stopped the truck's bumper inches from Vera's legs were an afterthought. That primordial scream was the show. Vera collapsed on the hot, dirty pavement and tried to catch her breath.

Is this my last image, she thought, *trash blowing down a hot street?*

She sat up and thumbed the dust off her wristwatch—the cute little female mouse face smiled up at her, its pink-gloved hands pointed to 12:15.

"Oh, Mandy," Vera said, "We're alive!" Vera said to the cartoon mouse face in her watch.

The crowd stared for a few seconds then moved on—it was lunchtime in L.A.

Jake L'Hommedieu rushed into the street, knelt down and clasped Vera's delicate hand.

"Are you alright?" he asked.

"I think so," Vera said, trembling uncontrollably. He put his arm around her and helped her to the sidewalk.

"Do you need an ambulance? Or could I call someone for you?"

"No thank you," Vera said as she squeezed the bridge of her nose.

"Would you be interested in auditioning for a movie? I think you're just what we need," Jake said, and handed her his business card.

"A movie?" Vera said, and glanced at the card.

"Be there tomorrow morning, eight o'clock sharp," Jake said and walked away.

~

Vera spent the next few hours decompressing in a coffee shop. She ordered a cup of chamomile tea and sipped the steaming drink as she gazed out the window from her booth.

No, she wasn't the best waitress, and yes, she'd messed up people's orders before, but lately she'd been doing really well: carrying three plates at once. She'd set down two plates but as she set down the third, the bank president, Mr. Cohen, had patted her butt. Vera had jerked and spilled hot matzo ball soup in his lap then spilled water on another guest. She'd been fired, almost crushed by a truck, and then offered a possible movie role.

Vera wished her mother and father hadn't died in a car crash when she was four because she needed serious comforting now. And she didn't dare tell her grandmother, *her Bubbe*[1], about this. Now, whenever things got too intense Vera went to the comfort of the sweet little entity within her wristwatch—a gift from her late grandfather.

A neighbor girl's wealthy uncle had taken her to Mandy Land, theme park, where Mandy Mouse supposedly lived, and the girl couldn't stop talking about it. Vera had wanted to go so badly but Grandpa, who made his living as a shoemaker—the only skill he knew from Germany—couldn't afford to take her. So instead, he bought her the female mouse watch—cute, innocent, Vera's solace now that he had passed

She missed Grandpa, her *Zaydeh*[2], her towering inspiration of bravery, truth, toughness. He'd shown her the numbered tattoo on his left forearm; told her of the inhumane treatment he and the other prisoners had endured, the double rings of electrified barbed wire, twelve-hour workdays in the gravel pits; and then, their incredible escape. He'd been one of only 144 to escape from Auschwitz alive. Vera thought of the advice he'd given her, she could still hear his warm voice, the deep Russian/Jewish accent, as he carefully chose his words.

"Terrible men will try to take your spirit. Vera, in your life you *never* become victim."

Zaydeh and Bubbe had never improved their English because they'd never felt the need. Much older than other parents in the neighborhood, surrounded by a culture they knew and trusted, Yiddish was mostly what Zaydeh spoke. Bubbe's English had gotten better since Zaydeh had passed, but Vera's world seemed so small, filled with Jewish traditions and fears Bubbe learned from Zaydeh. With her mother, father and now Zaydeh all passed, Bubbe raised Vera as her daughter. Vera loved Bubbe, but sometimes felt like she couldn't breathe.

Vera laid a fifty-cent tip on the table. She stepped out onto the sidewalk, into the sea of people, and walked the seven blocks to the bus stop. She quickened her pace as the city bus approached. Air brakes hissed as the crowd boarded. It was a slow walk to the front of the line, so Vera studied a flier stapled to a telephone pole. "Semi-Pro Women's Wrestling: Rhonda Roundhouse vs. Raggedy Ann in a woman-on-woman cage fight!" Two determined-looking women's faces stared at her from the ad.

---

1 Bubbe is a Jewish term of endearment for grandmother.
2 Zaydeh is a Jewish term of endearment for grandfather.

Vera wandered down the aisle passed a huge woman in gray sweats whose face looked familiar. She found a seat at the back, just as the bus lurched into motion, wafting the stench of perspiration. She realized she had a dried blob of gum on the bottom of one black patent leather Audrey Hepburn shoe. *The world can be so icky!*

Now that she had lost her job there was nothing to do but return to Bubbe's house. She thought how she should be out on her own by now, on a career track. College would have helped—too expensive. Vera checked her Mandy Mouse watch: 4:30 PM. She considered people's comments that the watch was juvenile for a woman of 23, but Mandy was cute and spunky, she had fashion sense and knew how to work it. With her petite size, black shiny hair and pale skin, Vera identified with the mousy diva. Vera got off at her stop and walked toward her grandmother's home two blocks away.

~

Rhonda Roundhouse watched the petite woman with the shiny black hair leave the bus stop. *What a pretty little thing she is.*

Rhonda reflected on what a long road it had been from her father's farm in Fort Scott, Kansas, to the Women's Wrestling Arena in Los Angeles. She'd been ten years old when she saw the look of disapproval on Daddy's face: the hogs weren't going into their pen—always because *one of them* led the others the wrong way. Despite Daddy's shouts of warning Rhonda had leaped into the mud with the huge animals and wrestled the bad hog into submission. She'd dragged it into the right pen and the other hogs, wanting no part of Rhonda's rough housing, had followed. She had never gotten badly hurt so Daddy stopped complaining.

At 16 Rhonda became a robust farm hand and took to wrestling bigger hogs, much to Daddy's and his friends' amusement. At 17 she'd told Daddy she wanted to move to Los Angeles to become a professional women's wrestler. Daddy's brow creased.

"Rhonda, those people aren't decent folks like us. I don't know how to tell you this, sugar, but some of them don't believe in the *Lord.* You'll get hurt if you go."

Her eyes had welled up. She couldn't imagine anyone could believe that, what with all the beauty in the world. After a couple of days, she'd brought up the subject at breakfast.

"Daddy, I want to go anyway. Nobody's going to sway me from what I know to be true. I'm a good hog wrestler and I reckon I can wrestle women just as well." So, Rhonda Franklin had waved goodbye to her family from the back of a Greyhound bus. She tried to summon strength from the stage name she had created: Rhonda Roundhouse, but she was scared.

They *had* hurt her: the big girl from New York City broke Rhonda's leg, another fractured her wrist. She'd had many injuries, but she'd healed and come back for more. Those women cheated, drank alcohol, took drugs, and did other things for money she couldn't believe. But Rhonda was a quick learner and soon she'd dish out some broken bones of her own.

~

Vera used her key, got inside, walked down the hall and into her room, a shrine to everything Mandy: Mandy Mouse poster, figurines of her in a red and black dress, a matching flower on her head, Mandy Mouse alarm clock and pink satin pillows with Mandy's likeness on them. Vera collapsed on her bed and pulled into the fetal position just as her grandmother, Zissell, entered.

"What, you don't say hello no more when you come home?" Zissell asked.

"Hi, Bubbe. Sorry, I'm tired."

"How was work? Did you make some goot tips?"

"I, I did alright. I'm going to go to sleep early tonight."

"You come and have dinner wit' me, do dishes, *den* you sleep."

After dinner, Vera showered and got into her satiny Mandy Mouse pajamas, kissed her grandmother on the cheek and went to bed and pulled the sheet into a little tent-shape over her ear. Zissell walked in and gazed as her daughter's toes curled up inside her pink Mandy Mouse socks.

"My silly Mouse girl. Why she puts the sheet like that?" Zissell whispered, but she felt only love as she watched her daughter's flawless complexion against black hair—her long eyelashes peacefully closed.

~

The next day Vera Googled the address on the business card. She knew Bubbe would watch from the window, so she walked toward the bus station. Once she turned the corner, Vera called a taxi from her cell. The cab arrived. The driver knew the address on Hollywood Boulevard and dropped her off ten minutes before her appointment. She glanced up at the gothic letters arching twenty feet above her head: *Falchion Films, Inc.*

Vera entered B studio and showed the receptionist Mr. L'Hommedieu's card.

"You want to see Felix," the pale-complected receptionist said. "The first assistant director."

Vera wandered countless corridors and peered into dusty doorway sets but saw no one. Finally, she saw two scantily clad women, one a flowing-haired brunette, the other a curvaceous, short-cropped red-head; both beautiful. Vera asked about Felix. An overhead intercom blasted, "Shelley you're wanted in makeup."

"There he goes now, honey," the redhead said, and pointed to a very thin blonde-haired man in skinny jeans and a purple European-cut shirt, briskly walking away. Vera caught up to him as he turned the corner.

"Excuse me, I'm Vera Horowitz, I'm here for an audition with Mr. L'Hommedieu." Vera produced Jake's card.

Felix turned on Vera with the sharp features and quick movements of a hawk and snatched the card from her. He examined it and checked his watch.

"You're the new girl? Hurry!" Felix opened an exit door, pressed Vera through and out into the sunlight. They walked a few feet and Felix again put his hand in the small of Vera's back and pressed her up two steps and through the open makeup trailer doorway.

"Mr. L'Hommedieu will be ready to see you at 8:45," Felix said. "Here, brush up on your lines. Your character's name is 'Lonnie.' Start on page four, and don't give the makeup girl any trouble." Felix shoved a script at Vera and pulled the trailer door closed behind him.

"Hi, I'm Shelley," said the pale-skinned stylist, who draped a plastic smock over Vera's clothes.

"But aren't you the receptionist I spoke with earlier? You were just—"

"Sure, I wear a lot of hats around here. Sit down, hon. Mr. Whitscomb wants the scream queens looking like fresh-scrubbed lab techs. You know, preoccupied with intellectual stuff and naively vulnerable. If the zombies didn't get you there wouldn't be a movie, right?"

"Zombies? I didn't know this was a horror movie."

"Jake must have seen something in you. There are dozens of actresses who would die to get an interview with Jake L'Hommedieu, much less a chance to meet the great Barry Whitscomb."

"Who is Barry Whitscomb?"

"He's *only* the most legendary director in B-horror movie history. Oh, and that *gorgeous* head of hair! He's retired from directing; he's a producer now but he still oversees the pictures. Jake's his protégé."

"Thanks for filling me in," Vera said. "I'd better study my lines."

~

Jake L'Hommedieu spoke with Barry Whitscomb, who sat behind his desk.

"Barry, we've made plenty of B-horrors together. Like I told you, I'm ready to make a romantic drama film, a rom-dram, and I want you to help me."

"You're never going to make dramatic films," Barry said. "Remember when you came to me? You pleaded for a chance to work with me, said you'd wanted to make B-horror movies since you were sixteen, how it was in your blood? You sold me, kid. You're still that nineteen–year-old who thinks with his id. That's all you're ever going to be. Like Dirty Harry says, 'A man's gotta know his limitations.' But look at you, working with the great Barry Whitscomb!"

"But, Dude, I've polished this script for five years now. It's ready. I just need the right female lead—"

"Uh, uh, uh—still talkin' drama?" Barry said and held up his index finger. "You just lost your 'dude' privileges. But I will let you do something I never let anybody do. Come here."

When Jake hesitated Barry beckoned with his beefy hands."I know you're looking at my hair. It's beautiful ain't it? I know you want to grab a big handful of it. Well go on, grab two hands full of it and give it a tug, kiddo,"

"Really? I mean your hair is legendary."

"Go on, this head of hair's like magic."

Jake grabbed a handful of Barry's hair.

"I said grab it, punk! Both hands and shake it! Give it a good tug! Really shake it around, boy!"

Jake reached over the desk, grabbed Barry's hair, and shook his head back and forth, side to side just as Felix opened the door.

"Excuse me, Barry, I—"

"Yes, Felix?" Barry said, looking out between thick strands of auburn hair.

"Oh, I didn't mean to interrupt anything—"

"Nonsense. What is it?"

"Well, the new girl, Vera Horowitz, is here. She's ready in make-up."

~

Felix grabbed Vera's wrist and dragged her to center stage. Bright lights and camera people, key-grips, gaffers, and various stagehands were visible through the glare of dusty air.

"Okay, Ms. Horowitz, Mr. L'Hommedieu and Mr. Whitscomb are ready to hear your reading," Felix said, who abandoned Vera onstage.

"Where do I begin? Vera asked. "With Lonnie's first appearance in the film?"

Felix, very annoyed, strutted back to center stage and snatched the script from Vera.

"Lonnie's lines, starting at the top of the page I *gave* you. I'll paint you a picture. You're a lab tech; you and the others at this facility have corralled a bunch of blood-thirsty zombies. They're chained against a wall. You recognize one of them as your best girlfriend, Sarah, from your old 'hood. You're trying to get through to her; you just *know* if you get her to remember you it will be safe to unchain her. A-a-annd, go!" Felix said and left the stage.

A homely, bored-looking actress with mussed up hair, reeking of cigarette smoke, strode over and stood next to Vera. Brian, a gaffer, leaned out from behind the key light and stared at the girl next to Vera.

"Lola, you are *so* ugly—I love you," Brian said.

"Shut up, Freak," Lola answered.

"Hi, I'm Vera," Vera said quietly, extending her hand to the girl.

"Lola. Now *focus!*" the girl hissed.

Vera dropped her hand and read from her script. "Sarah, I know you remember me," Vera said, holding the script in one hand, attempting an imploring gesture to the girl next to her, then lost her place and paused awkwardly. "I want to let you go. Remember when we loaned each other our clothes? Remember when we went to prom together with our dates?"

The actress fought against invisible chains and gnashed her teeth at Vera.

Barry leaned over and whispered to Jake in his director's chair, "Pretty bad."

"I trust you, Sarah," Vera continued. "I know you would never hurt me. I'm going to set you free. You're my best friend," Vera screwed up her face and looked into the lights. "Excuse me, but do you think anybody would talk like this? I mean,

I'm sorry, but I don't think anybody would really be this stupid."

Hushed murmurs echoed from the set. Jake L'Hommedieu silently chuckled from his seat, delighted by the girl.

"Young lady, do you know why you're here?" Barry said. "It's not for your directorial input. It's because Mr. L'Hommedieu thinks you have a good scream. So unlock the damned zombie and let's hear it!"

Vera simulated unlocking the chains. The zombie girl immediately tackled her and pretended to claw and tear at Vera's stomach. From her back Vera struggled to keep the aggressive girl at bay. She looked into the spotlights, pretended they were the semi's headlights from the day before, and let go with another terrific scream. It was high-pitched and clear. It elevated to a higher octave and sent shivers throughout the on-set staff.

"My god, she's good," Barry said. "Hire her quickly and get her an acting coach."

~

Felix grabbed Vera by the arm and led her to Jake and Barry.

"Hey!" Vera said, yanking her thin arm free.

"We'd like to hire you, Ms. Horowitz," Jake said. "There are two more pivotal scenes we need to go over. Here, practice page eight. It's the love scene just before you get devoured." Vera rehearsed her lines and took the stage again. This time a tall, broad-shouldered blonde guy with a broken nose joined her.

"Vera, Alex. Alex, Vera. A-a-annd go," Felix said.

"Tony, I don't know what to do," Vera said, "That female zombie is Sarah — we can't kill her."

"It's okay, babe," Alex replied. "That's not Sarah anymore. None of them are people anymore. Say goodbye and I'll put them down."

"She's my friend, Tony."

"It's for the best. I just don't want them to hurt anybody."

"I love you, Tony. Just give me a few minutes alone with Sarah, okay?" Vera consulted the script and looked uncomfortable.

"The kiss!" Barry yelled through his bullhorn.

Vera leaned over and gave Alex a quick kiss and looked back at the script.

"Okay, that's it everybody," Barry said. "Meet back here in an hour. Vera and Alex, I need a word."

The staff left the set. Vera, Alex and Barry stood in a little circle as Jake collected his papers and eavesdropped. Jake stole an admiring glance at Vera, then quickly looked away. *She's amazing*, he thought.

"Yes, Mr. Whitscomb?" Vera said, standing next to Alex.

"I've been a director and producer in this business for forty-five years," Barry said. "I like you, kid; you've got a great scream. But your chemistry with Alex isn't coming through. You'll make $16,000.00 on this picture, but we've got to get that kiss right. Might I suggest, since time is short, that you two sleep together tonight?"

Vera's mouth dropped open.

"I'm open to it, "Alex said, "I mean if you think it would help the scene."

"What? Whom I sleep is none of your business!" Vera said. She marched to the makeup trailer and slammed the door behind her.

Jake looked at Barry with disgust and followed Vera. He knocked on the trailer door. Vera yanked the door open and glared at Jake.

"What do *you* want?" she asked.

"I just wanted to say I'm sorry for Mr. Whitscomb's behavior. I was wondering if I could buy you a cup of coffee."

"What? Now *you're* hitting on me? You're a creep just like him."

"No. This is a sleazy business, and it must seem like a lot for your first day in movies, but you should be happy—you've got a real gift."

"I don't drink coffee. It makes me nervous," Vera said and closed the door.

In the stillness of the trailer, Barry's words echoed in her head "sleep together tonight." An outrageous thing to say in its own right, but it was her personal business that she was still a virgin at 23.

~

Following rehearsal, Felix and his beau, Andy, walked Vera back to her trailer. Felix and Andy lurked in the hallway, awaiting Jake's return from the cafeteria. Jake rounded the corner.

"That was *some* impassioned soirée you and Barry were engaged in," Felix said to Jake. "I wish Andy and I could make those kinds of sparks together."

"Yeah, I heard you touched his magnificent quaff!" Andy added. "I wish I had the chance. So, when's the wedding?"

"Will you knock it off, you two? I'm straight, okay?"

"Please, Barry's quite a catch" Felix said. "You must be gay; why else would he let you yank his head around like that?"

Jake became flustered and almost spilled his coffee.

"I'm not gay! I'm in love with Vera Horowitz!" he blurted out.

"We didn't think you were gay," Andy said, "We were just messing with you. But what was that *other* thing you said? You're in love with Vera? Oh, she doesn't like you at all."

~

That night Vera went home to her grandmother's house.

"Bubbe, you're never going to believe it—I'm going to be in a Hollywood movie! I'm going to make sixteen thousand dollars!"

"What? How you know dese people?" Zissell Horowitz asked.

"I was almost flattened by a truck yesterday and a man gave me his business card. He said I had a nice scream. He's a big deal in movies because everybody says how lucky I am."

"You was almost hit by a truck? Why don't you tell me? American movies is schwartz yor! You have 'nice scream'? What kind of chazzer makes such talk to decent young lady?"

Vera had learned several of Zissell's favorite Yiddish phrases from their conversations.

"I didn't want you to worry, Bubbe. American movies are *not* bad luck, and he's *not* a pig, he's an okay man, I guess. Besides, I didn't want to tell you I got fired from the restaurant."

"Oy vey! Now two things you don't tell me! I'm so ashamed. What will I tell your aunt? That was big favor you know."

"It was never going to work out. Besides, <u>Zombie Betrayal</u> is just the start for me. Mr. Whitscomb says he's got another movie he wants to put me in."

"Vera, you are young girl. You can only trust family. You need goot job so people see how hard you work; how else you meet goot man to take care of you?"

"I'm a grown woman, Bubbe; I don't *need* a man to take care of me."

"You quit 'dis nonsense! That nice Aaron Finklestein says he eats at restaurant, but you don't talk to him. Policeman is good, steady job. You go out wit' him."

"Why him? Why now? He's not my type, Bubbe."

"Oh, now you have a 'type.' *You*, who never has no boyfriend, so choosy!"

"That's because you never let me date anyone before! Leave me alone about it. I have a *real* job now."

"Listen to *family*, Vera. I come to work. *I* say if you go on with dis business."

"Bubbe, please don't do that. You'll ruin everything for me."

Chapter 2
Close Up

It was quiet at the restaurant as Aaron Finklestein entered in his police officer's uniform. He was looking for Vera Horowitz, the girl he had admired from a distance since elementary school. Another waitress tried to interest him in a table, but he'd waved her off—he would wait for Vera to seat him. He'd made that mistake before and ended up in another waitress's station—and *then* Vera would appear from the kitchen. She was so shy, but she was so hot!

Finally, Aaron got the attention of the owner.

"Is Vera Horowitz working today?"

"No. She doesn't work here anymore," the woman said.

"Where is she?"

"I have no idea. But may I interest you in a nice seat by the window?"

"No—no, thanks," Aaron said, looking angry. He stalked through the doorway, roughly shouldering a male customer on the way out.

~

"Barry!" Jake said, and stalked in the rotund man's direction. "We need to talk in your office." Barry was startled but then remembered two things: First, he *liked* being scared. And second, there was no reason to be scared because it was only Jake L'Hommedieu.

"Ooh, what's this about?" Barry asked. "You finally grow a set, think you're gonna' show me what's what?"

"Inside!" Jake said, and grabbed the larger, heavier man by the back of his brown pin-striped suit and pressed him through his office doorway.

"This is getting interesting," Barry said. "What's on your mind, sport?"

"Sit down, Barry."

"Don't mind if I do," Barry said and slumped into his wooden rocker.

"That lewd suggestion for Vera and Alex to sleep together to improve their chemistry, which there was *none of* by the way, was totally out of line. I had half a mind to tell Ms. Horowitz that Alex is your nephew, but I think we may still convince her that this business isn't a total cesspool."

"What's wrong with you, kid? You grow a conscience or somethin'? You trying to wreck yourself? I know you hate women as much as I do. God knows you've hacked up and mangled enough of them in your movies."

"I don't hate women! Portraying killing women on film symbolizes what society holds as precious—and how horrible it would be to destroy something so vulnerable and beautiful. Changing up *the thing* that kills them makes our films social statements."

"Yeah, right. You hate 'em just like me. Oh, I don't blame you, they get everything good; they get to walk around showin' off their bare skin, bat their eyelashes at ya', make you think you have a chance then dump you on your head on the concrete. Play their cards right, if they're pretty enough, they can get some sugar daddy to set 'em up real fancy—don't ever have to work. They live longer than us, get us to open doors for them, take 'em out to dinner—everything. So, I say, full steam ahead, slaughter 'em on film. Can't do it for real unless you want to end up behind bars."

"Barry, I don't hate women. This is art to me. I just don't know if I can go on making B-horrors any longer. Like I said earlier, I have this romantic drama I want to launch—"

"You shut your mouth about that thing. You're onto something good with this Vera chick. She's not your typical scream queen, is she? Right now, I have two barbies out in my trailer: big hair, big eyes, tiny noses, big racks, long legs and they can scream pretty good too."

"So why don't we cast one of them in the lead?"

"Because I don't care if they get slaughtered on screen. There's something about that Vera, like you said, vulnerable and beautiful once she talks, something human you don't want to see die. Then there's her scream. First time I heard it, it went right through me—shot up to the top of my skull and rifled right down to my toes. You know where it settled, kid? Right in my heart and I bet you thought I didn't have one. It was like listenin' to an animal in distress. That's why we've got to kill her in some horrible way on screen—that face, that scream, like somebody's daughter dyin', that'll put butts in theatre seats."

"I agree with you that she's got something special. I think she can really act, Barry, if we give her the chance and some good lines. There was a moment—that expression she made—"

"You damn well better stick with our two-movie contract, kid, or you ain't ever, ever gonna' work in L.A. again. Got me? You make horror movies. You show women get slaughtered on screen for all the frustrated boys and men out there to enjoy. You hate 'em, you know it, so don't pretend to get noble on me, 'cause I'll mess you over, boy.

~

Rhonda Roundhouse had just won her third semi-pro women's wresting match. Her temple still ached from the elbow "Raggedy Ann" had thrown at her when Rhonda had her pinned and Raggedy knew she had no way out. The roar of the crowd still echoed in her head: "Rhonda! Rhonda!" She sat in her dressing room on the rubdown table and stared at the gray cinderblock wall, her heart still beating hard from the match. As she waited for her coach, she savored the memory of the man she'd met last month:

She'd been recovering from a fractured shin while hobbling on crutches and wrestling a bag of groceries at the same time when she became aware of a benevolent presence walking beside her. She didn't normally speak with strangers, but this man had such kind eyes and such a pleasant way about him.

"Pardon me, Miss, could I help you with those groceries?" he asked.

He was not as big as her, but he didn't seem intimidated by her size or musculature. Rhonda had been tired. She'd half-expected if she handed him her groceries, he would run off with them—but he hadn't. He took the bag and slowed down to keep pace with her, even stepping in front occasionally leading with his shoulder to run interference for her against sidewalk traffic.

"You seem like a really nice person. Are you from L.A.?" he asked.

"No, I'm from Fort Scott, Kansas. Are you from here?"

"Yes, but I don't like to admit it. Do you have anyone to cook and take care of you?"

Rhonda hardly cared what came next. If he tried to manhandle her or rob her, she felt she could handle him. *But he might really be a nice guy.* She'd never had a boyfriend and she had just turned 22.

"No, I live alone and I *don't* have any help."

"Well, it would be my honor to make you a home cooked meal. I happen to be a great cook and it will give us a chance to get acquainted. All you have to do is relax. Deal?"

"Alrighty. I'm going to trust you. Please don't try any funny stuff though because I'm a professional wrestler."

He actually looked offended."I am a gentleman, Miss. What is your name by the way?"

"Rhonda. What's yours?"

~

Rhonda's trainer suddenly walked into her dressing room, jolting her out of her daydream.

"Good news and bad news: Which do you want first?"

"Good news," Rhonda said.

"That was a terrific match. The crowd loves you and you're on track to become a household name."

"And the bad news?"

"Your money's not here. I don't know *when* you're getting paid. Charles says he hasn't gotten the check yet."

"Yeah, right. I'll bet he's been gambling with our money again." Rhonda said and stalked down the hallway.

"Rhonda, wait! You're going to get your big shot! Just play the game. Be patient," the trainer yelled, but she had already rounded the corner.

Rhonda barged into Charles's office. He jumped in the seat and almost spilled his drink on a pile of racing forms.

"Rhonda—you could knock, you know. Hey, that was some match tonight. You keep winning like that and you're going places."

'Where's my money?"

"I don't have it yet. There's been a delay."

Rhonda shot out her arms and dragged Charles over the desk by his collar.

"I want my money, now!"

"You just cost yourself a wrestling career. Get out of my office or I'll call the cops."

"I want my money and I'm coming back for it, Charles."

~

Rhonda marched out the rear auditorium doors and down the back alley. The night air chilled her to the bone in her soaked sweats. She had worked hard to get this far, and she needed her man to console her. The only problem was that after a month of getting closer with him, letting him cook for her, give her shoulder and foot massages and even cuddle with him on the couch, *dog gone it*, he still wouldn't tell her his *name!* He'd tell her tonight, by golly, because she was in a mood.

Rhonda entered her apartment by unlocking all three locks, and was immediately hit with the delicious aroma of another wonderful home-cooked meal.

"Hey, Babe, I hope you're hungry because I've got these pork carnitas almost ready. I bought pork tenderloin and fresh veggies from the Farmer's market. I've been slow roasting them for hours. Hey, what's wrong? You look upset."

"I *am* upset. I won my match but then I lost my temper when I found out Charles gambled with our money again. So he fired me."

"That's terrible," he said. He started to hug Rhonda, but she gave him a firm cross arm.

"No. That's the *other* thing that's bothering me: Who are you? You come over to my place—I don't even know how you get in here. You are so good to me and you do all the right things, but you won't tell me your darn name. Now come on, what is it?"

"We've talked about this before. I *can't* tell you—it's not safe for you and if you know and tell anyone it will ruin my means of making a living."

"But it's not *normal,*" Rhonda said, taking her beau's hands and pulling on them.

"Just call me the name on my business card," he said. "That way if anyone asks about me and that's all you know, you'll be safe. And you won't compromise my position."

"It's crazy. I don't want to call you that. It sounds like an animal or something. What if we go out to dinner or meet someone I know? I can't introduce you with that name."

"Just try it."

"I don't even want to *say* it. It's a dumb-sounding name."

"Get used to it, Rhonda. In a few years I'll have enough money to retire and I'll stop using it."

"How many years?" Rhonda said, pouting.

"About five more. Now say it. For me, please?"

"I wouldn't do this for anyone else in the world, but you are such a sweetheart of a guy"

“Come on, Rhonda.”
“Alright,” Rhonda said, and mumbled the name of the man she loved.

Chapter 3
The Barbies

The trailer was spacious and well-appointed. There were two wide-screen, high-def televisions mounted on adjoining walls, and a table in front of them with a scattered pile of horror DVDs. It was 2:00 PM on a Tuesday and Serena Miles and Naomi Nivens, the two women Vera had met in the hallway her first day, or the Barbies as they were called, reclined in chaise lounge chairs and sipped Mai-Tais. The women, 35 and 37, respectively, watched *Gator Ate Her* on the left screen, but each occasionally flicked their eyes toward the green cardboard box on the table.

"I like it when you take time and make the drinks with crème-de-almond," Naomi said.

"Feel free to make them yourself, Sister," Serena replied. "Shh, my scene's coming up."

Both women watched the screen. The on-screen Serena, a fetching brunette, ten years younger, sat on the edge of a white fiberglass boat--at night--in a swamp--in a bikini--with her legs dangling off the edge-- her toes inches from the water. Suddenly, a thirty foot alligator exploded from the water, clamped her in its jaws and arced toward the marsh--not before an extreme close up on Serena's face: an expression of agony accompanied by a high-pitched scream--then she and the gator plunged beneath the murky depths.

"*That* was a classic scream. I've still got it too if Barry would just give me a chance," Serena said. She slumped in her chair and gulped at her icy beverage.

"As long as we're showing off, let me show you one of my gems from,when was it, '83? '84?", Naomi said. Anyway, here it is: *I'll Give You Something to Cry About.*" Naomi slid her DVD into the right player and stopped the left player. She clicked the scene selector and the one she wanted appeared: Naomi, a gorgeous 25-year-old redhead appeared onscreen. She was strapped to table, helpless, tears in her eyes. "I'm sorry!" her character shrieked.

"I'll give you something to cry about," the mad doctor said. It was Barry Whitscomb, with his famous head of hair. He turned and buzzed off Naomi's thigh with a surgical saw. Naomi let out a blood-curdling scream as the doctor laughed.

"Now *that's* how it's done," Naomi said. She beamed and arched her back to showcase her silicone breast implants.

"Barry's promised me I could be his next victim," Serena said.

"Uh—I don't think so, girlfriend. I've been keeping him warm at night."

"I've heard that promise many times from Barry over morning coffee."

"I need a little pick-me-up." Naomi said, and reached for the green box.

Serena grabbed her wrist just as Naomi opened the lid. The box was filled with white powder an inch deep. Rows of loose razor blades stood at attention in a built-in compartment, opposite another filled with thin white straws.

"Barry's going to be mad," Serena said. "He said never before 4:00 on weekdays."

"I don't care. I put up with enough from that man and what does it ever get me?" Naomi said and elbowed Serena's hand out of her way.

~

Vera stood inside Shelley's trailer, chatting with her over tea.

"I'm worried that I'll confuse Barry's and Benny's names," Vera said. "Barry's the owner, right? And Benny's the acting coach? They sound similar."

"I had the same problem when I first started here so I made up this little trick," Shelley said. "In my head I say 'Scary-Barry,' because Barry produces the horror movies. And 'Henny-Penny Benny,' because he reminds me of an aggressive little rooster."

"Thanks, I'll try that. So, what's Barry Whitscomb really like?"

"The ladies just love him. He could be a real bore, you know? I mean some producers are *so serious* all the time. Don't get me wrong, Barry wants things the way he wants them, but he's always laughing, joking, he makes people feel good. He's like a big, gruff teddy bear."

"Why did he make that vulgar suggestion about my sleeping with Alex then?"

"Method actors—Barry's one of the originals. He wants his picture to turn out right and I'm sure he didn't really think that one out before he said it. But I'll tell you what, he's launched a lot of girls' careers."

~

Jake had long thought Barry was tweaked. *What rational person makes movies where vapid, attractive young women are killed and tortured on screen for others' amusement? Those characters shouldn't be so naïve, one might say. These movies provide a heads up that not everyone is kind, not every situation safe. Besides, nobody really gets hurt.*

From a young age, Jake had taken dares from his friends to see scarier and gorier movies. It was a rite of passage to prove he wasn't afraid to confront the most horrible images. That was okay—then. But now, years later, Jake still made these wretched movies. What was worse was what Barry had revealed about himself today. Barry Whitscomb hates women. Add to that Barry's presumptuous remark, "You hate women as much as I do," and Jake realized he didn't even know who he was anymore. Hadn't he personally made several pictures wherein he deliberately portrayed women being killed in more and more gruesome ways? It had become nearly impossible to look at an attractive woman without picturing how to creatively slaughter her on screen. The damned *industry!*

Jake wanted a real relationship with someone as genuine, wholesome and attractive as Vera Horowitz, but first he had to get to the bottom of something. He would meet with a therapist at 3:00 PM to determine whether he did or did not hate women.

~

Barry strutted across the lot toward his trailer. Vera would make this picture a big hit and bring him a tidal wave of money. It was time to celebrate with the Barbies. It was perennially amusing to him to string the aging scream queens along with gifts and promises of stardom. The old carrot on the stick trick—with the prize just out of reach. Barry opened the trailer door. The startled Barbies looked up, mid-sniff; white powder clinging to their nostrils.

"It's a little early to party isn't it, Ladies?" Barry asked. "What did I tell you?"

"Not until four, Barry. I tried to tell her," Serena said.

"Thanks for warning me off, you innocent widdle thing," Naomi said and squeezed Serena's face.

"Get your whore nails off me!" Serena yelled, glancing at Barry for approval.

"Ladies, relax. I'll take you out for a fancy dinner. How does that sound?"

Serena and Naomi pouted from the far edges of their chaise lounges.

"What I want more than dinner is for you to put me in *Zombie Betrayal* instead of that little nobody Jake dragged in here," Serena said.

"Actually, that's *my* role you're talking about," Naomi said.

"Okay, you're both getting spankings," Barry said and spanked the Barbies, and as they tried to escape he tickled them both roughly. The women laughed until they could barely breathe.

"I let you girls live here. I feed you, buy you nice things, the least you could do is show me some spirit. Who wants a piggyback ride around the trailer?"

The women eyed each other like track runners.

"I do, Barry," Naomi said, before Serena could answer.

"Hop up," Barry said, and hoisted Naomi up onto his back. He kicked open the door handle and romped around the outside of the trailer. He galloped and whinnied while the vindicated Naomi laughed with delight.

Vera and the stylist stepped out of the make-up trailer and witnessed Barry's escapades.

"You're right," Vera said to Shelley, "he's just a fun-loving kid."

Chapter 4

Getting into Character

Aaron, Ira and Levi, sat at a park bench in their blue police uniforms across the street from the restaurant where Vera used to work.

"You guys know Vera Horowitz, right?" Aaron said, gesturing to the restaurant with his sandwich. "She used to work in there."

"Sure, little Vera. She was the pride of the neighborhood," Levi said.

"Little hottie as I recall," Ira said.

"Damn straight. I need some advice, my chavers. I've had it bad for her since grade school. I've got to find a way to schtup her but she's avoiding me."

"She's so hot—and you are the man, A-ron, shoo in for captain, going to own your own home soon," Ira said, "You're babe candy for a traditional Jewish family."

"Why do you guys have to talk about Vera like that?" Levi said.

Ira looked at Levi, shook his head and turned back to Aaron. "Talk up her grandmother, come on like you want to get married and have kids with her—she'll come across."

"Gotta' go," Levi said, "I'd hate to see you do that to a sweet kid like Vera, Aaron."

Aaron and Ira waited until Levi was half a block away then turned to each other.

"Boy scout," Aaron said.

"Remember at the community pool when Vera walked out on the diving board in that gold bikini? She was just sixteen but even then everything was in the right place."

"I remember. She looks even better now. I've only seen her in clothes, but I can imagine. I like your idea." Aaron took a big bite of his corned beef sandwich.

"You've got to nail her. Then you're gonna' give me full details over a beer."

"Done," Aaron said with a smile.

~

Jake was late for his appointment. He ran down the pale green hallway and slid to a stop a few feet from the door with the brass plaque that read: "Thelma Gladstone, PhD." He checked his watch; he'd made up the time. Jake stepped forward and knocked. He listened to the tufty wick of high heels crossing carpet from behind the door; lifting the legs higher to avoid snags made for slow stepping. How many of his "victims" had fallen prey to the vanity of high heels?

A thin woman with her hair in a tight twist opened the door and regarded him solemnly.

"You're quite punctual, Mr. L'Hommedieu. Come in," Thelma said, "Please sit down."

Jake entered and relaxed on the couch while Thelma sat diagonally from him, notepad open, pen ready, and peered over her cat glasses.

"What would you like to talk about?" Thelma asked.

Jake couldn't find the words. When he didn't speak, she lowered her notebook.

"You'd mentioned on the phone that you were concerned about your attitude towards women?"

"I make horror movies for a living. Its standard fare that attractive women are cast as victims and die in nasty ways."

"Why do you suppose the standard is to cast attractive women as victims?"

"I guess it's because most guys can't get them."

"They can't get them. So, they—kill them on film in gruesome ways?"

"It's not quite that. It's a form of art. At least that's what it used to be for me."

"Go on." Thelma said, and scribbled on her notepad.

"Well, I've wondered if there's some underlying reason why I make these movies. I wonder if I actually don't like—I wonder if I hate women." Jake huffed and looked exhausted.

"Do you feel like you hate women *while* you're making the films?"

"No, I'm always trying to up the ante, trying to make the gore more and more gratuitous. It's what the fans seem to want." Jake said, and stroked his silk lavender tie.

"How do you know what the fans want?"

"We bring in focus groups from horror fan sites to view the rough cuts. They fill out research forms after the viewing."

"I see," Thelma said and scribbled. "What initially attracted you to this work?"

"I'm not sure. I've been asking myself that lately."

"What leads up to a woman dying in one of your films?"

"She's always doing something stupid, or she's some place which is clearly dangerous and she's in a vulnerable position."

"What types of characters are these women?"

"They're either really naïve women who get lucky breaks in life because they're attractive, or they're total shrews willing to walk over anybody to get what they want."

"So presumably—they get what they deserve in your movies?"

"In a way. I mean, nobody 'deserves' what happens to these women. It's really quite horrible what happens to them. Hence the name: horror movie."

"Yes," Thelma said and scribbled more notes. "How would you describe your relationship with your mother?"

Okay, here we go, Jake thought.

"We're estranged. I haven't spoken with her for years."

"Can you expand on that?"

"It's because she was always sticking her nose into my business."

"And your father?"

"Divorced, when I was very young. No word from him since."

"Do you have any siblings?"

"Yes, five sisters," Jake rolled his eyes, "I'm the only male, and the oldest."

The questioning continued as Jake became more uncomfortable with having to answer.

"Our time is almost up," Thelma said. "We'll need to schedule several more appointments. Let me get my date timer."

"Several more appointments? No, I don't have that kind of time. You see, I'm in love with someone and I just need to know if I'm mentally stable enough to date her," Jake said. Thelma looked up from her date timer and shook her head. "I wouldn't advise asking out anyone of the opposite sex until we've gotten to the bottom of this. Now are you available next Tuesday at this same time?"

"You don't understand, she's going to get away! She's working in the movies now. There are lots of flashy characters around—"

"There are a lot of fish in the sea, Mr. L'Hommedieu. Is Tuesday at three convenient?"

~

Vera finished her tea as she watched Barry carry Naomi back inside the trailer. Just as she was about to thank Shelley and go home, she saw Brian, the director of lighting, from her first day. He walked across the lot, apparently deep in thought.

He's drop-dead gorgeous, Vera thought.

"Hi Brian," Vera called out, and waved. Brian glanced up at his name, waved and kept going. Vera closed the door and stepped back inside the makeup trailer.

"Shelley?" Vera asked, "What's the deal with Brian? Is he attached?"

"Oh, you're barking up the wrong tree if you're interested in him."

"Oh, it wouldn't surprise me if he's gay. Those eyes, that jawline—"

"No, it's not that. He's only into ugly women and you hardly fit the bill."

"What do you mean?"

"He's obsessed with the ugliest women he can find. He finds out where they work, gets a job there, all so he can spend his workday around them."

"Why would he want to—So who's he into here?"

"I don't mean to be unkind, but apparently Lola is the crème-de-la crème of ugly."

"Oh. I thought she was wearing stage makeup," Vera said.

Chapter 5
Take One

It was Vera's first full dress shoot. She wore a white lab tech's coat with pens in the pocket, a short skirt, her hair pulled back in a ponytail and a stylish pair of glasses. Lola, the zombie girl from Vera's first audition, had pale, mottled skin, sunken eyes, a patch of blonde hair missing and snaggly teeth. She was covered with dried blood and dragged one foot as she walked.

"It's a fine day for a splatter scene," Barry said, leaning back in his producer's chair and puffing his cigar. The barbies sat next to him and looked bored. Lola sat two chairs down from Jake and smoked a cigarette.

Vera's cell phone rang, and the screen read: "Bubbe."

"Hi, Bubbe. You don't have to come down here, everything is okay," Vera said into the phone.

"I will see what dis man is up to," Zissell said, "Now tell to me the address again."

Vera gave her grandmother the address and let out a huff.

"Okay, clear the set," Felix said and sneered in Jake's direction. "Everyone except Vera and Alex. Let the lovebirds have some space."

Alex lumbered onto stage where he dwarfed Vera.

Barry yelled through the bullhorn. "Felix, bring us up to speed. The fast version."

"Okay, Barry. Alex's character, Tony, warns Vera's character, Lonnie, that her best friend, Sarah, who is now a zombie, won't remember her—she is dangerous and has to be put down. Lonnie wants a moment alone with Sarah. Tony agrees. Just before the scene wraps, Alex and Vera embrace and—shall we begin?"

"Yeah, go ahead," Barry's amplified voice echoed from the audience.

"Places, people," Felix yelled, "*Zombie Betrayal*, love scene, take one, action!"

Felix snapped the black and white clapperboard dangerously close to Alex's broken nose. Alex and Vera melted into a passionate kiss as Jake filmed the scene.

Felix swept his hands up, like a game show host displaying a new car.

"Congratulations, young lady," Barry said with a grin, "Your on-screen chemistry has really improved. I could almost believe you and Alex were a couple just then."

Jake pulled away from the camera, looking sad.

"Okay, kids, everybody meet back here at twelve-thirty," Felix said. "Vera, you need to lie down on the set and let the makeup folks work their magic."

Brian turned to the zombie girl. "Lola, let's grab some lunch before your next scene."

"No, I'm saving my appetite for Vera's tummy," Lola said, blowing a smoke ring.

Vera lay down as the special effects crew knelt around her and untucked her blouse.

"First time, honey?" the first woman asked.

"Yes, it is," Vera said.

"This may be a little cold, Vera," a serious-looking woman said, "it just came out of the fridge a few minutes ago." She laid a red and pink veiny bladder over Vera's bare abdomen. It sloshed and slid around until the woman secured it in place with Velcro straps.

"We need you to be still until your scene, these fake intestines are very fragile," a man with a bristly black goatee said.

"You're doing great," goatee dude said, "just hold still while we tuck you in."

"This really is starting to make me shiver," Vera said.

"Sorry," the woman said. "Barry wants it that way, makes you seem more scared. Hold on, it's just ten minutes until your scene and we have to get it in one take."

"You make those guts with cherry paste like I asked you?" Lola yelled from her seat.

"You got it, Babe," goatee said.

Vera watched the minute hand on the wall clock creep around the face as her teeth visibly chattered. "I can't stand this cold much longer," she said.

Felix strutted onto the set. "Hang tight, Vera. We're ready."

"Lola, ready to chow down?" Barry asked, taking his seat and lighting a fresh cigar.

"I am so hungry, Mr. Whitscomb." Lola grinned with her gapped teeth.

"Then go get her," Barry said and swatted Lola's tush.

Felix stood above the shivering Vera while Lola crouched down to Vera's left.

"*Zombie Betrayal*, devouring scene, take one, action!" Felix said, then snapped the clapperboard and backed off set as Jake filmed.

Lola dived for Vera's midsection. Vera caught Lola's nasty claws in her hands, but Lola overpowered her and clawed at her stomach. She dug her fingers in like she was tossing a salad and pulled long strands of intestines out into the light for the camera to film. Vera shrieked as Lola chewed the globular strands, her face a bloody mess. Just as Vera slumped into supposed unconsciousness Zissell Horowitz walked in through the back door.

A powerful matronly shriek electrified the film crew. All heads turned to see Zissell holding her face in her hands. She suddenly charged passed Barry and Jake and leapt onto the stage. Zissell grabbed the bewildered Lola and threw her from Vera. Lola slid behind the curtain. Zissell dropped to her knees and tried to tuck Vera's intestines back inside her.

"Vera, my girl! What have they done to you?" Zissell cried.

Vera sat up and grabbed her grandmother by the arms. "Bubbe, I'm okay."

Zissell's eyes grew huge. "What is this?" she exclaimed.

"It's just pretend. It's my new job, Bubbe," Vera said, "It's for a horror movie."

Zissell squinted into the bright lights. "Who makes such a movie? Who does this to a nice Jewish girl?"

"Jake L'Hommedieu is the writer," Felix said, then coyly smiled. He ran a finger along his lips and pointed to Jake.

"Who is this Jake? What kind of man writes such filth?" Zissell yelled.

Jake stood. "Mrs. Horowitz, I hired your daughter because she has a gift. A lot of girls would be thrilled to be in her position."

"You, you are the chazzer who does this to Vera!"

Zissell marched into the audience and grabbed Jake by the ear.

"Aagh! Security!" Jake yelled, but the security guards were too busy laughing at the four-foot six woman to do anything.

Zissell twisted Jake's ear down to her level and marched him out the back door and into the sunlight.

"Let me go!" Jake yelled.

"Where is phone?" Zissell demanded.

Jake pointed to his trailer. Zissell forced Jake up the steps and made him sit at the writing table.

"We gonna' call your mudder. Dial to her now!"

"I don't talk with my mother. Besides I'm a grown man and—" Zissell cranked Jake's ear again. "Ouch!"

"Dial to her!" Zissell ordered.

Jake reluctantly pushed the button for "Jacqueline L'Hommedieu."

Chapter 6

Fade Out

Vera stood, let the bladder of fake intestines and blood splash onto the stage and dried her blouse with a towel as best she could. A stagehand knelt and swabbed up the bulk of the mess as Vera descended the stage steps to where Barry sat.

"I'm so sorry about my grandmother's behavior, Mr. Whitscomb," Vera said.

Barry's chest heaved up and down with laughter as he wiped a tear from his eye.

"That was the funniest thing I've ever seen. Don't worry, Vera honey, we got the money shot and that's all that matters."

"I just want to thank you for giving me this chance."

"Say, a bunch of us are stopping by a local pub called the Dolly Shot after work. Why don't you get cleaned up and meet us there? We can discuss your future in film. Say seven?"

"I'll be there. Right now, I need to go have a talk with my grandmother."

Vera ran out the rear stage door.

Lola gradually stood from the stage and smeared the back of her hand across her mouth, wiping away some of the red cherry paste. Brian noticed her flailing out from behind the curtain and leapt up on the stage to help.

"Lola, are you okay?" Brian asked.

"Yeah, what a freak Vera's grandma is, huh?"

"Right? Anyway, let me help you get cleaned up and I'll buy you lunch."

At the end of the corridor Brian held the cafeteria door open and Lola entered. They got what they wanted from the a la carte line and Brian stepped in front of Lola.

"It's on me," Brian said.

"Whatever," Lola said and led them to a table.

"Lola, I've been director of lighting for the last five years. I've worked for three horror companies and I've lit up a lot of 'ugly' people. In that time, I've only seen two other girls who come close to your ugliness."

"Let me guess. Catherine Brooks? Over at *You'd Better Run, Girl Films,* right?"

"Yeah, she's one."

"She's not natural—plastic surgery all the way."

"I know, right? She's not authentic and it shows. She doesn't know how to carry off looking that ugly. But you—"

"And the other one," Lola said, "Carrie Almos, exact opposite of Catherine. She only looks that way because she got in a head-on car crash and couldn't afford surgery. Now that's the only way she can earn a living—but that mental baggage isn't helping her acting."

"Right? So, Lola, I just want to say that for me to be sitting here in front of the ugliest girl for at least three hundred miles in any direction is *amazing*. And for me to have the privilege of lighting that face, so hideous that it's beautiful, I just—I want to be around you all the time. I know it sounds crazy, but what I'm saying is, I get you, and I want—"

"Listen, Brian, you *do* get me, and I'm flattered, but before you get any more tongue-tied why don't you go take a cold shower and I'll get cleaned up and I'll meet you at the cast party tonight? Thanks for lunch."

Those grey, gapped teeth. That pock marked skin. "Really?" Brian said. "That's awesome."

Lola stood and sauntered away. Brian wished she would grant him one glance over the shoulder, but she just walked out the door. *God, she's so confident!* he thought.

Vera was so flustered she didn't know which way to turn. She watched her hands, indecisively fidgeting in space. She had to find her grandmother, but what was she even doing here like she was an actor? She had never taken a single drama course in high school. She craved some normal interaction. Suddenly, she saw Brian sitting in the sunlight through the cafeteria window. He was smiling, in a good mood now—this might be her chance to get his attention. It just couldn't be true what Shelley said about Lola. Vera composed herself and opened the cafeteria door. Brian glanced up at her.

"Hi Brian," she said.

"Hey," he said, but he looked disappointed, gazing out across the quad.

Vera walked toward him. "You did an amazing job of lighting everyone today,"

"Thanks," Brian said, a bit distracted.

"I was just wondering if you'd seen my grandmother walking around here. You know, the woman who spazzed out back there?" Vera laughed.

"How could I forget? No, I haven't seen her," Brian said, smiling.

Just then Lola walked back into the cafeteria.

"Lola, you came back!" Brian said, his eyes aglow.

"I forgot my purse," Lola said, eyeing Vera. She stalked over and snatched her purse off the chair, glared at Vera, and walked back out the door.

Outside the cafeteria, Lola trudged away. She thought of Vera and spit into the bushes. What made her think she could ever hold onto a guy like Brian? He belongs with a pretty girl like Vera. I'm only in Hollywood because I've got a face for horror movies. Just as there is a universal ideal of a beautiful face there is its opposite—a face of universal ugliness. Lola knew she had such a face.

She had known as far back as she could remember. The boys got meaner as she got older and so did the girls. In fifth grade she had gone home and cried alone in her room after the boys had called her a "dog" and pelted her with rocks. A week later she had gone off and cried in private when a group of girls had surrounded her on the playground; the lead girl had asked Lola if her mother had turned to stone after giving birth to her and saw her face.

"They tease you because they don't know you," Lola's mother said, "that scares them."

Lola knew her mother was trying to spare her feelings, but she zeroed in on that verb her mother had used: "scares." She scared them.

The next day she approached the boys. She endured the first couple of stones and kept on walking. As she marched up to the leader of the boy gang his eyes widened.

"You're so good looking," Lola had said, then kissed him sloppily on the mouth.

The boys looked repulsed and stumbled backward as Lola walked away, smiling. When she again encountered the girl group, the lead girl approached her with the well-rehearsed lines:

"These flowers wilted when you walked up; you make me want to puke."

Lola punched the girl in her stomach, and the girl did puke. Both events resulted in trips to the principal's office, but Lola didn't mind. Students left her alone after that, which gave her the chance to focus on her classes. It turned out she was smart, but not smart enough for a scholarship and her parents were just scraping by.

She also needed spending money and her small allowance wasn't cutting it. Every summer when other kids got jobs at ice cream stores, stocking grocery shelves and babysitting, Lola was always passed over, only to learn one of her pretty classmates had landed the job. She guessed the job market would be the same if she ever got a college degree too—society was so hung up on appearances.

One night, alone in her parents' living room, Lola watched a horror movie where a hideously deformed woman played the villain's sidekick.

"I could act the hell out of that!" she said aloud.

Right after high school graduation Lola was Los Angeles-bound. She found her way through Hollywood to the You'd Better Run, Girl studios where she caught the attention of the casting director. She took one look at Lola and said:

"You are seriously ugly. I'm casting you right away. Sign here, and initial here."

Lola made her screen debut in *I'll Eat Your Face.* Nobody remembered her name, but You'd Better Run, Girl put her face on the movie marquee and the crowds poured in. Some gorgeous guy named Brian suddenly came to work at the studio, running the lighting. He hovered around her. Two movies later Barry Whitscomb stole Lola away with a bigger paycheck and fancier perks.

She'd never understood Brian's attraction to her. She'd been both flattered and freaked out that he confessed he'd come to work there just to meet her. Then he'd followed her to Falchion Films. Of course, she'd been attracted to him, and she'd liked other girls' being envious of her for the first time in her life, but there had to be something wrong with Brian.

~

Barry swaggered into his trailer. He ignored the startled-then-innocent looks on the snuffling Barbie's faces.

"Hi Barry," Serena cooed.

"Dinner was divine last night, Barry," Naomi said.

"Why don't you come with me down to the Dolly Shot, Naomi?" Barry asked.

"But it's only two-thirty."

"I can be ready in just a jiff, Barry," Serena said.

"No, I need to have a talk with Naomi, just the two of us."

Serena sat down, crossed her fishnet-stocking-clad legs and stared at the wall.

Naomi and Barry walked arm-in-arm around the block. Barry's size twelve extra wide alligator loafers rolled along while Naomi's four-inch-high-heels clicked double time to keep up.

"I knew this day would come," Naomi said. "All the times you promised me a part, all the special nights we spent together. Is it going to be a big film? Oh, it doesn't matter it's just a thrill to be acting again!" Naomi sighed. She squeezed Barry's arm through his shiny white and yellow reptile skin jacket and leaned her head on his shoulder as they entered the Dolly Shot doorway together.

The walls were covered with still shots of prominent L.A. directors' movies, as well as a few of Barry's. Naomi paused to gaze at a photo of herself in her 20s, holding her hands up defensively as a shadowy figure in the foreground brandished a chainsaw.

"Have a seat," Barry said, and motioned for Naomi to sit. A sharp-eyed waitress recognized Barry and almost hurt herself jostling by two other waitresses. She opened her order pad and nimbly maneuvered her hips past the maze of tables to the red leather booth where Barry and Naomi sat.

"Mr. Whitscomb, always a pleasure to see you and your friend," the waitress said.

"I have a name. It's Naomi Nivens. I'm in several of your movie photos."

"Would I have seen any of your recent films?" the waitress asked.

Barry smirked.

"We'll have two Long Island ice teas, sweetheart," Barry said.

Naomi studied her nails.

"Right away, Mr. Whitscomb," the waitress said.

"Naomi, life is funny," Barry said, once the waitress left, "It's funny to me how different media can teach us things about life."

"Like what, Barry?"

"Like, I know I have a few years on you, but I think you're old enough to remember two singers from the 80s: Juice Newton and Vonda Shepard?"

"Sure, Barry, I remember them."

"When expressing themselves on the subject of having their hearts broken, both women took drastically differing stands. Juice Newton released a song in 1982 entitled 'Break It to Me Gently' in which she attempted to cling to a dying love until the bitter end to savor the good times, even though she knew the relationship was ending."

Barry paused to take in Naomi's expression: typical scream queen face, whites of her eyes fully expanded.

"By contrast, in 1989 Vonda Shepard released a hit song called 'Baby Don't You Break My Heart Slow' in which she stated that if her heart was to be broken then the bastard should get it over with quickly and not drag out the pain. How would you want it, Naomi, babe?"

"Why are you asking me this, Barry? Did I do something wrong?" Naomi's eyes widened even more.

The drinks arrived and Barry slid Naomi's in front of her.

"How do you want it, kid? I can tell you I respect Miss Shepard's 'tude a lot more."

"Barry, all those times I slept with you, I mean, there were a lot of guys I could have been with, you promised me I was gonna' be a star again. You said when the right movie came along—you and Jake write the movies, don't you? Why are you doing this to me?"

"The trailer's getting a little crowded, sweetie. There's a fresh young talent in need of housing until she gets on her feet. Don't worry, you've still got a face and your body's not bad either. You'll do alright."

Naomi drew back her drink, about to throw it in Barry's face but he struck his hand out and caught her by the wrist.

"Whoa, this jacket is albino reticulated python skin—very expensive."

"We just slept together last night!"

"I know, and those screams left me feeling lackluster."

"Those were my bedroom screams, not my stage screams! I've still got it, Barry. Just give me the chance!"

"Nah, you've got to know when it's over, babe." Barry plied his fingers through his thick, shimmering hair. Naomi was momentarily entranced.

"I hate you, Barry! You're gonna be sorry you messed with me!" Naomi stood and left the booth, tears streaming from her eyes.

"Come back. Here's a little cash, last you for a week or two." Barry grinned.

Naomi paused at the door, then spun around, walked back and snatched the roll of bills from Barry's hand.

"Wait," Barry said. "Gotta' keep your nose tuned up too, right?"

"Damn you to hell, Barry Whitscomb," Naomi said, and grabbed the vile of coke.

~

The phone rang in Jake's inner ear, far away, on his mother's dresser in Creighton, Nebraska. *Maybe she won't pick up*, Jake thought. But in that instant she answered.

"Hello, this is Jacqueline." That charming lilt, the one he loved so much when he was a boy, echoed over the line.

"Hi, Mom, it's me, Jake."

"Jake, I'm surprised to hear from you. Are you alright?"

"Say what what you do to my Vera!" Zissell yapped, and twisted Jake's ear harder.

"Ouch! Stop that, dammit!" Jake yelled over his shoulder, but Zissell only grabbed Jake's hair and pulled it backwards over the chair. "Okay, okay." He returned to speaking into the phone. "We're shooting a movie where a fake zombie girl eats fake intestines from a young woman's abdomen and the young woman's grandmother saw it, she's here in my trailer, and has become so incensed that she made me call you. I suppose so she could hear you scold me."

"I never did understand why you make those disgusting movies, Jake. I'm afraid I'm on her side."

Zissell's head was near Jake's so she could hear the conversation. "Hah! I knew you was a pervert! What will your mamma do with you?"

"Mom, she wants to know what you're going to do to me—"

"I heard. Put the woman on, Jake."

"Hello, this is Jake's mother. With whom am I speaking?"

"I am Zissell Horowitz. Your boy drags my girl's insides out for the world to see! I raise Vera to be goot girl. When people see dis film what man will want her?"

"I'm sorry for my son's behavior, Mrs. Horowitz. He is really a good boy too, but he has a strange imagination. I will say that his films make a lot of money and your daughter will become a well-known celebrity."

"That is not what I want for Vera. It is unclean! I never hold my head up in synagogue now. Make him to destroy dis film and apologize to me and to stay away from my girl forever."

"I can't do that, Mrs. Horowitz, this is his business and that film is his property. I will ask him to apologize, however."

Jake listened and nodded. "I am so sorry, Mrs. Horowitz, for offending you, but what my mother said is true. The film is not entirely mine, I have a partner. Besides, Vera has signed a contract with us. She wants to do the film. Can you appreciate that?" Jake hung up the phone.

"No," Zissell said, "put her in different film. One where Vera has happy life, marries decent gentleman in synagogue and has many healthy children. Den I accept apology."

"It's funny you should say that because I would love to make that film. Unfortunately, I have to finish this one first, as well as one more, before I'm free to pursue my own career. I really have the utmost admiration for your daughter."

"You are big liar. Man who writes filthy movie has no morals, no respect for God or woman or family or nothing!" Zissell released Jake's hair and ear. "We see what you say to Rabbi Gilad!"

Zissell marched out of the trailer.

Vera spotted Zissell walking across the lot and ran towards her.

"Bubbe, what did you do to Mr. L'Hommedieu?"

Vera grabbed her grandmother by the shoulder. Zissell twisted Vera's arm until she caught her behind the elbow and marched her toward the street.

"You work here no more. You come to my house and bathe. Den we go to synagogue to pray with Rabbi Gilad. You gonna be pure again, Vera."

"Let go of me, Bubbe! This is my life; you can't tell me what to do."

"You are not shikse, dese people are tsuris, not kosher!"

Vera stumbled while trying to keep up with her vigilant grandmother.

"Now march, klutz!" Zissell said.

~

Jake rubbed his ear and massaged his scalp where the tiny woman had yanked his hair. *Why is my world filled with such weirdos?* Jake wondered as his cell phone rang. *Oh my god, it's Mom.* Jake answered.

"You just hung up on me!" his mother said.

"I'm sorry, I didn't mean to—I was trying to deal with Mrs. Horowitz."

"Jake, you realize there's a reason this happened. We need to talk."

Jake slowly released his breath.

"Let me start," his mother said. "It's been too long since we've spoken, we're mature adults. What did I do that was so awful?"

Jake reflected on the meeting with his therapist.

"The whole time I was growing up you were preoccupied with your girls, you never had a moment for me. Then when I struck out on my own you called me incessantly to give me unwanted advice. It was way too late by then, Mom."

"Do you know how complicated girls are, especially five of them? Dresses, shopping, worrying, crying, braces, periods, training bras, dating. You seemed like the only stable one in the family, so I never worried about you. When your father left, I had my hands full, Jake."

"Do you know what it's like coming home to a world of pink doilies and perfume, and giggling phone conversations and thirty pairs of little shoes underfoot? Ribbons, pom-poms, girls' underwear hanging in the shower, makeup all over the bathroom? It was like I'd crashed on planet estrogen!"

"You couldn't have blamed me for having girls. Believe me, there were times I wished I'd had a couple boys instead."

"I'll tell you what I did, Mom. I was pissed! I spent a lot of time in friends' basements watching horror movies, coincidentally where vulnerable girls got what some twisted B-movie director imagined they deserved. I sat on those couches and absorbed those movies. I'm not proud of it."

"That must have been rough on you. I did the best I could, honey. Do you still like what you do for a living?"

"No, and it shows in the quality of the pictures we make. And the worst of it is I'm in love with the daughter of the woman with whom you just spoke."

"Oh, Jake, that's never going to work out. Could you imagine having that woman as your mother-in-law? We're just too different."

"You want to have a relationship with me again?" Jake said, "You spent a lot of years dealing with females. Tell me how to win her over and I'll call you every weekend and fly home for Thanksgiving and Christmas every year."

"Wow. That's a tall order. Let me put my mind to it and call you back."

"Okay, Mom. I'm hanging up now."

~

Vera ran from the synagogue, flagged a cab and jumped in. She checked her cell phone: 6:45 PM. She could still see the scowling eyebrows of Rabbi Gilad as he glanced from Zissell to Vera and read the words of the Torah. Her grandmother's eyes had gleamed—believing she was guiding her daughter in the right direction. It had all made Vera feel like she was a child again. *To hell with that!* Vera thought. *I have a career now; I'll make my own decisions.*

She directed the cabbie to pull over. She paid and tipped him and walked two blocks until she found the Dolly Shot. Two glimmering limousines were parked outside: one black, one white. *The money, the status, not wondering where my next buck is coming from, I've tapped into something good here in Hollywood. Bubbe worries too much; I won't become a bad person.*

Vera opened the brass door and took in the movie stills around her. She saw a picture of Barry in a doctor's operating scrubs holding a scalpel in his latex-gloved-hand. A wide-eyed Serena lay on the operating table in the background. The title: *No Anesthetic for Annie.* Vera looked up and saw Barry, three-sheets-to-the-wind, beckoning her over to the bar. Vera composed herself and walked over.

Chapter 7
Stage Family

Vera wasn't tall, but she was well-proportioned and pretty and knew how to make a good impression. She put her shoulders back, stood up straight and strutted confidently toward the bar. When Barry was sure she was coming over he faced the bar and smiled at his reflection in the mirror; he was the devil himself tonight—two seconds from delivering the world's biggest pile of bullshit. He sensed Vera's proximity and, without looking, he slid his arm out around her waist and pulled her slight frame up onto the seat next to him.

"Vera, I'm so proud of you, we're going to make a lot of money together. You're going to be a movie star," Barry said, his face so red from alcohol it was practically purple.

"Thanks, Mr. Whitscomb," Vera said.

"You need to catch up. I think champagne is in order."

Barry poured a glass of Dom Perignon and handed her the crystal flute. Vera defensively accepted it as icy white effervescence overflowed and frothed onto her fingers. She tried to absorb it with a napkin, but Barry clinked glasses with her and splashed more onto her wrist.

"Drink up—" Barry commanded. He scowled, then realizing he must appear menacing, he morphed his expression into a grin, "—while I tell you about the family you're now part of." Vera sipped and swallowed.

"The family?" she asked, as Barry coerced her to drink by tilting her glass upward. Vera couldn't help staring at Barry's gorgeous hair. *So shiny, soft and layered—*

"Hey, I'm over here, sweetheart," Barry said and pointed to his eyes. "Yes, a family, now catch up."

Vera sipped, and breathed in the teeming bubbles that burst up her nose.

"Scream queens ain't like other actresses at all," Barry said. "The really good ones like you, with talent and innocent-good-girl looks, well, the audience just eats you up. You're everything they value. But strangely, you are the very ones they want to see sacrificed on screen. Like Billy Joel says, 'Only the good die young.' You gotta want it, Vera. You gotta give the camera everything you got: your emotions, your pain, your exasperation, your guts, and your very life. You gotta please the audience, but the audience ain't your friend. Capiche?"

"But we're making movies the public wants so they should be happy with us."

"The audience for these movies is the most depraved, malignant group of individuals you'll ever meet. They can't *wait* to see you get what's coming to you. This job is fun and even glamorous, but you've got to understand it. You'll make a lot of money. You'll be famous. But here's the catch: As long as you die well on film your career will have a long life. At the end of the day you need a family to pick you up and understand how much you've sacrificed for your art. Anything you need, you come to me right away, doll." Barry smiled warmly.

"Thank you, Mr. Whitscomb. I appreciate your confidence in me."

"So, it's thirty days until you get paid, right?" Barry said, looking concerned.

Vera tried to hide her surprise with a dainty sip of champagne. *Those bubbles.* She squeezed the bridge of her nose to stifle a sneeze.

"No, I didn't realize it would be so long."

"Yeah, it's tough, union rules. Tell you what: We start another movie in a week so you gotta be available. Apartments in L.A. are expensive, hell everything you gotta pay a lot around here. I got a vacancy in my trailer I reserve for real pros. Vera, this is one of the perks for somebody with your potential. You can stay in my luxurious trailer right here at the studio for free. What do you say?"

"It's too generous, besides, I mean, what would people say?"

"After they get over their jealousy you mean? After they realized that *you* really deserve to be here, that *you're* the real star on this set? I guess that's their problem ain't it?" Barry said.

"But I thought Serena and Naomi lived there?"

~

Jake entered The Dolly Shot, saw the film crew in two red leather booths, and scooted in next to Felix and Andy. He noticed Brian sitting next to Lola—resting his arm on top of the booth over Lola's shoulders and running the fingers of one hand through her dull, lifeless hair.

"Hey, you're late, Jake," Felix said, "You're missing the show, Barry's seducing the new hire right in front of us." Felix gestured toward the bar.

Jake saw Barry's arm around Vera and his heart sank.

"If she touches his hair it's all over," Felix said.

"You know something, you're a miserable little shit, Felix," Jake said.

"Sticks and stones," Felix countered, sipping his mojito and grinning smugly.

"When I'm directing my own films, I'll remember who was loyal to me," Jake said.

"You're no director. You have no power, Jake. Barry runs things around here. You're just sitting here watching him scoop up your girl. Now is that pathetic or *what?*" Felix said, and high fived Andy.

~

"It was time for Naomi to move out on her own," Barry explained to Vera, "I realized I was being cruel not to tell her that she wasn't gonna' be a scream queen no more. Can you keep a secret, Vera?" Barry leaned in close and whispered in her ear. "Naomi got lazy, she wasn't working on her craft and she had a bad attitude. Kindest thing I could do was to help her see she wasn't growin' no more. Besides, that trailer is reserved for movie stars, not ungrateful leaches."

"The poor woman. She was in so many movies. What's she going to do now?"

"I'm gonna pull some strings, see if I can get her some work somewhere. Don't you worry about her. You just stay focused on your craft, work with Benny, he's a great acting coach. You'll meet him on Monday. In the meantime, are you ready to start acting like the star you are and move into your luxurious trailer?" Barry cocked a mischievous eyebrow.

"I would be honored, Mr. Whitscomb. I accept." Vera flashed him a radiant smile.

"Outstanding! Well, we've got a lot to celebrate. Drink up, this is three hundred dollar stuff and I can't let it go to waste." Barry filled Vera's glass again. "But you've gotta do something for me or the deal's off."

Vera stole a quick glance at Barry's thick auburn hair. *It seems alive in this light.*

"Call me Barry."

Vera looked up at him with her big brown eyes and smiled. "Alright, then, I would be honored, Barry."

Barry smiled. The reticulated albino python jacket crinkled against his arm as he squeezed Vera's small body close to his.

~

Lieutenant Aaron Finklestein had finished his shift and turned in his paperwork. He could finally try out Ira's advice. As he drove toward Vera's grandmother's house he got an alert from Ira and picked up.

"Yeah?"

"Aaron, you've got to get over to manage this crime scene. 9000 block of Beverly Boulevard. Field Commander's detained and the inspector in charge is with his wife in the hospital—the Commissioner's asking somebody from our precinct to step in and handle it."

"My shift just ended, Ira."

"You want to get those captain's bars a little sooner? Here's your chance."

"I guess I'd better," Aaron said and swung left onto Santa Monica Boulevard.

Chapter 8
Out-Take

Naomi paced outside The Dolly Shot as the sun set. She sobbed until the temperature dropped and her tears became shivers. She unclenched her fist and counted the crumpled roll of hundreds Barry had given her: $2,000.00. The logic was simple: She was cold, limousines had heat, so she called a limo service. Per her instructions, the driver cruised through Burbank, and then through Beverly Hills until Naomi directed him to her old home. He parked and waited while she entered the trailer.

"So, did you get a movie deal?" Serena asked sarcastically.

"Barry kicked me out," Naomi said, "I'm just here to get my things."

Serena's expression softened. She sat up from her chaise lounge and touched her nails to her cheek.

"What?"

"He said he has to make room for Vera."

"Sweetie," Serena said, standing and hugging Naomi. "I really thought, after all this time—"

"I know. I'll talk to him. Where are you staying?"

"I don't know. Help me get my things I don't want to be here when he comes back." Naomi wiped her eyes as she entered her old bedroom.

~

Jake watched Vera hop down from the bar stool. He crossed the room and stood beside her. Barry stood too, wobbled, and tried to stabilize by planting one alligator loafer first behind him then to the side.

"Thanks for a wonderful evening, Barry," Vera said, "but I need some sleep."

"Come on, you can ride with me," Barry slurred.

"Thank you, but you've already been too generous. I'll see you tomorrow."

"Bring your things, you can move into the trailer in the morning."

"I'll give her a lift, Barry," Jake said. "I haven't had a chance to talk with our new star." Vera looked up at Jake and folded her slender fingers over his overcoat sleeve.

"Don't let him get fresh with you, Vera." Barry chortled as they left the bar.

Cold air rushed in as the bouncer held the door open for them—framing Jake's limo, gleaming silver against darkness, just beyond the filthy sidewalk. Jake tipped the muscular man and stepped outside. The driver, ever-alert, hustled around the luxury automobile, opened the rear door for Vera and Jake, and closed them inside with a "foomp."

The interior of the cavernous limousine was warm and smelled clean. The engine surged and pressed the couple back into soft leather seats.

"So how does it feel to be a movie star?" Jake asked.

"Great!" Vera shrieked with laughter.

"Whoa, my ears." Jake said, and cupped them with his hands.

"It never would have happened if you hadn't given me your business card."

"This film will put you on the map. But let me ask you something: Are these the kinds of movies you want to keep making?"

"It never occurred to me that I had a choice."

"I see a lot more potential in you than just making B-horror movies. I have a script, it's a romantic drama, it's my baby actually, and I want to cast someone wonderful in it. Are you interested?"

"Wow! But I can't. I've agreed to make another film with Barry."

"So have I. I'm suggesting that if you're game, we could work on my film nights and weekends. It will be a lot of work and you'll have to learn all you can from Benny to get your acting skills up to speed."

"A few weeks ago I was just a lousy waitress. Suddenly, I'm getting all these movie offers. I don't know what to say."

"Say 'yes.'"

"Yes!" Vera shrieked, then she giggled and rapidly tapped her toes on the plush-carpeted floor.

~

Naomi watched the garish L.A. tourist temptations pass outside the limousine window. She cruised through the seedy sections until the streetlights grew brighter. Bigger, taller palm trees now lined the streets, and world class stores with designer names she knew appeared.

"Pull over right here, please," Naomi said.

The driver parked, rounded the limo, and helped her step onto the wide, concrete drive of the Hilton Garden Inn. Naomi walked beneath the white canopy flanked by green broad-leaved palms.

Inside, she booked a penthouse suite and paid and tipped the driver and the bell boy. She spent the night ordering from room service, getting drunk, snorting lines, and watching herself in old horror DVDs on the 50-inch-flat screen.

~

Barry's limo driver dropped him off at his trailer. Serena heard a voice, parted the kitchen blinds and looked out. It was Barry who sang a drunken song as he stumbled toward the steps.

Barry worked his key in the slot and barged in—an absurd grin on his face. He fell over.

"Naomi said you kicked her out and Vera's moving in. Is that true?" Serena demanded.

"Yes, my dear. The show must go on," Barry said. He rolled over and stood up.

"Naomi deserves better, she's put in two decades with you and this circus!"

"It's happening. So, make our new guest welcome, Serena."

"Is that what you're planning for me too? You just use us then—"

"I think you've still got it, babe. Naomi's another story."

"Barry, are you listening? Is that how you reward loyalty? Is that how—"

"You've got a future here, doll. Naomi, not so much," Barry laughed, tossed his coat on a chair and strolled down the hall to his bedroom.

"Barry, you can't treat people this way!" Serena shouted.

But Barry just whistled down the hallway.

"Naomi's a human being!" Serena yelled after him.

~

The next morning Barry resembled a red-faced basset hound as he sat behind his desk. He swallowed ibuprofen and nursed a steaming mug of coffee.

"If we *have* to do another wretched horror movie together I vote we table *Bavarian Scalps.*" Jake said. "It seems absurd that Native Americans would A) want to travel to the Alps, B) would resort to tomahawks as weapons in the 21st century, or C) be interested in scalping German mountain climbers. I mean, what's their motivation?"

"Female German mountain climbers," Barry countered, his eyes squinted shut.

"Nope, still doesn't work for me."

"Okay, so we're down to *Machete Betty, Fifty Ways to Cleave your Lover,* or *The Organ Peddler,*" Barry said.

"Who would play Machete Betty? Lola? I don't buy it."

"Come on, when Lola walks down the sidewalk little kids scatter."

"I can't believe I'm saying this," Jake said, "but it doesn't fit what the public expects from us: women as victims, not villains. Did I mention I'm burned out on B-horrors?"

"Yeah, now could you keep your voice down? I've got a doozy of a hangover."

"So, my vote is for *Fifty Ways.* Another company just put out a film about stealing people's organs against their will so let's nix *The Organ Peddler* too. Then I am finished with this business. Then we're square, Bare, right?"

"Yeah, have Felix schedule *Fifty Ways* and see who we can get from central casting."

"What's wrong with Naomi for one of the victims?"

"News travels fast, eh? No, when I tell somebody they're off the lot that's it."

"You are rotten to the core, Barry."

"Sure, whatever you say, just pipe down, kid."

~

It was Friday at 11:00 A.M. when the manager of the Hilton Garden Inn escorted Naomi down the elevator and out to the curb.

"You can't do this to me! I'm Naomi Nivens! I've been in a lot of movies."

"And I'm sure they were good ones. But Ms. Nivens, if you don't have some means of paying your bill, I must ask you to leave. You still have an outstanding balance with us for five-hundred-seventy-five dollars."

"I've already paid you eighteen hundred. I just need to stay here a couple more days."

"When you come back with more cash or credit cards you will, of course, be a welcome guest. Now where shall I send your final bill?" the manager asked.

Naomi looked at her remaining funds $45.00. She hailed an approaching taxi, picked up her suitcase, and climbed into the back seat. She was sad, but her designer clothes were so nice. She smoothed her hand across the black, leather skirt, glanced down at her suede fuchsia platform peep-toe sandals, and smiled.

"Where to?" the cabbie asked.

"Just drive," Naomi responded.

After a few miles she peered over the cabbie's shoulder at the meter: $38.50 glowed in digital yellow numbers. Naomi's nose ran and her eyes were bloodshot from having run out of cocaine.

"You'd better let me out here," she said.

"No, no, Miss, you don't want to get out here. This is a very bad part of town," the cabbie said.

"Well, I'm out of money, sport."

"I will drive you to the corner. From there I suggest you make a hasty retreat to somewhere else."

The cabbie pulled over and Naomi handed him the $45.00.

"Keep the change," she said, and wheeled her suitcase down the sidewalk.

Two prostitutes watched Naomi approach and shifted their posture to business mode. Unaccustomed to the streets, Naomi made direct eye contact and smiled. "Excuse me, ladies," Naomi said as she tried to walk around them.

They cornered her between a brick wall and the sidewalk.

"Ladies, hell! What you doin' on our corner, bitch?" the first hooker asked.

"What up, ho?" the second hooker chimed in. "You must have *some* generous pimp. Check out that boob job and clothes on fresa here."

"I am *not* a prostitute! This skirt is an Alice and Olivia box leather skirt that retails for $495.00. These are Christian Louboutin peep toe fuchsia, red sole booties that retail for $1,095.00. I'm *in* the industry. Maybe you've heard of Naomi Nivens?"

The hookers regarded each other incredulously before launching a ten-minute beating and kicking frenzy on Naomi.

When she regained consciousness, Naomi's shoes and skirt were gone and her suitcase lay open on the sidewalk, her other clothing was missing, and her DVDs lay scattered in the gutter. Her eye ached and was nearly swollen shut. There was blood on her face and one of her hair extensions lay in her lap. She stood, barefoot, in her bra and panties, gathered her DVDs, packed them into her suitcase and snapped the clasps shut.

The driver of a sedan noticed Naomi. He slowed and pulled up alongside her. Naomi limped toward the car, her suitcase in tow. The sedan stopped and the window rolled down. Naomi peered in at the driver. He didn't speak, but tilted his head and gazed curiously at her.

"Excuse me, do you know where I could stay tonight?" Naomi asked and smiled.

The man parked. He got out, rounded the sedan, flashed his badge, and spun Naomi around. He pressed her face against the hood, and handcuffed her hands behind her back.

"You're under arrest for indecent exposure and soliciting prostitution. You have the right to remain silent. Anything you say can and will be used against you in a court of law—"

~

Jake and Felix sat at a conference table Thursday night and went over the call sheets.

"I need the establishing shots Andy took yesterday."

"He's on the sound stage with Benny," Felix said.

"I need those shots to get a feel for where we're going before we even *look* at the blocking. Now, who do we have from central casting today?"

"You want *names*? They're *extras* —bystanders and two cops for scene three."

Jake's phone rang. It was 7:45 P.M.

"Hello, this is Jake." Jake heard crying over the line.

"Jake, it's Naomi. I'm in jail. I need you to bail me out."

"What? I'm in a meeting. Can't you get someone else?"

"You're my *one* phone call. You were always nice to me on the set. I thought maybe—"

"Okay, okay, sit tight. Tell me which precinct and I'll get there as soon as I can."

~

Vera sat and studied her new lines in the cafeteria as she sipped a cup of tea. Lola studied Vera from across the room. Lola walked behind Vera's seat, around in front of her table and cleared her throat. Vera looked up.

"Oh, hi, Lola," Vera said.

"If it's not the new screama donna. Just because you're crashing in Barry's trailer doesn't mean you're anything special. A good friend of mine got kicked off this set to make room for you, pretty girl!" Lola said.

"Excuse me?" Vera said, and sat up straighter.

"Naomi had *real* talent. She could scream loud too. I know, only the pretty ones get to be victims, right? Where do you think you'd be without us uglies to slaughter you? Just because I'm ugly don't be thinking you're better than me."

"I never thought you were ugly, Lola, and I *don't* think I'm better than you. Where did you get *that* idea?"

"Barry. He always casts me as a wicked ghoul."

"Come on, we're giving you a make-over right now," Vera said.

"Ohmigod! You think I *want* to look like you? That's funny. You know what it takes to pull this off every day? *Pretty* is a dime a dozen around here. Your career is going to be in the toilet in a few years while mine will go on until I decide to quit. And you'd best quit checking out my boyfriend, scream queen, or you'll be screaming for real." Lola extended her middle finger, eyebrows raised, and marched from the cafeteria.

~

The driver pulled up in front of Precinct 7 and Jake got out. He inquired as to Naomi's whereabouts at the front desk and a deputy led him to a bench where Naomi sat, handcuffed next to a hooker dressed as Raggedy Ann, her deep-orange yarn wig hung down over her eyes.

"Jake, thank God. Get me out of here," Naomi said.

"How did this happen?"

"I spent the money Barry gave me. They kicked me out of the Hilton Garden Inn penthouse suite."

"You stayed at the *Hollywood Hilton*? That's over five hundred a night. Naomi, you have to live more frugally with no income."

"It's the only way I know how to live. They *beat* me, Jake."

"Who? The people at the Hilton?"

"No, two really mean hookers!"

Jake posted bail of $1,200.00 and helped Naomi into his limo.

"Thanks, Jake. I'm so tired. I just want to sleep."

"You can stay at my place until we can figure something out. I'll have some dinner delivered. Just take it easy," Jake said, and put his arm around Naomi.

"I'm *not* a hooker," Naomi mumbled.

"I know you're not," Jake said, as Naomi fell asleep against his shoulder.

Chapter 9

Intercutting

Vera couldn't concentrate on the script after what Lola had said about her. She left the cafeteria and walked down the Falchion Studio One corridor. She started to push the door open when a tingle edged up her spine. She glanced behind her.

Jake L'Hommedieu—at the end of the corridor—so tall and handsome. Hollywood director, probably has his pick of women. He was charming last night—lots of attractive women in L.A—why would he want me? Vera stepped into the chilly morning sunlight.

Jake noticed Vera and his heart raced. She'd seen him too—her big brown eyes had locked on his steely blues for a second. Whenever Jake thought of emotions, lately he thought in terms of writing dialogue.

What was that look? Interest melting into sadness? Disappointment? Run after her! But what would I say? That I might be deranged but I don't want to be? At least that's a healthy attitude isn't it? God, I'm a mess.

As she walked, Vera continued to indulge thoughts of Jake. *I'm so new to acting, we've just met—what if he did take an interest in me? Did he ask me out for coffee? Or did he just offer to bring me a cup?*

~

One of the cameramen who had been friendly to Vera yesterday now stared coldly at her as he walked past. Vera looked after him. *What's that about?*

She'd had a terrible fight with her grandmother last night over moving into Barry's trailer. *We've fought before—it's always better the next day.* Vera decided to take this time to collect her things and move into the trailer.

Barry's uniformed driver saw Vera cross the lot and strode to intercept her.

"Beautiful morning, Miss Horowitz."

"Yes, it is," Vera said.

The driver turned and walked in step with her toward the limo.

"Mr. Whitscomb has instructed me to drive you anyplace you want to go."

"Seriously? I don't have to pay you?"

"He said you are to be treated as one of the Hollywood elite."

The driver opened the rear limo door for her. Vera paused and looked up at the driver for reassurance. When he nodded, she giggled and got in.

~

Tuesday morning Naomi awoke and immediately wished she were dead. Her body ached from the beating. She staggered to the bathroom sink and splashed water on her face. Her reflection was awful: tangled hair, smeared mascara, and a black left eye.

"Has-been!" Naomi yelled at her reflection, "No prospects, no money, and no boyfriend! You were traffic-stopping gorgeous!"

The emotional outburst pushed her nerves over the edge. Naomi's fingers trembled. She involuntarily clawed at the countertop. *Oh, no—it's back.*

Her self-concept and self-pity, such important emotions a second ago, suddenly shrunk to nothing. What was once Naomi became an uncomfortable thing, crammed into a tight, small space—replaced by the animalistic craving for white powder.

This had happened once before when Barry had left her and Serena alone for the weekend. They'd snorted all the coke in the green box, then turned on each other like desperate vicious animals. It had been so upsetting they'd never spoken of it again.

Naomi's mind was gone. The body tore through drawers and threw them. The contents sprawled. The body fell—stood—lurched room-to-room and ripped Jake's condo apart.

~

At 8:00 A.M. Jake sat down at the conference table he'd left the night before.

"Hey, sunshine," Felix said.

"Let's get to the table read," Jake said, eyeing the actors seated at the table.

"*Fifty Ways to Cleave Your Lover,*" Felix announced, then opened the script's cover.

The five others at the table opened their scripts in unison. Felix read the narrator's part while the others awaited their character's cues. Jake folded his fingers behind his head, closed his eyes and leaned back to listen.

***

"FADE IN: EXT. NEBRASKA – DAY.

INSERT – A ROAD SIGN – "Welcome to Nebraska!"

INT. POLICE CAR – DAY

KELLY MCGUINESS, lead investigator, steps from the police car.

EXT. SUBURBAN FRONT YARD – DAY

Yellow plastic "crime scene" tape stretches across the yard. Police officers stand guard as Kelly steps over the tape and inside the front doorway, his trench coat aflutter.

INT. SMALL RANCHER – DAY

KELLY: "Where's the body?"

COP #1: "Back here."

They walk down the hallway into a back bedroom.

Close Up: A blood-drenched bed with hacked-up sheets and mattress. Beside it: an enormous seven-foot-tall blender—filled with pureed human remains.

COP #1: "We found the murder weapon."

The cop holds up a zip-locked baggy which contains a bloody cleaver.

COP#1: "We figure the assailant hacked his wife up on the bed then fed her into this blender."

KELLY: "I was afraid of this. I.D.?"

COP #1: "Mary Goround, recently married."

KELLY: "And she took her husband's last name?"

COP#1: "Affirmative."

KELLY: "The victim before this one's name was a Mrs. Elle Pee. The one before her was a Mrs. Tori Anado. This has got to be the work of The Cuisinart Killer."

COP #1: "Excuse me, Sir?"

KELLY: "The killer's taunting us. He picks his newest conquest based on her vulnerability and her *first name*. He courts her, marries her, gives her his latest *fake last name*, and then when he loses interest he kills her and feeds her body parts into this industrial-sized blender. The fake name al ways has a circular theme: like 'Merry-Go-Round,' 'L.P.,' or 'Tornado,' to indicate his M.O. This psycho's going through women like a lawnmower through spring succulents."

COP#1: "I think I get it. But why does he care what her *first name* is, sir?"

KELLY: "He works the *first name* into the mix too. You see it all blends together."
Cop nods thoughtfully.

COP #1: "What about forensics reports?"

KELLY: "At the last two crime scenes there was a bloody latex-gloved print on the first setting. 'Stir' at the next crime scene, a bloody print on the 'chop' setting. Now I see a print on the 'mix' setting at this crime scene. An industrial blender like this one has five settings."

COP#1: "There are only: 'pulse' and 'liquefy' remaining. What does that mean?"

KELLY: "It means after the next two killings the trail ends and *Cuisinart* disappears forever."

COP#1: "We don't have much time."

KELLY: "Exactly. I'll look into who has access to industrial blenders like this one. You get your hands on a wedding registry, Lieutenant. Look for newly weds with circular last names. We've got to beat *Cuisinart* to the punch!"

COP#1: "Human smoothie punch."

KELLY: "Shut up and get going, Lieutenant!"

COP: "Yes, sir."

***

"Hold up there, everyone. What do you think so far, Felix?" Jake asked.

"It's got a solid hook. When does *Vera* die?" Felix asked and smirked.

Jake looked irritated. "Vera dies last, but *Cuisinart* is a polygamist so the murders pile up as he courts Vera—to build the suspense."

~

Vera arrived at her grandmother's house and saw all her things piled out on the lawn. Mandy Mouse laid face down, her nose in the mud, her dress over her back in a very undignified way. Vera's mouth dropped open as she trudged to the front door and used her key in the lock. Her key wouldn't work so she rang the doorbell. After a minute, an eye looked out the peep hole.

"Bubbe, open up, my key doesn't work," Vera said.

"Heh? Go away strange girl, I don't know you," Zissell yelled through the door.

"Come on, Bubbe, open up. What are my clothes doing in the lawn?"

"I said go, strange girl, before I call de police."

"Bubbe, it's me, Vera, your daughter!"

"I don't have no daughter no more, be gone!" Zissell snapped the brass circle shut over the peep hole.

Vera carried armfuls of her clothes and her Mandy Mouse keepsakes to the limo and put them in the trunk. She got in and the driver pulled away from Bubbe's house.

~

Jake needed a break from the bustling activities on the set. Wherever he went someone assaulted him with needless questions. It was the first day of preparation for the new film, and if he wasn't around he knew Felix or Andy could handle things. Jake collapsed into the comfort of his limo seat and pulled his black sleep mask down over his eyes for the short ride.

"My place, please," Jake told his driver.

When he reached his condo and started up the walk, Jake noticed something that didn't look right: his curtains were torn down from inside and someone was running around frantically in there. He was so tired it didn't register at first. Then he remembered. *Naomi.*

Jake used his key and entered. Naomi ran up to him, grabbed him by his lapels, and hung on him with her full bodyweight.

"I need it, Jake. I need it now!" Naomi croaked, eyes sunken, her face pale and waxy.

"Oh—I don't keep any of that stuff here. What the hell did you do to my place?"

Naomi curled into the fetal position on the floor and whimpered quietly. Jake stepped to the door and waved for the driver to come in. He found a blanket and wrapped it around Naomi and told the driver to sit with her on the couch for a few minutes. Naomi tried to fight but she was too exhausted.

Jake pressed "Rehabilitation Centers" into his smartphone and ten popped up. He found the closest one and called.

"Yes, I need to get a friend of mine with a substance problem admitted immediately. I can drive her there. Yes, I can pay. We're leaving now. Jake L'Hommedieu."

Naomi had gained new strength and Jake and the driver had to struggle to walk her out and into the back seat of the limo. They drove to the rehab center and Jake filled out the forms and paid to have Naomi enter a treatment program.

"So much for a break," Jake said. He climbed back into the limo and returned to the set.

~

Felix knew nothing of consequence happened the first day of shooting. In fact, *he* was the instigator who had whipped everyone up into a questioning frenzy and sent them Jake's way. His plan had worked, and Jake left the set for a few hours—freeing him up to have a leisurely brunch of crepe suzettes with Andy.

"That was fabulous," Felix said as he and Andy clocked along the sunny sidewalk.

"Right-o, Old Bean, but you've got a little powdered sugar on your face," Andy said and wiped it off with his silk handkerchief.

~

Rhonda's cell sounded with two boxing bell dings. She had a text message from her trainer:

"Rhonda, Charles says if you'll apologize to him you can come back to work."

Rhonda texted back: "Tell him he's got that backwards—I'll be back when he apologizes."

I'd better get off my high horse, Rhonda thought. *The bills are piling up. If I'm not a wrestler, what am I?* She ran down the list of skills that might make her employable. *I'm strong, loyal, I'm a hard worker and I can get a crowd worked up in the ring—I guess that means I can act.*

Rhonda stepped off the bus and looked up at the huge gothic lettering mounted 20 feet above the lot: *Falchion Films, Inc.* She stepped inside and spoke with the pale-skinned receptionist, who gave Rhonda a business card. Rhonda crossed the lot to the main building.

Felix and Andy strutted in perfect synchronization with each other on the sidewalk across the lot as a large, muscular woman in t-shirt and sweatpants approached them. They tried to walk around her, but she kept adjusting her path to intercept them.

"Excuse me, gentlemen, is one of you Felix Short?" the woman asked.

"I am. What do *you* want?"

"My name is Rhonda Roundhouse. Well, that's my stage name. I'm a professional wrestler. Anyway, I'm looking for work. I can move heavy set pieces, yard work, and of course I can act. Can you use my services?"

"You'll want to speak with a man named Jake L'Hommedieu. He's usually here during the day."

"Thank you for your time. I'll try to catch up with him," Rhonda said.

As she walked away Felix leaned over, his lips grazing Andy's ear. "Did you see those *nails*? Oh, and those *clothes*, how *awful!*" he whispered.

Simultaneously, they saw Barry's limo pull up in front of the trailer. Vera got out and carried her bunched-up clothes toward the trailer door. Felix and Andy glanced at each other and smiled smugly.

"Hey there, Ms. Starlett! What's the news?" Felix called, as he caught up to Vera.

"What? Oh, I'm moving into the trailer," Vera said.

"Well, hold up honey, because I've got some *news* for *you*. What do you think of Jake L'Hommedieu?"

"He seems nice, very professional. Why?"

"Because he's got it *bad* for *you*, girlfriend."

"What? No, you must be mistaken. We talked just last night, and he didn't make any—"

"Andy will back me up on this. He said, and I quote, 'I'm in love with Vera Horowitz.' Isn't that right, Andy?"

Andy nodded.

"When did he say that?" Vera asked.

"The first week you joined us."

"He must mean, as an actor—or he 'loved' me in the scene—"

"Oh no, he had that lovesick look young boys get when they have a crush on a pretty young thing. I *know* it when I *see* it," Andy said. "But you know, Felix, what do you think happened to Naomi? She had to go to make the vacancy, right?"

"I forgot to mention, I heard she moved in with Jake," Felix said, his poker face intact.

"Really?" Andy said, "Well, I can't blame him, she is extremely attractive."

"Enough of that. Are you up on your lines, Vera?" Felix asked.

"No, but I will be soon," Vera said, shifting her slender hips under the weight of the clothing.

"Well, snap it up, sweetheart. We make horror movies here, back-to-back!" Felix slapped the back of his hand into his palm.

"I will, soon as I get settled in."

Felix scowled at Vera.

As they strutted away, Andy leaned in and whispered to Felix, "Look at you crack that whip, mister."

~

Jake's smart phone emitted a staccato electric guitar riff trailed by Sting's high-pitched chant— *"I can't stand losing you"*—Jake's reminder of his 3:00 P.M. appointment with his psychologist, Thelma Gladstone, Ph.D., the whole point of which was to get well—so he could date Vera. Jake grabbed his papers, pushed "therapy" and fled to his limo. Thelma's number rang—

"Doctor Gladstone."

"Hi, Thelma, I'm on the way. I was just wondering if you'd had the chance to read my romantic drama screenplay."

"I did, Jake. It was very revealing. We'll talk about it when you get here."

"I'm on the way."

Jake pocketed his cell and jumped into the back of his limo. His driver accelerated. Thelma's office was just a few blocks away. They arrived. Jake got out at the curb and took the steps two at a time. He dashed down the pale green tiled hallway and slid around the corner. He saw his therapist's door plaque at the end of the hall and sprinted for it. Jake walked the last few steps, slowed his breathing. He knocked and Thelma opened the door.

"Thank you for being on time, Mr. L'Hommedieu. Come in."

Jake sat in the comfortable cushioned recliner. He appreciated the low lighting, the chance to be still and quiet for a change. Thelma sat across from him. She crossed her legs and positioned her notepad and pen.

"I'm sorry, but I have to know. What did you think of my rom-dram script? I think it's going to be very empowering for women."

"You *do* eventually get your heroine to a state of higher status, but only after she subscribes to demeaning customs and acts subservient in the male-dominated workplace. And for some reason you have other women getting slaughtered who don't want to play along with the sexist protocol."

"But don't you find it romantic?"

"Not in the least. I've researched your condition and based on your questionnaire answers and my personal observations of you I've found your symptoms to be consistent with individuals of the T-type, or 'thrill-seeking' personality.

"What personal observations?"

"Both times you arrived here I heard you run down the hallway just seconds before our scheduled time, then you walked the last few steps. It's thrilling to race the clock isn't it, Mr. L'Hommedieu—to risk being late?"

Jake glanced away. "So, what if I *do* like thrills in my life?"

"When brains of Type-T persons are exposed to arousing images, an area called the 'insula' activates. Images, such as the ones in your films, stimulate strong emotional responses of fear and pleasure which trigger internal chemical reactions that lead to a 'dopamine fest' in your bloodstream, giving you temporary feelings of euphoria and intoxication followed by the inevitable downer."

"What are you saying, doctor?"

"You're addicted to horror movies. It's warped your attitude towards women."

"Really?"

"Do you ever watch films *other* than horror movies?"

"No. I was afraid it might contaminate my creative process."

"Since you're a director I'll show you what I'm talking about in a way you'll be able to relate. I'd like to show you some short films of different genres. I'll stop the projector just before the climax. Tell me, as a director, what you think would logically come next.

As Thelma dimmed the lights, a projector screen lowered from the ceiling. A girl and a boy in their late teens flirted with each other in a tree house as the moon rose through an open window. Thelma stopped the film.

"Alright, Jake, what do you think happens next?"

"That's easy, a werewolf reaches in the window and rips the girl's head off for being promiscuous."

Thelma switched the film back on. The couple gradually started making out and promised their undying love to each other.

"What kind of plot is that?" Jake said, "there's no moral retribution."

"The girl expresses her emotions toward the boy physically. It's natural. They're both young healthy teenagers."

Jake shook his head. "What kind of sick film is this? I feel nauseous." He swallowed while blinking and holding his forehead.

"Let's try another one."

Thelma flipped the switch. A young woman is hired at a prominent Wall Street firm. She makes many sales calls and closes lots of sales. The boss praises her hard work and she gets a promotion. She smiles as her co-workers look on in admiration.

Thelma switched the film off. "What happens next, Jake?"

"Late at night, as she's working on paperwork, a psychopath stalks down the hallway with a chainsaw and slaughters her for her co-workers to find the next morning."

Thelma switched on the film. The woman stood before a chart at a board meeting where she demonstrated how her team shattered all previous sales records. She is promoted again and finally becomes the C.E.O.

"She's newly hired! She hasn't paid her dues," Jake complained. "Why does she get all these breaks? Did you see how happy she looked? Like she didn't have a care in the world. She should be punished for being so presumptuous, so headstrong, for being—"

"Strong, talented and confident? Listen to yourself. You have serious issues regarding women, Mr. L'Hommedieu."

"I'm going to be sick," Jake said. "Where's your restroom?"

"Second door down the hallway on the right."

Jake bolted out the door. Moments later he stumbled into the room looking ill.

"I don't *want* to be this way. Please help me, doctor."

"Overcoming your addiction to years of watching only horror movies is going to require total abstinence from these images, then a re-wiring of your mental pathways."

"But it's my job! I must create enough of those images to finish two more movies. That rom-dram script was my way out."

"You have no concept of such films. It's going to need a re-write."

"That was five years of work!"

"The way you love to race against time you should find a deadline challenging. I'm willing to help you, but I *have* to know you are putting in the effort."

"If I do, will I be well enough to ask out that girl I was telling you about?"

"We'll see. First, let's get you registered for the program. I'm talking about ninety uninterrupted days of counseling. Can you commit to the program, Jake?"

"Whatever it takes to ask out Vera."

~

Barry strolled through the special effects warehouse. He perused the trays of faux weaponry: axes, machetes, bowie knives, sickles, and finally the one he wanted: the cleaver. He lifted it. It had a heavy black nylon handle with a flat, shiny blade. Over the blade there was a rubber edge spray-painted a high-gloss silver. It looked real. The blunt rubber edge wouldn't kill anyone if it accidentally hit them, but it delivered substantial weight and left female victims with ugly painful bruises that sometimes lasted a week or more. Barry swung the cleaver at a wooden shelf. Despite the rubber edge, the cleaver left a half-inch-deep dent in the shelf top.

My last couple of horror films—might as well go for broke. I can't wait to see Vera suffer for her art, Barry thought.

~

Vera knocked on the trailer door. The driver stood behind her, crumpled clothes in his arms. Serena opened the door with attitude: all serious scowl and hand on hip.

"Oh, it's *you,*" Serena said, "Come on in, get used to your new place."

"No," Vera stated flatly, "We're not starting out this way. Ask me nicely."

Serena dropped her arm and stared at the woman, 12 years her junior. Serena smiled.

"Please come in, dear. I'm so happy you've bumped off my long-time colleague, Naomi Nivens, who's been a beautiful scream queen and matinee idol since you were in diapers."

"I accept. I was invited to move in here by Barry just like you were."

Serena stepped aside as Vera and the driver paraded passed her.

"Your room is at the end of the hall on the left, just past Barry's"

Vera jerked her head slightly to the right. *Barry lives here?* The driver left, and Vera busied herself organizing her room. After a half hour of eerie silence, Serena appeared in Vera's doorway. Vera stood with her back to Serena and held Mandy up at face level.

"We're in Hollywood, Mandy," Vera said quietly to the stuffed mouse.

"That's adorable. A room dedicated to Mandy Mouse," Serena said. "You *are* young, aren't you? I apologize about earlier. Naomi's been a fixture around here for years. Could I fix you a drink? I make a mean Mai Tai."

Vera set Mandy on her dresser and smoothed the mouse's silk skirt.

"That would be great but Felix just got up in my face about learning my new lines."

"Vera, nobody does anything the first day of a new film. Felix is good at his job but he just likes to hear himself talk. You're not going to see him for the rest of the day. Now how about that drink?" Serena smiled and cocked an eyebrow.

"Okay, I'm sorry too," Vera said, "I'm pretty nice once you get to know me."

"Come on. I'll have these babies mixed up in a jiff."

Vera stood next to Serena in the kitchen. *Wow, this place has everything,* she thought.

"I'm not going to feel bad that Naomi isn't here anymore," Vera said. "Barry told me she had already moved out."

"No, it's not your fault. I guess you only get so many years to make your mark in the industry. It's just that Naomi and I were housemates for so long it's hard to get used to her not being here. Excuse me for a sec." Serena pushed 'puree.' The blender whirred loudly and filled the air with fragrances of rum and exotic juices.

"Speaking of Naomi," Vera said, "I heard she moved into Jake's place."

"I haven't heard from her. Good for her, she deserves some fun for a change."

"You're not going to believe this, it's probably just gossip, but Felix told me that Jake has a thing for me. That can't be true though, I mean, he wouldn't ask Naomi to move in if—"

"Hmm? Jake was never interested in Naomi when she was seeing Barry. Now that she's hit the skids, I guess she's easy pickings," Serena said.

"Jake's like that? That's pretty lame."

"I love Naomi, but she's not the sharpest tool in the shed and Jake's a *really* smart guy. You do the math."

Serena poured their drinks into two ice-filled glasses, plunged pineapple spears through the dark layers of rum and into the liquid-yellow centers—two golden hearts impaled.

Vera looked down at her shoes and followed Serena into the living room. The women reclined in the chaise lounges. Serena reached out and clinked glasses with Vera.

"Welcome to first class, my dear, for as long as it lasts."

Vera looked more hopeful. "Serena, I have to tell you, I can't even believe this has happened to me."

"When Barry first invited me to move in, I was totally thrilled too. He'd picked me out of a lineup of thirty girls. He told me what a big star I was going to be and how much money we'd make together. That was no bull. I became a star, we made money. But the funny thing was, all I wanted to do was run my fingers through his gorgeous head of hair."

"You mean that's his real hair? I thought it was a wig."

"It's real. At first you think *it's only hair,* but then it's so lustrous and thick you'll find yourself dreaming about it. You're going to touch it eventually and then—you'll see, you'll just fall in love with him. Then it's 'Yes, Barry this, and Yes, Barry, that.' That's what kept Naomi and me around so long." Serena cast her eyes to the heavens.

"You're putting me on, right? He's got to be in his fifties—gross!"
"He's sixty-three, honey, and trust me, you won't care when it hits you."
The door opened and Barry walked in.
"Well, it's good to see my two stars are getting to know each other!"

Chapter 10

Double Take

"I have a couple of rules since both you two girls are going to be co-staring in *Fifty Ways,*" Barry said.

Serena held her hand to her neck and gasped. She swallowed and slowly set her glass down. "Me too? Barry, are you serious?"

"You've earned it, kid. Tell Vera the scream queen's rules before a new shoot."

Serena's face morphed into nearly robotic memorization mode. "No sugar, no alcohol, no fatty foods. Go to bed early and eat healthy," she said.

"Yep," Barry agreed. "So no more Mai Tais for a while. I need you looking good for your slaughter scenes. Now, how about a tour for Vera, here?"

"My pleasure," Serena said, turning to Vera, "The trailer is over eighty feet long. You'll notice everything is padded and covered with the softest calf skin."

"So no drunk girls hurt themselves," Barry added. "We don't need no accidents here."

Vera noticed the subtle yellow and white faux finished walls and ceilings and cream-colored crown molding as Serena continued the tour.

"We each have our own Sealy Posturepedic queen-sized beds, our own Wi-Fi hook ups, hideaway sofas in our rooms, imported alpaca carpeting throughout. Two bathrooms with showers, Jacuzzi tubs, our own dressing rooms with California closet systems, full mirrors and lights that come on when you open the door. Cable TV in every room. In the living room we have our own high-def flat screens to watch the dailies on. Two fully-stocked bars, a completely accessorized gourmet kitchen, an on-call chef, Barry's limousine—but we have to check that he's not using it first—and whatever *other arrangements* you and Barry have," Serena said.

"That was real good, sweetheart. If your acting career ever goes south you can always become a tour guide," Barry said, and laughed heartily.

~

Jake sat across a desk from the on-call staff member at the rehab center.

"It's going to be three days until the cocaine is out of her system," her bloodstream, even her hair," the man said. "After that withdrawal symptoms will persist. She's been an addict for so many years it's going to be a daily struggle. Check back with us in a couple of days."

"Can she have a normal life again?" Jake asked.

"She'll have a better chance if she has something else to focus her energy on."

"She's an actress," Jake said.

"That's good. We'll need next week's expenses for Ms. Niven's care paid in advance."

Jake cleared his throat and pulled out his wallet.

~

Vera jogged slowly across the foggy morning lot as she waited for Serena.

"You are *killing me*, little girl," Serena yelled, barely shuffling her feet along.

"Come on, Serena, we've got to get our cardio up. Benny said to expect some really physical scenes," Vera yelled behind her.

Vera jogged in place and checked her Mandy Mouse wristwatch while Serena caught up: 7:25 A.M. "I don't mean to be rude," Vera said, "but we're going to be late. We still have to get showers and be there by 8:00. Come on or I'm going ahead."

"Go on, I can't act if I'm dead," Serena stammered.

Benny Edwards was a little bulldog of a man. Most people's first reaction was to laugh at him, with his old school short, white crew cut and suspenders. But one look at his serious stare and those impatient leathery lips quickly changed their minds.

Wet hair clung to Vera's face as she and the panting Serena arrived at the set.

"You're late, ladies," Benny said. He checked his gold Rolex against his tan wrist.

"We're sorry, Benny, it won't happen again," Serena said.

"I am not playing around here," Benny replied. "I could just as easily coach people who *want* to grow as actors. I'm on retainer. There are other actors on this lot. If you waste my time again, I'm going to go train them and *your* acting will suffer." He allowed several heavy seconds to tick by before he spoke again. "New girl, have a seat and learn. Serena, it's been a while since you were in the saddle. You ready to get real?"

"Yeah, Benny," Serena said.

"What we're going to work on, Vera, is having Serena get in touch with how open and vulnerable she can be in front of the camera."

Benny abruptly faced Serena. "Are you currently in a relationship?" he asked.

"Not really, I'm—" Serena answered.

Benny stepped closer to her. "It doesn't surprise me. I've known you for several years now. You don't bring much to the table. You don't have any type of degree, you're 35 years old and it shows, you don't take care of your body, you're not a good conversationalist, you aren't funny, you're not clever, you aren't particularly bright—"

"I'm actually not quite 35 and I'm jogging now," Serena replied, her brow creased.

"Jog? What's the point? *Look* at you. Your arms are saggy, you have lines on your face, I think you're downright ugly, if you can handle the truth. You haven't been in a movie for years and I *don't* know what makes you think you can act." Benny's eyes gleamed brightly.

"I *am* interesting. I know fashion," Serena offered, her voice quavering.

"That's pathetic. What man wants to hear about fashion? You must be a huge disappointment to your parents: you've never been married, never given them any grandchildren. They must think you a very ungrateful daughter."

"My parents have both passed away," Serena said, close to tears.

"Well, I'm sure they're happier not to be disappointed anymore—"

"That's enough!" Vera suddenly shouted, "I'm no acting coach, but that's too personal."

"I don't care if she hates me, look at the results," Benny said and gestured to the shaking, sobbing Serena. "Now *that's* vulnerable."

Vera stared open-mouthed at Benny.

~

Jake had just arrived on the set. Felix spotted Jake and walked down the corridor in his direction. *A man on a mission,* Jake thought. Jake's cell phone vibrated. The caller's name: "Jacqueline." Jake flipped his phone open.

"Hey, Mom."

"Jake, I think I know the approach you should take with Vera. It's simple."

"That's great! Just a minute, Mom,"

Felix was a few feet from Jake now and he began to speak, but Jake held up his index finger, closed himself inside an empty conference room, and locked the door behind him. Rapid knocks came from outside the door.

"Go ahead, Mom," Jake said into the phone.

"I know you think I was emotionally unavailable when you were younger, but I watched you interact with your sisters. You know, the sisters whose femininity drove you to make those dreadful movies?" Jacqueline said.

"Yes, Mother," Jake said.

"I've given some thought to why it's customary to cast beautiful women as victims in horror movies. Why a beautiful one if she's just going to get killed right away? I think it's because the frustrated men who make these movies feel they can't ever get the beautiful girl—so if they can't ever date them or marry them then they'll kill and degrade them on screen."

"Okay, go on."

"Well, I have good news for you. When you were an adolescent you were no prize, Jake. You were tall and skinny, you had acne and let's face it, honey, you had issues. But now you are so handsome and accomplished, and from our talk I can see you *really* want to be normal. Jake, there's no reason now that you can't have the beautiful girl!"

Jake thought back to the time when he was the hot new director in L.A., when he had slept with several attractive wanna-be actresses. But they had just used him for what they thought would be a leg-up in the industry.

"So that's it? Just like that I can have Vera?"

"Not quite. When you were younger, on rare occasions when you got out of your own head, I admired your ability to really listen when one of your sisters had a problem. I could tell you didn't like it one bit, but you did it. Remember what it's like to be decent, Jake? That's all you have to do with Vera. Take her out and then don't do what most directors do: go on and on about yourself. Just *listen to her.* If you get into a relationship it's a skill you'll need anyway."

"That sounds like it might just work. Thanks, Mom, I'll try it."

"And when it works, remember our deal, mister. You're coming home for Thanksgiving and Christmas *every year.*"

"You're on. Thanks, Mom, gotta run," Jake said, and hung up.

~

Jake opened the door and watched Felix rapidly move his lips. As Jake walked down the hallway, Felix fell in beside him in locked step. Jake only caught snippets of what Felix said:

"—schedule—inadequate lighting—really bad extras—"

Jake's mind was on Vera. *It must be a quiet dinner with a window seat, candlelight. She'll have problems, all women have problems. Of course, I'll listen to Vera and help her.*

"Jake!" Felix finally yelled. "There's someone I want you to meet. She's here right now."

Jake snapped out of his trance. He looked at Felix, who smirked.

"This way," Felix said, and led Jake into a back office.

Jake expected to see yet another of Felix's painfully thin girlfriends he'd met at a fashion show—and promised Jake could cast her as an extra. Jake entered and was taken aback by the large muscular woman who stood before him.

"Jake, meet Rhonda Roundhouse, a castoff from the Women's Wrestling Association."

Jake glanced at Felix and back to the woman who had to weigh 250 pounds, but she had such a pleasant face. Jake winced from her firm handshake.

"A pleasure. What may I do for you, Ms. Roundhouse?"

"For political reasons I am currently unemployed by the W.W.A. I am available for work here—anything you need. Set pieces moved, yard work, riffraff tossed off your property. Obviously, I can act too. Ever watch women's wrestling on TV?"

"No," Jake said. "Do you have a card? If I can think of someplace to use you, I'll be sure to give you a call?"

Felix was beside himself with barely contained giggles.

"Sure, here you go," Rhonda said, and handed Jake her card. "Nice meeting you, gentlemen. Have a nice day, now."

The woman left the office, closing the door behind her.

"I'm sure you're very amused with yourself, Felix," Jake said, "but if you ever waste my time like that again there's going to be a problem."

Felix held a finger to his lips and grinned.

~

"Okay, Vera, it's your turn," Benny said. "We're not going to go through *that* exercise until just before your big scene. Today is just about boundaries. You seem defiant to me or defensive, I'm not sure which. You don't want boundaries—it's no good for scream queens."

"What, just let people run over me?" Vera asked.

"No, as an actor, there's power in vulnerability. A man wants to do horrible things to you in this movie. What *I* care about is that you control the scene by telling the killer, 'Okay, you do whatever you're going to do to me, but only when I give you permission—see?' Then it seems real."

Vera didn't like the way Benny seemed so pleased with himself.

"You're the acting coach, so let's get on with it, I guess," she said.

"New girl, *lose* the attitude," Benny said, "we're going to practice now. No talking. You put up your hands and no matter how close I get you let me push your hands out of the way. You've gotta be like putty. Now get vulnerable, Vera."

~

Benny walked briskly to the back soundstage. He opened the solid gray steel door and stepped inside where Alex waited for him.

"Looks like you've put on ten pounds of muscle since the last movie," Benny said.

"Twelve," Alex said, and puffed out his chest.

"Ready to get into character?" Benny asked, and stepped into his padded suit.

"Yeah," Alex said.

"I'm gonna come at you and I want you to throw me around the set. You can't hurt me, but I really want you to try. For every bruise you give me through this padding I'll give you twenty bucks. Deal? There's just one more thing: I don't want Serena or Vera to see you until the day of their big scenes. Got it?"

"Sure, Benny," Alex said, and shoved the small, stocky man across the set.

~

Vera and Serena walked back to the trailer in silence. Vera couldn't believe how exhausted the boundaries exercise had left her. *I feel vulnerable alright. And confused.*

Inside the trailer, each of the women freshened up in their respective bathrooms then joined each other side-by-side in their lounge chairs.

"I guess we'd better get ready for tomorrow," Serena said.

They picked up their scripts and read. After a while they were able to concentrate. Serena was in three scenes before she was to get whacked, and Vera was in five. Vera read her lines and got lost in wondering how best to portray Alex's wife since she had never actually dated anyone.

An hour later, Barry walked into the trailer. Vera and Serena sat in the chaise lounges and nibbled paper-thin rice crackers while they studied their scripts.

"Wow, so solemn. How was your day, girls?" Barry asked.

"Tiring. Benny's really cruel, you know?" Serena said.

"You want to star in my films—you work with Benny."

"Sure, Barry, I just forgot how intense he can be."

"Toughen up, doll."

Barry walked by and brushed the back of his hand against Serena's cheek.

"Vera, how do you like your acting lessons so far?"

"Great, Barry. I mean, it's definitely hard work."

"You work hard, you play hard. Once this shoot is done, we're going to have a good time. What would you ladies like for dinner?"

"Just a little salad for me, Barry," Serena said.

"That sounds good," Vera agreed, still unaccustomed to Barry's generosity.

"You two aren't just having *salad*. You're stars! I'll order up the best gourmet salads you've ever tasted. Just sit right there and study. Work up a good appetite and I'll be back."

Vera watched Barry's auburn hair shimmer in the chandelier light. It bounced as he descended the steps and exited the trailer. *Like an impossibly soft, shiny forest.*

After Barry left the trailer Serena stood from her chaise lounge, excited.

"Guess what I have? It's your first dailies from *Zombie Betrayal*. Let's watch it."

Serena slid the DVD into the player mounted near the ceiling above Vera's lounge chair.

"Wow, they developed that fast," Vera said.

The images flowed across the hi-definition screen in vivid color. Lola's eyes looked wild, her zombie face ravenous, as she attacked.

"That's me," Vera said. "Gross! It looks so real. Ooh, that's mega-disgusting."

"Agreed, but that's how we get paid. You'll get used to it. We study and learn how to do it better next time. Jake calls it performance art."

"No wonder Bubbe freaked out."

~

The next day the film staff crowded the set. Barry strode onto stage—a warehouse with a framed-in three-sided bedroom and no ceiling. He looked up at the large, fuzzy microphone suspended ten feet above his head. Beckoning with his beefy hands for the key grip to lower the mic, Barry resembled a fat cat that wanted a dangling toy. The mic dropped and he spoke.

"Okay, people, quiet down," Barry said. "Today is an auspicious occasion. Serena Miles has been out of the spotlight for *quite* a while. I told her we had to wait for the perfect movie for her to come along and I keep my promises, don't I, sweetheart?"

Serena smiled.

"Look at that, she can still blush even after all this time," Barry said.

Polite laughter followed.

"Anyway, let's hear it for one of our greatest scream queens: Miss Serena Miles!" The set echoed with clapping as Serena nodded graciously to the staff.

"Barry, I'm going to skip the shoot today," Jake said. "I'm not going to attend any more shoots that involve slaughter scenes. You'll have to direct." Jake stepped sideways between the seats to leave the building.

"What are you talking about? Do your job, man," Barry feigned. He wanted fewer people on set for what was about to happen.

"I'll write them," Jake said, "I'll do auditions, edit, whatever but I'm not going to actually *watch* the slaughter scenes anymore. I *am* doing my job."

"Fine. Just make sure you follow through on our deal."

"No problem. I'll see you later."

Barry waved his hand and made a disgruntled face in Jake's direction then faced the stage and smiled.

Stagehands ran like tennis ball boys. They snatched stray film canisters, cotton balls, sandwich wrappers, anything that looked out of place in a domestic bedroom. The call squawked through the bullhorn: "All quiet on the set!"

"Why isn't Vera here?" the make-up woman asked the key grip.

"She isn't supposed to see Alex before her slaughter scene. It amps up the intensity, so she stays scared, doesn't get too chummy—"

Barry slapped the grip on the back. "Quiet!" Barry hissed.

Serena took her position next to the bed, while Alex stood outside the doorway, out of her sight, and Felix paced onto the set.

"*Fifty Ways to Cleave Your Lover.* Kara Sell slaughter scene, take one, action!" Felix snapped the clapperboard together and backpedaled off screen.

Serena took on the persona of her character, Kara, as Alex entered the room. When Serena saw Alex, her eyes widened. *He looks so powerful since his last role as a lab tech.* Serena had rehearsed this choreography with a stunt double, but not with Alex.

"I can't believe we're finally married. I have a lot of plans for the house. You'll see, I'll make it really cozy here," Serena said.

"How do you like your new name?" Alex asked.

"I love it, *Kara Sell,*" Serena said.

"Say it again for me," Alex said, a knowing look on his face.

"Kara Sell," Serena said. Slowly, the significance of the name seemed to dawn on her. Her eyes widened as she backed away.

"This isn't happening; you're *him*, aren't you—the Cuisinart Killer!"

"Yes, Ma'am." Alex said, and pulled a cleaver from behind his back.

Serena and the stunt double had always hit their marks perfectly. *This is so irresponsible for Barry not to let me rehearse with Alex!* Serena thought.

Serena faked left. Alex charged her as she ran to the right. He reacted so fast she couldn't believe it. He shoved her backwards onto the bed.

Alex swung and actually struck Serena's wrist with the rubber-coated cleaver. The heavy object stung her wrist. Her nerves shot a pain signal to her brain. Serena couldn't scream—so shocked she only gasped. Alex drew back and struck her shoulder. Serena gasped again, then remembered to scream.

"Stop!" Serena yelled.

Felix consulted his script and leaned toward Barry. "There's no dialogue on page thirty—only screaming," he whispered.

"Sure seems real though. I like it," Barry whispered back.

Alex swung and struck her thigh.

This hurts! He's hitting me every time! Serena wanted to curl up in a ball, but she wanted to be a star even worse. Despite the pain, she emitted her obligatory shriek with the final chop of the cleaver to her other wrist.

"That's a wrap!" Felix called.

Serena stood and rubbed her bruises—deep, purple bruises—on her shoulder, her wrists and her thighs. Alex turned and walked away.

"Hey, you sonofabitch," Serena yelled.

Alex slowly turned around. "You talking to me?" he smirked.

"Yeah, that was *way* too rough! Look at this, you really hit me!"

"Sorry," Alex said, and left.

Barry turned his head to hide his smile. Brian, Lola and the other staff members glanced uncomfortably at each other, then looked away.

Chapter 11

Jake & Rhonda

After leaving the set, Jake wandered the sunny lot. *Serena's slaughter scene—just another simulated attack on women. Sitting one out won't erase them from my memory, but it's a start.*

He strolled to the cafeteria, bought a cup of coffee, then went back outside. It was peaceful with nobody asking questions. Jake sipped his coffee and checked his watch: 12:30. They *should be wrapping things up in there by now.*

He sat on a bench and watched as acting hopefuls jogged toward B Studio for an audition with Benny. Jake glanced at the set doors for signs of life. A voice from behind him called his name and Jake turned around. He recognized the muscular woman from the other day.

"Excuse me, Mr. L'Hommedieu. I'd just like a moment of your time. You see, I'm a very capable person, very responsible, very loyal and a hard worker. I just need a break right now. I'd be happy to do anything you need around here: run out for lunch, coffee, dump the trash, clean up sets."

The double doors burst open and staff members flooded onto the lawn. Jake turned to watch. *They look disturbed,* Jake thought. *Must have been an intense scene. Glad I sat it out.*

Most of the crew followed the sidewalk toward the cafeteria, but Felix and Andy saw Jake talking with Rhonda. Their faces lit up and they walked directly for him.

"Oh, great," Jake mumbled.

"So, you couldn't stay for the slaughter scene, but you've found a friend," Felix said.

Jake nodded and glanced at his feet, hoping they would leave.

"I see what you have in common though," Andy said. "Your sense of fashion! You two would look adorable at a diner together. Eating—what?" Andy glanced at Felix.

"Corn pone, chicken chitlins and ham hocks." Felix said.

"Oh yes, and 'dumplins' and gravy, and don't forget the pie," Andy chimed in.

"Don't forget some chitlins for your chillens."

"Do you think they'll actually crossbreed?" Felix said. "What would those 'chillen' look like? Ma and Pa L'Hommedieu? You must send selfies. Promise?"

"It's been fun, but Andy and I are famished. We'll have to chat later. Ta-ta," Felix said.

Rhonda watched them leave then looked back at Jake.

"Excuse me, Mr. L'Hommedieu, but don't they work for you?"

"They do."

"Well, it's none of my business, but why do you let them treat you that way?"

"They've worked here so long, they're good at their jobs—I don't want to make waves."

"Alrighty, but there's such a thing as proper respect for your employer. It's fine if you don't want to hire me, but I suggest you call my boyfriend. He'll get those guys to show you the respect you deserve."

Rhonda pulled out a business card and held it out. Jake took it, a black and white card that read: ***Dark Snout Persuasive Services—the nicest guy you'll never meet. Results guaranteed.***

"So, what would your friend do? I can't have them hurt. I need them around here."

"He'll change their minds about the way they think of you. He's so charming they'll want to treat you better."

"I guess it's worth a try."

"You'll thank me. Then maybe you'll consider hiring me too."

"You seem nice. I'll try you out as an assistant set dresser for a week. You said you don't mind moving heavy things, right?"

"No, sir, no problem at all. Thank you, Mr. L'Hommedieu."

"Come with me," Jake said.

~

That night Serena cried as Vera helped her from the Jacuzzi and wrapped her in a terrycloth robe and slippers. Vera got four ice packs from the kitchen and helped Serena to bed.

"Ow, ooh, ouch, it hurts so bad. Thanks for being so sweet, Vera. *Ow, damn.* Just the special effects scene left, it's okay if I look unhealthy when I'm all hacked up. Make me a vodka tonic," Serena said.

"You poor thing."

Vera returned with ibuprofen and the drink, and helped Serena sit up in bed so she could take a sip. Serena swallowed, closed her eyes and winced.

"I'm sorry you're so banged up," Vera said. "Do you want to see a doctor?"

"No. But Vera when it comes time for your scene with Alex—be careful."

"It seems like it's every woman for herself around here."

"The stunt scenes are always a little rough. Accidents happen—but this is the worst. I think Alex was really trying to hurt me. *Ooh, ouch.*"

"There's no way those were all accidents. *I* wish *I'd* been there," Vera scowled and tucked Serena in for the night.

~

Aaron Finkelstein rang the doorbell of Zissell Horowitz's house. The brass peep hole opened, and a small eye looked out. The door opened and Zissell smiled up at the officer.

"Aaron! You look so handsome in your uniform. Come in, come in."

"Hello, Mrs. Horowitz. Is Vera here? I haven't seen her at the restaurant."

Zissell reached up and pulled Aaron inside by the back of his shoulder.

"You sit here. I will get us tea and Hamantasch." Zissell briskly walked into the kitchen and returned with triangular-shaped apricot and nut-filled pastries and two teacups.

"You come to see Vera? Goot. I like you, Aaron, you was always goot boy, goot jew and now look at you: a grown man, successful, handsome. *A policeman.*"

"Thank you, Mrs. Horowitz. I'm up for a promotion soon too: Captain. I've got a little house over on the Eastside, seven more years and it's paid off. I'm looking for a wife, a 'Mrs. Finklestein.'" Aaron laughed.

"Ooh. I wonder who will the lucky one be?"

"I was hoping to discuss that with Vera. Do you know where I could find her?"

"She goes wit business that makes disgusting movies. I kick her out until she gets smart." Zissell handed Aaron a name and address. "She is my Bas-yekhyde, di, Aaron."

The old Jewish words echoed from Aaron's childhood. "Your only girl child, right? Falchion Films, eh? Yeah, they make horror movies so shmaltzy they're almost comical. Thank you, Mrs. Horowitz. I'll see if I can find her."

Chapter 12

The Man With No Name

"This is absurd," Jake said, looking at the business card. From the privacy of his office, he dialed the number on the card. Two rings, a series of clicks, a modem sound. Then a recorded message from a distorted voice:

"Thank you for your call. This is a secure line. Once received, your message will be erased, and all evidence of this transmission will be washed from the system via state-of-the-art techniques. Leave the name and contact information of the party of interest, henceforth referred to as the P.O.I. Describe, completely, your desired result regarding P.O.I. and any pertinent relationships of which Dark Snout Persuasive Services, henceforth referred to as D.S.P.S., should be apprised. Leave desired mode of contact. D.S.P.S. will contact you within 24 hours. You have two minutes to leave your message. Have a nice day."

After the beep Jake took a deep breath and left his message. "Hello. The person of, I mean the P.O.I.'s names, are Felix Short and his partner, Andy Faull. I don't want them harmed or threatened in any way. The problem is they are constantly making belligerent, disrespectful remarks to me, their employer. They are both very good at their jobs, but they've made me dread coming to work. I'll need a text as to your rates and methods before I'm comfortable giving any more information about the, the P.O.I."

Jake read over his rom-dram script for the hundredth time in five years. This was it—he had to do the hard work, the excruciating rewrite his therapist said would heal him. *Must think differently. I'm not comfortable with how some of the women characters are beginning to seem so uninhibited. At times they seem like they're not even afraid of the bad guys. There, I've taken out the last slaughter scene. The script seems so bare now—just women achieving their goals, standing up to men. This is it—going to get sick!*

Jake ran into his bathroom just as his breakfast backed up in his throat and launched out into the toilet. He went to the sink and washed his face with cold water then toweled off.

This rewrite's going to be the end of me, he thought, brushing his teeth. *Got to work on something else.*

He organized his desk and unrolled the proposed blocking sheet from Felix. *No, Felix, the dolly won't fit into a three-foot space against the wall.* Jake wadded the sheet into a ball and took a shot at the trashcan: Two points.

There was a knock at his door. He answered it and a buff-looking policeman stood there.

"Are you Jake L'Hommedieu?"

"Yes, what can I do for you, officer?"

"I'm looking for Vera Horowitz. I understand she works here?"

"Yes. Here's Felix Short's card. He's somewhere on the set," Jake said. "Just call him. He should be able to track Vera down. If Felix doesn't know check with Shelley, the receptionist at the front desk. She knows everything that goes on around here."

"Thank you," the policeman said. Jake closed the door behind him.

That's weird, Jake thought, *why is a cop looking for Vera?*

Two hours later the text arrived. The number read: RESTRICTED.

"D.S.P.S. Rate $300.00 per hr. plus expenses. Billing begins at initial contact. Methods = my own, but P.O.I. will not be harmed. That said, if accosted I reserve right of self-preservation. Need personal details, description P.O.I., require time & place for initial contact. I am mobile in East L.A., require one hr. notice. Let's begin."

Jake sent what he knew of Felix's and Andy's personalities, taste in clothing, music they had mentioned, and job titles. Then downloaded two photographs of them and texted D.S.P.S.

"What the hell's this guy think he's going to do?" Jake murmured.

The next day after the blocking session, Felix and Andy left the set to make way for the lighting crew. Jake followed them on foot from 50 yards away, tapped his cell phone and texted Dark Snout: "Get ready. Tailing P.O.I.s down Hollywood Boulevard. Will send time/place for initial contact soon."

"Waiting/Ready" the reply text shot back.

Jake saw Felix and Andy hail a cab and get in. He pointed to his chauffer, who climbed into the limo and revved the engine. Jake got in back.

"Follow that cab," Jake said.

"How original, sir," the chauffer said.

After 15 minutes, the cab left 101 south and turned onto I-110. *I know where they're going,* Jake thought. He was right. The cab swerved into the Santee Alley Shopping district. The cab parked and Jake followed Felix and Andy on foot. They entered a store. Jake texted: "Contact point inside Rapunzel Fashion Showroom, Santee Alley Shopping District."

A minute after Jake pushed send, he received another text: "Thank you. Location confirmed. Leave vicinity immediately. Will take it from here."

Jake looked around. He just wanted a *glimpse* of this Dark Snout guy. He tried crossing the street and watching from a distance. His cell buzzed. He looked at the screen. "Leave now."

Jake got into the back of his limo and drove away.

As the limo pulled out and turned left at the corner, a man with movie star good looks emerged from behind a group of teenagers, who danced to a beat box while a young man rapped. Dark Snout strode directly through the doorway of the Rapunzel Fashion Showroom where he stood behind rows of paid seats next to two security guards. Beyond the seated patrons was an elevated shiny white runway. A curtain ruffled in the background shadows.

He spotted the backs of Felix's and Andy's heads, where they'd apparently paid top dollar for front row seats just in front of the runway. He adjusted the hearing device in his ear and dialed in the frequency, then fine-tuned another dial to eliminate every sound except Felix's and Andy's voices.

The thumping beat of the music flowed from the speakers and the show began. A girl and her mother stood in front of Dark Snout.

"Why is this place called Rapunzel's?" the girl whispered.

"Because all the male models have really long hair—like in the fairytale."

On stage an overhead light followed a young man with blonde hair to his hips. He strutted onto the catwalk, wearing a loose shimmering long-sleeved shirt with bold, vertical stripes, graduated from graphite to charcoal into medium gray, each with mini squares of three shades of shiny gold running the length of each stripe, worn with black skinny jeans and severely tapered black Cuban heels.

The young man stopped just in front of Felix and Andy, posed then turned abruptly, his golden hair splaying gloriously in the light. He then strutted into the shadows. Andy touched Felix on the sleeve.

"Snap! That's the one, on the very first model. I'd *kill* for that outfit. What's the price?"

Felix read aloud from his buyer's schedule, "Number 1, Celestial Catnip, $6,750.00."

"No! Well, you have to pay for nice things." Andy squeezed Felix's arm.

"I know," Felix said, "Wouldn't you *love* to get inside Adriano Moretti's head at the moment he created a new look?"

"There would be nothing more exquisite," Andy said.

Dark Snout stood and discreetly exited the show. He stepped outside, read from his program and texted: "Giovanny, need Adriano Moretti knockoff #1, Celestial Catnip. Whole outfit. Nice commission 4 U., D.S."

~

The next day at Falchion Films, Lola sat in the break room and blew a perfect smoke ring that quavered and grew in mid-air. It hung there, six inches in diameter. Brian approached her, reached out and slid his hand through Lola's brittle hair and pulled her misshapen lips to meet his through the smoke ring. She pressed her chipped, ratty nails to his face and lightly pushed him away.

"That was an unusual first kiss," Lola said.

"That's the way I always see you, through a haze of lights. Through this smoke ring you look—enchanted ugly," Brian said with a kind of wonder. When Lola smiled, actually a frown, one of her moles disappeared behind thick, cracked lips, and her eyes squinted like dull raisins. "Let's get to work. But you can keep talking to me that way if you want. We can make out at lunch behind the dumpster."

Brian and Lola left the break room as Andy crossed the quad.

"The lighting's better, but I want more diagonals," Felix said.

"I told Brian that *yesterday*," Andy said. "There he is now!" Andy said and turned to Brian.

"Brian, you'd better do your job. You can flirt with that hag later."

Just then a handsome man of an unreadable age (maybe late 20s, early 30s) with coppery-brown hair that hung below his waist, strode confidently down the sidewalk right in front of them, his nose in the air. A loose shirt with shimmering wide stripes of charcoal, graphite and light gray, punctuated by multi-hued gold squares, floated around his torso while black skinny jeans hugged his hips and those same ruthless Cuban heels propelled him away.

"My god, he's *gorgeous!*" Andy gasped.

"He's wearing Celestial Catnip! I didn't think anyone could even buy those outfits yet," Felix said.

"Well, go find out who he is!"

Felix walked after the stranger. *I don't want to have to run, but who walks that fast?* Felix caught up to the man and cleared his throat.

"Excuse me, that's an Adriano Moretti original you're wearing, isn't it?"

The man turned, his beautiful locks spun, and he posed, one hand on his hip.

"Yes."

"It's remarkable. How you were able to purchase one so soon? We just watched the launch of the new line yesterday."

"I am a personal friend of Adriano. He's a lovely man."

"But what are you doing here? This is a sorry little B-horror movie lot. If you know Mr. Moretti surely you have better places to be than—"

"My dearest friend in all the world is a director here, Mr. Jake L'Hommedieu."

"You're friends with *Jake?* I mean, of course. Jake's a great guy."

"Jake and Mr. Moretti and I are attending a private showing of his *newest* line. *This* fashion candy will only be available in Milan for the first year."

"Jake likes fashion?"

"Jake likes me. Mr. Moretti *adores* Jake. So I convinced Jake to come with. I've told Jake if he wants to bring along a special guest, he's welcome to but he's yet to take me up on the offer. Excuse me." The man walked away.

"Wait, what's your name?" Felix yelled before he could stop himself.

The man walked briskly back.

"I'm Clark Clout, and you are?" The man extended his hand.

"Felix Short." They shook. "It's a pleasure to meet a friend of Jake's."

~

The next day at lunchtime Jake sat alone. Felix and Andy approached him.

"Jake, what are you doing sitting here by *yourself?*" Felix said, sitting across from him.

"I can't imagine a *director* eating lunch alone," Andy said, and sat next to Jake.

"Okay, what do you guys want?"

"Nothing," Felix said. "Can't your assistant directors hang out with you?"

"Seriously. I know there's some big joke coming so let's get it out of the way."

"Jake, I know we've teased you a bit too much, but we'd like to make amends.

We met your friend earlier, Clark Clout?"

"Who?"

"He *said* he was your dearest friend. He knows Adriano Moretti?"

Jake pondered the name. "Clark Clout, yeah. Where did you run into Clark?"

"Right here on the quad," Felix answered. "Mr. Clout said you could bring a friend to see one of Adriano Moretti's shows. I just want you to know that Andy and I are *very* available."

"Let me have a little peace, quit nagging the crap out of me and I'll *consider* it."

"Sure thing, Jake. Enjoy your lunch," Felix said.

That night Jake received a text: "D.S.P.S. Invoice: 10 hrs. @ $300.00/hr. = $3,000.00 + $750.00 expenses = Total Due: $3,750.00. Visa, MasterCard & AmEx. accepted. Thank you for your business."

Jake slid his credit card through his smart phone app, entered his information and pushed "send."

"Best three grand I ever spent."

Chapter 13

Reveal

A distant scream jolted Vera awake. She instinctively reached for her cell phone: 12:47 A.M. The scream reverberated again—far away, but not too far—it came from inside the trailer. Vera stumbled out of bed, made her way down the hall into Serena's room, and flipped on the light. Serena sat up in bed, dark circles beneath her eyes, damp hair stuck to her face.

"I can't stand this pain, Vera, look!" Serena gasped.

The purple bruises on her wrists and shoulder had spread and become a swollen potpourri of reds and fuchsias.

"I'll take you to the hospital," Vera said. "Come on, let's get you dressed."

Half an hour later, Vera talked with a nurse while Serena, who wore a hospital gown, sat on the edge of an exam table. She rocked back in forth in an attempt to deal with the pain.

"These are some very suspicious-looking injuries," the nurse said, and held up one of Serena's wrists, "How did she get these?"

"We're actors at Falchion Studios," Vera said, "She got them during a movie scene from a rubber-coated cleaver,".

"They might as well have used the real thing. Who did this?"

"The actor's name is Alex Boxwell."

"Blunt force trauma like this can cause blood clots or nerve and tendon damage. I'll need to photograph these injuries for our records. This is abuse—something Ms. Miles may want to pursue in court." The nurse focused the camera on Serena's wounds.

Vera left Serena with the hospital staff for overnight observation. She had the nurse make copies of Serena's injury photos and took them with her on the drive back to the trailer. *If Alex hit Serena in front of all those people, why didn't anybody do anything?*

I don't want to see him, Vera thought of her obligatory pre-shoot acting lesson with Benny Edwards. After a fifteen-minute ride, the limo swung into Barry's parking spot and Vera trudged toward Room 3B. She opened the door and there he was. The automatic door closed behind her.

"Come in," Benny said, "You're late. Wasting my time already!"

"Sorry, Benny."

"Just shut up and listen. I saw the rough cut of your last 'performance.'" Benny's fingers made air quotes.

"Wasn't my scream good enough?"

"Your scream was the only thing that *did* work. Your *attitude* is all wrong."

"My attitude?"

"Don't you know what you're supposed to be? When you set foot on that stage you become *nothing. Worthless.*"

"I'd just been torn apart by a zombie and she ate my intestines."

"Yeah, but you didn't sell it with your eyes. Whoever comes across that stage at you is much more powerful, much faster, much more a survivor, and therefore much more *deserving* of life. Whereas you are weak, insignificant and worthless—just like in real life."

"What's *that* supposed to mean?"

"I heard before your lucky break you got fired from your job as a waitress."

"That's not fair."

"You're twenty-three and you lived with your grandmother."

"But that's because—"

"That's because you're like a baby. Weak and helpless. Can't hold a job, can't earn a living, no friends. I heard your grandmother came in here to fight your battle against Jake—of all people."

"I didn't *ask* her to come in here."

"All you had to do was cry for help. And scream. You fell out of the nest, Baby Bird. You're on the ground, waiting for a predator to come along. *That's* what I mean by just like in real life. Everybody senses you're weak. You want to get fired from this job too?"

"No." Vera hung her head.

Benny jumped up in her face. "Then the next time a killer comes at you on that stage let us all see what you really are: eyes wide open with terror, no fight in your worthless little body, like you're scared to *death*. Because that's what you were born to be, Vera Horowitz: *a victim.*"

~

It had been three weeks since Naomi was admitted to the rehab center. Jake sat across a glass coffee table from the counselor assigned to her case.

"How is she doing?" Jake asked.

"She really *wants* to get better. Not like some patients. It's in their eyes: the scheming, the gears turning, obsessed with getting their next fix."

"Is she okay to go back to work?"

"We've reduced her night sweats and cravings with proper nutrition, sauna sessions and regular exercise to eliminate toxins from her fat cells. She's had more depression-free days. You can take her out of here any time, but she needs to stay busy or she's going to revert to her old behavior," the counselor said, "I definitely would not leave her alone. She needs to stay connected. She needs structure and supervision."

"Gotcha," Jake said, and considered this. "And if I wait longer before I pick her up?" Jake said.

"Same deal, she needs a lifestyle change."

"Alright, I'll take her today," Jake said, but wrinkled his brow.

~

Jake and Naomi rode in the back seat of the limo on the return trip to the Falchion lot.

"Wow, Naomi, you're in such good shape," Jake said.

"Thanks, Jake. They worked me out like crazy on that Stairmaster. I don't know how to thank you for helping me."

"*I* do. Do you really see yourself as an actress or were you just hanging out at Barry's trailer because it was easy?"

"I've always wanted to be an actress.My first shoot with Barry was when I was seventeen; I starred in *Face Invaders.*"

"I remember. And since then we've made a lot of bad movies together. Still, you had some decent acting moments over the years. In *The Memphis In-Law Mangler*, for instance, you nailed your character. Can you act that well again?"

"Just give me the chance, Jake."

"I'll give you that chance right after lunch."

The limo turned into the Falchion Studio lot and into his private parking space.

~

Vera showered, changed clothes, and crossed the lot. She entered the set and glanced up on stage where carpenters built a fake fireplace in a bedroom. She would be portrayed as a victim there at 12:45 that afternoon. Vera walked through the doorway, down the hall, and into the break room.

Framed Plexiglas-covered Screen Actors Guild Safety notices hung on the wall. Vera scanned the intro: "As an actor, you are ultimately responsible for your own safety and the safety of your fellow cast members. You have the absolute right to say no to any stunt or scene you think might be dangerous. You have the right to request a stunt double. Support your fellow performers who say no. If you have a problem call the guild." Vera programmed the Actors Guild phone number into her cell and left for Barry's limo.

~

Jake and Naomi strutted along one of the sidewalks that crisscrossed the lot. Jake checked Naomi's balance. Despite her ordeal, she was so fit that she resembled a runway model in the designer outfit he had brought her to change into. It briefly occurred to him that he and Naomi were each in their own kind of recovery. He frowned, then put on an upbeat face for her sake.

"Let's get some lunch," Jake said.

"Why do we have to eat at the cafeteria, Jake? I don't want to run into Barry."

"I can bring anyone I want there. Besides, I have to stay on the set today and the new script's in my office so you can study your lines there."

Studio employees came and went from the cafeteria doors like bees from a hive. Jake and Naomi approached a petite young woman from a diagonal sidewalk. She had dark shiny hair and a figure reminiscent of Audrey Hepburn's. *Vera!* Vera saw Jake with Naomi, clucked her tongue, and looked away. Jake's heartbeat raced. He felt alive, and gave chase.

"Vera, wait a minute," Jake called out.

Vera never broke stride. Jake caught up and stepped in front of her. "Hey, I haven't seen you for a couple of days. How are you?"

"Just fine. You and Naomi make a nice couple."

"We're—not a couple."

"She moved into your place, didn't she?" Vera said, disgusted.

"It's just temporary. She doesn't have a job yet."

At Barry's limo, Vera waved off the driver and opened the rear door herself.

"Nice of you to help the girl out," she said. See you later," Vera turned away.

"Wait! You have the wrong idea. Where are you going?"

"I'm concerned for everyone's safety after what happened, and somebody's got to take action around here," Vera said as she climbed into the back seat.

"We'll go with you. What happened anyway?"

"*You* should know, Jake. Serena's in the hospital. People are getting hurt on your movie. And no, I'll go alone, you two have fun together."

Jake stared as Vera pulled the door closed and the limo purred away.

~

Barry sat in the cafeteria by himself at his usual spot: a table on an elevated platform where he could watch the action. He dug into a deep dish of pasta. He stabbed a meatball with his fork and twirled it until he'd ensnared it with a three-inch ball of spaghetti. He admired his glistening prey for a second before he engulfed it with his mouth. *Good heavens, how delicious, grated cheese, garlic, mushrooms, tomatoes, spices. Wonder what kind of meat this is?*

Barry became aware of the bundle of frenetic, impatient energy that was Felix, who hovered over his seat and wrung his hands. Barry chewed and slowly looked up at Felix, one eyebrow raised—a predator interrupted while feeding.

"What?" Barry said.

"Serena's slated for her special effect shots and she's nowhere to be found," Felix said.

"So, handle it, that's what you get paid for."

"Okaaay, well, Vera's slaughter scene is next and I can't find her either. Neither one is answering their cell phones."

"I'm not going to babysit you, Felix. Find them or you're fired."

Felix started to speak but then turned on his heel and left the cafeteria. The seated diners' faces turned in unison and stared as Jake and Naomi entered the cafeteria—from Barry to Jake and Naomi then back to Barry again—like a herd of gazelles who watched one of their own about to get pulled down by a cheetah. Barry stood, wiped his mouth, patted his belly, and watched Jake cross the room with the tall, striking redhead.

"Hey, Kid, come here!" Barry bellowed across the room.

Naomi glanced, saw Barry and quickly looked away. Jake turned to Naomi and saw the miserable look on her face.

"Get what you want, I'll be a minute," Jake said to Naomi, then approached Barry.

"I'm not sticking around to talk with him," Naomi said from the a la carte line.

Barry grinned and beckoned to the air as Jake walked over.

"Is this what you've been doing instead of directing our film, Kid? She's looking good." Barry gestured to Naomi. "Maybe I let her go too soon."

"Did you know Serena is in the hospital?"

"No. For what?"

"I don't know. Vera said something happened to her on the set."

"She had a stunt scene with Alex, but I didn't realize she really got hurt."

"I'm going to go," Jake said.

"Do your job, Jake. *Fifty Ways* isn't going to shoot itself."

~

Vera's cell phone had buzzed for an hour, but she couldn't allow any distractions—she had to talk with Serena. She glanced down. The last fifteen calls were listed as: "Felix, Felix, Felix."

The limo pulled up in front of Malibu Memorial and Vera ran inside. She got Serena's room from the front desk and pushed the "2" button on the elevator floor panel.

Vera heard two nurses conversing as she waited for the elevator. They lowered their voices slightly as they stepped behind her and waited for the elevator.

"You watch out for that Mexican woman I saw in here last week," one nurse said.

"The one trying to get drugs? Or the one fishing for plastic surgery candidates?"

"The one fishing for face job patients for her uncle in Tijuana. If you see her call security immediately."

The elevator doors opened, and the three women stepped inside.

"I'll call security, but is she really doing any harm?" the other nurse asked.

"Absolutely! She puts patients at risk, robs the hospital of revenue and promises people they're going to be beautiful again after major facial trauma. Gives them false hope."

The elevator doors slid open and Vera stepped out. She found the on-call nurse who led her to Serena's bedside. Serena looked exhausted. Her wrists and shoulder were wrapped in white gauze, and a clear line ran to her arm from an IV bag hung on a stand.

"Ms. Miles is on a blood thinner and a morphine drip. She can talk but she might not make much sense right now," the nurse said and left Vera alone.

"Serena? Serena, can you hear me?" Vera said.

Serena opened her sleepy eyes. "Vera," Serena smiled.

"Listen, Serena, you have to talk with the Actors Guild. You have to press charges."

"Vera, you're adorable. Don't you know this is my big chance? If I make a fuss I'll never act at Falchion again. You're sweet to come down here," Serena trailed off.

"Serena! Acting schmacting! You could have died. I'm calling. Talk to them."

"I'm *not* talking to them. You have a big scene today; better get ready. You're young, if you want to call the Actors Guild for yourself go ahead, just don't mess things up for *me*."

"Serena? Serena, listen to me," Vera said, but Serena's smile faded, her eyes closed, and she quietly snored.

Vera's phone buzzed again. She looked down: "Felix." *I could die today!* Vera thought. She looked around the room like a trapped animal. She called Shelley.

"Shelley, what's the mood like on the set? Is Felix losing his mind?"

"Uh, yeah, sweetie, he's upset. And some policeman came around looking for you. Good-looking guy if you like the type. A lieutenant Finklestein. Left his number for you."

"Give it to me."

Shelley read as Vera programmed the number into her phone contacts. *I've done a lot to avoid Aaron all this time, but this is an emergency*. Vera dialed him.

"Lieutenant Finklestein," the voice said.

"Hi, Aaron? This is Vera Horowitz, remember me?"

"Vera, I've been looking for you. Calling to ask me out?"

"I know it's been a while, but could you help me this afternoon? I'm in a real jam."

"My shift ends at two. Why, what's going on?"

"I'm in a scene with an actor who just put a girl in the hospital. I'm scared. If you were there it would make me feel a lot better."

"What time's your shoot?"

Vera glanced at her Mandy Mouse watch: 1:15 P.M. "I'm an hour late for it right now, the first assistant director keeps calling me but I'm afraid to pick up. Please, Aaron."

"My beat's ten blocks from there. Tell you what—I'll be there, but you owe me a cup of coffee sometime, Vera."

"Great. Promise me."

"I promise, Vera. You can always count on me." The line went dead.

Vera hung up. Immediately her phone buzzed again, and she picked up.

"Hello, this is Vera."

"Vera, where the hell are you? Your slaughter scene is ready to go and you're holding up the whole film crew!" Felix's voice spewed over the line.

"Sorry, I'll be there in fifteen minutes."

"Hurry. You're costing Mr. Whitscomb *money,*" Felix said and hung up.

~

Vera arrived at the lot and walked toward the set. Felix hustled her into makeup.

"Fifteen minutes. Move it!" Felix yelled as he shut the trailer door behind her.

~

Jake and Naomi had eaten a quick lunch and gone to his office. They sat down and Jake imagined leaving Naomi there by herself.

"Alright, Naomi, here's my script. It's perfect, it's my baby and whoever gets the lead is going to have a big career. Are you ready to focus and take charge of your life?"

Naomi took a deep breath. "I'm ready, Jake."

"I need to go watch a shoot and I've got to leave you here by yourself, but you've got plenty to do so you won't cause any trouble will you—like at my condo?"

"No, Jake, I'll just study my role."

"I trust you. There are snacks in the fridge, ice water, tea, the bathroom is right there. I really went out on a limb for you so don't let me down. I'll be back in a couple of hours, okay?"

"Sure, Jake, no worries. Bye-bye." Naomi waved to him.

Jake gave her the script and locked the door behind him. Jake thought how he was about to break his promise to himself by watching a slaughter scene. *But this is the woman I love. An acceptable exception.*

~

Vera looked like a Midwest ranch woman as she emerged from the makeup trailer. Her tiny cowgirl boots click-clocked as she entered the set. She nervously glanced at her watch: 1:45 P.M. She scanned the film crew, the doorway. *I'm going to end up like Serena!* Suddenly, Vera saw Aaron in his deep blue uniform and let out a huge sigh. She ran over, hugged Aaron tightly, and directed him to sit in the third row of the audience. Barry watched as Vera returned to the stage. He put a hand on her shoulder and leaned in close.

"Who's your friend in the audience?" Barry whispered in Vera's ear. "We don't need nobody watching us film."

"The policeman is here to make sure nothing like what happened to Serena happens to anybody else," Vera explained.

"What happened to Serena?"

"Seriously? You *know* what happened to Serena!"

"I know she got a couple bruises." Barry's face was filled with compassion.

"She's in the hospital, Barry. She's really hurt! How could you not know that?"

"We've used these props for years, nobody's ever—I can't deal with this now, I've got to conduct business. I'll go see her after this shoot."

Vera looked at Barry like he'd just sprouted feathers. Barry shook his head as if he was upset, and approached the cop in the third row.

"Hello, Officer," Barry said. "This is a closed set. It's for employees only so I'll have to ask you to leave."

"I've had a really bad day, buddy. Ms. Horowitz is a friend of mine and she's expressed concern for her safety on this set. Does that sound like I've got probable cause to be here?"

"I guess it wouldn't hurt for you to watch just this once."

"That's better."

"That's fine, Officer. Please enjoy the shoot."

Barry turned to the staff and lifted the bull horn to his lips. "Okay, everybody, take five. I'll be right back then we're going to shoot."

Barry walked behind the curtain. He quickly ducked out the back and double-timed it across the lot to Alex's trailer. He knocked once, then barged in. Alex was startled and stood.

Barry glanced at Alex's poster-covered walls: a great white shark burst from the water, a seal clamped in its jaws; a cheetah pulled down a gazelle; a python squeezed the life from a wild pig; an American eagle grabbed a bird from mid-air with its talons. The block letters "Apex Predator" hung on all the walls.

"It's off, champ," Barry said. "I know you're disappointed, me too, but you make sure you don't make contact with Vera and that cleaver or we're all in trouble."

"Awe, come on, Uncle Barry, I'm all pumped." Alex said and slumped in his chair.

"You just do like I told you or we're all going to jail. It's a bummer, I know. We were right on the cusp of getting life to imitate art. Now hustle, they're ready for you on the set."

Felix walked onto the set and stood in front of Vera and Alex in their cow-folk attire. Barry sat next to Jake, aware of the cop's presence two rows behind them. Shelley ran out and adjusted the angle of Vera's cowgirl hat.

"There, you look real cute, hon," Shelley said. She winked as she backed off stage.

"All quiet on the set," Barry yelled through the bullhorn.

Vera swallowed hard.

"*Fifty Ways to Cleave Your Lover*, Nastasia Carr slaughter scene, take one," Felix yelled. He snapped the clapperboard and backed off stage.

The spotlights shone through the diffuser and gave Vera and Alex a warm glow in their comfortable living room. A fire crackled in the fireplace as they toasted each other.

"I've never been so happy," Vera said. "I have to admit I was a little apprehensive though, what with all the talk about that awful 'Cuisinart Killer' on the loose."

"Did you run your new name past your girlfriends to make sure you weren't marrying a psycho?" Alex said and laughed.

"Oh yes, there's nothing circular about my new name, Nastasia Carr."

“I guess out here in the country that automobile racing is pretty big. I forgot what they call it. Do you remember?” Alex asked.

“Oh, you mean NASCAR?” Vera suddenly looked stunned.

“Yes, that’s it.” Alex pulled the cleaver from behind his back.

“That’s not fair. Nobody ever calls me Nas as a nickname! We were going to be happy!” Vera shrieked as Alex advanced on her.

He brought the cleaver down to a couple of inches from her shoulder, but didn’t touch her. Then he swept it down to her hip, but didn’t make contact. The chopping went on—each time accompanied by an ear-piercing scream from Vera.

“Cut! That’s a wrap!” Felix yelled. Aaron rubbed the goose bumps from his forearms, and Barry tried to get his neck hairs to lie down—both caused by Vera’s screams. Vera walked down the steps toward Barry’s seat. Barry leaned in close so he could talk quietly with her.

“Vera, I want to go check on Serena. Which hospital is she staying at?”

“Malibu Memorial. I don’t understand. You were there. Serena said she yelled at Alex for hurting her.”

“Actors banter all the time. I’ll see you at the trailer for dinner,” Barry said.

Aaron saw Vera and side-stepped through the seating to go talk with her, but she left.

“You see, we run a very safety-conscious set here,” Barry told Aaron.

“Make sure of it.” Aaron replied.

In the commotion of actors, stagehands and lights being dimmed, Vera had slipped out the back stage door. Jake, who stood outside the set, held up a hand to try to get Vera’s attention, but she just glared, walked into the makeup trailer and closed the door behind her.

Aaron stormed out the back stage door and looked frantically around for Vera, but he was alone on the lot as the strange movie people walked away.

“Shelley, I think everybody’s crazy around here,” Vera said.

“I know. You get used to it. Actors, directors, producers, you’re all are wound pretty tight. You’ve got to calm down, hon. Let me fix you a cup of tea. You like chamomile, right?”

“You’re the only one I can trust around here, Shelley. I’d love a cup of tea.”

“Oh, and before I forget, here’s your first check.”

Shelley handed Vera an envelope. Vera tore it open and pulled out the blue-green check with the tax receipt. She unfolded it and read the amount: $16,000.00.

“This is more money than I’ve ever had at one time.”

“Congratulation, hon. Now go buy yourself some nice clothes.”

~

Jake returned to his office and found Naomi sobbing into the script. Opened sugar packets lay on the floor next to two empty diet soda bottles and energy bar wrappers.

“Naomi, are you having a relapse?”

"No, this script is the saddest most beautiful thing I've ever read. I never knew you could be so romantic, Jake."

"I told you. It's going to be a big hit. Do you think you can act convincingly?"

"I wish we had gotten to know each other sooner. I wasted all that time with Barry when you were here all the time." Naomi gazed dreamily at Jake.

Jake involuntarily did a once over of Naomi's figure. She stepped closer to him—big green eyes behind short wisps of red hair, full lips parted—and wrapped her elegant fingers around the back of his neck.

"Okay, hold on. We're not doing this, Naomi. You're just substituting one addiction for another. Besides, like I have to keep telling everyone: I'm in love with Vera Horowitz."

"Really? That's a shame, Jake, because I don't think she likes you back."

~

Barry sat patiently next to Serena's bedside. He had given her face some gentle pinches followed by a few gentle slaps. Finally, she opened her eyes.

"Barry, you came to see me." Serena smiled and rubbed her face.

"You okay, kid?" Barry asked.

"Yeah, Barry. You know what Alex did was wrong, don't you?"

"It's business. You're okay, right? You want to be a star again, right?"

"Yeah, Barry." Serena's eyes were downcast.

"You ain't gonna say nothin' stupid, right?"

"No, Barry."

"Good girl. You got a special effects scene, then we put this film in the can and we all get paid. I see a big come back for you, sweetheart," Barry said, and left Serena's room.

~

Vera showered. She was alone in the trailer. She heard noises from the kitchen. *Whatever, I'm taking my time. This has been one stressful day.* She had dried her hair and changed into her lounge clothes when she smelled a delicious aroma waft down the hall.

Vera stepped into the kitchen just as the gourmet chef left and Barry uncorked a bottle of deep red merlot with a resounding pop. He poured two glasses, handed Vera one, and clinked glasses with her.

"Looks like it's just you and me tonight, Vera. I had the chef make us a little dinner."

"How is Serena?" Vera asked.

"I feel so bad about what happened. She's on pain killers, but they say she'll be okay."

"How did that happen? With Alex I mean?"

"I had a stern talk with Alex. It's my fault. I get people so stirred up and insist they get into character, and Alex went too far. I can't believe one of my people got hurt." Barry turned his head downward and slightly away from Vera.

"I'm starting to question what the hell I'm doing, you know?" he continued. "Jeez, and Serena—this was supposed to be her big comeback." He wiped his eyes.

Is he crying? Vera thought, then took a small sip of her wine. This is excellent *Merlot.*

As Barry entered the living room, he clicked the tiny remote in his palm. Quiet symphony music flowed from the surround sound system as the room temperature raised two degrees. Barry sat on the light tan suede couch and tucked the remote between the pillows.

"Barry, there's no harm done. We'll throw Serena a big party later," Vera said.

She sat next to him on the couch. Barry turned away so only the back of his head was visible. It shimmered. *The layers, so thick.* Vera gazed deeper. It seemed the deeper layers were even shinier than the outer ones. *They look so soft.* Barry's head gently bobbed up and down. *I think he's really crying.* Vera watched as her hand reached out and stroked the back of Barry's head, her fingers splayed, reached, explored and got lost in the depth. *It's somehow even more luxurious than I'd imagined.* A sob escaped Barry.

"You're a very kind girl, but I think I'd better go lie down," Barry said and ambled down the hall to his bedroom.

Vera watched him go, then rose to her feet, and followed him. The chandelier light played upon his gorgeous hair as Barry flopped onto his bed.

"You'd better go, I don't need no young girl watching me cry," Barry said.

But Vera was entranced and approached the bed. She almost sat when she saw Barry's yellow and white python jacket hung on a coat tree, the reptile skin neatly camouflaged against the pale yellow and white faux finished walls and ceiling. Vera felt she was inside a giant snake's lair. She backed up, and carefully traced her footsteps through the alpaca carpeting.

"You're right, Mr. Whitscomb, I'm going to give you some privacy."

She quickly changed clothes, grabbed her coat, and started to walk outside when she smelled the gourmet dinner in the kitchen. As scared as Vera was, she was also 23 and always hungry. She walked into the kitchen and took a bite of grilled salmon and rice from the oven. *Delicious.* Vera walked outside and rapped on the limo driver's window. She woke him up, but he quickly stepped out and opened the door for her, while yawning. He fought it but his whole face yawned too.

"Where are we going this evening, Ms. Horowitz?" the driver asked.

"Take me to The Dolly Shot," she answered, and climbed into the warmth of the limo.

Chapter 14

Jake & Vera

Vera entered The Dolly Shot. There were no wait staff in sight at this hour. She scanned the dimly lit room, encircled by red leather booths. She saw a tall, handsome man and his date, a stunning red head with short-cropped hair, seated at a center table.

Jake and Naomi. Vera watched them for a moment. *I guess they do make a nice couple.* When Jake excused himself to go to the men's room, Naomi glanced around. Vera tried to leave before Naomi noticed her, but it was too late.

"Vera, over here," Naomi called. She tipped her chin back in a welcoming gesture.

Vera reluctantly walked over.

"Vera, sit down, we need to talk."

"Thanks, I'll stand."

When Naomi looked annoyed and pointed to the chair, Vera sat.

"Listen, Jake's really got feelings for you," Naomi said. "You should talk with him."

"He's got a funny way of showing it: by inviting you to move in with him."

"Vera, my world had just crashed. That sweet man paid to put me through rehab." Naomi paused to take in Vera's expression, then continued. "He's good looking too isn't he? I'm not stupid. I made a move, but he turned me down."

Vera's mouth dropped open.

"I know, right? What man turns *me* down? He says he's in love with *you.*"

"What are you two doing here together then?"

"I'm not supposed to be left alone because of—my condition. I told Jake to go find you, but he said I needed to eat to keep up my strength."

Jake emerged from the men's room, his head down. He didn't see Vera until he'd almost reached the table. When he saw her his face lit up.

"Vera, awesome! Join us," Jake said.

"You know what, I think I will."

"I'll eat at the bar while you two catch up," Naomi said, but Vera grabbed her hand.

"Give us a minute," Vera said, "we should *all* have dinner together."

Naomi nodded and walked toward the bar. They both involuntarily watched her leave in her tight designer skirt.

"We shouldn't leave her at the bar. She might be tempted to drink," Jake said.

"Okay, enough of the noble act. You've got my attention. We're not going to leave Naomi alone. Just tell me, no games, Jake. Are you really interested in me?"

"Terribly."

"Okay." Vera smiled and looked down. "We'll talk later. Get your girl back over here."

Naomi read the menu while Jake and Vera stole amorous glances at each other.
"I'm starved," Vera said. "I walked away from a gourmet dinner with Barry."
"Wow, you've got *some* will power. Why'd you leave?" Naomi asked.
"Because Barry's so weird. I'm just glad to get out of there."
"Why? Did he do something out of line? "Jake asked.
"No, he's just creepy. I don't want to talk about it. So, when do I get to read this famous rom-dram script of yours, Jake?"
"We'll stop by and get it from my office after dinner. I'd love for you to read it."
Jake paid for dinner and the three of them climbed into his limo: Jake sat in the middle between Naomi and Vera, with Vera on his left.
"So, when did you first realize you were attracted to me?" Vera said softly, as she brushed her pinky against his hand. Jake held her hand and faced her.
"Honestly, it was the day you told off Barry for his suggestion about you and Alex. I thought: That girl's got a spirit."
"I'll take that," Vera said and smiled. She checked Mandy: it was midnight.

~

Barry grabbed a bottle of bourbon and two plastic cups as he left the trailer. He entered the main building, speed dialed Alex, and strolled the empty corridors. His cell was squeezed between his chin and shoulder as he the twisted cap off the bourbon.
"Hey, Uncle Barry, what's up?" Alex said over the phone.
"You want to see what your handiwork looks like? I've got a copy of the dailies. Meet me in the viewing room."
"I'll see you there," Alex said and hung up.
Barry shivered with excitement.

~

Vera, Jake and Naomi entered Falchion Studios. They passed the conference, editing and dailies viewing rooms, as Jake led the way to his office.
"I hope we can find time in your schedule for a read through tomorrow," Jake said, as he unlocked his office. He grabbed the script and they walked back toward the exit doors.
"Excuse me," Naomi said and entered the ladies' room.
Time stopped, as Jake and Vera suddenly realized they were alone.
Vera stared at Jake. Jake stared back. The heat between them was palpable. Without speaking, Jake opened a dailies viewing room door and guided Vera inside. It was nearly dark where they stood in the back of the balcony. All the seats faced the huge movie screen, below and to their right. Jake glanced at the faint light coming from behind them through the dark glass. Someone had apparently left the projection room light on by mistake.
Jake held Vera by her shoulders. He could just make out the curve of her face and her dark eyes which stared up at him. He moved one hand to her waist, then barely touching her face, he slid the fingers of his other hand through her hair and

pulled her lips to meet his. They embraced in a lingering kiss. Slowly, they pulled apart and gazed at each other.

"I've thought about this moment for weeks," Jake whispered.

"Why did you wait so long?" Vera whispered back.

Suddenly, a brilliant cone of light and sound erupted from the projection room and lit up the huge screen in the room below. Male voices emanated from the lower sets of seats. Jake strained to identify the men. He recognized the silhouettes: Barry and Alex. They were sitting in the fifth row from the front. Jake gently covered Vera's mouth and moved closer to her.

"Come on, quietly," he whispered.

He took Vera's hand and led her between the rows of seats to the edge of the balcony where they crouched, watched and listened. The images of Alex and Serena appeared ten feet tall and in vivid color on the screen. Alex shoved Serena backwards onto the bed. She held her hands defensively as Alex struck her wrist with the cleaver.

"That's not acting. Look at that, you can tell she's in pain," Alex said, fascinated.

"Yeah, and the look on her face is pure shock. Oh, *now* look at her, she's really scared," Barry said, "We're probably going to win some special effects award with this one. I can almost hear them: 'How did you get it to look so real?'" Alex and Barry laughed out loud.

"I wish I could have been the one," Barry said, "but I'm cursed to play the part of the responsible producer. So how did it feel, Alex?" Barry's cheeks expanded in a winning grin.

"Like an apex predator. Like I could do anything!" Alex gazed arrogantly and smiled.

Barry poured bourbon into a plastic cup, gave it to Alex, then took a gulp of his own.

"I envy you," Barry said. "Just look at that expression on your face. You look noble or majestic or somethin'. I'm *glad* one of us got to experience it. All these years of faking it—don't get me wrong, the fantasies were great too but *this*—I can only imagine the *power*."

"How are you going to keep Serena quiet about this?" Alex asked.

"It's her big comeback, she won't risk it. I'll turn her out to pasture soon anyway."

"Oh, really? I was looking forward to having another 'accident' with her."

"We've still got Vera. Just be patient," Barry said, and patted Alex on the shoulder.

Jake and Vera looked at each other open-mouthed. Jake held a finger to his lips and took Vera's hand. Together, they ascended the carpeted stairs and eased the exit door open.

"Look at that! I got her *good* with that one!" Alex yelled, as Barry snorted.

"I feel like a kid in a candy store!" Barry laughed.

Vera and Jake quietly closed the door and stood panting, their backs against the corridor wall. Vera closed her eyes and shook her head.

"Jake, this is a sick, sick place," Vera said under her breath. "They're basically talking about plotting murder! I want to kill those bastards!"

Jake stared at the far wall just as Naomi approached from the end of the corridor.

"I *wondered* where you two had gone." Naomi yelled.

Jake and Vera held fingers to their lips to quiet her. Naomi tip toed toward them.

"What's going on?" she asked quietly.

"We need to go someplace where we can talk privately," Jake said.

They checked behind them as they left the building, stepped into the cool night air, and got into Jake's limo.

"My place," Jake said to the driver. Jake pushed a button and a glass partition rose between them and the driver.

"Come on, spill," Naomi said.

Jake filled Naomi in on the ride home.

~

Jake, Vera and Naomi sat in Jake's living room.

"I still can't believe it," Naomi said. "I always thought Barry was kind of a rat. All men are kind of rats. But he was also really good to me and Serena a lot of the time. And now you say he's talking about whacking us? It's so crazy."

"We both heard them, Naomi," Vera said. "The question is, what are we going to do about it? What would the Guild do about it, Jake?"

"If they could prove it wasn't an accident? They could stop the film. Serena would have to press charges, or one of the staff would have to admit what they saw, but they're all afraid of crossing Barry," Jake said, "If I'd been there, I would have stopped it right away."

"Why weren't you on the set that day?" Naomi asked.

"I—I don't watch the slaughter scenes anymore."

"Why not?" Naomi asked, "your therapist doesn't want you to see the scenes you wrote?"

"I just don't. I don't want to talk about it. Something I'm working through."

"And Barry let you off the hook with *that* excuse?" Naomi asked.

"Yeah. But he did seem awfully relaxed about it—hey," Jake said, his eyes wide open.

"We're like lab rats," Vera said. "Barry promises us we're going to be stars, treats us like we are as long as we follow the rules, then Benny breaks our spirits, then Alex carries out their sick fantasies by actually hitting us. It looks like he's been using you too, Jake. I don't think he wanted you to see that's why—"

"Yeah, I've got it now, Vera," Jake said.

"I'd like to give them a taste of their own medicine," Naomi said.

Jake's eyes suddenly lit up. He searched through a stack of business cards until he found the one he wanted.

"What's that?" Vera asked.

"Her name is Rhonda Roundhouse," Jake said, "I have a crazy idea, but we all have to act like everything is normal."

Vera looked at Naomi then back to Jake. "Go on, we're listening."

~

At 11:00 AM the next, day Jake and Barry faced each other across the conference table.

"What's so important that you had to get me in here on a Saturday?" Barry asked.

"I'm changing the way *Fifty Ways* ends, Barry." Jake flipped through the script and scratched out paragraphs of dialogue and exposition.

"What's wrong, kid, you seem mad? What don't you like? It's perfect."

"This Cuisinart Killer. I hate him. I say he dies at the end."

"I love the guy! He's runnin' things. He's master-minded the whole string of murders in a really clever way. Now I want to see him get away clean. Maybe open the door for a sequel."

"I want him dead or this film isn't moving forward one inch," Jake insisted.

"Are you crazy? It's too late in the schedule. We've got a hit on our hands. Think about it, kid. He's a fun character, you know, campy—"

"If you want me to sign off on it, Cuisinart dies."

"Okay, kid, you've gotten weak anyway. Good thing you're getting out of B-horrors," Barry said, "Go on and do your girlie movies, leave the heavy lifting to the big boys."

"Whatever. I'll have the rewrite ready Monday. Table read right here Monday at four. Does that work for you?"

"Sure, kid."

"I'll have Felix arrange it."

~

Vera and Naomi sat in Jake's kitchen finishing up breakfast.

"I want revenge, but I was just getting started in this business," Vera said.

"Trust me, Vera, you'll have a great career ahead of you. *Zombie Betrayal* was a big hit and your scream still gives me a splitting headache. Other directors will want you."

"I don't know if I can stand to work around Barry on the rest of the scenes."

"This is where your acting skills will come in handy. You've got to follow through with your special effects scenes, so nobody suspects anything."

"I'd better get showered and get into costume. See you later,"

Vera hugged Naomi and walked toward the front door. Just as she was about to open it Jake walked in.

"Vera. Where are you going?"

"Back to the trailer to get ready for my F/X scene."

"Do you really want to go back to that trailer with Barry?"

"No, but I have to."

Naomi listened from the couch. Jake glanced at Naomi.

"Come back here with me for a minute," he said and led Vera down the hall to his bedroom. They stepped inside and Jake closed the door behind them. He looked into Vera's eyes and let the moment settle over both of them.

"I feel incredibly lucky to have gotten closer with you," Jake said. "And I know things are moving fast. But I don't like the thought of you living with that whack-job. Would you like to move in with me? You could have your own room."

"Are you sure? I mean, Naomi lives here already, and I can't imagine Serena's too keen on staying with Barry now either."

"Just looking out for my cast. But for you, I'll chisel an engraved invitation."

"That's not necessary. I accept," Vera said, and then gazed at her feet.

Jake gently lifted her chin and they melted into a kiss.

~

At 2:00 P.M. Jake met the heavy-set woman in the lobby of Malibu Memorial Hospital.

"Thank you for meeting with me," he said.

"I appreciate the opportunity," Rhonda said, "I'm a crazy-hard worker, you'll see."

"This is not going to be what you were expecting, but I think once you see the whole picture you'll understand," Jake said.

Rhonda looked at him quizzically, but followed him into the elevator. On the second floor Jake looked both ways, only a lone nurse at the end of the hallway. He peeked into Serena's room, she was asleep, so he entered and motioned for Rhonda to follow him.

"This woman was nearly killed by a man who enjoys battering women," he whispered. Rhonda scowled. "Why doesn't she report him?" she asked.

Jake led Rhonda back to the hallway. "She's afraid of losing her job as an actor."

"I've got no respect for men like that, but what do you want me to do?" Rhonda asked.

"I want to advance your wrestling career. I'm sure you need money for training. I'm willing to provide you with a place to practice and a training partner, and I want to compensate you with enough money to make it worth your while," Jake said, and scanned the hall again.

"You want me to beat up the guy who did this to her?"

"I didn't say that. I want to donate funds to your wrestling training. This schmuck is going to be your first partner. How much money do you need?"

"I'm trying to earn five thousand dollars to pay off my double-wide."

"I think that's a fair price. How about payment in cash once the job is done?"

"Five thousand dollars? That's a lot of money—but I'd end up in jail."

"You can wear a mask. I'll make sure nobody sees you. Five thousand for a few minutes work. Do we have a deal?"

~

Monday, after neatly packing all her clothes and Mandy Mouse collectibles into the trunk of Barry's limousine, Vera got into her same fake-blood-splattered cowgirl outfit, pulled on her boots, and walked onto the set. Barry and the special effects team were already there.

"Vera, you're right on time," Goatee Dude said, "Lie down, we'll get you set up." Vera lay down on the blood-soaked bed while a woman positioned a brace behind her shoulder blade with a fake arm attached that stuck straight up.

"Tuck your real arm into this cut out opening in the mattress," the woman said.

The sleeve on the fake arm matched the material from which Vera's blouse was made. It took a moment to hook up the clear plastic tube that would spray fake blood from the pump, but Vera was finally in position for the first shot.

Andy strutted onto stage. "*Fifty Ways,* Special Effects, Nastasia Carr, Lose the Arm Scene, take one, action!" Andy snapped the clapperboard.

Alex raised the cleaver, swept it down and chopped off Vera's fake arm. Vera felt the vibration go to the brace behind her shoulder blade as the prosthetic wrist and hand fell to the floor and fake blood sprayed all over her and Alex.

"Cut!" Andy yelled. "Wrap. Get set up for the next scene. Step it up, people."

The special effects team turned off the pump to the blood tube and worked on Vera's hip, the focal spot for the next special effects shot, while she lay still. Alex winked and grinned at Vera as he left to take a cigarette break.

~

After an already busy day, at 4:00 P.M., the actors sat around the conference table, a script before each of them. Jake sat next to Barry while Felix cleared his throat and clapped his hands together to quiet the chatter.

"*Fifty Ways to Cleave Your Lover*, rewrite. Everybody open to page seventy-three," Felix said.

The actors flipped through their scripts and found their places. Felix took a sip of water and read:

FADE IN: EXT. WYOMING – DIRT STREWN FRONT YARD - DAY

INSERT – YELLOW PLASTIC "CRIME SCENE" TAPE FLAPS VIOLENTLY IN THE BREEZE

INT. FARM HOUSE – DAY

Close up: A blood-drenched bed with hacked up sheets and mattress. Beside it: a seven-foot-tall blender filled with pureed human remains.

COP #1: "Looks like Cuisinart got away, sir. You were right, there's a bloody latex-gloved print on the 'liquefy' button.

KELLY: "Damn. They have eyes but they cannot see."

COP #1: "With all due respect, sir, they don't have eyes. See, their eyes and everything else got all mixed together when Cuisinart pushed 'liquefy.'"

KELLY: "Shut up, Lieutenant!" I meant we had all the clues, but we still failed these poor women."

CUISINART (O.S.): "Hee hee."

INSERT – SKYLIGHT ABOVE BEDROOM
A shadowy figure flees from the skylight. Kelly and Cop #1 look up.

COP #1: "What was that?"

KELLY: "It came from the roof. Come on!"

INT. FARM HOUSE – DAY
Kelly and Cop #1 run toward the front door.

EXT. DIRT FRONT YARD – DAY
Kelly and Cop #1 run to the side of the house and look up.

INSERT – WOODEN LADDER LEANS AGAINST THE ROOF

EXT. LADDER – DAY
Kelly and Cop #1 climb to the roof. Kelly pulls his gun from the holster in side his trench coat.

INSERT – CUISINART PEEKS FROM BEHIND THE CHIMNEY

KELLY: "F.B.I.! Come out with your hands over your head. It's over, Cuisinart!"

COP #1: "Yeah, it's over, Cuisinart!'

KELLY: "Shut up, Lieutenant."

COP #1: "Yes, sir."
Kelly moves around the edge of the roof, his gun held ahead of him. Cuisinart darts from behind the chimney, the bloody cleaver held in his hand.

INSERT: THE FARM HOUSE ROOF TOP
Kelly, Cop #1 and Cuisinart run in a big circle as Kelly aims at Cuisinart.

KELLY: "Stop or I'll shoot!"
Cuisinart runs but holds the broad face of the cleaver defensively toward Kelly.

INSERT: Kelly fires his gun. The bullet flies in slow motion and strikes the cleaver which knocks it out of Cuisinart's hand. The impact knocks Cuisinart off balance and he crashes through the skylight as the cleaver spins above his head. Kelly and Cop #1 run to the edge of the skylight and look down into the bedroom.

INT. BEDROOM – DAY
Cuisinart plunges into the bloody blender.

INSERT: THE CLEAVER FALLS AND STRIKES THE "LIQUEFY" BUTTON ON THE BLENDER

INSERT: CUISINART IS LIQUEFIED WITH HIS LATEST VICTIM

CUISINART: "Arrgh!"

COP #1: "That's gross, sir. I'm skipping lunch today."

KELLY: "We got him, Lieutenant. You know what they say…"

COP # 1 holds his stomach and looks sick.

COP #1: "What's that, sir?"

KELLY: "What comes around goes around."

CLOSING IMAGE: Camera pans out of bedroom, up through the skylight and above the roof where Cop #1 retches over the side of the building.

FADE OUT.

Felix closed his script and collected the rest from the group. Jake stood to leave but Barry grabbed him by the arm.

"I don't like it, kid," Barry said. "What are you tryin' to do to this picture? C'mon, this guy Cuisinart's a winner. He's like Freddy, or Jason or Leatherface. I'm talkin' franchise."

"That's it, Barry. If you want to make a lame movie where Cuisinart comes back from 'liquefy' that's your call, but once this movie's done I'm out of here."

Jake walked away from Barry onto the set just before Vera extracted herself from the bloody bed. Her wrists and one leg were missing, and her face was splattered with gore.

"Nice," Jake said to Vera and smirked.

"Shut up," she said, and smiled back at him.

Alex laid down the cleaver and wiped fake blood from his face with a towel.

"Oh, Alex, good, "Jake said. "Benny said he wants you in training room 3B right away. He says it's urgent."

"Really? Can't it wait? I'm a mess."

"He says now. You get Benny mad at your own risk."

Alex wiped himself off and changed into clean tennis shoes before he trudged down the corridor. Jake watched him round the corner and followed from a safe distance. There was nobody at the far end of the corridor where training room 3B was located. Alex was almost to the door when Jake heard two cast members walking up behind him. It was Brian and Lola. They headed for the end of the corridor. *I can't let them interfere!* Jake thought.

"Hey, "Jake said. "I could really use some help if you two could spare a few minutes."

"Sure, Mr. L'Hommedieu," Lola said.

"Great, come on, this way. I need a couple objective viewpoints on my new movie." Jake turned them around toward the other end of the corridor and put an arm over each of their shoulders.

"Do you think you might have a part for me?" Lola asked.

Jake glanced over his shoulder as they walked. Alex had just entered room 3B and, as the door closed, Naomi emerged from the janitor's closet across the hall and set out "Caution—Wet Floor" signs.

Chapter 15

In Costume

Alex entered 3B, but it was empty. As he strolled toward the center of the room, someone who stood just inside stepped in behind him and closed the door. Alex spun around. He faced a heavy woman who wore a red Mexican luche libre mask. She leaned against the padded wall with her arms crossed and regarded him.

"Where's Benny Edwards?" Alex asked.

The woman shrugged but didn't speak.

"What's with the mask, you fat cow? I asked you seen Benny?"

"No, but I'll handle your training today," Rhonda said calmly.

"I don't train with women."

"Huh? That's funny, I heard you like to beat 'em," Rhonda said, and lunged at him.

"Maybe I do. You wanna—"

Rhonda lifted Alex over her head in a fireman's carry and slammed him onto the padded floor on his back. A dull ache throbbed through Alex's torso.

"You gonna hit me, or what?" Rhonda asked.

She yanked Alex to his feet, and bludgeoned his face with her elbow. Alex held his jaw with both hands as Rhonda swung an upper cut into his ribs with a "crack."

"That's what I'm talking about!" she said.

"No more." Alex squeaked, his breath nearly gone.

"I'm just getting started."

Rhonda lifted Alex and brought him down sideways on her bended knee with another "crack."

"These will all heal. Trust me, I've had every one of the injuries I'm gonna give you."

Alex groaned from deep in his gut. He rolled onto his side and curled up a ball.

"Sport," Rhonda said, "when I finish with you today you're gonna be wrapped in a *whole* lot of plaster."

It was 5:15 P.M. when the masked woman stalked passed Naomi and out the exit doors. Naomi wanted to peek inside 3B but she resisted. Instead, she put the "Wet Floor" signs back into the janitor's closet and left the building.

She crossed the grassy lot to the break room. Once inside, she dropped two quarters into one of the last coin-operated telephones left in L.A. and dialed 911.

"911, what's your emergency? Police, fire or ambulance?" the operator said.

"Ambulance. There's a badly beaten man in room 3B at Falchion Studios. He needs an ambulance. Now."

"State your name," the operator said.

Naomi hung the heavy phone on its cradle. She pulled out her cell phone and dialed a taxi, then waited at the far side of the lot. After a few minutes she heard the siren. She watched as the square blue and white vehicle parked. Its lights flashed.

EMTs ran. They eased Alex onto a backboard and loaded him into the back of the ambulance just as Naomi's taxi arrived.

~

Jake sat across the dining room table from Vera, his forehead wrinkled, his hands in fists.

"What's wrong?" Vera asked.

"Have you ever had to do something bad to end up doing something good?"

The doorbell rang. Jake opened the door and Naomi entered without speaking.

"Did the person—deal with Alex?" Jake asked Naomi.

"Yeah, that's a wrap," she answered.

"You look really ticked off," Vera said.

Naomi sat, then abruptly stood and paced. "I can't stand the way Benny's talked to us all these years. He's just as responsible for Serena's condition as Alex."

"I've heard Benny was a bit harsh, but I didn't know he was *that* bad," Jake said.

"I've never heard anyone speak so cruelly to anyone," Vera said.

"I'd like him to see how it feels like to be a victim for once," Naomi said.

"Hey, hold on," Jake said.

"Jake's conscience is bothering him about Alex," Vera explained.

"Fine, we'll handle things ourselves, right Vera?" Naomi said.

Vera's cell phone rang. "Oh, hi, Bubbe, I thought you weren't talking to me anymore."

"Listen to me," Zissell said. "That nice Aaron Finklestein says people getting hurt where you work. You stop dis movie business and go out with Aaron. You marry him before I die. Don't you want to make your Bubbe proud?"

"Right now I want my Bubbe's voice to disappear!" Vera said and hung up.

Vera lips tightened. She scowled at Jake, scanned the room, and marched to the wine cabinet. She grabbed a random bottle of wine and twisted the corkscrew into the top.

Jake crossed the room and peaked at the bottle Vera had chosen.

"Vera, that's a $250.00 burgundy," Jake said, "I was saving that for a special occasion."

"Oh, I'm not worth it? Barry, Benny, Alex and now you too?"

"That's not fair—I'm nothing like them."

"You like my spirit? We're getting some payback on Benny Edwards alright, and it'll have nothing to do with any *man's* ideas." Vera uncorked the bottle.

"What do you mean 'man's ideas'?" Jake asked.

"This whole place is run by men. Sick, demented men."

"I'm glad you said that, Vera, because I've got one hell of an idea," Naomi said.

Vera poured wine from the vintage bottle into her's and Jake's glasses, while Naomi hoisted a glass of sparkling soda water.

"I've got a confession," Naomi said.

Jake and Vera leaned forward and listened.

"Serena once put something in my drink that made me, let's say, very suggestible. It wore off after twenty-four hours, but when I was back to my old self she showed me that I'd written out a check to her for ten thousand dollars. We tore it up and had a good laugh."

"Where are you going with this?" Jake asked.

"Serena gave me a couple of the pills. They're tiny, but they pack a punch. If we could get one of them into Benny's drink we could learn his weaknesses and use them against him."

"Okay, but he's not going to sit down and have a drink with any of *us*—he's really guarded," Vera said.

"It can't be one of us. It has to be a stranger," Naomi said.

"Ladies, stop for a second and think," Jake said.

Vera ignored him, crossed the room and sat by Naomi.

"Benny's no fool," Naomi said, "He knows he's not the most approachable."

"I like the idea of someone else talking with Benny. A stranger," Vera said.

"I don't like this at all," Jake said."

"So, who invited you?" Vera said. "I just got paid for my role in *Zombie Betrayal.* I'll finance everything myself."

"Vera, remember me?" Jake said. "I've done nothing but help you, and Serena, and Naomi, since I found out about this whole mess,"

"Fine, you want to help? You've got connections don't you?"

"Don't get so hot," Jake said, "I'll ask around." He didn't have to ask around, but he couldn't believe what he was considering.

"You don't understand," Vera said. "Somebody controlled us. They're plotting to beat us on film. Benny kills our spirit so we can't even fight back!"

"I know what he put me through. Are you up for some girl power, Vera?" Naomi said.

"Absolutely." Vera said and high-fived Naomi.

~

Barry's dream from last night had been fantastic. He was the world's largest python and he had cornered Naomi, Serena and Vera in a dead-end rock canyon with sheer walls. He had already swallowed Naomi and Serena, and now there was only Vera left. Barry savored every second of helplessness in the tiny scream queen's eyes as she waited for the inevitable.

He awoke and whistled as he strutted to the kitchen and poured himself a cup of coffee. *Serena's in the hospital. She can't finish her special effects scene with Alex. Unfortunate timing having Alex hit Serena with the cleaver. Couldn't think of another way to catch the attack on film. If she can't* perform *in her F/X scene it will delay shooting. I need cash.*

"Better return that big blender to the rental place," Barry said and laughed for no reason.

~

Vera got a call from the hospital: Serena was well enough to leave. Everyone drove to Malibu Memorial. They entered Serena's room as a nurse helped her into her crepe designer wrap.

"How are you?" Vera asked. She put her arm around Serena as they walked into the hall.

"I'm still sore, but I'll be okay." Serena leaned her head on Vera's shoulder.

"There have been big changes since you've been gone," Jake said. "Tell me what you want for dinner and we'll fill you in."

"I'd love some sushi," Serena said as they helped her into the limo.

~

Half an hour later they relaxed around Jake's dining room table. Everyone dipped California rolls in soy/wasabi sauce and ate.

"There really are no more jobs at Falchion—for any of us," Jake said. "My contract is up after this film. There's no love lost between you and Barry, Naomi. And as for you two, Barry's made it clear he's waiting for a chance to whack you."

"It seems mean," Serena said. "Why should I get involved in this? I just need to set up some job interviews."

"You have the *most* to be mad about," Naomi said.

Serena's face hardened. Vera reached out and touched Naomi's knee to quiet her.

"I asked myself the same thing, Serena," Vera said. "But if we don't take a stand more girls are going to get hurt. Alex is no longer a threat, but Benny and Barry are getting worse."

"So, I just have to read the script?" Serena said, "That's all?"

"No, you'll have to get into character. You have to sell it," Vera said.

The sound of a boxing bell chimed on Jake's cell phone. He opened the new text that simply said: "Plaster."

Jake texted back: "Awesome, have ur $. Have new job for U & D.S. Need to meet you and D. S. in person."

"No can do. U know rules," was texted back.

"Trust you, Rhonda. Make exception 4 bonus?" Jake texted.

"If in person U will have gun on U. Nothing funny or else."

"Nothing funny. U hold cards."

"Here's address, C U @ 8:00."

"I've got your 'stranger,'" Jake said to the women. "I've gotta run."

"I don't think so," Vera said." We're going with you."

"I can't bring all of you with me. I'm meeting the person who worked Alex over."

All three women scowled at him, their arms crossed.

"Alright, come on," Jake said, and led the way to the limo.

~

The film crew moved to studio set H where Serena's slaughter scene was shot. Dust and cobwebs were everywhere. The crew cleaned around the articles in the room, careful not to disturb them for the final F/X shoot. Barry sat up front and unwrapped a Cuban cigar.

"Hey, anybody seen Alex today?" Barry yelled.

The stagehands looked up and shook their heads. Barry lit up and puffed a trail of white smoke as he approached the exit doors.

"No? Well, have him call me when you do," Barry said and stepped out into the sunshine. *This waiting around is boring. Where's Benny?*

Barry strolled down to the training rooms. *Benny can always make me laugh. If ever two guys were on the same wavelength it's me and Benny,* Barry thought. He entered and expected Benny to chew him out for not knocking first, but the room was empty. *No actors, no stunt people, huh?* Barry walked toward the other wing. *Maybe he's in 3B.*

~

Jake knocked on the door to the empty warehouse. Rhonda opened it and stared at Jake, Vera, Naomi and Serena.

"Wait a minute, who are all these people?" Rhonda asked.

"These are my partners. Three very angry women."

Rhonda sighed. "I know better than to fight those odds. Come on in."

Jake glanced at a man who wore a black furry wolf mask and sat cross-legged in a lawn chair in the corner, a .44 Magnum in his hand. Jake shook his head slightly, turned and handed Rhonda a thick envelope.

"Go ahead and count that if you want. It's all there."

Rhonda took the fat envelope. She counted the $5,000.00 and smiled. "I can't believe this. Thanks, that was the best job I've ever had."

"Is your 'wrestling' partner okay?" Jake asked.

"Let me put it this way: I made sure you got your money's worth."

Jake looked worried and tensed his shoulders.

"Look," Rhonda added, "it's nothing *I* didn't go through when *I* learned the ropes."

"Excuse me, but I don't have all night," the man in the wolf mask said.

"I think I know who you are," Jake said to the black furry face.

"That gun is loaded," Rhonda said. The masked man nodded.

Vera took the lead and addressed the stranger. "I hear you're a good salesman."

"People just like me," the man behind the mask snuffled.

"It's true. People let down their guard around Snout," Rhonda said.

"Why the mask?" Vera asked. "I'd like to see who I'm doing business with."

"You said, 'unknown to the film industry,' you folks are in the biz, correct?"

"You can't wear that around the guy we want you to get close to," Vera said.

"I'll show my face when the time is right. Let's talk money," Dark Snout said.

"Okay, Mr. Snout, I'll fill you in on the creep we want you to get close to," Vera said.

~

Alex lay in the Critical Care wing of Malibu Memorial Hospital. The orthopedic surgeon had finished the operation to repair his broken leg with titanium screws and plates an hour ago, and now wrapped the final plaster layer on his broken wrist.

"Good Lord, whoever beat this man couldn't leave well enough alone. It's like they went down a check list," the surgeon said.

"What do you mean?" the post-grad assistant asked.

"One broken femur, one broken ulna, one broken clavicle, one broken phalange, one fractured costae spuriae and finally —not broken, no no—but a severely sprained back. None of these injuries are life-threatening, but whoever did this was very methodical."

~

Benny sat in the Farmers Market section of The Grove at a table in his crisp white short-sleeved shirt and cream-colored slacks, and sipped an espresso from a tiny white cup. It was cool beneath the dappled shade of grape leaves interspersed with tiny white lights. *It's a beautiful day to manipulate some stupid people,* Benny thought.

The crowd had thinned as tourists' gradually stood from their tables. "—and the man at the restaurant told me Jessica Alba is here all the time—" a mother's words trailed off as she and her family left.

Only a pleasant looking man, in a pale green shirt, sat at a nearby table. Benny checked his Rolex: 5:45 P.M.. He squinted at the waiter, snapped his fingers, and held up his cup. The young Latino waiter walked over and took the cup from him. Benny had devised a game—he'd put the boy through his paces every weekday after work. From the second he handed the boy the empty cup, Benny timed him. If the boy delivered a new espresso within two minutes, he earned a nice tip. A second later—nothing. The boy walked rapidly back toward Benny, the small cup and saucer held at arm's length to reduce spillage, his face tense.

"A minute, fifty-three seconds, fifty-four, fifty-five, fifty-six—you're not going to make it," Benny said, as he watched the thin gold second hand sweep the face of his watch.

The boy handed Benny his espresso.

"Congratulations, punk," Benny said and handed the boy a dollar.

Benny drank the scalding liquid in one rapid gulp. *Intense.*

Satisfied, confident laughter rolled out from the table to Benny's left. *This is my game, my private game, who dares to laugh?* Benny thought, and turned. The man in the green shirt faced him directly. He smiled broadly, naturally, all white teeth and dimples.

"Something funny?" Benny challenged.

"You really worked that kid. You did him a favor, he's got to learn about the world sometime, right?" the man said.

"You've got that right," Benny murmured.

Benny stood. The crowd was gone, and Benny was alone with his buzz. His ears rung as he turned to leave.

"Excuse me, friend," the man said, "but could you recommend a bar with decent atmosphere around here?"

Benny looked startled. *People don't talk to me.*

"I'm heading to such a place right now. It's two blocks down on the left once you reach San Vicente Boulevard," Benny said and left.

Footsteps echoed behind him, then to the side.

"Would you mind if I tagged along?" the man asked. "I'm not terribly good with directions and I'd be happy to buy you a drink for your trouble."

"Look, it's simple. Right down that street on the left, a child could find it."

"Too bad I'm not a child then," the man smiled.

Benny looked down and admired his highly polished cordovan penny loafers which clocked in a straight line down the sidewalk.

"Are you still here? I'm not much for company, look, what do you want?" Benny asked.

"Where did you get those penny loafers? I've looked all over. I used to own a pair and I miss them?"

"I've had this pair for thirty years—I maintain my belongings. I have them resoled and polish them regularly."

"You really have your act together," the stranger said.

Benny stopped and faced the man straight on. The man stopped too. Benny stepped up one inch from the man's face.

"Do you know who you're talking to? I am one squared-away, meticulous, organized bad-ass son of a bitch. So, if you want to buy me a drink you'd better be ready to buy me several because my time's too valuable for some panty waist," Benny said and held his stare.

"You've got my attention, colonel," the man said and saluted, "if you want to do some drinking, I'm down, lead the way."

Benny shook his head and smiled in spite of himself.

~

Barry entered the corridor and was surprised to find the same cop from Vera's shoot thrust the heel of his hand into his chest.

"Who are you?" Lieutenant Finklestein asked.

"You remember me, I'm Barry Whitscomb, the producer of the film you watched."

Aaron dropped his hand. "My training. Automatic. Who occupied this room during the last twenty-four hours?"

"You could check with Felix, our First Assistant Director. He keeps track of those things. Why?"

"Do you know an Alex Boxwell?"

"Of course, he's an actor here."

"Does he have any enemies? Anyone who would want to do him harm?"

"No, he's just one of the gang. He's worked here for years."

"I'm in charge of his case, here's my card. Call me if anything should come to mind." Barry took the card as Aaron walked back inside 3B with his notebook and pen.

"Wait, what happened to Alex?" Barry asked and opened the door.

"Are you a relative?"

"Yes, I'm Alex's uncle."

"Can you prove that?"

"My last name's Whitscomb, my late sister's maiden name was Whitscomb. Boxwell is her married name." Barry produced his I.D.

Aaron took the I.D. and nodded. "That checks out. Why didn't you say that? Mr. Boxwell was badly beaten by someone. He's under observation at Malibu Memorial Hospital."

Barry grabbed his license, turned and ran outside.

~

Dark Snout bought Benny the first round and they raised their glasses to toast.

"I know you're selling *something*, so you might as well just get it out," Benny said, his tumbler of brown liquid held in mid-air.

"You've got me, I sell life insurance. Everybody needs life insurance."

"No, I'm not buying life insurance from you. I'm single, no children, no living relatives. Who would I leave it to? Here's to strangers buying me drinks." Benny said, and gulped from his drink.

"Do they have menus here?" Dark Snout asked.

"Of course, they have menus here, are you blind?"

As Benny reached two bar stools over to grab the menus, his glass held out for balance, Dark Snout dropped a tiny brown pill into Benny's drink. Benny slapped a menu against the stranger's chest and held up two fingers to the bartender.

"Didn't turn out the way you hoped, eh, Sport?" Benny said. "Since you're buying, let me tell you something. People are my puppets. I would never humiliate myself like that kid did for a lousy dollar. And I'll tell you something else, *you're* my puppet too if I want you to be." Benny swigged his drink.

The stranger waited and smiled amicably at Benny. Benny's face took on an expression that was so calm it was comical. Dark Snout laid $25.00 on the bar and knocked to get the bartender's attention.

"Didn't turn out the way you hoped, eh, Sport? You'd like to show me your home now," Dark Snout said.

"Oh. You'll be impressed by how neat and clean everything is," Benny said.

"I'm sure it's every bit as disgustingly sterile as you are. Now move."

~

Jake, Vera, Serena and Naomi found four realistic-looking mouse costumes with gray heads and ears in the prop and wardrobe room. They tried them on and posed for each other.

"Are you sure Benny's going to believe all this?" Vera asked.

"Those pills are so strong I'd have believed I was Beyonce that night if Serena told me I was," Naomi assured her.

"I've checked out the disc-dubbing room," Jake said. "Nobody's booked any time in there today. I just need a film or a disc to work with."

"Great," Vera said. "That's all we can do for now. We should get some snacks, I think it's going to be a long night."

~

Benny opened the front door to his home. He gestured to a tabletop.

"This is my pride and joy, my ivory chess set. You can't get these anymore unless—"

"Get me your home movies from when you were a boy," Dark Snout commanded.

Benny led the way to his bedroom and reached up onto the shelf in his closet.

"Oh my God, they're alphabetized and cross-referenced by year, you anal-compulsive sociopath. Give me the ones with your mother in them."

Benny handed Dark Snout three discs. In the living room, Dark Snout slid one into the DVD player attached to Benny's TV and pushed play.

"Point out your mother when you see her," Dark Snout said.

"There she is, there's the old witch."

Dark Snout checked the DVD time counter and wrote a note in a small notebook: "Mother shows up at a minute 17 seconds." He repeated the procedure with the other two discs, then he called Vera on his cell.

"Hello?" Vera said.

"I'll meet you at the corner of Colgate and Fairfax Avenues, I've got the discs," Dark Snout said and hung up.

"Would you like to play a game of chess?" Benny asked Dark Snout? "I'll show you a move where I can keep taunting the king at QR1 over and over again with a knight while the queen is helpless to do anything about it, stuck at QR8." Benny beamed.

"No, show me where your home security camera recording device is."

Benny led Dark Snout to the garage and pointed to the box. Dark Snout opened the lid and took the disc. Dark Snout made Benny sit on the couch.

"Stay there until I return."

Benny nodded and slunk down. The stranger took a wolf mask from inside his shirt, pulled it over his head, and stepped outside.

~

Barry walked into Alex's hospital room and his jaw dropped. Alex lay unconscious, his wrist in a plaster cast, his neck and rib cage heavily bandaged, his leg in traction and a tube connected to his arm. Barry approached the bed.

"Alex? Alex, can you hear me?" Barry touched Alex's face. No response. "I'm gonna find out who done this, Alex. This is *my* set. I *demand* proper respect!"

Barry took the stairs two-by-two, and got outside and into his limo.

"To the set, man, move it!" Barry yelled at his driver.

~

Dark Snout stood at the corner in his wolf mask as Jake's limo pulled up. Vera, Naomi and Serena stepped out and joined Dark Snout at the curb, boxes of costumes in their arms. Jake took the three discs from him, got back inside and raced away.

"Come on, this way," Dark Snout said. The women followed him into the house.

"Don't you think wearing that mask will attract attention?" Vera asked.

"In L.A.? Hardly."

They got inside Benny's house and shut the door.

"What a clean place," Naomi said. She saw Benny on the couch and jumped a little.

"Over here," Dark Snout said, and ushered the women into the kitchen.

"Are there people in my kitchen?" Benny asked.

"You are calm and relaxed," Dark Snout said, "just stay on the couch."

Benny smiled and closed his eyes as Dark Snout joined the women in the kitchen.

"I've delivered on my part of the deal. Pay me and I'll be on my way."

Vera handed him the envelope filled with hundreds. He counted them, saluted with two fingers, and left. The three women stood in a circle.

"I feel funny being here," Serena said. "I mean what the hell are we doing?"

"These guys won't stop until they've killed someone on film, so if you don't have any chutzpah, Serena, at least don't cause us any trouble," Vera said.

Naomi pulled out a candy bar and munched it while she stared Serena down.

~

Jake had combined the best clips of Benny's mom speaking to the camera onto one disc. Then he'd programed a synthesized version of her voice so when anyone read into the microphone it would sound like Benny's long deceased mother. He loaded up the portable synthesizer with the other equipment and jumped back into his limo.

He arrived at Benny's place and carried the jumble of wires and devices inside. The room was darkened as the women, in their gray and white mouse costumes, pinned bed sheets to the window frames, and Benny sat contentedly on the couch. Jake changed into his mouse costume in the kitchen, then returned to the living room and inserted the master disc into the DVD player. He had hooked the wires to the DVD player and handed a long wire with a microphone to Serena, who also wore a mouse suit.

"What's going on?" Benny said.

"Everything's fine, Benny," Jake said. He clicked on the synthesizer and patted Serena on the shoulder.

"Benny, I want you to pay attention to the TV," Serena said through the microphone.

"M-Mom? Is that you?" Benny asked.

"Yes, Benny," Serena said.

Benny watched the image of his mother speaking on the wide screen, high-def television.

"Benny, we've played this game long enough," the voice from the TV said. "I think you're old enough now to face what we really are."

"What game, Mom?" Benny asked, his eyes wide open.

"The game that you are an acting coach."

"But I am an acting coach, Mom. They're all afraid of me because I'm so tough."

"You're not tough, you're the opposite. Benny, we're a family of mice and we have to be very careful."

"We're mice? What do you mean?"

"You, and I, your father and sisters, are all mice. I've let you pretend all this time so you could enjoy your youth, but I was always watching you," Serena said slowly.

"You always watch me, you never let me do *anything*. You're always mean to me," Benny pouted.

"I had to be mean to keep you safe. The world is full of predators who want to eat you. Your sisters know how to survive, but you've got to learn. You must always be alert or a hawk or a cat or a snake will catch you out in the open and eat you."

Benny glanced around the dark room at the silhouettes of mouse heads behind the couch.

"But why don't I look like you?" he asked.

"You *do* look like us. You just can't see it. You've fooled yourself all this time."

"Oh my God, it's true? I'm a mouse?" Benny gasped.

"Say it and accept it if you want to live, Benny. Say 'I'm a scared little mouse.'"

"I'm a scared little mouse," Benny said.

"Good. Now we're going to practice until you know it by heart. Then you'll be ready to go after your first piece of cheese."

~

Barry's limo tires slid and bounced into the Falchion lot with a stuttered honking noise. The driver parked in Barry's spot. Barry got out, slammed the door, and marched to Jake's office.

Somebody knows something about this—Alex's injuries are no coincidence! Barry thought as he stalked down the corridor. He knocked on Jake's door, but there was only silence. Barry dialed Jake. No answer. Then Vera. No answer. Then Serena. No answer.

"Nobody ignores Barry Whitscomb!" Barry yelled.

He glanced up at the mock-up poster of *Fifty Ways to Cleave Your Lover* on the wall. The caption: "He slices, He dices, the Machine Does the Rest!" Alex's maniacal face loomed in the foreground, the huge blender behind him.

~

"How long has it been?" Jake whispered in Vera's ear from behind the couch.

"Two hours since we gave him the pill."

"Come with me for a second." Jake said. He took Vera's arm, led her into the kitchen, and closed the door behind them.

"That was unfair what you said about me earlier. I'm nothing like those sickos and I am *with you*, Vera. How far do you intend to take this?" Jake said, holding Vera by the shoulders.

"You're right, Jake. I just wanted Benny to see what it's like to be scared. I mean, the police wouldn't do anything if we told them how cruel Benny was."

A high-pitched scream from the living room jolted Vera and Jake. They walked in. It was Naomi who'd screamed. The front door was open. Jake looked out in time to see Benny run down the driveway.

"Benny got away," Serena said.

Jake, Vera, Naomi and Serena all ran after Benny in their mouse suits. Jake gained on him, but Benny heard him, glanced over his shoulder and ran for the shadows.

"Eek! Eek!" Benny screamed.

"Benny, stop!" Jake yelled.

As Jake caught up, Benny doubled back on himself and ran in the opposite direction. *Impressive,* Jake thought.

Vera and Naomi tried to corral him. Benny, wide-eyed with terror, jumped left—blocked by Vera. Then sprung right—blocked by Naomi.

"Eek! Eek! Eek!" Benny screamed, his hands held like little paws.

Jake tried to grab him. Benny looked up, darted between Vera and Naomi, and slipped by Serena. He scurried down an embankment and into a culvert beneath the road.

"Benny, get back here!" Jake yelled.

They ran to the mouth of the culvert and looked into the dampness. There was only the splash of Benny's quick feet and the echo of his voice.

"Eeeek! Eeeeek!" Benny screamed as he disappeared from view.

"I've never seen anyone run so fast," Naomi said.

"I think we went too far," Vera said.

"Ya think?" Jake said.

Chapter 16

Benny

Aaron Finklestein arrived at Malibu Memorial Hospital, showed his badge, and was led to Alex's room.

"Mr. Boxwell is on a morphine drip right now," the nurse said. "You can have a few minutes with him, but he needs to rest."

Aaron pulled up a chair next to Alex's bed. "Mr. Boxwell? I'm Lieutenant Finklestein, I'm charge of your case. Do you know who attacked you?"

Alex opened his eyes.

"Yeah, some big she-beast did this. I can't blame her though—after what I did." Alex grinned winningly from his morphine high.

"And what *did* you do?"

Alex smiled deliriously, all his teeth on display. "I beat up a lady with a rubber-coated cleaver—really messed her up. The big lady must be a friend of hers."

"I'm going to forget you said that since you're under medication and it would get thrown out of court. Would you recognize the woman if you saw her again?"

"No, she wore a red mask. I don't *want* to see her anyway. Do you see me, cop? You see what she did to me?"

"Yes, I see." Aaron said, and let out a sigh.

~

Jake helped Vera up the embankment and over the guard rail at the top of Fairfax Avenue.

"Get this stupid mouse head *off* me," Jake said, and together he and Vera yanked it off.

"What now?" Serena asked.

"What *now?*" Jake said. "We find Benny, that's what. Come on we've got to find out where that drainpipe lets out." He opened the back door to the limo, and everyone climbed in.

"Drive slowly we need to look down the hill to see where the tunnel appears."

The driver put on the flashers and cruised along at 20 miles per hour. All four sets of eyes peered out the side window, down the yellow grassy ridge to the right.

"There he is! He just ran across that yard," Naomi yelled and pointed ahead.

Everyone looked. A flash of Benny's cream-colored slacks and white shirt vanished behind a large home.

"Follow that man," Jake yelled at his driver.

The limo turned the corner and accelerated. When they reached the next street, Benny was gone. Jake pressed the privacy button—the glass partition rose between them and the driver.

"Dammit, what if something happens to him? "We put him in this position," Jake said. Vera and Naomi regarded Jake evenly, while Serena bit her fingernail and looked out the window.

"That's right, Jake, we did, and he thinks he's a mouse. Mice hide when they're scared. He'll probably find someplace safe to sleep it off," Vera said.

"I hope you're right, because he's not a mouse—he's a human being."

"Stop worrying, Jake," Naomi said.

Benny ran hunkered over, along South Highland Avenue with the big lawns and the huge homes. He stayed in the shadows of the palm trees whenever he could. This route was familiar to him, maybe it was instinct, but it seemed like the way home.

~

Barry found Felix and Andy in the conference room discussing scenes for The Organ Peddler.

"Felix! Where is everybody?" Barry said, grabbing Felix by the shoulders.

"Ouch, Barry, you're hurting me. I don't know, but I heard Serena's out of the hospital."

Barry released his grip. Felix adjusted his shirt with a few brisk tugs.

"And Alex is *in* the hospital," Barry said, "so they still can't finish their F/X scene. Have you heard anything from Jake? He's short on backbone, but that boy's a whiz at film editing."

"I haven't seen him, but we have plenty of clips of Alex swinging that cleaver."

"Listen, *Fifty Ways* is dragging out. That means until it's in the can Falchion doesn't get paid. Do you have a handle on the blocking for *The Organ Peddler* yet?"

"We both like the idea of—once the organs are procured—the killer rides one of those ice cream freezer bicycle thingees around the black-market section of town with the chilled organs inside," Andy said.

"I love it!" Barry said. "A play on words— peddler and pedaler," Okay, roll with that. I want the script in my office first thing in the morning."

~

Jake and the women scanned the Hollywood streets until 8:30 P.M.

"Jake, how much longer are we going to search?" Serena said, yawning. "I think Vera's right, he's probably hiding somewhere."

"I guess you're right. It's too dark to see now anyway. We'll have to get up early and go look for him."

Jake and the women drove back toward Jake's place in silence.

~

Benny ran a couple of miles and turned right onto Santa Monica Boulevard. He sensed safety lay at the end of this memorized route. After a half a mile, he turned left onto North Wilton Place. Close to the buildings, crouched over, he moved swiftly through the shadows. Loud cars zoomed by several yards to his left but didn't seem an immediate threat.

After a couple miles Benny veered right onto West Sunset Boulevard. He panted heavily but ran faster, spurred on by the possibility of safety and food. He turned right onto Hollywood Boulevard and saw a familiar sight. He could no longer read, but shapes looked familiar—huge gothic letters 20 feet in the air. He stood on his toes, his hands held limply, and licked the salt off his nose.

He entered the lot and searched for a comfortable place to nest for the night. A little rooting yielded a mildewed blanket behind a dumpster. Benny curled up and closed his eyes. No food tonight but this place felt like home.

~

Jake unlocked the door to his condo and everyone flooded in. Naomi and Serena plunked down on the couch. They bumped against each other but didn't seem to care.

"We need to crash, Jake," Naomi said.

"You two will have to share a room, Naomi, you know where it is."

"Good night. Don't wake us too early," Serena said as the two women shuffled down the hallway. Naomi wrapped her arm around Serena's shoulder as they turned the corner.

"Vera, we need to talk," Jake said.

"I'm pretty worn out from today too, Jake. Could we talk in the morning?"

The doorbell rang. Jake looked out the peep hole and turned to Vera. "It's a cop."

Jake opened the door half-way but found he couldn't speak. The officer showed his gold badge and put it away.

"Good evening. I'm Lieutenant Finklestein. I understand Vera Horowitz lives here?"

Jake turned to Vera, obscured by the door, and she nodded.

"May I ask what this is about?" Jake said.

"Official police business. Is Miss Horowitz here?"

Vera stepped in front of Jake and opened the door fully. "Hi Aaron. I never got the chance to thank you for helping me last week."

"I have some questions for you, and then you owe me a cup of coffee."

"Come in, I'm sure Jake has some coffee."

"No, just you. Down at the diner. I won't take much of your time."

"We won't be long, Jake," Vera said. She pulled on a sweater and walked down the sidewalk with the rugged-looking cop.

"There goes the woman I love," Jake muttered quietly.

~

Rhonda reclined in the queen-sized bed in her double-wide, while perusing a home decorating book, while Dark Snout, sitting beside her, read a surveillance gadgets magazine.

"Snouty?" Rhonda asked quietly.

"Yes, Rhonda?"

"I know I don't measure up to those beautiful movie stars you hung out with earlier, but do you still find me attractive? I know I'm kinda big and—"

"I think you're beautiful. And if you do anything to try to change yourself I'm going to be very upset with you. Now, let me see those guns."

Rhonda flexed her biceps and smiled.

"There's my wrestler girl," he said as he hugged Rhonda tightly.

"I love you, Snouty. I've never felt so secure, what with the trailer being paid off and you getting paid so well. I'm worried about those show biz people though. They don't know what they're doing and they're not bad folks."

"No, they're not. Don't worry. They're adults, they can make their own decisions."

~

The diner was quiet as Vera and Aaron entered.

"I was kidding, I don't let a lady buy me coffee. What would you like?" Aaron asked.

"Thank you, I'll have a cup of chamomile tea."

"Okay, business first, then I have a couple questions of a personal nature. Why didn't anyone report Alex Boxwell's attack on Serena Miles? It would have been a lot smarter than the way somebody schlepped their way through it."

"Honestly, I think everybody's afraid of getting fired by Barry Whitscomb."

"So, Barry knew about it all along? He sure seemed shocked to find out his nephew got beaten up. Showbiz people are tight—bad news moves through the grapevine fast. It's not hard to find a motive. I'm not pursuing this questioning much further because nobody's pressing charges. I *know* you know something about what happened to Alex Boxwell and I'm here to tell you you're out of your league with these actors meting out justice on their own."

The waitress set down two steaming cups and walked away. Vera waited for her to go before she spoke.

"But I don't know anything about that."

"Vera, you're a terrible liar. That's because at heart you're a good girl. These movie people are all nuts. Now, you come from a good family, you've got your grandmother sick. She just wants to see you in a good relationship. I don't have to tell you I've had feelings for you for a long time. I've got a good job and I'm about to earn a promotion to captain. All I want to do is take care of you and make a nice home for us. I've sure put in my time—since fifth grade, remember when you had braces? How about a nice dinner, some normal conversation?"

"I'm flattered, Aaron, you're a nice guy, but I'm seeing someone right now."

"Who? That goof back there in the doorway? L'Hommedieu? What's that, French? He looked so scared I thought he was going to pee his pants. If I were seriously pursuing this case he'd be the *first* one I'd question. What religion is he anyway?"

"I don't know, we've never talked about it." Vera suddenly looked puzzled.

"What does a clown like that even *stand* for? Don't you want a normal life, Vera?" Aaron stood and picked up his cop's cap. Vera slowly stood too.

"Just think about it," Aaron said. "Come on, I'll walk you back." He laid seven dollars on the table.

He always left me good tips, stable guy. I could do worse, she thought. Aaron smiled his sad smile and Vera smiled back as he opened the diner door for her.

"How about throwin' me a bone here, Vera? You might find out you like me," Aaron said, as they walked along.

"It's tempting. Maybe if I'm ever single," Vera said as Jake's condo came into view.

~

Jake watched from the peephole as Vera and Aaron approached. He noticed Aaron leering at Vera's back side, lingering with each step she took up to his front porch. Jake opened the door, ushered Vera in, and briskly pulled the door closed behind her.

"What was that all about?" he asked.

"He was questioned me about Alex. It sounds like the police are dropping the case."

"Just like that? No suspects? They aren't checking us all out?"

"It doesn't sound like it. I'm really tired, Jake. I could sleep on the couch—"

"Nonsense. You can have my bed. Come on." Jake led the way and gave Vera a clean, folded t-shirt. "I keep extra toothbrushes in the bathroom."

Jake left the room. After a couple of minutes He knocked.

"Come in," Vera called.

Jake opened the door and saw her in his bed: her shiny black hair spread out on his pillow, brown doe-like eyes gazing up at him. He wanted to kiss her in the worst way, but it had been dark in the theater. With the light on she was too perfect to touch.

"Oh, Jake, would you cover my ear with a sheet."

"With a sheet?"

"Yes, or I won't sleep. My ear must be lightly covered with a sheet."

Jake obliged her, then bent down and kissed her on the forehead. He turned out the light. The moonlight through the window illuminated Vera's pale complexion and perfect lips.

"Good night," Vera said.

Jake left and closed the door behind him. Vera thought about Jake and all he had done to help her. Staring in Hollywood movies—all the cat and mouse escapades had been exciting, but she was getting tired of the uncertainty. *This business is so crazy.*

Aaron. He was a bully in school, but he seems more mature. Maybe he's grown out of that stage. What would life with him be like? Solid, stable. I guess I could have given him a chance instead of avoiding him. Vera fell asleep dreaming of Aaron in his deep blue uniform.

~

Jake's feet hit the floor the second his alarm sounded. He brought a hot cup of tea from the kitchen and handed it to Vera.

"What time is it?" she asked.

"It's seven. Come on, we've got to find Benny."

"Okay, just let me brush my teeth."

Jake and Vera climbed into the back seat of his limo just before his driver could open it for them. *God bless him, he's up early and clean shaven,* Jake thought.

"We need to search Santa Monica Boulevard," Jake said as he sipped his coffee.

~

Benny heard the commotion of humans: walking, talking. He rose up on his hind legs and peered around the dumpster fence. The humans walked through a glass double doorway with the sun glinting off it. When the human traffic slowed, Benny ran over and sniffed under the doorway—there was *food* in that big room. This way was too dangerous for a mouse. He would have to find another way in.

~

Jake's phone rang and he picked up.

"Jake L'Hommedieu," he said.

It was Felix. "Jake, where have you been? Barry keeps asking me where you are. By the by, have you heard about Alex? It's really nasty. Some giant apparently broke his bones to make their bread."

"What? Where is he?"

"Malibu Memorial," Felix said, "We're all going to visit him this afternoon if you want to join us. But now, you're needed on the set to put together Serena's and Alex's F/X scene."

"We'll be in in about an hour."

Vera could hear their conversation in the quiet limo.

"Who's 'we,' Jake?" Felix asked.

Jake glanced at Vera since no one on set knew about them yet. Vera nodded and smiled.

"Miss Horowitz and I," Jake said. He listened for Felix's reaction."

"Wha—?" Felix said.

"It seems she really likes me." Jake smiled and snapped his phone shut.

~

Naomi and Serena awoke to the smell of coffee.

"I'm getting a cup of that," Naomi said. She returned with two cups and gave one to Serena.

"Listen, I'm not worried about Benny. Why? Because you gave me the same drug and it wore off and I was fine. So, what I want to do instead is carve out our future together. Jake's written this beautiful script, he said there's a role for you in it. Let's practice so we're ready."

"Are you sure it's okay if we read it without asking him?" Serena asked.

"Yes. I've got the script right here. I'm a pregnant single mother and you're my supportive B.F.F." Naomi opened the script to page one.

~

Jake and Vera quit the search and headed into Falchion.

"Let's grab a bite in the cafeteria, then we need to find Benny," Jake said.

"Okay, but I look terrible. I just want to get the rest of my things from Barry's trailer."

Jake and Vera walked hand-in-hand to the cafeteria. The line inside was long. It wound behind a yellow tiled wall into the a la carte section. Suddenly, a scream rang out. Women shrieked and stood on top of their chairs as Benny scampered from under a table. He snatched a cheese Danish off of a woman's tray, then crawled under a table with it.

"Somebody call security! Some vagrant dude's crouched under my table," a gaffer said.

Jake stepped out of line and approached Benny with his palms held upward.

"Benny, it's me, Jake. Come out. I'll get you a decent meal and a change of clothes."

Benny bared his teeth and gripped his cheese danish so tightly the filling squished out between his fingers.

"Eeek! Eeek!" Benny yelled and ran out of the cafeteria in a crouch. He rammed into a couple's legs that had just walked in. Benny jumped to his feet and forced his way out the door and across the lot. Jake ran after him and caught up to him just before he reached the fence. He lunged and brought Benny down with a flying tackle.

"Eeek! Eeeeek!"

"Yeah, I know 'eek'. Well, you're coming with me, pal."

Jake strained to hold on. Vera ran up to help hold Benny. Together they shuffled him toward the parking lot.

"Get him in the damned limo," Jake mumbled.

Vera and Jake held the wriggling Benny in the back seat. The driver turned around.

"Excuse me, sir, but are you holding that man against his will?" the driver asked.

"Yep, he needs our help. Now drive—my place."

By the time they reached Jake's, both he and Vera were fatigued from restraining Benny. They got him inside and walked him past the open-mouthed gapes of Serena and Naomi, to a back bedroom where they collapsed on top of him on the bed.

"Where did you find him?" Naomi asked.

"Later. Help us," Vera panted.

Jake knelt on Benny's chest and held his arms together while Serena bound Benny's wrists, ankles and legs with bed sheets. The whole time he shrieked and gnashed his teeth.

“Do you have more sheets?” Naomi asked.

“Here,” Jake said, “Tie him to the bed.”

“Wow, he’s strong,” Vera said. “Somebody cover his eyes with something.”

Serena folded a t-shirt, so it covered his eyes. Naomi tied sheets together, lashed two across Benny’s chest and two more across his legs, then tied the ends to the bed frame.

“There,” Jake said with a satisfied exhale, his hands on his hips.

Everyone released their grips from Benny and backed away. He thrashed at the sheets, but he was secured.

“Okay, turn out the lights,” Jake said.

Benny continued to squeal as they closed the door behind them. Jake sat at the kitchen table and ordered brunch for everyone from a local deli. The squealing from the bedroom slowly diminished as Benny calmed down.

“I don’t know about you girls, but for my money that wasn’t worth it at all,” Serena said.

“I’ve got to get to Benny’s place to remove all the evidence,” Jake said, “Save me some food, I’m going to be hungry.”

At Benny’s house, Jake scanned the neighborhood, but nobody seemed concerned with his presence. *I guess Benny doesn’t have any friends,* Jake thought. He entered and unplugged and dismantled all the equipment, took down the sheets and, in three trips to his limo, he’d loaded everything into the trunk. He locked up and headed back to his condo.

Inside, Jake sat down and dug into a sandwich.

“Well? Is everything okay back there?” Vera asked.

Jake nodded and munched. “Everything’s in the limo. Wow, this is great curried chicken—” Jake was cut short by a yell from the bedroom down the hall.

“Benny’s awake!” Naomi said, and stood up from the table, “Come on.”

Jake eased the door open, and he and the actors tip-toed up to Benny. He was still tied.

“Where the hell am I? Who’s there?” Benny said.

Jake looked uncomfortable. “You apparently either had too much to drink or you were delirious with exhaustion.”

Jake uncovered Benny’s eyes. Benny jerked his head around as he adapted.

“Jake? What am I doing bound to your bed?”

“You were flipping out in the Falchion cafeteria. We brought you here to calm down.”

“Thank you—I think. Untie me, please.”

Benny stood and rubbed his wrists and ankles.

“Are you okay, Benny?” Vera asked.

“I think so. I don’t *do* things like this. I *never* lose control.”

“It’s okay, Benny, it happens to the best of us,” Naomi said, fighting a smile.

“I’ll call you a cab,” Jake said.

Benny sat in stunned silence while he waited. They watched out the window as the cab took him away.

"If he didn't leave peacefully I was going to call Orkin," Serena said and laughed.

Chapter 17
Out on the Town

Jake awoke early, showered, shaved, and got dressed. It was Thursday morning and he should probably handle the editing of *Fifty Ways,* but he had to make an impression on the amazing girl still asleep in his bedroom. He thought about the advice his mother had given him: *Listen to her, don't just talk about yourself.*

"Why not pull out all the stops while I'm at it?" Jake whispered to the silent kitchen.

He buttoned his shirt as the cup of water for Vera's tea spun behind the microwave window. On the way to his bedroom, he saw Naomi return from the hall bathroom to her's and Serena's room. *It's like I'm running a hotel here,* Jake thought, tapping on Vera's door.

"Come in," Vera called.

Jake entered and Vera pulled the blanket around her neck.

"Here, I know you like chamomile tea, but it's morning and this peppermint has caffeine."

"Thanks," Vera said, and wrapped both hands around the steaming cup.

"I want to show you the sights. Get ready and wear something nice."

"Oh really? Cool!"

Vera stood and opened the closet—she didn't *have* anything nice. Faded blue jeans, a pink blouse, old threadbare black skirts, tank tops from her job at the restaurant, and of course, her patent leather Audrie Hepburn shoes. She had the check for $16,000.00 in her purse but she hadn't had time to deposit it at the bank or shop for clothes.

She showered, dressed in the black skirt and faded pink blouse and met Jake in the foyer. Jake and Vera sat in the back seat of the limo.

"Where to, sir?" the driver asked.

"The Urth Caffe for breakfast. You're hungry, right?" Jake asked Vera.

~

Felix and Barry met on Lot B to discuss blocking. Andy rode in circles on a shiny beige ice-cream-vending tricycle with matching umbrella.

"Snap! This is the one," Andy said, "How do I look?"

"Like a peach," Barry said, "How much did that thing cost us?"

"Four thousand online," Felix said, "It arrived this morning. We assembled it ourselves."

"Congratulations. We need someone gnarly looking for the villain. Any ideas?"

"Some bad guy types from central casting. Like to have a look-see?" Felix asked.

"Yeah, parade them past me in the conference room in an hour."

~

Jake and Vera had just finished breakfast. The remnants of Jake's organic scrambled egg spinach burrito and Vera's tomato-basil quiche were whisked away by the server—clink-clink, Jake thought, improvising sound effects in his head. *Stop it! This is not a movie!* he scolded, taking the last sip of his Spanish Latte.

"I've never tried a green tea Boba before," Vera said, dabbing her mouth with a napkin.

"It's great to try new things isn't it?"

"I know, right?" Vera tried to sound upbeat. *Jake, you're what's truly a new thing in my life—the closest I've come to dating was a boy I held hands with when I was fifteen!*

"Let's get you some new clothes. There's world-class shopping a few blocks away."

"I'll need to stop by the bank first to deposit my check."

"Your money's no good here. It's on me," Jake said as they stepped into his limo.

The driver parked at the curb in front of The Beverly Center, he walked around and opened the door for Vera and Jake. They walked up to the multi-level, upscale shopping mall and entered through Macy's.

"Where do you usually shop?" Jake asked.

"I've never shopped *here* before that's for sure," Vera said.

"How long have you lived in L.A.?"

"All my life—I've just never been here." *Because I've never had the money.*

Her previous shopping experiences had been in the dingy consignment shops, the same mildewed buildings where her grandmother had shopped growing up.

This is amazing, Vera thought. *High ceilings, gleaming tile floors that stretch for acres, a sea of circular racks filled with colorful clothing, elegant white manikins, faint scent of perfume*—she felt she didn't belong here but she was willing to roll with it.

"How about some nice dresses?" Jake said, entering the petites department. He lifted an Adrianna Papel one shoulder chiffon off the rack. "You'd look stunning in this."

Vera walked slowly, taking in the colors, reaching out and feeling the textures.

"That's beautiful, but I'm more conservative." Vera said, picking up a Calvin Klein scuba lace flare dress.

"Nice. 'Winter Rose'?" Jake said as he read the tag.

"I like pink."

"I'm learning. Pick out some more. Let's get you completely outfitted today. Something formal, casual, something for a night out and something you can dance in," Jake said.

"I can't believe how nice you're being," Vera smiled, "What's the catch?"

"You're a movie star, you should look the part."

~

Barry sat back and swilled straight bourbon from a tumbler as the first villain candidate lumbered in. Felix arched his eyebrows hopefully in Barry's direction.

"Naw, get him out of here—he's built like a lumberjack," Barry bellowed.

Felix held the door open for the man as he exited.

"Next!" Felix called into the hallway.

A muscle-bound man in his 20s with a shaved head and tattoos entered. Barry waved his hand dismissively.

"No, what is it with these buff guys in perfect health? I want a bad guy, gnarly, bashed-in-looking, out of shape, you know, from the streets—" Barry's mind locked onto an idea.

"Thank you, you may go. Next!" Felix called.

"Don't bother, I think I've got our man," Barry said, shouldering past Felix and stalking away.

~

It was 2:30 P.M. when Jake and Vera finally walked out of the Beverly Center. Vera wore a bright pink Alex Perry ruffle mini dress and carried three more bagged dresses, while Jake carried another dress and two boxes of shoes.

"You *do* like pink don't you?"

"This is really too much. I'm going to pay you back for all these."

"Nonsense. This is my treat. That was a lot of shopping though. How about some lunch? I know a great sushi place called Katsuya. It's right by Capitol Records. We could go there afterwards."

"Wow. This is the best time I've had in years," Vera said.

After lunch and a tour of Capitol Records, Jake suggested they check out the Avalon Club. Jake looked at Vera, so excited she was all but hopping up and down on her toes. The line wrapped halfway around the building, but he and Vera walked straight by everyone. Vera was duly impressed that Jake knew the bouncer—who waved him and Vera through.

Inside, the laser lights and blaring techno pop music took some getting used to—but just as Vera's eyes adjusted, Jake pulled her to the center of the bouncing crowd. Vera found her rhythm and they joined in the dance as the music morphed into a slow, carnal beat.

Jake felt he was doing a lot of things right and Vera was a good dancer—really good. He suddenly worried that he had made a blunder by bringing her here because she had caught the attention of several handsome, young men—younger and in better shape than him. But she wasn't paying any attention to them. She gazed at Jake through dark strands of hair which swung back and forth as she gyrated to the beat. Sudden passion flooded his body. *Is it my imagination or is that the most sensual stare a woman's given me in years?*

~

It was 11:30 P.M. when Barry and his limo driver quietly entered Alex's hospital room. It was deathly silent and there were no nurses in sight. Barry seemed to roll across the tile floor in his alligator loafers, unnaturally quiet for such a big man, like a predator in stalking mode, until he stood above the sleeping Alex.

"Psst, wake up, Alex," Barry whispered.

Alex opened his eyes and wiped away the crust. "Uncle Barry—you came to see me."

"Yeah, now get up. We've got to get you onto the set."

"What? No, Uncle Barry, I can't leave here—I'm just starting rehab—I'm in way too much pain," Alex's eyes grew wide with fear.

"Grab his IV rack and help me get him into this wheelchair," Barry told his driver.

"No, Uncle Barry, don't move me," Alex said, but two sets of hands were upon him.

"You shut up or I'm gonna hit you."

Barry and the driver lifted Alex and lowered him into the wheelchair, hooked the IV rack to the back of his chair, and wheeled him out into the hallway and into the elevator.

~

It was 1:30 A.M. when Jake and Vera carried her new clothes into his condo.

"That was so much fun today. Thank you, Jake."

"I wanted to show you the Santa Monica pier today, too."

"Are you kidding? Today was packed. I haven't danced that much since high school."

Jake held Vera by one shoulder and motioned to the sofa. They sat facing each other as they let the shoe boxes and dresses slump to the floor. Jake gazed into her eyes—looking for that sensual expression she'd made on the dance floor. He leaned in and kissed her. She didn't resist until he slid his hand up over her right breast. Vera inhaled and pulled his hand away.

"I'm sorry," Jake said.

"It's okay."

What's that look? Jake wondered. *It's not quite scared—not exactly angry— apprehensively scolding.*

"I'm going to get ready for bed," Vera said.

She stood, moving Jake's arms as if extracting herself from the unsavory tentacles of an octopus. She composed herself before she walked into the hall bathroom. Jake followed a few steps behind, holding his face to his hand—looking out between his fingers as he entered the guest bathroom at the end of the hall. *What have I done?*

As he brushed his teeth, Jake reflected on the models and actresses he'd met over the years. In the early days of his being an L.A. director, Jake and a young woman he didn't know, had made out at a party, as far as he could figure, because they both realized they were the two best looking people there. They'd even discussed it briefly.

Many of the actresses had very pretty faces, with fit, amazing bodies, collagen lips, top-of-the-line boob jobs—and such ambition! It hadn't been his idea to have sex with them—but they'd wanted the roles so badly; they hadn't wanted to leave anything on the table—and who was he to turn them down. He'd never promised them they'd be in one of his films—he'd only hired the ones that fit the character he'd envisioned for the slaughter scenes. But the sex had seemed almost obligatory, casual. Jake had never experienced such modesty with a woman of 23 in L.A., and Vera's reluctance and shock at his advances left him stunned.

Jake stepped into the hallway just as Vera walked into his bedroom. She left the door open behind her. Jake stared at the open doorway. *What is this? We've been kissing, she likes me, and she's moved in with me but—*

"Are you coming?" Vera's voice called.

"You want—to sleep in the same bed?" Jake asked.

"Yes, 'sleep,'" Vera replied.

"Right, 'sleep,'" Jake conceded.

Jake turned out the lights and approached the bed.

"Come on, hop in," Vera said.

Jake climbed in and pulled the covers over them. She giggled, hugged Jake, and pulled him close—her delicate fingers touching his ribcage. He gently felt around until he found Vera's face and pulled her lips to his. They kissed for a long time, then a little more. Then quite nimbly, Vera spun around—her back to him. Jake couldn't believe how well today had gone. The girl of his dreams right here in his bed, living with him. He just couldn't figure her out.

I'm just moving too fast—this is special. Slow down—don't want to blow this.

"Good night," Jake said.

It was good to have her here. It was comfortable having his arms around her—she seemed almost weightless—her back curled against his chest. He breathed in the scent of her hair as his thoughts morphed into a warm sunlit sandstone passage. His mind floated down through the roughly carved opening into a sultan's pillow-filled sanctuary with Vera's brown eyes and sweet face blossoming through the walls over and over—Jake had almost slipped into unconsciousness when Vera spoke.

"Jake? Do the other girls have bad dreams when they see themselves in horror movies?"

"What? Sometimes. But I think once they get used to it and they know—you know, that everything is just a series of special effects—it doesn't bother them anymore."

"Because I've had bad dreams after I saw myself in *Zombie Betrayal.*"

"It's just a movie," Jake said. He hugged Vera and kissed the back of her head.

~

As Barry and the limo driver wheeled Alex through the doors and onto the set, the night crew was in full swing. The set was a grimy city street, dented trash cans sat at the curb, closed rental shops lined the streets and an overhead streetlight flickered. In the foreground sat the now filthy ice cream tricycle, the umbrella on top, all painted a sickly green-grey color to simulate mildew.

"Come on, help me get Alex into the saddle," Barry roared.

Three stagehands scooted their hands under Alex who let out a groan of pain. They lowered him onto the tricycle seat, Alex's face twisted into a rictus of agony.

"Uncle Barry, take me back to the hospital. You can't believe how much this hurts."

"Good, use that pain. You wanna be a star? You look great, kid, all bashed in and grey. And that face you're makin', freakin' perfect, just the way I imagined this villain. Here, read over your lines—they're just a few—then we'll take you back to the hospital."

Barry handed Alex a crisp, new script and pointed to his lines, highlighted in yellow. Alex strained, he read, then grimaced in pain. He gave the now crumpled script back to Barry.

"I've got it—now hurry—this is excruciating."

Barry and the staff backed off stage. Only Andy remained. He slid an oversized dirty trench coat sleeve over Alex's wrist cast, wrapped a black raincoat over his leg cast, pulled a stocking cap over Alex's forehead, tied his good foot to the tricycle pedal so he could ride it, then backed off stage.

Felix cued the misty-rain machine then stepped out into the drizzle.

"*The Organ Pedaler*, selling scene, take one," Felix said, snapping the clapper-board together and backing off stage.

Alex pedaled with one leg in a slow, painful circle in the street. He grimaced as a sketchy-looking character approached.

"Do you have any eye-candy this evening?" the man asked.

"We're all out right now. How about a nice lung pop?" Alex croaked.

"No, I am more in the mood for a liver sorbet."

"We have a liver sorbet and we also have a tasty frozen heart custard this evening."

"Okay, I'll take the liver and the heart. The usual rate I assume?" the stranger said, looking both ways.

"That's right, ten thousand," Alex groaned in utter distress.

The man handed Alex a wad of bills and, with a monumental effort, Alex leaned forward and retrieved two plastic lunch boxes from the cooler. As he withdrew them, ghostly dry ice fingers flowed from the cooler to the man's hands.

"Cut! Felix yelled and everyone applauded.

The misty rain machine stopped, and bright lights came on. Barry's driver, Andy and a stagehand lifted Alex off the tricycle. Barry smiled as the crew helped Alex back into his wheelchair.

"Well done, Alex, you're so sickly and waxy—just what the scene needed."

~

Jake awoke and Vera was gone. He knew it: *it had all been too perfect.* She was perfect and now she had left him already because he was a freak! A no-good freak. And why not? He didn't deserve her she was so—

Vera walked into his room wearing one of his t-shirts and carrying two steaming mugs.

"I made you coffee," she said, sitting on the edge of the bed.

That beautiful voice! Jake smiled and made room for her on the bed.

"Good morning," Vera said, clinking cups with Jake.

He leaned in for a kiss then pulled away, taking in her eyes, her smile. *This is some good acting—like I didn't think she just kicked me to the curb.*

"I have to go into Falchion for a few hours to edit *Fifty Ways*" Jake said. "But I want to take you out to lunch—and to see the Santa Monica pier. What do you say? Can you be ready by eleven?"

"Yeah. I'll just go deposit my check and I'll meet you here."

"Okay," Jake replied, brimming with confidence—*as if I were in control*, he thought.

~

Barry saw Brian and Lola kissing behind the dumpster and sneaked up on them.

"I can't get enough of you," Brian said, "You smell like rotten apples. Touching your hair is like running my fingers over corn husks—There are so many textures to you." Brian said, and held Lola in his arms, then inhaled deeply as he kissed his way up her neck. As Lola smiled her lips folded over a large mole which disappeared into a crease—her eyebrows tilted upward, her lips downward. The results: a sympathetic frown. A fly circled her head.

"What are you *doing* to me?" Lola gasped.

Brian ran his fingers across Lola's elbow—a rough patch of skin and a dime-sized wart. He kissed her again.

"Your body has so many surprises—I want to unwrap you inch by inch."

"I feel like I'm torn between two worlds—uglies and pretties. I'm so confused. You're one of the pretties, Bri. Why don't you find yourself a model or some bimbo actress?"

"If you don't want me around just say it."

"No, I *do*. It's just that you're—"

Barry stepped in front of Brian and Lola. "It's just that you can take this up on your own time. Do you *like* working here?" Barry interrupted.

Flushed and startled, Lola pushed Brian away.

"*Yes,* Mr. Whitscomb," she said.

"Then I need you to do something for me—*if* you want to keep your jobs."

"What?" Brian said.

"Follow me."

Barry led the way into the Building C set piece storage facility. He unlocked the door to the chilly rentals room and flipped on the lights. Row after row of florescent overhead lighting flickered on until the room hummed. Brian and Lola took in the twenty-foot-tall ceilings—the aisles of industrial equipment on the bare concrete floor. There was the seven-foot-tall Pyrex glass blender from *Fifty Ways* splattered in fake blood and organ pieces crusted in oozing shapes. Brian approached the blender; just beyond his face, separated by the thick, blue-green glass, clung fake bone fragments and gelatinous gore.

"I need to cut some costs," Barry explained. "I can either get rid of employees or equipment. This industrial mixer is rent-with-the-option-to-buy. Funny how they phrase that—it means if it *looks* used, we bought it. You make it look brand new or find yourselves new jobs. I need it sparkling clean by Monday, two days—plenty of time. Let me know when you're finished, and I have a *paying* job for both of you. Adios."

Barry closed the door behind him. Lola and Brian walked up and looked at the eight-foot ladder, the mops and long-handled bristle brushes and the wash tub in the corner, buckets, rags, bleach, and detergent.

"I guess we'd better get started," Brian said.

Chapter 18

You think You Know Someone

After Jake and Vera spoke, and even after the peppermint tea, Vera had laid down on the bed and fell asleep. From the bedroom, Vera heard the front door to Jake's condo close; then the sound of a large vehicle pull up, women's voices, doors shut and a well-tuned engine quietly cruising away. Suddenly, she remembered Serena and Naomi saying they were going shopping at 9:00 A.M. Vera's Mandy-Mouse watch read 8:45A.M. She pulled on one of Jake's bathrobes, which hung to the floor, and walked into the kitchen, lifting the robe as she went. She found still-steaming water in the kettle and made herself a mug of chamomile tea.

Jake emerged from the hallway in a pale gray Gorgio Bissoni suit and leather portfolio held in one hand. He beckoned Vera to follow him as he walked toward the front door.

"Come on, walk me out. I'm going to meet with a banker about a loan. I'll be back in a couple of hours. Can I bring you anything?"

Damn handsome man I've nabbed, Vera thought.

"No thanks. I'm just going to chill."

Jake leaned over and kissed her then gently touched his index finger to her nose.

"See you later, beautiful," Jake said, with his pearly white smile.

What's not to like? Vera thought. Looking adorable, she waved two fingers from her tea mug as Jake pulled the door closed behind him. The way he'd just left—in a suit, with a briefcase—reminded Vera of a husband just leaving for work. *I wonder if Jake would be good with kids? What's wrong with me? I'm being ridiculous!*

For the first time Vera was completely alone in Jake's condo. She set her teacup on one of the glass tables flanking the leather couch. It was too dim in the room—then she laughed as she remembered the retro "clap-on" device Jake had had installed in all the rooms, and clapped her hands together; immediately the table lamps glowed warmly through creamy lampshades. She glanced over at a fanned-out stack of magazines on one of the end tables.

She noticed a well-worn, laminated copy of *HorrorMeister* magazine and picked it up. It was dated March 2000.

I wonder why Jake kept such an old copy?

The cover photograph was of Barry dressed as a pirate with a bloody hook hand. He stood above Naomi, his boot heel on her hip while he pulled a twist of Naomi's hair in his good hand. Naomi, in her early twenties, her hair long, dyed blonde, lay helpless on the deck of a wooden ship—dozens of bloody holes in her body. She looked up at Barry with a terrified expression. The movie's title was *Meatooks Some Liberties with the Lady.*

"Sick," Vera said, and flipped to the article on page 15.

The article was entitled: "Meatooks—in sick hands with new director Jake

L'Hommedieu at the helm." There was a photo of Jake and Barry, their arms across each other's shoulders, looking like old pals.

Hmm, 15 years ago, Barry was just 48 back then. What's with that excited look in Jake's eyes? Gross! Vera thought.

The interview between *HorrorMeister,* Barry and Jake followed.

HM: Barry, this movie is a lot of fun: Lots of screams, plenty of gore! One noteworthy quote—the pirates' references to "skull duggery." What inspired you to get into the cannibalistic pirate niche?

BW: I can't take the credit. This fellow right here is responsible. He's twice as twisted as I ever was.

HM: Jake, the degree of violence here, and the number of puncture wounds even tops the sleeper hit from You'd Better Run, Girl pictures: *Rhino Where You're Camping This Summer.* Your picture was slammed with an NC-17 rating and it still set new box office records. Do you consider that a risk? I mean, with this being your first foray as new director and all?

JL: I'm not afraid to crush boundaries to give fans what they want.

HM: Shame on them if that's what they want. I mean that in a good way, of course.

BW: Jake's demented alright. I can't tell you more, but with the sick ideas in this kid's head, fans can expect superb nightmares over the next few months.

HM: I'm a Barry Whitscomb fan from day one. Won't you miss directing?

BW: I always said if I couldn't deliver a movie that gave me chills and kept me awake at night I'd take a back seat. I'd like to hang in there, but how can I compete? This kid is sick, sick, sick.

Disgusted, Vera slapped the magazine shut and tossed it onto the table. She reflected on her daydream of raising children with Jake, and pictured them stumbling across this movie online. *What kind of role model would Jake be?*

The phone rang from across the room. After the third ring a woman's voice echoed from the answering machine. "Hi Jake, it's Mom. I'm just calling to see how things are going with your lady friend—"

Vera crossed the room and snatched up the phone. "Hello?"

"I'm sorry, I must have dialed the wrong number."

"No, this is Jake L'Hommedieu's residence."

"With whom am I speaking then?"

"I'm Vera."

"Oh, I've heard wonderful things about you. I'm Jake's mother. I hope to get a chance to visit there some day. It's so cold here in Nebraska."

"You mean you've never been here—to visit Jake?"

"Oh no, dear. I guess you didn't know—Jake and I have been estranged for years. It's only since he's met *you* that we've begun talking again. His sisters and I miss him terribly."

"He hasn't seen any of you? For years?" Vera asked.

"No, but I have you to thank for his calling me. I think we're all patched up again."

"I don't mean to pry but why haven't you—?"

"I don't feel comfortable saying any more. Jake can tell you."

"Of course."

"It was nice talking with you, Vera. I hope to meet you some day."

"Thank you. It was nice talking with you too." The line went dead.

Vera walked over, slumped down on the couch and closed her eyes. She wanted to look at that picture of Jake smiling again to determine whether it was a posed shot or real. As she sat up she noticed there was another laminated magazine beneath the first.

She slipped it the from beneath the others and glanced at the cover of *Shrink Rap* magazine. There was an article about *Meatooks* on page 25. Vera flipped to it and dug in. At the top of page 25 Vera read the title: "*Meatooks,* Sad Statement on Morality: An Interview with Phillip Thompson, Ph.D. (SPOILER ALERT)"

The article began: "It was my privilege to interview Dr. Phillip Thompson on the subject of the decline of our society's mores brought on by the new breed of graphic horror films. Dr. Thompson is not a practicing psychiatrist, but is a respected and prolific researcher and contributor to professional psychological journals."

SR: Doctor Thompson, you actually contacted our office with regard to the new blockbuster film entitled *Meatooks Some Liberties with the Lady.* How is this film different from other sensational horror films?

Dr. T: I felt the need to express myself on this disturbing trend in entertainment. I would hope a well-adjusted person in our society would be taken aback by the total lack of compassion indicated by the movie poster and the adolescent humor of the tagline.

SR: There is a school of thought which maintains horror movies can provide a healthful release of one's anxieties; a form of self-therapy. Would you care to weigh in?

Dr. T: This movie goes far beyond a place where one vanquishes mental angst. The plot is a thinly veiled device which exalts a two-hour visceral display of the execution of six barely-clothed women aboard a 1690's wooden pirate ship. The women—young, beautiful, responsible—go about their business in town. The pirates—an illiterate, filthy hoard—sneak into town to "get fresh meat for the voyage." They abduct the women, drag them aboard their ship, and set sail.

SR: Often times, films of this genre mete out justice based on the victim's apparent sins. Would you say that's true of this film?

Dr. T: These are "nice" girls; kind, happy, industrious, and from all outward appearances completely innocent; one doesn't want to see anything bad happen to them. Instead, this director assaults viewers with two hours of the terrified girls' hiding in the ship's holds, being found, dragged out one by one and torn apart with the pirate's hooked-hands and eaten alive while the other women are forced to hide and watch, knowing they are to be next. This film holds out no hope, all the girls were killed. I found it morally reprehensible.

SR: The film set new a horror movie record for largest grossing opening week. That must say something about our society's craving for these types of films.

Dr. T: It's like giving a child hot dogs and macaroni and cheese or giving them a balanced meal. The first appeals to the base instincts of immediate gratification, but soon the fatty, low nutritional value decreases the individual's health, subjecting them to myriad maladies. Whereas a nutritionally balanced meal requires discipline but results in a more healthful person.

SR: Do you have an opinion regarding the director of this film?

Dr. T: I haven't met him. A Mr. Jake L'Hommedieu, as stated in the credits, but judging by the material in his film, he displays flagrant nihilistic, misogynistic tendencies. He has given every advantage to the pirates, so it is clear from the onset he intended to kill all the females in the film. In my opinion, the creation of this film is a desperate cry for help. I hope this individual will read this article and seek out professional counseling.

Vera slowly closed the magazine and laid it on the end table.

He read this. He saved it and still—I'm dating a monster.

~

Jake met with a banker and secured a new line of credit for his romantic drama then he drove to the meeting he hadn't told Vera about: the one with his therapist. Jake felt different—calm, confident as he opened the glass door, entered the building and slowly walked the length of the hallway. He came to a complete stop, exhaled and knocked. The door opened and his therapist, apparently speechless, dabbed at her eyes with a tissue—her normally pale complexion now splotchy and moist. She motioned Jake inside.

"What? No running up to the door?" Thelma said.

"I take it you read my screenplay?"

"Yes, I just finished it," Thelma sniffed.

"Well?"

"You've taken out all the slaughter scenes and degrading, misogynistic moments. It's sad, it's funny, it's tragic, and it's empowering for women. I've never seen anyone with an eighteen-year-long addiction turn themselves around as you have."

"Really? I was really hoping you would say that because I've started seeing the woman I've been so infatuated with. In fact, she's moved in with me."

"Hmm? That was quite a leap of faith for someone with your condition. I advised *against* dating. I want to warn you that it's possible for you to revert to your former behavior patterns. Can you honestly tell me that you can look at a beautiful woman and not imagine all the different gruesome ways you could have the special effects people dismember her, or impale her, or slice her up?"

"Stop it! Stop it! Yes, I can honestly say I'm through with all of that demented thinking. What kind of therapist *are* you anyway? Don't you want me to get better?"

"Of course I do. I just want you to be aware that you've reinforced this behavior for eighteen years; with what do you plan to replace that behavior?"

"With love. With consideration and politeness and romance. You just said I'd pulled a 180 with my screenplay!"

"You've got to take it one day at a time."

"I can do that."

"You can't take women for granted anymore. They're your equals, in some cases, your superiors."

"Okay."

"And if you *do* find love you've got to monitor it every day."

"Will do."

"If you're willing to do all of that then you may be one of the lucky ones. I'll see you next week to evaluate your condition. Of course, if you feel you need guidance sooner, then my door is always open. Now, let's talk about your relationship with your mother."

~

Brian and Lola strolled arm-in-arm in downtown L.A., past the shops, not seeming to notice the people, just gazing at each other occasionally. It was then that Felix and Andy noticed them. Felix touched Andy on the arm and walked briskly in their direction.

"Hey, you two. Lola, mind if I have a word with Brian for a sec?" Felix said.

Brian and Lola looked bewildered, but obliged him as Felix took Brian by the arm and led him half a block away and into an alley.

"What's this about, Felix?" Brian said, "I'm trying to relax on my day off."

Felix appeared stern. "Look, mister. There's something very wrong in Camelot. You are an unbelievably handsome young man and Lola is like—well, I don't want to be cruel, but her face makes children cry. I've seen it. You two are not a Hollywood match. And don't try to feed me some malarkey about how deep she is."

Brian stared open-mouthed for a second. "You really have no clue, do you? Yes, Lola is the queen of ugly. Yeah, she is the probably the ugliest woman on the planet—and she's conquered that. You wouldn't last ten minutes being that ugly, Felix. But she pulls it off movie after movie—listening to Barry insult her, seeing how you and Andy cluck your tongues at her. She has more character than any of us. I would love her for that alone, but there's so much more to her than that."

Brian spoke over his shoulder as he walked back toward Lola and Andy. "Just get away from me; you're taking time away from me and my girlfriend," he said, nearly within earshot of Lola and Andy as he walked rapidly, and Felix kept pace.

"I don't understand. You're really good looking, Brian. We're in L.A.—think of waking up to that face twenty years from now."

Lola twitched then looked away.

"Come on, Lola," Brian said, "you don't have to make small talk with Andy,"

He took Lola by the hand, leaving Felix and Andy to gape after them.

~

Jake arrived at his condo and whisked the door open.

"Vera, are you ready to check out the Santa Monica Pier?"

Vera sat unmoving on the couch, flicking the laminated magazine cover nervously up and down with her fingernail.

"No," she said.

"Why not? It's a landmark—the Ferris wheel is solar powered. It's so cool."

"How did you get into this business?"

Jake glanced at Vera's suitcase at her feet. "What? Why? And what's your suitcase doing in here?"

"Because this movie you made in 2000 is disgusting and you look depraved in the photo," Vera waved the magazine back and forth as evidence.

"Oh, *Meatooks?* I had to make a big splash. Barry told me 'Go big or go home!'"

"It's sick!"

"You've been in a zombie movie and been eaten alive. You've been chopped up with a cleaver and fed into a blender. How was that movie any different?"

"Because in those movies bad people die at the end, some good people who learn to overcome risks live, and the plots have some humor in them. This one is mean-spirited. The article says the movie is about defenseless, barely clothed girls, trapped, torn apart by meat hooks, then eaten alive. How could you make a movie like that?"

"I'm the oldest—of five sisters with no male role model. Their girly behavior—I had to get out of the house or go crazy. So, I watched a lot of horror movies in my buddy's basement."

"Your mother called here today," Vera said. "She said you and your sisters have been estranged for years. You've never even had her out here to visit."

"My mom? My mom doted on those girls. They didn't need me around."

"She says they miss you terribly. What about bullies? What about brotherly advice? Your sisters needed you, Jake."

"That was a long time ago. Besides, we're talking again. We're good now."

"How old were you at the time?"

"I was sixteen—just a kid."

"How old were you when you stopped hanging out at your friend's?"

"Nineteen. After that I pitched myself to Barry. What a long shot—a Hollywood director taking a chance on a kid with a quarter-million-dollar movie! I had to hit the ground running."

"And apparently you're still a kid. You were nineteen in 2000 and hadn't talked with your family for three years; now it's 2015, you're thirty-four and you're just *now* talking?"

"I didn't have it figured out. I mean, thank god your grandmother forced me to call. We talked it all out. I wanted to change for *you,* Vera." Vera counted on her fingers.

"What are you dense? Eighteen years without talking with your family? Here's a check for the clothes—$1,700.00"

Vera grabbed her suitcase and walked toward the front door. "I need stability."

"Those clothes were my treat. Wait, don't move out—that's a stupid idea."

"You'd know a stupid idea when you saw one, right? Make Benny think he's a mouse."

"I did that for you—to get even. Where're you going anyway?"

"I'm moving in with Bubbe for a while—we both need to get things sorted out."

Jake followed her across the room. "Until we get what sorted out, Vera? Vera, wait."

"I looked up 'nihilism,' the word the psychiatrist used to describe you. It means 'a rejection of all religious and moral principles.' I can't be with someone like you! Get help."

The door slammed. Jake ran across the lawn and into the street as the taxi pulled away.

"But I *did* get help! I've been to a therapist! I'm mostly cured!" Jake yelled, but it was too late.

Neighbors stared at him as he bowed his head and walked back toward his driveway.

Chapter 19
The Break-up

Brian and Lola had just finished breakfast at a deli across from Grauman's Chinese Theater. They stepped outside to the medium rush of traffic on Highland Avenue. The wide sidewalk was divided lengthwise between the warmth of the morning sun and the chilly shade of the buildings. Lola pulled her turnover sweater collar to her neck.

"Why bring me all the way down here? What's this big secret?" Lola asked.

Brian paused and fidgeted with something in his jacket pocket. He smiled nervously at Lola then took her hand and led her into the sunlight.

"I wanted you to remember today so I thought let's do this in a place that says 'L.A.'"

"Do what?" Lola said, she looked dubious as Brian dropped to one knee on the sidewalk, half in and half out of the shade, and offered up a small, black velvet box.

"Oh, I don't know about this, Bri."

Lola was vaguely aware of a group of twenty-something females approaching from the left; they were all designer footwear, sequined short skirts and tanned toned tummies, $500.00 highlighted feather cuts, and porcelain-veneer smiles.

Brian opened the lid and the diamond sparkled. As he began to speak, he was cut off by comments from the passing girls.

"Boo," a girl said: her one-word assessment of Brian's apparent proposal.

"I know, right? He could do so much better," said another, mid-strut.

"Really?" one girl paused, hand-on-hip, and spoke directly to Brian, "You could date my sister, Dude, she's way prettier."

Lola stared as the girls strutted away, laughing, and tossing their hair. She was so stunned that she barely pulled her head back in time to avoid being hit by a teen-aged male on a moped. He buzzed down the sidewalk, forcing the privileged girls to scatter. The boy wobbled to a stop and cut the engine. Lola heard the girls' rants.

"Hey, idiot! You almost hit us!"

"Sorry," the boy responded, "I know you're in a hurry to shop at Baby Gap."

"You drive like a baby. Call us when you reach puberty!" the lead girl shouted.

The boy parked and ducked into a store doorway, escaping further insults.

Lola had heard cruel remarks all her life, but since she'd arrived at Falchion Films they had slowed to a trickle. The staff was comfortable with her role; she was the ugly girl, the bad girl who played the villain's edgy, snarky sidekick, who gave the films their snap. Since she'd started seeing Brian, however, the cruel remarks had picked up momentum—and lately, that old feeling of not fitting in had crept up the back of her scalp.

She joggled from her musings and gazed at the kneeling Brian—*ridiculously handsome.*

"Lola, I love the person you are inside and out. You're the one I've searched for and I can't imagine spending my life without you. Will you marry me?" he said, plucking the ring from its box and presenting it to her.

"I can't, Brian. Didn't you *hear* that? Society really has a problem with gorgeous guys and ugly girls getting together. The opposite is okay. You've studied film: King Kong, Beauty and the Beast, Phantom of the Opera, Cyrano de Bergerac, Hell Boy. Ugly dude/beautiful girl, okay; Ugly girl/gorgeous dude, not okay. Besides, I heard what Felix said: my face isn't going to get better looking with age."

"None of that matters! I'm not going to get better looking with age either."

"Bullshit. You'll age like George Clooney or Clint Eastwood. The pretty girls will eventually wear you down and you'll take off with one of them."

"No way! That'll never happen."

"Look, I can't do this. I especially can't do this for a lifetime. If you want to keep seeing each other *privately*, then okay."

"Remember when you accused me of being shallow—just liking you for your looks? Well, it's you who's being shallow now. I love you, and *why* is nobody's business but ours."

"This is too intense. I've always been alone—it works for me." Lola backed up a step.

"What? It doesn't work for me! I love you. I want to spend my life with you."

"Give me some space, Brian. A couple of weeks at least." Lola turned and walked away.

"Wait!" Brian said.

"Seriously, back off!" Lola said.

She stared longingly into the distance. Half a block away the sidewalk turned the corner. If she could only reach it—to be alone—to *think!*

Lola walked quickly, glanced behind her, and saw Brian jogging after her. She ran. The teen, just ahead, had stepped out of the store. He turned the key to his moped. The motor started, the vibrating bike propped on its kickstand. As he paused to pull on his helmet, Lola reached him, shoved him hard against the brick wall. She straddled the moped, rolled back the throttle, and took off. Brian's hand clutched at the back of her sweater—but slipped as she pulled away.

Her reality became a moped-charged wind tunnel. Air chilled her face, rushed through her hair, as she accelerated. She swung wide and sped past the girls. Where the sidewalks converged, just ahead, nothing blocked the glorious sunrise and the far buildings in the backdrop glowed. *Freedom!* Lola sneaked a quick peak behind her at the panting, running Brian. She exhaled with relief. She leaned and accelerated into the corner.

Eager for new scenery, but cautious of pedestrians, she braked to 15 mph and cruised into the blinding sunlight of the new section of sidewalk. It was too bright. Sunrise shouldn't be this bright. Her heart stuttered.

This is straight up horror.

Just ahead, blocking the whole sidewalk, two men carried a six-foot-long plate glass mirror. Lola yanked the handlebars left toward the street, but it was too late—she skidded—abandoned the handlebars and threw her hands up defensively—only one hand between her and the glass—her face took the brunt of the impact. Hot and cold crashing, glass everywhere, engulfed her—people screaming. Everything went black.

Chapter 20

Group Reaction

Jake stood in the center of the street and stared where it curved out of sight—where the taxi had whisked his love away. A sick void gathered in his gut.

"I guess that's it," he said, hating the sound of his own voice.

But it's true—there's no way to convince Vera I'm a decent person now. I could call mother for advice, but she would probably say to let Vera cool off first. With no social life that just leaves work. I should finish editing Fifty Ways, get paid and rid myself of my obligation to Barry. If Vera's gone at least she helped me extract myself from that wretched relationship with Barry. How long will the editing take? A hundred hours? I've done it before on deadline. Immerse myself in work to kill the pain.

As Jake trudged back toward his driveway, he heard an engine surge up behind him. He spun around as the tires screeched to a stop. The rear door of his silver limo opened and Naomi stepped out.

"Jake, get in quick. Lola's been in an accident."

"What? How?"

"It's really bad. Just get in."

Naomi slid over and Jake climbed in next to Serena. As the driver took off, Naomi and Serena explained the accident at the same time, talking over each other.

"— and I don't think I can take it if one more thing goes wrong. First Barry dumping me, Serena, then rehab, I feel kind of bad about Alex, that Benny thing, and now Lola" Naomi said.

"Wait, where did she get the moped?" Jake asked.

"She 'borrowed' it from a kid to get away from Brian," Naomi said. "The poor guy was proposing to her and it freaked her out."

"How did you find out about this?"

"Brian. He called me, just totally losing it in the phone. He said he knew Lola and I were good friends and he didn't know who else to call."

At Malibu Memorial Hospital, the receptionist directed the group to the second floor.

"Come on," Naomi said, as the elevator doors closed them inside. "Brian said they're in the trauma I.C.U. and we can't see Lola yet, but let's go see what Brian knows."

The elevator opened and they walked toward the I.C.U. double doors, apparently locked from inside. A voice called out to them.

"Over here," Brian said, from a couch near tables and magazines. Jake approached him.

"Hey, buddy," Jake said, reaching out and squeezing Brian's shoulder, "we're here for you. Have you heard anything?"

"They took her from the ambulance—I followed them. They took her back, said I had to wait out here. A nurse told me they were trying to get her stabilized.

I'd just proposed, I don't understand what happened." Brian's brows were bunched, his hands in fists.

"Come on," Naomi said, "you need to relax." She sat at the far end of the couch and massaged Brian's shoulders. "This used to relax Barry."

"Jake, could you get us a cup of water?" Serena asked, pulling a bottle of ibuprofen from her purse.

"Brian, take it easy," Naomi said, "She's going to be alright."

"I never expected—"

"I'll bet Lola never expected you to propose either. She's a very independent girl."

"I just want to hear that she's alright," Brian said, writhing his shoulders and standing. "It's nice of you to massage me, but I should be ready when they come out."

Jake returned with a paper cup of water and handed it to Brian just as a young man in light blue scrubs walked through the sealed doorway and approached them.

"You're waiting to see Miss Lola Grubb? We've done all we can for now. She's stable and under sedation, and unless one of you is a family member, I can't permit any of you to see her now. Besides, she won't be able to speak at this time."

"Can you tell me how bad it is? I'm her fiancé," Brian said.

"She's undergone a lot of trauma. Check back with us tomorrow and we'll know more."

The young man returned through the doors using his card. The pneumatic doors sealed closed behind him.

Chapter 21

Barry's Reaction

The following morning, Helena Gutierrez watched through the hospital doorway. She imagined that the female facial victim must be very attractive to be involved with such a young and handsome American man. This man got up off his knees beside the bed, sobbing. He held the patient's good hand, the one not in a plaster cast, and kissed it over and over. As the *hombre americano guapo* exited the room with tears in his eyes, Helena stood back, walked a few feet away into the hallway, and pretended to text someone on her tablet.

A nurse entered the room and checked the tubes and monitors attached to the woman with the ravaged face. She made some notes on her hanging chart, walked into the hallway, and took a quick right—a woman on a mission. Helena peered into the doorway, hoping she could finally enter and introduce herself to the poor injured woman.

She had seen the woman with the terrible facial trauma wheeled in the day before. She always found out about them because she had a friend who drove an ambulance. This was the time to approach her—as the medication began to wear off—before the hospital staff got to her with their plastic surgery options. As she was about to enter, she felt the presence of a dominant male approaching from the hallway. Helena walked a few steps away and pretended to read one of the regulations hung on the wall but glanced as the heavy man entered the woman's room. His hair was so long and thick and lustrous. Never had she seen such hair! She was equally repulsed and attracted by the overweight man.

Barry looked down at Lola—the mass of facial bandages that must be Lola—a plastic straw secured to her lips to allow her to take in liquids, two tubes to give her nose some structure, her heart monitor and intravenous leads disappearing under the sheets.

"Wow, Lola. I have to take my hat off to you. You really live your craft." Barry said, as he pulled out a handkerchief and dabbed at his tearing eyes. "You've always been ugly, ugliest girl I'd ever seen, but you took it one step further. You, starring opposite the beautiful girls, who get hacked up, somehow made you uglier. You, you was always the showstopper."

"Makin' beautiful gals ugly, that's my trade, but you was always the yin to their yang. I always thought of you as, as like a daughter. But deliberately crashing your face through that mirror, well, that's life imitating art. It's like the best gift you could ever give me. You'll always have a job with me. I can't wait to see them bandages come off—it'll be like unwrapping a Christmas present."

Barry leaned over and kissed Lola's forehead bandages. Lola's mouth and nasal cavity filled with outrage at what Barry had said. She wanted to curse him out, go back to elementary school and summon the most disgusting expressions to show her contempt. But she couldn't speak. She could only sort of honk through the tube. So, she crumbled. Through the wrapping, the mouth tube, the straws where her nose had been, came a low, sustained, echoed sobbing.

"You get better now—we need you on the set, doll," Barry said, and left.

Helena rubbed the chill running up her shoulders and neck, as the big man lumbered away. With a glimpse at his bouncing, shimmering auburn hair, she entered Lola's room.

"Hello? Excuse me, but I heard what that monster said to you. Thank God he is gone. May I come and sit with you?" Helena asked.

Lola could see the woman, brown skinned and plump, through a single layer of gauze half covering her left eye. Lola would have nodded, but her head was held fast by a neck brace, so she beckoned with her arm—the one not in a cast—for the woman to approach. Lola tried to stifle the sobs, but everything just felt like sloppy suction.

"I am Helena Gutierrez. Can you see, through those bandages?"

Lola gave a thumbs-up.

"Good, because I have something to show you in just a moment. First, why should you listen to me? Because I have been in your position myself. I am twenty-nine now, but on my quinceañera my father presented me with what I wanted most in the world: a beautiful burrito. You would call it a baby donkey. I adored her and named her Lucinda—or Lucy.

"Because we were poor, every member of the family, every animal, had to do their part. Lucy pulled a cart, sometimes filled with dirt, sometimes vegetables. Anyway, I loved her. I brushed her and kept her hooves clean, fed her, gave her water, and how did she repay me? One day as I checked her back foot, she kicked me right in the face. Yes, it is true. She broke my cheek bone, my nose, knocked out my teeth and dislocated my jaw. Do you see why I am talking to you, my dear?"

Lola gave a thumbs-up, her wet snuffling subsiding for the moment.

"I was truly fortunate because only three hours away in Tijuana I had an uncle who was a world-class plastic surgeon. My father rushed me to see him. He restored my beauty—just like it was before. I am beautiful, yes?"

Thumbs-up.

"You don't have to settle for looking 'below average' anymore," Helena said, using air quotes. "Are you wealthy?"

Thumbs-down.

"No matter. You can be as beautiful as medically possible. As long as you pay in cash it will be affordable. You have a narrow window of time—before the swelling goes down—to decide. If you get the work done here in the United States it will be too expensive. My uncle is a brilliant surgeon. Let me show you."

Helena pulled out her smart tablet. "All of these women had terrible accidents, just like you. Here I have before and after pictures of them. Ugly from accidents, you see? Then after my uncle worked his magic on them. You see? All beautiful again. And the last picture is of me. This is what Lucy did to me when I had fifteen years. And here is me on my sixteenth birthday. Beautiful again, no?

Thumbs-up.

"Here is my uncle's card with the phone number of his office. Think about it, but don't show anyone at the hospital—they want you to use their doctors, of course."

Helena gently squeezed Lola's good hand, "We gonna take good care of you, sweetie."

Lola read the card: "Horatio Alvarez, Cosmetic Surgeon, specializing in facial reconstruction." She tucked the card under her pillow as a nurse entered.

"You are not supposed to be in patients' rooms, and you know it," the nurse said.

The nurse put her body between the patient and Helena and forcefully strode toward her. The nurse pressed Contacts on her smart phone as she stalked down the hallway after the retreating Helena.

"You're like a scavenger," the nurse said to Helena. "Well, you're not getting away with it this time."

The nurse glanced down at her phone as a voice answered. "Yes, I need security on the second floor," the nurse said into her phone. "That facial trauma freak is at it again."

She looked up, but Helena was gone.

Chapter 22

Aaron's & Vera's Date

Zissell Horowitz fox-trotted around her kitchen and sang an old Yiddish song of joy while she cooked. She had gotten the call from Vera that she was moving home, and Zissell had wasted no time calling Aaron to invite him to dinner. *My stubborn daughter, wasting so much of her life to collect girlie mouse things. Vera is the kosher beheyme, the trusting little cow, to follow the American, gonif. Gah! Even after all her Zaydeh went through in Auschwitz. "Never become victim, Vera," he said. Well, now we fix things. My new son-in-law in the handsome uniform. A homeowner soon, too."*

Zissell stood back and inspected the dining room table. She adjusted the angle of one of the napkins and let out a sigh.

The doorbell rang and Zissell ran to answer it.

"Vera, you don't have to ring bell to your home. I leave door unlocked for you."

"Right, Bubbe." Vera trudged in; her clothes held in her arms.

"Give dese to me. Your room is nice and clean. It is so goot to haf you home again. Away from dose bad people."

"What are you cooking?" Vera asked.

"Dinner for tonight. I invite a friend to join us."

"Who's that?"

"You know 'dem too. Aaron Finklestein." Zissell grinned.

"No, Bubbe. No, I'm not interested in him."

"You be polite to Aaron. He did you big favor I hear."

"He did, that's true. But just this one dinner then no more."

Vera hugged her grandmother and walked down the hall to her bedroom. Zissell smiled.

~

Aaron cruised into the old neighborhood, past his parents' house where he had lived down the street from the Horowitz's house. Living so close to the erotic girl, seeing her every day on the playground and in school had been exhilarating. Her allure hadn't diminished over the years, and now his lust and his obsession for her, was almost more than he could bear. He'd watched over the years as she'd chosen to socialize with loser after loser. He'd shown her how weak they were, besting them on the schoolyard for everyone to see. It baffled him how she never seemed impressed. The other girls were though. Easy conquests, most of them.

Tonight, despite all the years of her dodging his attempts, he had positioned himself so Vera wouldn't be able to turn him down. He'd take his buddy Ira's advice to play up wanting to marry, have a family. He already had Vera's grandmother wrapped around his little finger. Ira's strategy made sense: Vera was a little older now, past the rebellious stage; she would listen to her grandmother and let the handsome man in the uniform sweep her away.

Aaron parked and glanced at his reflection in the rear-view mirror: *Oh yeah, square jaw, tan from days on the street busting punks, full head of hair, how can she resist me?*

~

Vera showered and dressed. Her petite-yet-voluptuous figure filled out the Tragically Hip t-shirt, and the beige, tight-fitting capris showcased her toned calves. She helped her grandmother carry the dishes into the dining room just as the doorbell rang.

"You go! Go, girl. Answer the door," Zissell said.

Vera made a face and opened the door. Aaron stood in a suit, holding a bouquet of red and purple garland flowers.

"Welcome home, Vera. These are for you."

"Thank you, Aaron. They're beautiful," Vera said and hugged him.

"Thank you for coming, Aaron. Have a seat," Zissell said.

The three of them sang blessings, led by Aaron.

"Dat was nice, Aaron," Zissell said.

"I never properly thanked you for all your help last week," Vera said.

"Maybe we could go out after dinner. I know of a nice little place where we could have a drink and listen to some jazz. Do you like jazz?"

"That sounds nice."

"Aaron says soon he gets promotion to captain."

"Congratulations," Vera said.

"Well, it's not definite, but I'm ninety-nine percent sure."

After dinner Aaron offered to help with the dishes.

"No, no. Such a gentleman. You two young people go haf fun. Go on. Don't make me get the broom," Zissell teased.

"I'm sorry, but I'll have to ask you to ride in the back," Aaron said.

"You're kidding?" Vera said.

"Sorry, regulations. I'm getting a second car as soon as I get my mortgage paid down."

Inside Aaron's squad car, Vera took in the dispatch radio and the secured equipment.

"I've never been inside a police car before."

"You would have eventually if you kept hanging with those movie freaks."

"That's not fair, Aaron. Some of them are really good people."

"You're much too good for them, Vera," Aaron said, as he pulled into traffic.

"Nice of you to say. I'll miss being in movies though," Vera mused, "it was exciting."

"You thought it was dangerous as I recall," Aaron said, his forehead wrinkling.

"I had to do something with my life besides waiting tables."

"Do you like kids?" Aaron asked, as he turned onto Santa Monica Boulevard.

"Sure, but what does that have to do with anything?"

"I was just thinking outside the box. You seem like you would be a great little mother."

"Thanks, I guess. I was thinking about a career though."

"Raising kids is the best job on the planet I've heard," Aaron said.

"I'm too young to think like that. Besides, I can't even support *myself*."

"I know it's not fashionable, but I've heard a lot of times husbands still support their families." Aaron glanced in the rear-view mirror at Vera.

Vera rolled her eyes. "Well, I haven't exactly had any marriage proposals."

Aaron looked at her again until he got her to notice his stare. He smiled devilishly and cocked an eyebrow until she blushed. Aaron was so tickled at having gotten a reaction out of her that he let out a satisfied sigh. They reached their destination.

At the entrance to the nightclub, Aaron tipped the bouncer who had a word with the hostess who immediately seated them right up front just as the jazz quintet began to play.

"Perfect timing. You've got clout here, I see."

"I've been a cop for long time around here."

Aaron held up his hand and a waitress walked over with a tray full of champagne flutes. He handed the waitress a twenty and waved off the change. He took two glasses and handed one to Vera. After a few minutes, Vera relaxed.

They had a few more drinks as Aaron stole glances at Vera. She turned abruptly and caught him checking her out, but she didn't seem to mind. Two strands of shiny black hair fell across her eyes—eyes so dark brown Aaron struggled not to get lost in them. She turned to him; she apparently liked the music, a slow sensuous number. Her full lips bloomed into a pure crystalline smile and Aaron was powerless.

Damn, she's even hotter than in my dreams! Finally, I'm gonna score. Just keep playing the gentleman card like Ira said.

They walked outside and Aaron opened the squad car door for her. Vera checked her Mandy Mouse watch: 11:30 P.M. They drove toward Vera's mom's house and parked a block away, near a vacant grassy lot. Aaron got out and got into the back seat next to Vera.

"What are we doing here?" Vera asked.

Aaron leaned over and tried to kiss her, but she turned her head slightly. Not in a mean way, but it still stung Aaron's feelings.

"What's wrong?" Aaron said.

"My head is all mixed up. This is all I can offer you right now," Vera said.

She enveloped his hand in her small hands and closed her eyes. Her fingers and palms did a slow-motion dance in the moonlight, like warm silk rolling over and under his fingers and along the contours of his forearm, and then she smoothed her palm along his face.

"Good night," she whispered.

She started to get out of the car when Aaron's hand shot out and grabbed her by the arm.

"Where're you going? We're just getting started," Aaron said, dragging Vera back in.

"Stop, Aaron, you're hurting me."

"I saw the way you looked at me earlier."

He pulled her close, wrapping his arm around her and reaching down along her leg, groping along the inseam of her capris.

"You misunderstood me. Aaron, stop. Stop!"

"I know you want me, Vera. Come on. Nobody's going to bother us here."

Vera struggled and finally slapped him.

"Okay, I can handle it rough." Aaron felt along Vera's capris until he came to the metal button and unsnapped it."

"Aaron. Aaron! You've got to stop," Vera said, and opened her clutch purse and flipped the safety off her canister of mace with her thumb.

"You've been playin' cat and mouse with me since grade school," Aaron said. "Enough's enough."

"I'm a virgin!" Vera said, tears in her eyes.

Aaron froze. He loosened his grip on Vera's arm.

"Bullshit. You're—you're the same age as me, twenty-three. I mean—"

"I'm not kidding. Let me go. I don't want to use this on you." Vera aimed the mace.

"You mean you and that French punk L'Hommedieu, you two never did it?"

"That's none of your business!"

Aaron sat still, uncomprehending, as Vera buttoned her pants and backed out of the car, the mace pointed at his face at arm's reach. She stood outside the car and adjusted her blouse.

"Then why shouldn't I be the one, Vera? Why not me?" he asked, his voice softening.

Vera wiped her eyes with the back of her hand. She turned and walked along the crooked sidewalk, her legs brushing through the weeds growing up between the cracks.

He hadn't meant for her to walk to her grandmother's house—he just parked here so—

Aaron stared after her, his mouth hanging open in silent protest. Vera reached the front door and disappeared inside. He didn't realize it at first, but he had begun repeatedly smacking his fist into his other palm. He heard his voice rise to just below a yell inside the confines of the squad car.

"You're gonna tease me? You and me knockin' boots is WAY overdue, baby!"

Aaron climbed into the driver's seat, started the engine and pressed the accelerator to the floor—the tires squealed. He muttered to himself as he raced from the neighborhood.

"That's not the way it's goin' down, Vera. You can leave director-boy out in the cold and nothin' happens, that's okay because the punk's got no stones."

The big V-8 surged up over 80 miles per hour, the tires occasionally lifting slightly off the pavement, coming down hard with a chirp, as Aaron reached the interstate. The speedometer made jumps to 90 and 100 as he passed cars in the left lane, then the right.

"But you don't leave one of L.A.'s finest with a fourteen-year-old case of blue balls without a cost, Missy. Gonna cost *somebody*."

Aaron slowed down to 35 mph and crisscrossed his way across town until he reached a stretch of nightclubs and bars. He slipped the cruiser a couple of streets over, behind the main drag where there were more neon-lit bars and sketchy-looking pedestrians. He slowed to just above idling speed, watched the occasional drunk walk in or out of one of the ragged bar doors. He had a certain type of drunk in mind as the car crawled along the back street.

"Big guy, gotta be—to be worth my time."

Aaron had tired of hearing people tell him to pick on someone his own size. So now he always erred on the large side—just to be fair.

Just then two big men staggered out of a bar and in front of the blacked-out window. The smaller one, who wore a Giant's baseball cap, lit up a smoke.

"That's just a gift," Aaron said, putting the car in park. He grabbed his flashlight and nightstick and paced toward the men. He snapped on his flashlight and shined it into their faces.

"Hey, whoa. What's wrong, dude?" said the smaller man.

Aaron stepped in close and extended his nightstick between the two men, pressing it against the neck of the man in the baseball cap so he had to step away from the larger.

"I've got no problem calling a cop," the man said, fumbling with his cell.

"I am a cop," Aaron replied.

"If you're a cop why are you in a suit?" the smaller man said.

"Undercover. You guys are drunk in public and we've had complaints. You stand over there." Aaron pointed to a wall several yards away.

The smaller man reluctantly stepped away.

"We, we've had a few, yeah," baseball cap said.

Aaron stepped up in his face, directing the flashlight into the man's eyes. "What? Your big buddy can't speak for himself? Your quiet friend's probably going to spend the night in jail. You take a walk unless you want the same. Get me?"

"Man, this is bullshit!" As baseball cap pulled out his phone again and tried to video the scene, Aaron lunged out and grabbed the phone from him.

"Give me my phone!"

"You leave—right now—or I cuff you. I'll give your friend your phone later."

The man in the cap walked off down the street, looking over his shoulder. "Call me later, Pete," he called behind him.

Aaron turned back to the other man.

"Big man, I need you to walk down into that alley." Aaron saw the man hesitate and yelled, "Move!" so loudly that the man jumped and began to walk.

"It's too dark to see back here. Don't you just give me a breath test or— "

"Get going." Aaron said, and poked the man in the back with his nightstick. "That's far enough, stop. Turn around. Now here's the deal: You and me are gonna fight. You win, I let you go. I win, you go to jail." Aaron leaned the nightstick against the wall.

"I'm not going to hit a cop. You think I'm stupid?"

"That's okay—I'll go first," Aaron said, and punched the big man in the jaw.

Chapter 23
Team Effort

Vera stepped inside the front door and locked it behind her. She rubbed her hands over her bare arms, chilled from the night air, and realized she was still holding the canister of mace in one hand. She pressed the plastic safety back into position, tucked the self-defense tool into her purse, and quietly walked down the hallway.

"Vera? Is dat you?" Zissell's voice echoed from the front bedroom.

Vera entered Zissell's doorway. "Hi, Bubbe, I didn't want to wake you."

"No, bother. How was your night?"

Her grandmother sat upright in the small bed that she and Zaydeh had shared for so many years, the lace nightgown up to her neck, her back against the carved wooden headboard. Vera glanced at the framed 19th century cracked oil painting by S. Karski, hung on the tattered wallpapered wall, of a courting Russian couple in a horse-drawn wagon. Her eyes took in Zaydeh's old armchair, the one he used to sit in while he held her in his lap and told her stories. Time stood still in this room.

"The music was really good," Vera said.

"And Aaron? He was nice too?"

Oh, yeah, a real peach. Good son-in-law material, Bubbe. Vera thought.

"I'm going to get some sleep, okay?"

"Wait. You will see him again, soon, yes?"

"I just ended a relationship earlier today. I'm going to bed now. Good night."

~

Naomi got out of the limo and walked toward the door to Jake's condo. Jake waited a beat before glancing at Serena, still sitting in the middle of the back seat.

"Aren't you getting out, Serena? I'm going into Falchion to do some editing."

"No, Jake. It was draining, that whole thing with Lola, seeing Brian. He was so upset. It would be nice if you and I had a talk. Let me buy you a drink down at the Dolly Shot."

"I'm a little wound up right now. A drink sounds good."

The driver nodded and backed out of the driveway.

Inside the Dolly Shot, Jake's regular waitress seated them in his favorite red leather booth and took their drink orders.

"Jake, first, I'd like to thank you for getting us away from Barry and taking us all in. I don't know what I would have done otherwise."

"You're welcome. I couldn't have left you in that condition."

"I'm ready to work again but I have a question: You make horror movies. How do you go from a decade of that to doing romance films?" Serena said.

"The business wore me down and warped my perception of women—I needed a change."

"And you think you have a winner with this screenplay?"

"It made Naomi and my therapist cry. How's that?"

"Sounds like a good movie," Serena smiled. "Are we going to start shooting soon, because I'm starting to feel like a mooch, crashing at your place, eating your food—"

"The financing is in place. Rehearsals start on Monday—a studio on Pacific Avenue. I'll text you the address."

The drinks arrived: for Serena, spiced iced tea; for Jake, a dry martini, cold and cloudy—bright lemon wedge. They took sips, comfortably sitting in silence for a moment.

"There's just one more thing that's troubling me," Serena said, "What about you and Vera? You two were so cute together."

"Remember *Meathooks*? Vera found an old magazine I'd saved and read the article about it and thinks I'm a sicko. That's why she broke up with me and moved out."

"Oh, Jake. That's so sad. Well, she has the wrong idea about you."

"The thing is she wasn't wrong, that's why I was in therapy. My therapist says I'm mostly cured—I tried to tell Vera, but she was so mad—"

"I'll talk with her. I'll bring Naomi with me. Hell, she was in *Meathooks*, she knows you're a good guy."

"Would you? That would be great. But she'll think I sent you. It won't work."

"Jake L'Hommedieu, you are the best man I know. I'll make sure she listens to me. It's the least I can do after all you've done for me."

~

Barry's limo whisked him up into Benny's driveway; the expensive suspension system smoothed the bumps to a slight vibration. His driver knew Barry was often in a bad mood, but he seemed particularly peeved today.

"Excuse me, sir, but is something troubling you?"

"We only have half a staff. I want my people back on set!" Barry barked. He grunted as he heaved his bulk up into a standing position and lumbered to Benny's front door.

Barry knocked once, twice, three times, and then he yelled out loud—echoing off the houses in the quiet suburban neighborhood.

"Benny Edwards, get your ass out here, now!"

Quick footsteps echoed from within.

"Who's there?" the thin voice behind the door responded, not at all like Benny's normally harsh tone.

"It's me, Barry. Now open up, dammit."

Barry heard the deadbolt slide open as the door parted one inch followed by the sound of footsteps scurrying away. Barry swung the door open and strutted inside letting glaring sunlight blaze into the sanctity of the darkened home.

"Where are you, man?" Barry said, scanning the living room and flipping up light switches in the hallway and kitchen.

"No lights!" the timid voice uttered.

Barry saw the top of Benny's head peek above the couch. Immediately, he advanced on him and dragged Benny to his feet.

"What do you want with me, Barry?" Benny whined.

"I want what we had: You, me, Alex, on the set kickin' ass. You sick or what?"

"I'm, I'm scared, Barry."

Barry noticed that Benny had lost weight.

"Since when you scared of anything? You're the one makes people scared. I'm already tired of this so let's get you up and out of here."

Barry watched with disgust as Benny's hands slowly rose into limp wrists, held defensively in front of him, his head turned away. Benny seemed unaware of his behavior.

"What's with the girly hands, man? Benny Edwards is tough, tough, tough!" Barry shouted, shoving Benny in the chest.

Benny stepped back and leaned against the dining room table, holding his chest, and looking fearfully toward the open doorway.

"Everything wants to kill me, to ea-eat me," Benny whispered, eyes darting around.

Barry approached the smaller man, speaking a word with each heavy step.

"No—it—don't," he said, poking Benny in the chest with his finger on the last word. "Somebody's messed with Alex's head too, and you can bet we're going to straighten *that* out. I need my team back. I'm slappin' you around until you remember who Benny is. When I'm too tired to slap you even one more time, and you haven't manned up, you're dead to me. No more workin' at Falchion Films. Capische?"

"No, Barry, please—

~

Aaron awoke. His head ached, his ribs ached, and, as he held his fists above him in the morning light, his knuckles, swollen and purple, really ached. He thought about the night before. *Putz got some lucky punches in before I knocked him out.*

Aaron hadn't made good on his threat to arrest the man after he beat him. How could he? He'd been off duty, in his street clothes, not even on his regular beat. There'd have been no way to justify the arrest. So, after checking the street and sidewalks for witnesses, Aaron had simply picked up his nightstick, and left the scene. He'd crushed the smaller man's cell under his heel and thrown it in a dumpster. Aaron knew his temper was a liability, but he always managed to cover up the damage. It was okay; he was still next in line for captain.

Aaron checked his alarm clock. 6:30 A.M. His shift started in half an hour. He'd have to lie low for the day, drive around the back neighborhoods, and then hope nobody at the precinct noticed his swollen hands when he delivered his daily report.

After a quick shower, he strapped on his holster; the night stick hung below, *good smell of worn leather.* He checked his gun for bullets, checked the safety, grabbed his headset, and walked out to the squad car.

As soon as he'd started the engine his cell phone buzzed. The name read Levi, his childhood pal and now fellow cop. Aaron picked up.

"Hey, bud."

"Aaron, you need to meet me in the park on your break. I've got to tell you something."

"What is it?"

"Not over the phone. Meet me at ten-thirty, our park bench, you know the one."

"See you then," Aaron said and shifted the car into drive.

Levi was nothing if not level-headed. He was a good cop, did his job well, and tried to keep Aaron on an even keel. This sounded serious, and Aaron was uncomfortable not knowing information which might involve him. He drove with his left hand, his right resting on the seat, wrapped in a flexible ice pack. *Come on, ten-thirty, can't get here soon enough*

~

It was a sunny morning in Vera's room. With the way she felt it was good to be surrounded by so many fluffy Mandys; all smiling down at her, making her feel safe. She'd always known Aaron Finklestein was a bully, but he would have sexually assaulted her last night if she hadn't stopped him. Bubbe obviously had no idea what Aaron was like. It would be all too easy to let him lead her down the path to marriage and children, and wouldn't that make Bubbe happy and wouldn't that be the end of Vera's short-lived independence. Her cell rang.

"Hello?"

"Vera, where've you been?" Naomi said, "I've been trying to reach you since yesterday."

"I turned my phone off. I didn't want Jake to call me. We broke up."

"What? We need to talk about that. But listen, Lola's been in a horrible accident."

Naomi filled Vera in on the details. As she hung up, Vera dialed a taxi to pick her up in 15 minutes. She scrambled out of her clothes and hopped in the shower.

Lola and I have had our differences, but nobody deserves to be in an accident like that with no support.

~

Lola wiped the crust away from her eye, the one that was able to see through the single layer of gauze. She thought about the conversation with Helena Guitterez two days ago.

What is ugly? Lola pondered. *My stock in trade, my means of financial support. A source of fear and loathing to passersby. And beauty? Something people want. Something I've never had and don't deserve? Helena says it's possible for me. You can have anything you want in America, I've heard it said. How would it feel to be beautiful? Helena's been through the surgery. It must be okay.*

Lola's head felt woozy and two sizes too big. The drugs were starting to wear off again and her face ached so deeply. She inhaled, and heard and felt a sloppy gurgling in her nasal passages and throat. Both her broken arm and her neck ached. Now pain was coming from everywhere at once. Pretty soon the nurse would be in to administer another round of meds. Lola had to act before she arrived.

She uncomfortably slipped her good hand beneath her pillow and retrieved the business card. She laid the card on the sheet and groped over onto the nightstand and reached her cell phone. She couldn't speak with her jaw wired shut and the tube affixed to her lips, but maybe the plastic surgeon would get her text. She carefully tapped out a message while glancing over at the doorway every few seconds.

"Dr. Alvarez, I'm facial injury patient, Lola Grubb, at Malibu Memorial Hospital, L.A. I've met Helena Guitterez. Need ur surgical services. Have $. Need transportation today. Can u provide? Don't call, text me. Hospital cannot know. Heard people say my room 2nd floor. May be medicated—but get me out today."

Lola pushed "send" as the nurse entered her room. She shoved both the card and her cell under her pillow, ignoring how it stretched her sore body, and rested her hand on the bed again. The nurse approached her bed with a clipboard.

~

Aaron scanned the streets on his beat, killing time. He didn't want to see any crime that required action from him. He'd do his job, of course; he was a responsible cop. But running down a perp on foot, grabbing him and cuffing him would be rough on his aching hands today. He checked the time: 10:15 A.M. Just enough time to drive to the park where he'd meet Levi to schmooze.

Traffic's slow. Must be fans in town for the Laker's game tonight.

As Aaron turned, he saw across the park, that Levi was already sitting on their bench, tensely sipping from a Styrofoam cup. He flipped on his lights and tapped his siren. Seconds later cars on the narrow street pulled up onto the curb to let him pass. He was able to drive down the center of the street, taking minutes off his time. He parked at the curb, left his flashers on, and strode across the sidewalk toward the bench.

"Levi."

"Sit down, bro," Levi said. "You're in trouble, man. That dude you rolled last night had a buddy. Looked at the number on your cruiser, filed a complaint at the station."

"So? Anybody can say something happened involving a certain cop car. What proof does he have?"

"I heard about it, didn't I? Let me see your hands."

Aaron reluctantly held them out.

"I thought so. Pretend I'm an officer of the Civilian Review Board. I see those swollen hands, I have your car at the scene of the beating, I have the dude you roughed up and his buddy? Say you get off; you think this is the type of thing the chief hears about? Chief's not promoting someone to captain with that rep. Come on, Aaron, get your head out of your ass. You've worked too hard for this promotion."

"You really think I'm not going to get my bars now?"

"You get out of this, you're a lucky bastard. I'd do every little thing by the book."

"Thanks, buddy."

"You *do* have an alibi, right?"

"Yeah, I was with little Vera. Everything was going great then I tried to just, just kiss her and she pulled away. Pissed me off."

"Uh-huh. So that's why that poor schmuck had to get his bell rung. I tell you, Aaron, you'd better muzzle that temper."

"Yeah. Thanks, Levi." Aaron slapped Levi on the shoulder and returned to his cruiser.

~

Smack, smack, smack, smack, echoed the sound of a beefy palm against human cheeks.

"Stop!" Benny cried out, covering up, hiding his face, and curling his body into a ball.

"Who are you then?" Barry roared. "Man or mouse? Don't know yet?"

Thup, thup, thup, thup, the sounds of a hand echoed against the side and back of his head.

I deserve to be beaten and eaten. All I can do is cry out.

"Barry, stop it!"

This hurts! It's beginning to irritate me too.

"What's your name? I heard you was squealin' like a mouse in the cafeteria."

"Benny Edwards." *Now I'm a little more irritated than afraid.*

"You don't act like Benny. Benny I knew don't take crap from nobody."

Smack, smack, smack. Benny rolled over and got up onto his knees. *He's slapping me in sets of four—I avoided that last slap. I don't have to be totally helpless.*

"I guess you still need a wake-up call," Barry said and began a fresh set of slaps.

Benny's hand shot out with a vise-like grip on Barry's wrist. Benny's feeble thoughts, backed into a confining corner of his brain, were transformed into the concentrated actions of a prowling tiger. His eyes became predatory as he bent Barry's fingers backward, spun him around, climbed onto Barry's back and got him in a choke hold.

Barry gasped and grabbed at Benny's forearms but couldn't get him off. Barry sunk to his knees as Benny's legs wrapped around his ribs and he continued constricting his arms around Barry's throat. Seconds from Barry's passing out, Benny released his grip. Barry, red-faced and sweating, rolled over onto his side and gasped for air.

"If you ever slap me again, I'll kill you, fat man," Benny snapped, kicking Barry in the ribs for good measure.

"That's my man," Barry wheezed. "Welcome back, Benny."

"Now, get up, you corpulent, salacious slug. Like a drink?" Benny snarled.

"Yeah, water," Barry wheezed. "I knew you was in there, Benny."

Benny rubbed his face—still red from where Barry had bitch-slapped it.

"Fat man, I don't know what I was thinking, letting you talk to me like that. You think you're somebody because you make those rotten scare movies?"

"Thank heavens, you're back. I could just lie here the rest of the afternoon and listen to you bad-mouth me. But we don't have time for that. Now that you're better, we have to go rouse Alex from his hospital bed. The pyramid of terror is almost erect again: you, me and Alex. We need to bring Falchion Films back from the dead. I've missed you, man."

"Oh, I'm getting all weepy-eyed. Don't even think of hugging me because I'll kick you square between the bee-bees, Tubby. And why don't you get a haircut? You look like a red-headed sheep dog."

Barry had had a glass of water with a bourbon chaser and his color seemed better.

"Come on, Benny, we need to go check on Alex. He looked like hell the last time he worked on the set, but he made the best bad guy you've ever seen."

"He's your nephew, you go see him. When you have someone for me to coach, call me."

"No, let's go have a drink down at the Dolly Shot then. I miss things being normal. Come on, drinks are on me—since I roughed you up. I feel bad."

"If I weren't under hypnosis or a drug or—I don't know what it was—you could never slap me. I'd sooner suffocate you—stuff your sausage-sized fingers up your nostrils."

"Well, whatever then. Just come with me and have a few drinks."

"Okay, okay. Anything to stop your whining," Benny said.

He closed the door behind them, and triple locked his front door.

Chapter 24

Shelley

Shelley paused from scrambling through old financing leads; she needed a loan to keep Falchion Films afloat. *Barry has a spending problem.* She glanced at the papers overflowing her desk; it was a real mess alright. Being messy was okay when business was booming, it was a part of being productive. But being messy now was not okay—she was getting nowhere.

Her job title was Film Production/Receptionist, and she was supposed to have post-production skills, but after a few failed attempts it was clear she was lacking in this regard. Luckily, Jake was such a control freak he'd taken over the editing so Shelley could concentrate on what she did best: gossip. "Heads-up-your-job's-on-the-line" texts; or "I know you're hung over, hon, but you've got to be on the set pronto," phone calls; and, of course, the predictable "Guess who's doing whom from the set?" buzz. She was the ultimate gossip, whose talents lubricated communication in this sad excuse for a film studio. She also filed, did hair and makeup, and answered phone calls.

Her trailer door burst open and Felix and Andy entered without saying hello.

"Shut that door, you're letting in the sunlight!" Shelley scolded, shielding her ivory pale face with a manila folder.

They breezed by her desk toward the bright red $1,200.00 cappuccino machine Barry had bought last month.

Felix set two tiny porcelain cups below the dual spouts and pressed "espresso, 2." With the seeming high frequency of a fighter jet, the machine ground the Arabica beans, funneled and steamed them under high-pressure, and filled both cups with jets of dark steaming espresso infused with deep tan crema. A rich aroma filled the room as Felix and Andy sat across from Shelley, rested their elbows on her paperwork, sipped and stared at her.

"You must be in heaven with that scent in here all day," Andy said.

"It's nice. But since the staff found out about the machine the romance has worn off. What can I do for you girls?" Only Shelley got away with calling the assistant directors by this unflattering moniker.

"Andy and I need stars to manage, not bad understudies. Barry doesn't like the new talent and he's gunning for anyone who's not making the studio money."

"He stormed in here the other day. He wants Vera back and so do the fans," Shelley said.

"Well, how do we get her back? Wait—fans? Really?" Felix said.

"You bet'cha. Since Vera Horowitz arrived, Falchion Films receives fan mail again."

"I mean, she's not without talent, but fans?" Felix said.

"*Zombie Betrayal* was such a hit the sicko fans couldn't wait to see her get dismembered and killed in another film. I've highlighted the best quotes from Falchion's website posts for Barry to see. Listen to this, 'that ethereal scream left me breathless,' one says; 'her petite size pitted against much larger forces of evil was all I could ask for,' says another; and 'that beautiful face—go for facial damage in your next film.' Profits from that film took us a long way, but after payroll, bonuses, taxes and all the partying, we're nearly broke."

"What's holding up *Fifty Ways to Cleave Your Lover*? They'll get to see Vera hacked up and fed into a blender," Felix said.

"I know, but Jake's not around to finish editing. I'm trying to drum up investors, but—"

"No, forget investors. This is a no-brainer, get Vera in here," Andy said.

"She's not answering my phone calls," Shelley replied.

"Last I heard she was camped out at Jake's place, then, update, they broke up," Andy said, and then looked back and forth from Shelley to Felix. "What? A little bird told me," he said, glancing away and clucking his tongue.

"I suggest a personal visit," Andy said, "Come on, Shell, our livelihoods are on the line."

"A good-looking cop asked about her," Shelly said, "I have his card.
"That's a good place to start," Felix said, then reached out to pat her hand. "Do a little digging, Shelley. Nobody wants a mad Barry stalking around here."

The twosome stood and left the little cups on her desk, crusting froth clinging to the rims, for her to clean up later. As they crossed the room and opened the door, Shelley automatically raised a folder against the harsh sunrays. Felix pulled the trailer door closed behind them with a rush of dry air and Shelley lowered her shield. Her perfectly pale skin unharmed.

She found the policeman's card and dialed.

"Lieutenant Finklestein," Aaron answered.

"Officer, this is Shelley Arcongioli from Falchion Films. I was wondering if you were able to catch up to Vera Horowitz. She's needed on the set."

"All I can tell you is she's moved back into her grandmother's place. Gotta run—"

"Wait, Officer. Could I meet with you in person to ask a few questions? I'd be happy to buy you lunch for your trouble."

"Kind of a strange request, but yeah. It'll have to be dinner though—busy day. Meet me at 6:00 P.M. at Brando's Bar, on Vine Street."

"See you there."

Shelley sensed she'd find the angle to get Vera back, but that cop was a fine-looking man. Even though she was 38 to his probable twenty-something, working around striking young starlets had kept Shelley up to L.A. standards. It was a death sentence to look your age around here. No problem, thanks to lasers, line-smoothing shots, contour-restoring hyaluronic acid fillers and collagen lip injections; she could easily pass for an edgy 26-year-old. She'd get Vera back, but not without having another look at that hunky cop.

~

As Naomi and Vera stepped out of the elevator on the second floor of Malibu Memorial, they saw a commotion at the far end of the corridor.

"Hey, that's Lola's room," Naomi said.

As they got closer, they saw a woman in a navy-blue uniform instructing a man and a woman in light blue uniforms as she checked off a form on her clipboard.

"Have you tried to contact Miss Grub on her home phone?" the ward leader asked.

"Yes, ma'am, no answer," the man in light blue scrubs responded.

"Attempted to contact her next of kin?"

"Yes, ma'am, they haven't heard from her," a woman in light blue said.

"And security's conducted a search of the hospital grounds?"

"They're searching now."

Naomi and Vera paused a few feet away; the Ward Leader impatiently regarded them.

"Excuse me. We're here to see Lola Grubb. Is everything alright?" Vera asked.

"What is your relationship with the patient?"

"We're co-workers of hers," Naomi said. "Can we see her?"

"We're not at liberty to disclose anything about the patient right now. Leave your contact information with the nurses' station and someone will call you when we know more."

"But she was just here yesterday," Naomi said.

"Are you saying Lola's missing?" Vera asked, her mouth open.

"Leave your contact information at the desk." The Ward Leader then turned to the two in light blue. "You two, step inside. Close the door."

Vera and Naomi watched them disappear behind the closed door.

~

At 4:00 P.M. Aaron got the call from the dispatcher that he'd been dreading. He was to report to the chief tomorrow at noon to answer questions regarding civilian complaints of his whereabouts the previous night during a midnight police assault on a civilian in the 7000 block of West Sunset Boulevard.

Noon tomorrow. If I ice my hands a lot tonight maybe I can say I hurt them in the gym.

Everything's in the crapper, he thought, then remembered the receptionist who wanted to interview him and buy him dinner. She was a little hottie as he recalled. *Maybe after a few drinks—who knows?* Aaron drove home and changed into his civilian attire. He was hungry.

~

At 6:00 P.M. Shelley opened the cab door just enough to telescope a black umbrella skyward between the crack. It flared and stretched out, snapping the fabric into place, blocking out the afternoon sun. Shelley stepped out of the cab, and quickly pranced up onto the curb under cover of Brando's Restaurant's awning. Unlike most women in L.A., Shelley always hid from the harsh sun rays by wearing strong sunblock, covering up with large hats and sunglasses by day, and mostly venturing outside only in the evenings, keeping her skin ivory pale.

Inside Brando's a few couples were seated at tables and two men at the bar. No Aaron Finklestein in sight. It was essential that she make an entrance, so she went to the ladies' room to stall. The truth was, she wanted to get another look at herself even more than she wanted to pick up the cop. After all, this was quite an exotic look she'd put together.

In the ladies' room, she passed a partition which revealed a bank of full-view mirrors. Shelley felt a shiver of excitement as she faced her reflection, delectable as a piece of shiny, wrapped holiday candy. Gazing at herself in the mirror was something Shelley liked to savor, so she started with her feet. Her toenails, pale pink; her feet, delicate, fine boned, ensconced in pale pink platform sandals from which faux coral and pink leaves and vines emanated and wound up her toned calves.

Above her knees she appeared nude in transparent undergarments, wrapped in shimmering pale peach lace with randomly scattered coral-colored spots, which revealed her toned tummy, thin waist and rounded hips—all thanks to sad, single nights with salads, and nightly torture sessions on the Stairmaster. Next, her impressive triple-C cup cleavage came into view, which she'd financed from her share of the blockbuster *The Memphis In-Law Mangler*, a few years back. Her breasts were actually bare, but veiled under the thin gossamer of lace.

Allowing her eyes to rise upward, she gazed at her long, elegant neck, enwreathed by a pearl necklace. She admired how her pink lipstick and blue eye shadow played off her flowing mother-of-pearl-highlighted hair which hung loosely over her shoulders. Satisfied, Shelley lifted her pink manicured nails to her lips, winked and blew a kiss to her reflection. *Providing he has a pulse, Aaron will drop Vera once he sees me.*

As she returned to the restaurant, she immediately spotted Aaron, sitting at the bar in jeans, bulging biceps hanging from his white t-shirt sleeves, and sipping the froth off a mug of beer. Quite the gentleman to wait for me.

She strolled to the center of the room with her best Bambi-lost-in-the woods imitation complete with blinking eyes, and pretended not to see him. She smiled inwardly as Aaron did a double take, stood, and crossed the room to meet her.

"Whoa, you look amazing. Right this way, I see a table in the corner where we can talk." Shelley allowed him to rest his hand on the small of her back, feeling his palm against her bare skin through the lace, knowing he could smell the light scent of her perfume in her wake, as she led them toward the table. Aaron abruptly remembered his manners and stepped around to pull out Shelley's chair for her.

"Thank you for meeting with me, officer."

"No problem. Do you always dress up to question a cop?" Aaron scooted her chair in.

"I work around a colorful crew. I dress this way to fit in."

Shelley noticed Aaron fight to avoid looking at her thinly camouflaged cleavage, pressing against the lace. His willpower caved, his eyes flicked to her breasts, then back to her face.

"I'm not complaining," he said. "Now, let's get these questions out of the way so we can have a real conversation."

"Okay, I know you were looking for Vera and I know you caught up with her. Did you get what you wanted?" Shelley asked. She watched him hesitate, not sure how to proceed, then take a full gulp of his beer and unconsciously wipe the foam off with the back of his hand.

"There was the matter of the assault on Alex Boxwell," Aaron finally said. "I wanted to see what Vera knew."

"And that's all there was to it? She is quite an attractive girl. I'm only asking because I need to know how to get her back on the set. Her absence is affecting peoples' livelihoods."

"Yeah, there was an attraction. We went to the same school together. I'd always had a thing for her, but the feeling wasn't mutual."

She noticed Aaron's eyes unconsciously flick to her breasts again. *He's wondering whether he's seeing nipples through the lace or coral-colored spots,* Shelley thought. *They're in plain view but he can't tell, like when a shark's trying to target one mackerel from a school of hundreds.*

"I can't imagine why. I mean, you *are* a good-looking man," she said.

"If we're going to keep talking this way, I'd better buy you a drink," Aaron said, his pulse rising.

"No, a deal's a deal. I'm buying you dinner."

"Okay, but I insist on paying the tip."

Shelley raised her arm, getting the waiter's attention.

"Deal," Shelley said. "So, speaking of Alex Boxwell, did you find any promising leads? It's been quite a problem having him in the hospital."

"Nothing concrete. Perp's a big, muscular woman. Nobody's pressing charges."

"I need to know anything you can tell me to get Vera back on the set."

"She hated waitressing; she was lousy at it, so I don't think she'll be going back to that. She thought making horror movies was a slimy business, but she liked the other actresses."

"Yes, she lived with a couple of those actresses after leaving Falchion Films. Well, that gives me something to go on anyway."

"I don't mind the company," Aaron said, "but why not ask Vera yourself?"

"She's not answering my phone calls. I only have one chance to convince her in person and I can't afford to blow it."

"You seem pretty persuasive. You got *me* to meet with you. I'll bet you've got the boys lined up outside your door."

Shelley saw him zeroing in on her neck, which she knew to be both smooth and kissable-looking. She looked demurely down. "The problem is I'm kind of picky."

The waiter finished with the previous table and approached Aaron and Shelley.

"What kind of guys do you like?" Aaron asked.

"Big, rugged guys in uniform." Shelley smiled, staring evenly at him. Aaron stared back. Their eyes were still locked as the waiter arrived and pulled out his pad and pen.

~

It was half an hour after dinner, and three spiny cactus margaritas later, that Shelley turned her chair outward to accommodate Aaron as he moved around the table to the seat next to her. The kissing had begun. Shelley noticed, with one eye opened, that the waiter silently deposited the bill on their table. *He must have concluded we wouldn't be ordering dessert, she thought.*

"How do you keep your skin so freakin' pale?" Aaron asked, running his hand up Shelley's leg. "You look great and everything, I was just wondering?"

"The sun is my enemy. As soon as I learned that I took all necessary precautions," Shelley said, reaching out to squeeze his bicep. "How do you get these arms so big?"

"The gym. You want to get out of here? Back to my place? Back to your place?"

"Your place, I think. I'd like to see what a cop's house looks like."

~

The ambulance had driven steadily for 102 miles on I-5 South toward Santa Ana. As it turned onto the exit for I-805 South, Lola's sedated body gently rocked side to side, strapped to the gurney in the back of the ambulance. The ride came to a stop at what Lola surmised was the Mexican border. In a dreamlike state, she heard the driver and who she imagined to be a border agent speak briefly, share a laugh. Then the vehicle moved again.

She dreamed of becoming lovely under the surgeon's scalpel. Now she'd fit in—become one of the beautiful people. Barry wouldn't like her anymore, of course, but other people would. She could finally be what Brian wanted, although he wouldn't admit it: a beautiful girlfriend who would equal his good looks. A level playing field for someone like her, someone who had already proved she could take on any hardship. But that plainly wasn't enough. It would be okay. She would have a beautiful exterior—like every other actor in L.A.

The driver pulled up in front of a medical facility in Tijuana. A security guard and a second man in a white lab coat waited on the sidewalk. It was 1:30 A.M. as the driver parked. He got out and opened the rear doors. Together, the three men lifted Lola's gurney out of the back. As soon as the spring-loaded, stainless steel legs cleared the bumper, they snapped into position, locked in place, and the two from the facility let the wheels carry Lola's weight. They rolled her up to the glass doors where the doctor handed the driver a thick envelope full of hundreds. The driver got into the ambulance and drove back to L.A. to get some sleep.

~

Shelley and Aaron made out while stumbling sideways into his bedroom. All the while she felt him try to undress her.

"It's okay if you want to undress me," Shelley slurred. "But I can't even imagine what I'll do to you if you rip this lace. It's obscene what I paid for this outfit."

"It's okay if you do the undressing then. You can use the bathroom, it's right there."

Shelley strolled toward the bathroom, glancing to smile over her shoulder. She closed the door as she entered and spoke from inside.

"Why don't you get undressed while you're waiting?"

"Okay," Aaron climbed back under the sheets.

"Could you turn down the lights a little?" she called from behind the bathroom door.

"Sure thing." He twisted the dimmer dial. Shelley strolled out into the room, the moonlight cascaded over her form, caressed her in ethereal blue light.

"Lady, you look perfect," Aaron said, and held the sheet outstretched so Shelley could climb in. They let the reality of their warm, naked bodies touching each other gel.

"I've been thinking about kissing your neck for going on an hour now," Aaron said.

"Well, what's stopping you?" Shelley asked.

He ravaged her for hours.

~

Vera left her information with the main desk attendant and then waited outside Lola's room. Finally, the Ward Leader, in navy, opened the door, turned, and marched to the right, flanked by the two in light blue outfits.

"Excuse me," Vera said, following, "I need a better answer than the one you gave me."

The woman in navy responded as she paced, her head turned slightly over her shoulder.

"I don't have any information about the patient. Check back in the morning."

"A person, a human being is missing from your hospital and you don't know anything about it? That person has a family, co-workers and friends who care about her. Where is she?"

The woman spun around and faced Vera. "We sounded the code gray. Someone obviously assisted her in leaving her room. She was not capable of leaving on her own in her condition. It's not illegal for her to leave, she wasn't under lock and key, there was no guard assigned to watch her room. I don't know where she is, alright. We're trying to find out. We'll contact you once we know something. I'm sorry, but that's all we can do at this point, Miss." The woman turned and continued down the corridor.

~

Aaron and Shelley lay on their backs, sweating, panting, and staring at the ceiling.

Aaron got up to go to the bathroom. When he returned Shelley had composed herself, the sheet pulled up to her collarbone.

"Come back here," she said.

Aaron climbed back under the sheets. "Something else I can do for you?"

"What didn't Vera like about you? What did you do to put her off?"

"I tried to jump her bones. After all, I'd had a thing for her since grade school."

"Is she that particular? I mean, she did agree to go out with you knowing you had feelings for her?"

"You want to know why? The girl's a virgin. I was actually jealous of that French punk, L'Hommedieu, she was dating but no, she was never with him either."

"You're kidding?"

"Nope, I'm not kidding. Can you believe that? There's nothing wrong with that—I just don't understand, in L.A., at this age, how a chick gets this far in life without—"

"I know what you're saying. Well, she's a fool. She obviously doesn't know a good man when she sees one," Shelley said, and cuddled up to Aaron.

"Hey, that's great and all, but I've got to get up for work in," Aaron checked his bedside alarm clock, "Four hours, so you're welcome to get up with me at 5:30, take a shower, have coffee, I'll call you a cab, whatever, I just have to kick you out by 6:00."

"I understand. I have to get to work too. It would be nice to see you again. I mean since Vera's not taking up your time."

"That'd be great. I just need a little shut-eye is all," Aaron said.

Aaron wrapped one huge arm around her, and Shelley snuggled into his shoulder. A minute later he fell fast asleep. Shelley settled in as Aaron began to snore like a buzzsaw. She was tired, though, and soon faded off too.

~

The next day Shelley said a quick goodbye. She scribbled her number on a piece of paper, opened her black umbrella, and ushered herself into the waiting cab. Her outfit from the night before was mostly a jumble of vines and lace, wrapped around her in a gossamer wad, just enough to hide her nakedness from eager, early morning sightseers.

She paid the cabbie, walked into her trailer, washed her face, applied sunblock, changed into long-sleeved lounge wear, dark glasses, and an enormous hat. She called Barry on his cell.

"Huh? Who is this?" he mumbled through the phone.

"It's your number one employee, Bare. I've been working on our little problem—I just want to meet with you before I go talk with Vera. Can you meet me at the cafeteria for a bite?"

"Yeah, but I had a time with Benny last night and we really tied one on."

"I need to see what terms you're willing to extend to get Vera back."

"Okay, I guess some nosh wouldn't hurt. I'll see you there in fifteen, doll."

Shelley walked along the sidewalk which soon crisscrossed with three others as the morning stage hands, gaffers, actors, assistants, best boys, and extras made their way from building to building trying to get bad horror movies made. Foot traffic on the sidewalks became more crowded as she reached the double doors of the cafeteria.

She stood in the a la carte line to get a slice of honeydew melon, a bagel and cream cheese, and a cup of coffee. She sat stirring it as she saw Barry barge to the front of the line, nudge people out of line, grab what he wanted, then trudge over to plop down beside her.

"Okay, talk," Barry said, enveloping half a muffin with his mouth.

"Vera's in between men right now. She has no source of income and she's not crazy about living back at home with her grandmother. So, we have some negotiating room. The bad news is she's of the opinion that making horror films is slimy and she wants no part of it."

"Okay, so what do you think would get her back on the set?" Barry asked.

"Promise that we'll act decently, a safer set due to Serena's accident, and more money."

"Say we're sorry, we'll be careful, and offer her twenty thousand instead of sixteen."

"I think I can sell that. Hey, if we do get her back it would be kind of funny."

"What would?" Barry asked.

"You know how back in the day when they made movies showing natives who believed in volcano gods or fire gods or sun gods and so on?"

"Yeah?" Barry said.

"Well, what were the ultimate scream queens for them to sacrifice?"

"Virgins, of course. So?"

Shelley leaned in close and whispered in Barry's ear, "Vera Horowitz is a virgin."

Barry's eyes flew open wide. "Excuse me," Barry said.

Barry abruptly stood, staggered through the crowd of people until he reached the annex to the cafeteria. He had just made it through the double doorway when he felt his eyes roll back in his head and his loins erupt in a spontaneous orgasm, soaking his pants. In the background he could faintly hear Shelley calling, "Are you alright, Barry?" But his mind was racing. *Back in the day, hell! Vera's a virgin?! I'll have her back on this set and I'll have things my way again. I'm going to have a real-life sacrifice of a real-life virgin and capture it on film. The ultimate triumph: turning art into life! Consequences be damned!*

Chapter 25

The Perfect Victim

Barry was jostled by passersby as he stood in the double doorway cafeteria vestibule. He was annoyed by the hot wet stain soaking his pants, and annoyed by Shelley's attempts to steady him with her thin arms and delicately boned hands. He barged his way through the courtyard crowd with Shelley along for the ride, clinging to him like a baby albino possum.

"Barry, Barry, are you alright?" Shelley asked.

"Yes, get off of me!" Barry said, grabbing Shelley by the shoulders. "I need you to promise me, like your life depends on it, that you'll get Vera back on this set."

Shelley wriggled from his grip.

"Offer her whatever it takes," Barry said. "You know how I said we could go twenty thousand a picture? Make that twenty-five if all else fails. Get me?"

"Sure, Barry. I was just worried you were having a seizure back there."

"I'm fine, doll. Now scoot."

Barry swatted for her tush, but Shelley stepped away. He watched her for a second, then chuckled and lumbered off. He fished around in his baggy pants pocket until he found his cell. He thumbed Contacts, found *Benny* and pushed "call."

"What do you want?" Benny said over the phone. "The next time you ask me to go out for drinks I'm going to tell you to shove that idea— "

"Listen, Benny. You like humiliatin' women, right? You like seein' them broken down like they're fish gulpin' for air?"

"Yes, so?"

"Get ready for this. Vera Horowitz is a *virgin.*" There was no response on the other end of the line. "Benny? Benny, you there?"

"I was just processing what you said," Benny stammered. "Little Vera Horowitz, the ultimate victim! I don't know what to say, fat man. Thank you."

"You're welcome. Now strap on your thinking cap and come up with a way to warp her brain before we get her up on that stage. I want her ready for slaughter."

"You've got it. Call me when she's back on the set," Benny said.

~

Quarter to twelve, Aaron thought, glancing at his wristwatch, and turning into the precinct parking lot. *Must compose myself before I meet with the chief.* Aaron didn't realize his car was still coasting and bumped his front tires into the concrete parking block, jolting him.

I never hit those!

Inside, he saw the door at the end of the hall, the frosted window, the gold lettering that read "Chief of Police." He checked his watch again, 11: 56 A.M.. *Oy vey. This ain't gonna be pretty.* He counted his steps. When he got to 13, he'd reached the door. Now it was 11: 57. This is torture. *Maybe he'll appreciate my being early, shows I've nothing to hide.* Aaron curled his swollen fingers into a fist and rapped on the door.

"Come in," came the deep voice from beyond the door.

Aaron wiped the sweat from his palm onto the back of his uniformed leg, twisted the knob and entered. He brought his body to rigid attention, heels together, and saluted the man behind the desk.

"Officer Finklestein, reporting to the Chief of Police, sir."

The chief stood and half-heartedly saluted back, letting the salute fade away at the end, like he was slinging something offensive from his hand.

"Thank you for being punctual, Officer Finklestein, but we don't run that formal of a department. Close the door. Have a seat. I have a few questions for you. Where you were this Tuesday at twelve midnight?"

"I was on a date with Miss Vera Horowitz. We were at Jazzsters, a night club at the 3000 block of Santa Monica Boulevard, sir."

"Nowhere near the 7000 block of West Sunset Boulevard? When did your date end?"

"About one-thirty, sir."

"I assume you can get Ms. Horowitz to fill out this form, swearing to your whereabouts?"

Aaron hesitated, then shot out his hand to take the form. "Yes, sir."

"Would you mind showing me your hands, Finklestein?"

"No, sir," Aaron said, and held his hands palm side up.

The Chief cocked an eyebrow. Aaron flipped his hands over, knuckles side up. The chief held one of them to inspect.

"These look pretty scarred up and swollen. How did this happen?"

"In the gym, sir. I forgot my gloves at home before I hit the heavy bag."

The Chief looked dubious as he released Aaron's hand. "I've interrogated a lot of perps on the way to becoming Chief. I'm a good judge of when someone's trying to bullshit me. I'll bet you're pretty good at it too. Know how to spot a lie, know how to tell a lie?"

"Yes, sir. I think you could say that about lots of cops."

"You've been with the force for over five years. I approved you when the psychological evaluations came in that year. You were on the high-strung end of the scale, with tendencies toward violence. We had a lot of trouble with gangs back then."

Aaron evaluated the confidence, the patience, of the older cop with salt and pepper hair and gray eyebrows.

"Yes, sir. My partner and I had to subdue a lot of gangbangers the first couple of years I was on the force. I'm proud of my record, if I may say so, sir."

"I would be too; you took a couple of bullets, Medal of Honor. But the political climate's changed since then, and being captain requires a different skill set than those of a beat cop."

"Yes, sir."

"I don't entirely believe your story about your date and the gym. I've got two citizens who swear up and down that you were at their twenty, that you gave that man the headache and dental bill. Ever heard of the Three Strikes Rule?"

"Yes, sir. Enacted in 1994, the law requires a defendant convicted of any new felony, having suffered two prior convictions of a serious felony to be sentenced to state prison for twice the term otherwise provided for the crime."

"You know your stuff. But because becoming captain under my command is so important, I am enacting, for you only, a One Strike Rule. You have the potential to make one helluva great captain, but if I hear even a rumor of you roughing up a civilian again, you're out. I'll make sure you get the worst shifts, the crappiest territory as well as a demotion. You understand me?"

"Yes, sir."

"Now get out of my office and see if you can earn back my respect, Finklestein. Oh, and bring me that form—signed."

"Thank you, sir. I will.

~

Vera sat on the opposite side of the back seat of the limo from Naomi and stared out the window.

"Why does everything have to suck," she said.

"At least you've got a boyfriend," Naomi said.

"Not anymore. I broke it off with him. I've moved back in with Bubbe."

"Are you crazy? Jake really cares about you. He's had lots of opportunities too, with all the actresses around L.A., but he's never been so smitten by—"

"I don't want to talk about it, okay?" Vera interrupted.

"Whatever. I'd accept his offer to be in his rom-dram. Rehearsals start Monday."

"I'm out. I'd be too uncomfortable now that we're not dating," Vera said.

"Excuse me, Miss Principles, but what do you plan to do for money? From what I've seen your grandmother's not going to put up with that for long," Naomi said.

"I know. I do need a job."

"I'd put that high horse you're on out to pasture. People like us, without work, without money, get eaten alive in L.A. You saw what happened to me."

"You're right," Vera said with a huff.

~

Barry found Alex in his hospital room, slowly and painfully trying out a pair of crutches.

"Uncle Barry, check it out, I'm out of bed."

Barry watched as Alex slowly made his way forward—the round, rubber stoppers of his crutches squeaked as he went.

"The physical therapist says if I work hard, I can walk on my own in two more weeks!"

"That's great, kid. Listen, something amazing has happened—"

"Hold on," Alex interrupted, looking up at the TV mounted near the ceiling. "You have to see this."

Barry followed Alex's line of sight to the TV. Dreary music accompanied by a deep voice-over blared into the room from the TV.

"If you want to be scared out of your mind this summer you must see the new horror movie release from You'd Better Run, Girl Pictures, *The Sharpest Tool in the Shed.*"

As Barry watched, the superimposed bloody letters *Sharpest Tool in the Shed* dissolved into a dew-covered suburban back yard at dusk. A frantic, bare-footed young woman in short-shorts looked over her shoulder at something pursuing her. The fabric of her halter top strained to contain the bouncing of her oversized breasts as she whimpered and ran. She glanced behind her as a large shadow fell across her face, which caused her to scream in terror. A second later a blade swept sideways and decapitated her. The voice-over continued as her head flipped end-over-end in slow motion, trailing blood.

"What's beheading all these women?" the voice-over said. "The sharpest tool in the shed, that's what. Why is it always so sharp? Who sharpens it? What is it? It's a medieval weapon called a falchion and it's slicing its way into a theatre near you this summer." A swooshing sound-effect followed, slicing the screen in half revealing the letters S.T.I.T.S., dripping blood.

"Those bastards at You'd Better Run, Girl Pictures have gone too far this time, Uncle Barry. They're taking a jab at us by using our name in their picture! "

"What? The weapon they use, a falchion? That's lame. Did you hear that scream? Didn't do anything for me. You'd Better Run, Girl isn't a threat to us. Besides, the horror movie game is just about played out. Are you ready to play in the big league, Alex?"

"What do you mean?"

"I mean we have the chance to kill an actual virgin on screen, on film. I can sell it on the black market for a fortune. And the honor could all go to you. Somebody robbed you of your destiny the first time around, but I think we can show them that you're made of tougher stuff than that, right?"

Alex looked dubious.

"Right?" Barry said more forcefully.

"A virgin? Really? Well, the thing is, Uncle Barry, since I've been in here, healing my body, I've also done some reading, you know, to also heal my mind—"

Barry quickly slapped his nephew's face. "You're gonna get a grip, is what you're gonna do. You, we, are right on the cusp of greatness. Turning life into art. Making a lousy actress into a real-life victim. Apex predator versus prey. Heal your mind? Do you think a lion needs to heal its mind? Or a boa constrictor? Or a great white shark? Those animals do what comes naturally to them. Just because we've 'evolved' doesn't mean we have to give up those primitive rights. I want us to get back in touch with our roots, man. That Vera needs killing. We have the equipment, the know-how. Why not document it on-screen and make a bundle while we're at it?"

Barry realized his voice had risen when a nurse leaned her head into the doorway, looking concerned.

"You were talking about a virgin—then you said Vera needs killing. I don't understand, Uncle Barry."

A twisted smile spread across Barry's face. "That's who I'm talking about, Vera Horowitz is a virgin. Ain't it amazing? Look, Alex, it's either gonna be you or I'll get someone else and you've already paid too high a price to be denied the honor."

"Vera, huh? Well, how much would I get paid?" Alex asked.

"I'm going to guess that I could sell the snuff film for around two million. Your share, the lion's share if you will, would be about $666,000.00 a third, because I have a lot of other people to pay off to get this thing done. Well, you in or out?"

"I'm in, Uncle Barry."

Barry watched with satisfaction as a proud new expression crossed Alex's face.

Pride melting into greed, Barry thought.

Chapter 26

Let's Make a Deal

Aaron sat in his squad car, shaded beneath a palm tree, near the entrance to Vera's grandmother's house. He read the Witness Statement form over and over out of boredom. *Make it or break it time,* he thought. *It'll take a miracle to get Vera to fill this out.*

A silver limo pulled up into the driveway and Vera and a long-legged, red-haired lady with a body to die for stepped out. Aaron wasted no time. He got out and jogged, not so fast as to scare them, just enough to catch up before they got inside the house. The women walked and talked on the way to the front yard.

"I just thought it would be nice for you to see where I grew up. Hang out, get a break from rehearsing, you know, meet my grandmother," Vera said.

"Yeah, great. Why not," Naomi said.

"Vera, wait up," Aaron called.

Vera turned at the sound of his voice with disgust. Naomi turned and smiled.

"Go ahead, Naomi, I'll be there in a minute," Vera said. "What do you want, Aaron?"

"I need a favor. I need you to fill out this form, saying you were with me on a date last Tuesday from 11:00 P.M. until 1:30 A.M."

Vera burst out laughing. "That's hilarious. Yeah, I'll fill out your date *rape* form and I'll be sure to include *everything.*"

"No, you got the wrong idea about that. That was passion, spilling over from so many years of wanting to be part of your life. What about how I looked out for you on the set? I'd still like us to be together. But how can I make a life for us if the Civilian Review Board thinks I was involved in something bad. Something you know I *couldn't* have done because I was with you. Right? Vera? Just please fill it out. You'll see I'm a much nicer guy than you think."

"Goodbye, Aaron," Vera said and turned to walk inside.

"Can we talk later today? I deserved that, but this is my career. I'll wait out here—"

Aaron's voice was cut off by the slamming of the front door.

Inside, Zissell marched in from the kitchen. "What you tink 'dis is, a barn? You don't slam door to my house, Vera!"

"Sorry, Bubbe. I'd like to introduce you to one of my friends from the set. This is Naomi Nivens, Naomi, this is my grandmother."

Naomi held out her hand as Zissell eyed her suspiciously.

"You work wit' dose bad people making movies?"

"I did," Naomi said, shaking hands. "Now I'm hoping to act in romantic dramas."

"Goot', no girls should make dose' bad films. Now, why do you slam da' door, Vera?"

"Because there's someone I don't want to talk with outside."

Zissell immediately walked to the door and looked out the peep hole. "It's Aaron Finklestein! Go get him and I will make us something to nosh. Go, Vera."

"No, Bubbe. We're through."

"But why not? Naomi, you are a friend, talk some sense to her. Dis man wants to marry her. A homeowner, soon he gets promotion. Why you don't like Aaron?"

"We're not right for each other," Vera said, wanting to avoid her grandmother's rage if she knew the truth about Aaron. "I don't want to marry anyone. Now, please, just forget about it, Bubbe."

Zissell seemed heartbroken, her small face even more old and tired than a moment ago.

"But you don't have nobody, Vera. After I am gone, nobody to take care of you. No little Horowitz grandchildren, no family to tell how your grandfather escaped the camps. No—" Tears appeared at the corners of Zissell's eyes.

"Bubbe, don't." Vera said, and wrapped her arms around her grandmother and rocked her side to side. "I'll find somebody, some day. Just not Aaron. And you're not going anywhere, Bubbe."

~

From the back seat of his limo, Barry instant messaged his connection on the dark web from a disposable cell phone. He wrote freely because his words were immediately scrambled then deciphered on the other end—untraceable.

Barry's Message: *I have a virgin selected for murder on film. Pretty, petite. Asking two million. Details?*

Response Message: Murder? *Why waste virgin with regular murder? Unique offering. Client will pay much more for Mayan style sacrifice—cut out heart while still alive. Your take: four million. Yes?*

Barry thought for a second before answering.

Barry's Message: *Yes. I'll be in touch tonight.*

Response Message: *Look forward to it.*

Barry had his driver turn around—he had to get Alex onboard now. He knew Shelley could get Vera back, but Alex, the kid was so damned dumb, and he'd never actually killed anyone. The limo chirped to a stop in the emergency lane and Barry lumbered inside. *I need a way for Alex to practice so he doesn't screw this up,* Barry thought.

As he entered Alex's room, he found him squeaking back and forth across the tile floor on his crutches, red-faced and sweating from the exertion.

"Hey, Uncle Barry. I'm putting in some extra P.T. so I'm ready."

"That's great, kid. But there's a new twist. I could turn that six hundred thousand into a million if you were to make one change."

"What change?"

Barry closed the door to the hallway and stepped into Alex's personal space.

"I need you to cut out Vera's beating heart while she's still alive. No biggie, killin's killin', right?"

Alex stepped backwards; he retracted his chin and turned pale. "Uh, no. That's really messed up, Uncle Barry."

"What's the difference? Dead is dead. When are you ever in your lifetime going to make a million dollars all at once? Don't you want to have nice things?"

"Yeah, but what if I want to get married? How am I ever going to be normal after that?"

"Compartmentalization, I do it all the time. Do Vera, then shove it away into a compartment in your head and forget about it. Save the 'nice' Alex for your new wifey. Get it?"

"It's too horrible. I don't think I can do it."

"Horrible?! Oh, right. Why would there be something horrible in a horror movie?" Barry shot out his hand and squeezed Alex's face. Alex, unable to react with both arms supporting his weight on the crutches, was defenseless.

"You're doin' it," Barry said. "That's it. I told your mom I'd look out for you—best way to do that is to set you up with a million bucks, maybe a house, new car. But I can't do that if you don't step up and do this. You're doin' it, right?"

Alex stared wide-eyed but didn't move. Barry began to move Alex's head up and down in a nodding motion, Alex's lips squeezed out like a cartoon fish.

"Say it. I'll do it, Uncle Barry. I promise you."

"Agh'll duh ett, U-le Ba-we, Augh Pwomith yau."

"That's better. Now get back to your exercises. You may have to run Vera down the day of the shoot. She sure ain't gonna stand still for this."

"I have to think about this. I only said yes because you were squeezing my face."

"Yeah? Well, here's some incentive for you. You do it: you get a million bucks in cash. You don't do it: Benny and I are going to cut *your* heart out and sell the film to the highest bidder. It won't bring the same price because you're just a big dumb lug, but we're still going to cut out your heart while you're alive. Is that what you want?"

"You wouldn't really do that, right? You're just trying to scare me."

"You don't step up and do this, you're dead to me, dead to the rest of the world and you'll also be heartless. Huh? You like that image: you staggerin' around a dark set with your heart ripped out? I'll personally make sure you see it before you kick off too, bozo. You'll never get married if that's what you want. You'll stop breathing, walking, talking—"

"Okay, okay, I get it. It's still wrong though. I mean, even if I say yes, I wouldn't begin to know how to do a thing like that."

"Say, yes. Say, I have your word on it and Benny and I will walk you through it. Make sure you do it right. Okay?"

"Yeah, okay."

"Alright. You're gonna love spending a million bucks, Alex. Just nothin' like it," Barry said, shaking his nephew by the shoulder. He gave Alex a hard stare and left.

From the back of his limo Barry called Benny on a pre-paid "burner" cell phone.

"Benny, it's a go. Alex is onboard."

"What about Vera?"

"That's no sweat. Shelley'll schmooze her back into the herd. The problem is gonna be Alex. Somehow you and I have to show him how to cut out a live girl's heart. We need something as close to the real thing as possible."

"I'll find out what medical students practice on. How soon are we ready for a trial run?"

"Whenever you get us a fake Vera," Barry said.

"What's my budget?"

"Don't go over, oh, two to three thousand."

"I'll see what I can find. Later."

Barry drove back to his trailer for a nap. He loved to set the wheels of mayhem in motion then doze; to wait for the cell phone's chimes from Shelley and Benny to wake him from a dreamy state of anticipation. Like a snake warming its cold body on baking-hot rocks, confident that when his body has warmed the heat will rouse his unfeeling mind into action, then dinnertime would be soon to follow.

~

After a moment, Vera held her mother at arm's length. "You're okay, Bubbe. I'm going to talk with Naomi in my room. Come on, Naomi."

"It's nice meeting you, Mrs. Horowitz," Naomi said, as Vera took her by the elbow and pulled her down the hallway.

"Yah, nice to meet you too," Zissell said to the girls' backs, as they vanished behind the bedroom door.

"I see you've got your fabulous Mandy Mouse metropolis all set up again," Naomi said, looking around.

The female mice, adorned in all sorts of fluffy, frilly dresses and bows, smiled down on the women.Naomi found it strangely comforting.

"Yeah, Mandy's seen me through thick and thin."

Just then, Naomi's phone rang. "Hello? Oh hi, Shelley. What's up?"

"Don't answer, just say 'okay' if Vera's with you," Shelley said quietly.

"Okaaay," Naomi said, "but why are you calling me?"

"Because I already called everybody else and Vera wasn't with them. Vera hasn't been returning my calls, but if we could just talk I have a very lucrative business offer for her. So where are you two?"

"We're at Vera's grandmother's place."

"If Vera asks say I called about paperwork for a film. Be a lamb and keep her there for the next half an hour. You'll be doing Vera a big favor and I'll owe you one, Naomi."

"Okay, bye," Naomi said.

"What did Shelley want?" Vera asked.

"She wanted to know where you were. Says she has a lucrative film offer for you."

"She's not coming over here is she?"

"It sounds like it to me."

"I don't want her coming over here. I don't have anything to say to her. She's just Barry's mouthpiece. Especially with everything else going on and Bubbe so upset."

"She said she has a deal for you. You *do* need a job."

"But not working for a maniac who wants to *kill* me, Naomi!"

~

Shelley had heard about Jake's chauffer taking Vera back and forth from her grandmother's place. Shelley heard all sorts of gossip from Jake's chauffer because he was terribly smitten with her. She'd only had to flirt with him once and she'd started receiving roses and invitations to coffee. With a quick call to the chauffer, she'd gotten Vera's grandmother's address and wasted no time entering it into her GPS and speeding there.

Upon arriving, she was surprised to see Aaron parked at the curb in his police car. She got out, raised an umbrella against the mid-day sun, and strutted by his open window.

"I guess you're not over the little virgin yet," Shelley said.

"What? No, that's not why I'm here." he protested, but Shelley never broke stride.

She rang the doorbell and waited. She opened the tri-folded leather binder to the page with the triplicate carbon movie contract, complete with adhesive plastic X's where Vera needed to sign. When nobody answered, she rang again and followed it up with a couple of knocks.

"Yah, who is dere?" Zissell called, peering through the peep hole.

"Shelley Arcongioli, from Falchion Films. I have a very generous business offer for Ms. Vera Horowitz, if she'll come out and speak with me."

"You are white like ghost. No wonder, you're from da people who makes disgusting movies. Go away! Vera don't need you."

Another voice came from behind the door, followed by urgent arguing. Shelley heard the first voice shouting: "Go on, 'den, be a fool!"

The door opened and Vera stood there.

"What's this about, Shelley?" Vera asked.

"Your fans have spoken, and they want you back. Mr. Whitscomb is willing to increase your pay substantially to have you act in *The Organ Pedaler*. I've brought the agreement right here. All you have to do is sign."

"No, I'm pretty disgusted by the whole business to tell you the truth. Is that all?"

"Vera, what will it take for you to come back? Just for one film?It wouldn't even be that many scenes? How about twenty-thousand dollars?"

Vera seemed to consider this. "No, it's not enough. Serena got badly injured and somehow nobody, including you, seemed to care. The business is repulsive, I had to wait six weeks to get paid and put up with all those sleazebags. How can you stand to be around them?"

"That's neither here nor there. What would you consider fair compensation? We could get you an advance, that's not a problem. Twenty-two, twenty-three thousand? That would pay for a few month's rent in advance while you searched for a job you like better."

"How about forty thousand?"

Shelley gasped. "You've been watching too much TV. Nobody who's a starting actress gets forty-thousand dollars to act in a movie where seventy-five percent of the film has already been shot. How about twenty-five?"

"If the fans want me that badly how about thirty-five?"

"Be realistic, little girl. We're willing to offer you twenty-six."

"Thirty-four."

"Get out of the thirties, for god sake! Twenty-seven."

"I can live here with Bubbe. She's against my working for Falchion in the first place."

Vera turned and began twisting the doorknob. Shelley's hand reached out and grabbed Vera's hand before she could stop herself.

"Vera, wait! I'm going to say what our offer is. Just once. You don't counter me. Then we sign. Thirty-thousand dollars. Five thousand in advance. Deal?"

"Thirty-one thousand. Ten thousand in advance and you have a deal."

Shelley's pale face turned bright red and her jaw clenched. "I'm not authorized to offer that much. I just can't."

Vera folded her arms and gazed at Shelley without speaking. Ten painful seconds passed with neither woman saying anything. Finally, Shelley opened her collagen-filled lips.

"Alright. Can we go inside in the shade? The sun is seeping through this umbrella."

After Vera had signed and initialed by all the X's, and Shelley had written her a check for ten thousand dollars, Shelley tore off a copy, folded it and gave it to Vera.

"We'll see you on the set at six A.M. Monday. Don't be late," Shelley said, and scampered to her car beneath the shade of her umbrella. As she passed by Aaron's car, he called to her, but Shelley kept moving, got inside and drove away.

Vera saw Aaron's black and white cruiser and had a thought. She slowly approached him. He got out, the now-wrinkled and sweat-damp witness statement form held in his hand.

"Aaron. I have a proposal for you."

"Oh, god, anything, Vera. Just name it."

"I'm going to be acting in a bad horror movie for Falchion Films again and there is a really good chance that someone plans to murder me during shooting. If you want me to sign that form, then I want you to be present at every single shoot for the entire time I'm being filmed. I want you to have a gun with you. I want the gun loaded. I want you to be awake and alert. If I sign your form and you are not there while I'm being filmed, I'm calling your supervisor, the, what did you call them? The Civil Board?"

"The Civilian Review Board," Aaron muttered.

"Thank you. I'm calling the Civilian Review Board and the media and anyone else I can think of to tell them what you tried to do to me. I'll say I lied because you threatened me if I didn't sign the form. Do you understand me?"

"Yes. But Vera, I *do* work. I don't know how I can be at every shoot while I'm supposed to be at work."

"That's your problem. I understand there are just a few scenes left so make it to every one or I told you what would happen. It's only my life we're talking about here after all."

"Okay. You win. Now please sign here and I'll tell you how to fill in the open spaces."

Vera signed and copied down the words Aaron recited and handed it back to him.

"You recognize my phone number?" she said. "You'd better pick up right away when you see my number. I'll give you as much of the schedule ahead of time as possible, but sometimes they switch up on us. You'd better be there when I tell you. Swear that you will."

"I swear I'll be there when you tell me. How many days do you think it will take?"

"Who knows. Probably about two weeks. Get out of here and watch for my call."

Aaron closed the door to his cruiser, closed his eyes, and let out a sigh

~

"Hello?"

"Barry, it's Shelley. I got Vera back. I had to sign her for a lot more than we talked about to do it though. Thirty-one thousand and a ten-thousand-dollar advance."

"What?! I said no more than twenty-five! And nobody gets a ten-thousand-dollar advance! What are you thinking?"

"She was going to walk. Is that what you want? She's scared, disgusted, and complained that she didn't get paid for so long before. You said get her back—that's what it took."

"If this picture doesn't make a killing then you're paying me back that extra six grand you paid Vera."

"You're welcome. Vera will be there Monday morning. Goodbye, Barry."

Barry chuckled to himself. *Vera's not going to be around long enough to collect anyway.*

He walked to the kitchen for a snack. His hard work was paying off. He unloaded an array of sandwich fixings on the counter, laid out in rows, and began slathering on mayo, mustard, lettuce, tomatoes, then the slabs of meat: ham, beef, and chicken. He wrapped the bread around the conglomeration, something too large for a human mouth to accommodate. But Barry did it; he engulfed a quarter of the sandwich and bit through it and then worked it in his jaws as tiny tear drops formed in the crinkles around his eyes, which had become slits.

After the sandwich, Barry needed to sit alone to digest his meal. This was when he was most vulnerable: bloated, slow to react, contented, a sitting duck for another predator. But here in his lair he felt safe.

His phone chimed. *Benny!*

"Yeah?" Barry said.

"I got us one. It's called a High–Fidelity Human Patient Simulator, or HPS. It's a dummy with realistic bodily functions. It comes in adult, child, and infant sizes. I ordered us a child-sized one to approximate Vera's dimensions. The chest moves with respiration, lungs, heart, pulse, realistic fluids all flow, filled with blood and guts, just like a real human. If you cut it or hit it, it screams out in pain. To get to the heart you've got to get up under the ribs, just like a real person. You listening, fat man? The limbs try to protect it too, just like Vera will do. It's not cheap, though. You ready for the price tag?"

"I guess. Hit me."

"Forty-thousand. I put it on your plastic."

"You stupid sonofabitch! I can't afford that!"

"You can't afford to have Alex screw this thing up because the punk gets squeamish. Am I right or am I right? You are talking about millions, correct?"

"Correct. But only if we pull this thing off."

"I'm having the HPS sent on two-day Express for another hundred and fifty. It'll be here Wednesday afternoon. Now it's up to you to find a time and place for us to coach Alex."

"I guess I should thank you, but right now I'm just thinking of that thirty-day billing cycle and that forty-thousand-hundred-and-fifty-dollar bill. I had other things charged to that card too—"

"Shut up, step up and let's get this thing done and you won't have any worries, tubby."

"Yeah, okay," Barry said and let the swirl of endorphins and cholesterol carry him into a high calorie slumber as the cell phone tumbled from his beefy palm.

Chapter 27

Trial Run

It was 1:00 A.M. as Benny wheeled the oblong wooden crate, strapped to a dolly, down the corridor to set piece storage (S.P.S.). Barry stepped in front and unlocked the metal door so Benny could pass, then locked up behind them.

"Okay, let's see what my money bought," Barry said.

Benny pulled out a crowbar and got to work prying boards off the crate.

"Help me, fatso," Benny said.

As Barry pulled the end of a board, the nails at the far end bent and the board came loose in Barry's hands, sending him spinning across the room.

"Quit screwing around and help me," Benny yelled.

Barry walked back over. "You'd better remember who you're talking to."

"You're my employer. Now move," Benny snarled.

With the top boards removed, the men stared down into the crate at thick, blue-tinted plastic, hermetically sealed over the four-foot humanoid body within. Benny slit the plastic with a razor knife and pulled the plastic back, then reached in and pulled out chunks of padding from around the head and body. Finally, he cut away a thin white foam layer revealing the face.

The men gazed at the body which lay on its back in the crate. The complexion of the face was clear, the eyelids peacefully closed, short-cropped brown hair encircled the young masculine-looking face.

"Hey," Barry said "it's a dude! It's supposed to be a chick, like Vera."

"No biggie. The size is right, that's all we need, so Alex gets the moves down."

"Help me," Barry said.

They slid their hands inside the crate and, together, lifted the body up and gently laid it onto the floor where Benny cut away the remaining foam layer. The anatomically correct and naked body lay motionless on the cold concrete floor.

"Kind of eerie, no?" Benny said.

"Whatever. Read the instructions."

Benny scanned the instruction manual and flipped the pages, all the while mumbling aloud. "Most sophisticated blah, blah—enjoy improving your surgical skills with the high-fidelity human patient simulator (H.P.S.) blah, blah—something about ethical mode—What? Here's a menu of symptoms I can program: abdominal aortic aneurysm, blah, blah, brain abscess, blah, blah, ankle, broken, arterial thrombosis, avian flu, jumping ahead here, let's try heart attack."

"Yeah, that's good. Give him that."

"Says he'll flop all around if I do."

"Scrap that then, just get it working," Barry said.

"First, I've got to boot it up," Benny said.

When Benny activated the remote-control the H.P.S. emitted whirring and beeping sounds. With a loud static burst the H.P.S. opened its eyes and propped itself up on its elbows.

"It is cold in this room. I feel chilled," the dummy said in a young male semi-robotic voice, its lips moving in perfect synchrony. "I would like to go home. I am not wearing any clothing."

The dummy stood and swayed between its heels and the balls of its feet, getting its balance.

"It freakin' stands up?" Barry said.

"Yeah, it's like a real human," Benny said under his breath. Then, to the dummy, "We need you to sit up on this table."

Benny dragged the wooden crate off, letting it slam to the floor.

"I do not feel comfortable," the dummy said. "I am naked, and I do not know you men. Are you doctors?"

"That's right. I'm Doctor Benny and this is Doctor Barry. Now sit up on the table."

Barry looked at Benny, a wry glint in his eye.

The dummy hopped up onto the stainless-steel table. "Ouch. I have a splinter in my buttocks. It hurts."

"Oh, for god's sake," Benny said. He found the splinter and pulled it out.

"That is much better," the dummy said.

"Why's it acting like such a little pansy?" Barry asked.

"It's programmed to mimic human emotions."

"I have a feeling it's really gonna scream when Alex guts it."

"That'll be good practice because that's sure as hell what Vera's gonna do."

~

Lola awoke in a soft bed in a small, clean room with Mexican paintings on the wall. She noticed a glass beside a blue ceramic water pitcher on a bedside table. Condensation beads had formed on the outside of the pitcher, which caused Lola to feel the severity of her thirst. She poured a glass of water, and a couple of cubes of ice splashed into the glass. *Thank god!* She realized she still had a tube affixed to her lips because her jaw was wired shut. She picked up the glass and lowered her straw into the water. *What am I, a hummingbird?*

She sucked the cold water until the glass was empty. There was a rap at the door.

"Miss Grubb?" said the voice behind the door, "I know you cannot answer, but this is Doctor Alvarez, the one you came to see. I am coming in now."

The door swung open and a short trim man with thick hair, as shiny and black as Armor-Alled tires, entered. He wore an all-white, formal-looking outfit, and approached her bed. He abruptly stopped and put his hands behind his back.

"Good morning," the doctor said. "I understand you had quite an adventure last night: escaping from the hospital, then driving through the night. Yes?"

Lola gave the thumbs up sign.

"Mm-hmm," the doctor affirmed. "First, we were unable to get your X-rays before extricating you, so we will have to take some of our own. Second, I can see that you have minimal inflammation, which is good. The swelling has gone down, hopefully sufficiently that we may repair that part of your face. We have some decisions to make. Do you have any photographs of yourself prior to your accident? Perhaps in your cell phone? You will find it in the small drawer in the night table."

Lola gave the thumbs up sign, opened the drawer, and withdrew her phone. Doctor Alvarez stepped in closer for a look as Lola found her photos. She gave the phone to the doctor who scrolled through the matrix of pictures, expanding each image and screwing up his face.

Doctor Alvarez cleared his throat. "Miss Grub, I understand you are an actress who makes horror movies."

Lola gave the thumbs up sign.

"So, you wear stage make-up and prosthetics to look unsightly and frightening in these movies?"

Lola gave the thumbs down sign.

"Oh, I see. So, then these are actual pictures of you before the accident?"

Thumbs up.

"Miss Grub. You have an opportunity here to significantly improve your appearance. You could easily be made to look much more attractive than at any other time in your life. Would you like that?"

Thumbs up.

"Alright, then I am going to give you some catalogues to look through of famous American actresses and celebrities as well as some more exotic-looking actresses from outside the U.S. I need you to select one or two looks that you would consider for your own appearance and present them to me or my assistant. Then we will see what is possible for you, alright?"

Thumbs up.

"Alright. Now, we need you to transfer the funds for your care thus far. You may use a wire transfer. Will you be able to wire us three-thousand five-hundred dollars from your bank account from your phone if I give you the routing number?"

Thumbs up.

"Alright, we are off to a good start, Miss Grubb."

~

Aaron's patrol car cruised to a stop. He got out and strolled across the precinct lot. His feet practically bounced up the three steps and down the corridor to the chief's office. *What a difference a day makes*, he thought as he rapped on the chief's door. He heard talking growing closer on the other side. The chief whisked the door open and motioned Aaron in, then continued his phone conversation, as he returned to his chair behind the desk. Aaron stepped inside and quietly closed the door behind him.

Aaron looked out the window so as not to be rude, but the chief pointed to the seat opposite his desk and Aaron sat.

"Look," the chief said into the phone, "we don't have the manpower to oversee *two* protests on the same day. Don't you ever watch bank heist movies? That's when perps pull them when the cops are spread too thin. No, I'm only partially joking. Maybe it's not the best time for jokes, but my point is still valid. Just bump one of the protests a couple of days and there won't be any problems. Okay? Alright. Bye."

The chief hung up. Aaron thought he could see the gears turning as the chief eyed him.

"Finklestein, is that the 'you're still in the running for captain form' I asked you for?"

"Yes, sir." Aaron tried not to smile.

"You know you're still not out of the woods on this. I'm going to present your alibi as evidence and speak on your behalf, but the victim may want to pursue things further."

"Yes, sir."

The chief's eyes stared evenly at Aaron through his crosshatched grey eyebrows. "Aaron, I'm going to shoot straight with you: I'm scared for you, son. I know how hard you worked to get this far, so don't walk out that door and go freewheeling into the streets. You got lucky this time—don't blow this, the department can use the good Aaron I know is inside you. I have no use for the bad Aaron, and I won't hesitate to shoot him down in flames if I ever see him again. Understand, Lieutenant?"

"Yes, sir. Sir?"

"Yes?"

"I hate to ask this, but I'm overdue for my two weeks' vacation. The captain needed me to fill in for crowd control last week during the President's visit, and then that string of jewelry store break-ins happened, and my vacation kept getting postponed, but I—"

"No, that's fine. I think it would be good for you to take some time off, clear your head. Remember why you became a cop in the first place. Go ahead and take your vacation."

"Thank you, sir."

"And, Finklestein, when you get back I expect you to make the department proud."

Aaron nodded, quietly pulled the door closed behind him, and let out a huge sigh. He lumbered down the hallway. Not until the parking lot did he dare to speak under his breath.

"I did it. I did it. I did it. Yes!"

Inside his cruiser, he snatched up his cell and pulled out his wallet, found the scrap of paper with Shelley Arcongioli's number written on it. He dialed and waited.

"Hello?"

"Shelley, hi. It's me, Aaron. How would you like to get together for some dinner?"

"No, I don't want to get mixed up with some guy who's hung up on a virgin who doesn't want him," Shelley said.

"That's not the reason I was at Vera's mom's house. I needed her to fill out a witness statement form regarding the night we went out. That's all. I have no interest in her anymore."

"What did she witness?"

"Nothing you'd be interested in. Just police business."

"Uh, huh. So, you're totally over her?"

"Yep. She's nothing compared to you anyway. I like 'em more experienced."

"You think I'm experienced?"

"Oh, yeah. You taught me a couple of things the other night. I'm a good student, too."

"Well, I'm busy, Aaron. Besides, I think you need to cool off for a while and decide what it is you really want."

"I've got some free time now. I have two weeks' vacation, so if you could take some time off then we—"

"I don't *have* any free time right now. I'm sure you'll find some girl to chase out there."

"I'd be happy to chase you, Shelley."

"I have to go, Mr. Policeman. Maybe we'll talk later."

~

Jake plopped down behind his desk and began editing *Fifty Ways to Cleave Your Lover.* He looked over each scene through the D.I. or digital intermediate, where he could then optically scan the negative into the computer and then compile a cut list. He'd heard the grumbling through the grapevine that this was no time for him to get artistic with the editing because Barry had (once again) squandered too much of Falchion's money and revenue from the film was needed to pay people's salaries as well as the company's bills.

Jake was the entire post-production crew. He had to handle the editor's cut, director's cut, and the final cut himself. Fortunately, he liked it that way—no arguing over what some editor's idea of a montage should look like or represent. Jake liked the pressure (normally), but this situation wasn't normal at all.

He was going to have to watch and edit a series of scenes of the woman he loved having an arm chopped off with a cleaver, a reaction shot, a leg chopped off with a cleaver, a reaction shot, and so on until she appeared to be a lifeless mess on the floor; and then another series of shots wherein her body parts were tossed into a blender and pureed. He set his smartphone alarm to sound in an hour. He would have this wrapped up in an hour and then reward himself with a coffee break. This film wouldn't win the Oscar for best editing, but Jake might leave the room without losing his marbles, or since his therapy, tossing his cookies.

~

Barry entered Alex's hospital room and smiled at the sight before him: Alex was very carefully walking under his own power; no cane, no crutches.

"Uncle Barry. Check it out. The physical therapist says he's never seen anyone with injuries as bad as mine walk on their own so soon. He warned me to take it easy for a while."

"That's good, kid, real good. You need to come with me now, because we have to practice before your big scene with Vera."

"Uncle Barry, the last time you pulled me out of here early it set me back two weeks."

"You look pretty healthy to me. Come on, let's go."

Barry pulled Alex by the back of his arm while Barry's limo driver grabbed Alex's other arm, and together they escorted him out into the hallway toward the elevator.

Inside S.P.S. Barry locked up and Alex slowly turned to face Benny and the dummy.

"Alex, my man, you're looking well," said Benny. "Come over here and let me give you a little anatomy lesson." Benny gestured to a laminated chart of internal human organs.

Alex walked over and stood before the chart. He glanced at the dummy, which sat on the gurney, eyes closed.

"Now your job is to make a cut with this scalpel under the rib cage, then shove your hand up under those ribs. There are a couple of things that are *not* hearts, which may get in your way. First, the stomach, kind of small under the dummy's left ribs. Get your hand on top of that one and keep shoving. Then there's the liver, way bigger. You should feel that on the back of your hand. Keep shoving, get your hand *way* up in there, when you feel the one that's beating that's your target."

"Now, guts are like fish," Benny continued. "Kind of slippery, so you're going to be wearing these chef's grade cut-resistant gloves, so you can get a good grip on that heart. Grip it good, yank it out as far as you can, if it won't come out cut whatever's holding it back and hold it up so the camera can film it. What do you think?"

"I can't do it," Alex said, turning pale.

"Alex, Alex, Alex," Barry said, grabbing him by the shoulder. "We've been over this. Benny and I are gonna flat out kill you if you don't. Ain't that right, Benny?"

"That's right, Alex, we're going to kill you if you don't. Sorry to be so blunt."

"So, you want to give us another answer? A million-dollar answer?" Barry said.

"Okay," Alex said, looking at the floor.

"Good. So, this is practice time. We spent forty grand on this dummy for you to get it right. It's gonna *fight* you so Benny and I are gonna help hold onto it so you can get that heart. Put your gloves on and take your scalpel. Oh, almost forgot, even though this is just practice, we all have to wear these masks. Don't want to be recognized."

Once Benny saw Alex was ready, he booted up the dummy, which opened its eyes. Benny grabbed one of its arms and Barry grabbed the other.

"Excuse me, but why are you restraining me?" the dummy said.

"So you don't fall off the gurney, Dummy," Barry said.

"Jeez, I didn't know it talked," Alex said.

"Yep, it does everything Vera's gonna do. Now come on."

"Like, how do I start?"

"Make the cut."

"Who are you?" the dummy asked. "Why are you wearing those masks?"

Alex braced one hand on the dummy's shoulder and cut into its side with the other. It screamed and thrashed its arms about. It wrenched an arm away and, in the process, elbowed Benny in the temple. Benny let go of the arm and held his head, pulling off his mask. Barry held fast to the other arm as Alex looked bewildered.

"You cut me! My abdomen is in a lot of pain!" the dummy screamed.

"Get in here and help me, Alex!" Barry yelled, as the dummy flailed its free arm into Barry's nose.

"Dammit, Dummy!" Barry yelled, his nose dripping blood.

"Hey!" Alex yelled. "Nobody hits my Uncle Barry."

Alex dived and tackled the dummy onto the floor. He pinned it and reached up inside it and grabbed the heart and pulled. He pulled again, then wrenched it downward.

"There is pressure—it feels like something is squeezing my heart," the dummy yelled.

"That's right. That's me!" Alex yelled and pulled the heart out into the light, still pumping, as blood and fluids covered the floor.

Barry and Benny both slipped and fell on top of Alex and the dummy. Barry pulled himself into a sitting position, pulled the gore-soaked mask off, and smiled.

"Alex, you've made me so proud today," Barry said and kissed Alex on the forehead.

"We forgot to put down plastic first. What a mess," Benny said.

Alex carefully stood up. With a final a convulsion, the dummy's leg thrust out and kicked Alex in the groin. Alex dropped the heart, fell to his knees, and curled into the fetal position.

"I think we'd better tie Vera up the day of the shoot," Barry said.

Chapter 28

Melodrama

Jake put the final touches on *Fifty Ways* and selected *finish* so the computer could turn the film into a digital product. Now everyone could get paid. His job was done, and he was free of his obligation to Barry. Jake let out a huge sigh; he had earned his reward of a cup of coffee at that bistro he loved. To sit alone quietly, to people-watch would be bliss.

Jake said "limo" into his smart phone and knew by the time he reached the end of the corridor James would be outside the exit door, waiting. He listened to the rhythm of his footsteps echoing off the cinderblock walls and thought how he should be grateful for the life he had: a beautifully appointed condo in Beverly Hills (already redecorated after Naomi's cocaine rampage), a limousine and a loyal driver, a fresh start in a new film genre, money in the bank, a stock and bond portfolio that grew larger every time he checked it, and a greatly improved relationship with his mother.

But without Vera I'm still miserable.

His phone vibrated.

"This is Jake."

"Mr. L'Hommedieu. It's Thelma Gladstone returning your call. How are things going?"

"Thelma. Unfortunately, after all the work you and I did, Vera saw an old movie magazine of a horror movie I made, a really rough one, back when I wasn't afraid to make a piece of trash like that—and she dumped me. I was only nineteen when I made that film!"

"Jake, I'm sorry. But even if she truly is one in a million, there are one-hundred-fifty-eight-million women in the U.S. alone. Even if it's too late to win her over there are one-hundred-fifty-seven more just as good as her out there."

"Yeah? I'm not holding my breath."

"You'll find love. You're a much more mentally healthy man now."

"I called to schedule a session—for some maintenance. How are you by the way?"

"That's a good sign, Jake. Asking about another's welfare shows you're not too wrapped up in yourself—even though you're hurting. I'm fine. How about Tuesday at three?"

"I'll see you then."

~

Brian sat on the edge of a bench in A studio rocking back and forth, massaging his temples. Felix had just threatened to fire him for being late to shoots three times in a row. He was still hovering over him, still yelling in that tinny, condescending voice. The cast members stopped what they were doing to watch the show.

"It's not just the lateness," Felix yelled, "or the disrespect you display toward me and the staff, the quality of your work has taken a nosedive, mister! My glaucoma-ridden, arthritic, wheelchair-bound grandmother could light a stage better than you lately. Some Director of Photography. Look at me when I'm talking to you, Brian! Do you think this is a game?"

"No, I think you're serious. So why don't you fire me? I've lost the love of my life and I really don't care. Thanks for your compassion by the way," Brian said, standing and walking toward the exit.

"You walk out that door, Brian, and you no longer have a job at Falchion Films."

Brian reached the door, twisted the knob, and stepped into the bright L.A. sunshine.

"That's it. You're fired!" Felix screamed, the veins standing out on his neck.

As the door closed Andy walked up and whispered in Felix's ear. "We've got to get him back, you realize?"

"Yes, dammit," Felix hissed, "but he can't act like that in front of the staff. If he wants to apologize, he can have his job back."

"That's my tiger," Andy said.

Brian shuffled along the sidewalk. He plunked down on a bench in the middle of the quad and slid on his sunglasses to ward off the merciless sun. Jake's limo was there, and he was about to get in when he saw Brian sitting in the distance. Brian's posture made Jake hold up an index finger to his driver, in a *give me a minute* gesture, and approach Brian. Jake assessed Brian's appearance: absurdly handsome, thick head of hair, white t-shirt, black jeans, black Ray Bans, arms crossed, looking bummed out. Brian stared at the sidewalk when he saw Jake approaching.

"Brian, you look like you're ready to play Tom Cruise in *Risky Business 2.*"

"Hey, Jake," Brian said, managing a smile.

"Lola, eh? The hospital doesn't know anything else?" Jake said.

"They've looked but no dice. The police haven't found anything either."

"I wish I could help. I'm in the same boat. I don't know if you heard but—"

"You and Vera? Thanks to Shelley the cast has known for a long time. Sorry, Jake."

"It doesn't look like I can get her back, so I've thrown myself into work. It helps."

"I just got canned, so nothing's going to help me but finding her," Brian said.

"Who fired you?"

"Felix. Nice that he did it in front of the whole crew too."

"I'll call a guy I know who specializes in finding people."

"I can't afford to pay anybody."

"Did I say anything about your paying? I'll cover it."

"Really? I just want her back, the way her nostrils flared when she was excited, the way when she smiled that wart would disappear into the crease in her smile and then pop back out again when she got serious, the way—"

"Um, I don't mean to interrupt, but what was I thinking? You just got fired, you're the best lighting man in the industry, am I crazy? You're hired. Remember that rom-dram I told you and Lola about? It's happening. Seven tomorrow morning. I'll text you the address."

"Thanks. I accept," Brian said

~

Monday morning, Vera caught a cab into Falchion. She stepped out and pulled her sweater collar up, as much against the sleaze she anticipated as the frigid morning. She walked down the corridor until she came to a paper sign, messily scribbled in red magic marker "Quiet! *The Organ Pedaler* shooting today."

As Vera opened the door, something was different. Everyone on the set stared at her. A couple of the older women smiled and tilted their heads to the side, the way one reacts to an adorable puppy. Two younger women watched her as if they were amused.

"Good to see you back, Vera. It must seem like your first time," Andy said.

This was followed by snickers from the staff.

"Not at all," Vera retorted. "I'm as experienced as anyone in this room now."

"That's not what I heard," yelled the sound man. (More chuckles).

"What's *that* supposed to mean?" Vera said.

"There's nothing wrong with it, Vera," one of the older women said.

"I think it's sweet that you waited," said another.

"Nothing wrong with what? What's sweet?" Vera demanded, her voice rising an octave.

Vera approached the first woman. "What did you hear exactly?"

"I don't want to say it out loud," the woman responded.

"What are you all talking about?" Vera said.

"How you're still a virgin. Vera the virgin," the sound man laughed.

"Whether I am or not, it's none of your business."

"Well, that's what we heard."

"Who told you that?" Vera shrieked.

In reaction to the unearthly piercing sound, everyone held their hands to their ears and rubbed their arm hairs until they lay down again.

"One guess," a younger girl said, tipping her head toward the studio entrance.

Vera looked behind her. She immediately recognized the long neck, the deathly white complexion of Shelley. Shelley, who'd been smirking a second ago, but whose pale face rapidly flushed red; Shelley, who disappeared out the door.

"Shelley, come back here!" Vera shrieked and marched toward the doorway.

Felix grabbed Vera by the arm. "Take it up with her later, Virg—I mean, Vera."

Vera wrenched his hand off her. "I'll take it up with her now and don't touch me."

Vera strode across the room and out the door into the corridor. She found Shelley sitting in her office, pretending to talk on the phone. As Vera stalked toward her, Shelley shrugged her shoulders and mouthed the words "Sorry, phone call."

Vera reached out, grabbed the phone and forced it onto its cradle on the desktop.

"No, you are *not* on a phone call," Vera said, "Who told you that about me?"

"Aaron Finklestein, your old boyfriend," Shelley said.

"First of all, he was never my boyfriend. Second, whether it's true or not it's none of your business. Third, even if it is true do you think I want everyone where I work to know? Fourth, how dare you! I thought you were my friend, Shelley. I guess that whole being nice and taking me under your wing thing was just an act."

A long pause followed as the women regarded each other, like the intense pause when Vera and Shelley negotiated her contract, but Vera sensed this time she wouldn't come out ahead.

"A long time ago *I* came to Hollywood with a dream," Shelley said. "Thinking I would become a star. Unlike you, I'd taken acting lessons at a good school first. I did auditions, but I never got a single call back. I bussed tables at restaurants, cleaned peoples' houses and kept auditioning. Finally, I got to stand in the background and laugh with two other girls while a prettier girl stood in the foreground, smiled into the camera, and said how much she liked baking with XYZ brand. That was *it*. That was my entire acting career. Oh, I kept trying, but it was always one of the pretty, petite girls like you who got the roles I'd rehearsed for.

"I took film editing classes during the day and waitressed at night. Finally, I convinced Barry that he should hire me to keep his office organized and clean up the dailies. He said no but finally hired me when I slept with him. So, there you have it, Vera. It was sour grapes for me to see you waltz in here, a no-talent waitress, but with a prettier face, and land a plum role your first day. And now you have a piece of dirt on me that you can spread all around the set if you want."

Vera's mouth hung open.

"I'm sorry, Shelley. I can't do anything about the way I look, and I wouldn't get any sort of kick from spreading a rumor about you. I have a question though. When I was in your trailer the first day and I asked you if Barry was a dirtball, you told me he was a 'teddy bear' and how everyone loved him here on the set."

"Barry is a teddy bear. I was a terrible secretary and my film editing skills were non-existent, but he hired me anyway."

"Only because you slept with him."

"Initially, but then he didn't kick me to the curb. He kept me on and that gave me time to improve my skills and learn how a film studio worked. Now, as you can see, I pretty much run the place. I've gotten bonuses and raises throughout the years too. So, he's not all bad."

"He's a monster," Vera stated flatly.

"What makes you say that?"

"Are you blind? I heard he stood there and allowed Alex to put Serena in the hospital with that rubber-coated cleaver. It was no accident either, I saw Barry and Alex laughing at the footage from one of the dailies where Serena got assaulted."

"I find that hard to believe."

"Don't believe it then, but I don't trust that man."

Vera gave Shelley a parting glance and returned to the studio.

~

Barry, Benny, and Alex spent four hours mopping up fake blood from the storage studio floor. They'd cleaned the human patient simulator, packed it in the crate with the remote control and instruction manual, and locked the crate in a storage room. Alex lugged a large trash bag filled with bloody rags toward the exit door while Benny did a final mop down with clean water.

"There!" Barry yelled, "Now next time we put plastic down first."

"But won't Vera be suspicious if she sees plastic, Uncle Barry?"

"It won't matter what she thinks since it'll be her last night on the planet."

"Won't there be other people around during the shoot?" Alex said.

"Normally, yes. But this is going to be an afterhours shoot. A martini shot if, you know your film slang," Barry said.

"Wow, I can't wait to get some sleep."

"No, you go grab a shower and report to makeup, Alex. We need you more like you looked right out of rehab for your scenes with Vera. And when you see her and the rest of the staff, you'd better not let on anything's not normal."

"That's right, Alex," Benny affirmed, a warning glint in his eye.

Barry and Benny watched as Alex unlocked the door and wrestled the bulging bag of soaked rags out the doorway. Benny waited for Alex to get out of earshot before speaking.

"Look, that heart-ripping rehearsal was a disaster. Your nephew's a clod. I want to do this soon before something goes wrong."

"We've got four more shots to get through. One of those is the scene of Vera getting her heart cut out for *The Organ Pedaler* that the *public* will see," Barry said.

"Right after that scene, tell Vera we need to re-shoot it. She must wear the same clothes she wore for her first scene or she'll become suspicious," Benny said, "She knows how particular you are. You need a second set of those clothes ready for the real heart cutting scene."

"I'll have Shelley order two pairs of clothes for Vera's scene. But where to shoot it? We need to have the set look the same—Vera's going to wonder about that too," Barry said.

"Change the script so Vera's tied up in the original scene—because as you just saw she's gonna fight back."

"We need a duplicate set in another studio. We do Vera, we clean everything, dismantle the set, get rid of Vera's body, and get paid. Our alibi is the staff was all there for Vera's scene in *The Organ Pedaler* and they'll all see her get up afterward and walk away. When she goes missing later, we'll all be drinking with the crew." Barry snapped his fingers. "A wrap party."

"Alright, here's the timeline. Real filming wraps at 3:00 P.M. We shoo everybody out at 3:00 sharp; tell Vera we've got to re-shoot her scene; get her dressed and make sure she's on the new set by 3:30. She's tied up by 3:45; we rip out her heart by 4:00, and start cleaning. Finish cleaning the room by 6:00 P.M.; dispose of the body by 6:30, get ourselves cleaned up, change clothes and get to the party by 7:30," Benny said.

"Tight schedule. Benny, how do we dispose of the body so nobody finds out?"

"I'll handle that. You see to the rest. Want me to write it down for you?"

"You think that's wise?"

"Just checking you're thinking," Benny said, grinning.

~

It was noon as Serena and Naomi sat in the courtyard, their eyes riveted on the exit doors to the *The Organ Pedaler* set. Suddenly, the double doors burst open and the cast came flooding out for lunch. Vera, looking small and annoyed, was seemingly carried along with the crowd, jostled by the hungry actors.

"Vera, over here," Naomi called.

Vera looked up with a wan smile. "Hi. It's nice to see a friendly face. What are you two doing here? Aren't you afraid of running into Barry?"

"We came to talk to you. Come on, we brought you lunch. We can eat over at one of those tables." Serena gestured to the picnic tables in the distance.

"How nice of you ladies," Vera said, "What's going on?"

"How's the new shoot?" Naomi asked.

"They all act like children—oh, you mean how I said I wanted out? I do but there's a little problem called making a living."

"Jake's ready to start reading auditions for his rom-dram. We're both in it. Why don't you join us?" Naomi asked.

"Uh—no. At least with this crew I *know* they're evil and I can take precautions. Jake's got romantic interests in me and he's a sicko. I made a clean break and it's better if I just make some money at Falchion, then see what the rest of L.A. has to offer."

"Listen, Vera. Jake paid to put me in rehab when I was homeless, broke, and strung out on coke. He took Serena in when she came out of the hospital. He listened to you and all of us about Alex and Benny and helped us get revenge and I hear he was very generous to you too."

"She's right, Vera," Serena said, "What you're mad at Jake about happened over ten years ago. He was just a kid, an ambitious kid at that. He's a good guy."

"Alright, alright! What's going on here? Did Jake send you to win me over?"

"Absolutely not. We just can't stand to see you head down the wrong path. Do you know what happens to a scream queen who makes a successful film? She goes back for more because it's all she knows," Naomi said.

"And with that on your resume how many directors are going to give you a shot at acting in a mainstream film? Zero." Serena added.

"Aren't you sick of this slime?" Naomi said. "We are."

"Okay, what do I have to lose? If I find out he's a creep after all I'm heading for the exit though," Vera said, and took a bite out of a sandwich.

Naomi plunked down beside her on the picnic bench.

"If you discover he's a creep then I have no faith in humanity, and we'll leave with you."

Chapter 29

Rom-Dram

Jake spoke quietly with Naomi and Serena in the kitchen of the Pacific Avenue studio rental.

"You're sure you talked with her? You're sure she said she was coming?"

"Yeah, she wants the work," Naomi said.

"And I put in a good word with her too," Serena said. "I told her how she had the wrong idea about you, how much you helped us."

"I just want another chance with her," Jake said.

"You'll get your chance, but I'm concerned," Serena said. "You've never done a film like this. Are you sure it'll make money?"

"I've poured my guts into this screenplay. It made my therapist and Naomi cry when they read it. I've got the financing in place and *you all* are the main cast. I've hired Brian as Director of Photography, but we need make-up, extras, a film crew, the works."

"I'm sure you could get Colin's crew to work with you during night shoots," Naomi said. "I've talked with him and they can't stand Barry."

"I'll invite him to lunch and schmooze him over," Jake said. "Come on, let's do this read-through. I've highlighted everyone's parts."

Jake left the kitchen, flipped on lights in the adjoining room, illuminating a huge peanut-shaped conference table. He rounded the table, laying a copy of the screenplay at each chair. Gradually, Naomi, Serena and several extras sat down, some sipping coffee and noshing on snacks. There was silence as everyone took off their coats and settled into reading mode. The door opened, and Vera entered.

Jake looked flustered and began to ramble.

"Oh, Vera. Thank you for coming. Please have a seat," he said, rounding the table, bashing his hip on a chair and stumbling onward. He grabbed her chair and pulled it out for her. Vera looked around and sat down as Jake slid her chair in. He returned to his side of the table and stood before his chair.

"Now, let me give everyone a brief account of what this script is. This is not what you're used to from Jake L'Hommedieu, no. This is not a horror movie, no matter how artistic some of them have been in the past, this is not my making some social statement film vis-à-vis *The Big Drill* or *Seven Flays in May*, no. As much as I put into those films, this is quite a departure for me. Although I've put five years of my life into it, this embarkment into the milieu of romance is Avant-guard, radical, if you will. It contains humor, but as those who have read it can attest, there are layers which, in that latter half of the film, will pull at your heartstrings, so although you may initially laugh, realize that you do so at your own peril because—"

"Jesus Christ! Are we going to read the thing or what? I have an audition in a couple of hours," one of the extras said.

"You know that's Jake L'Hommedieu you're talking to?" Serena said.

"I don't care. This is just a side job for me," the extra snapped back.
Vera smirked and rolled her eyes.
"Of course," Jake said, "everyone's parts are highlighted. Let's begin."
Jake read the narrator's part.

Angel in a Sea of Sharks

FADE IN:

INT. BUSTLING OFFICE BUILDING – DAY

MIMI TOO, a gorgeous redhead, stands with her girlfriend, IVY GOTCHBACH, in the lobby of an enormous office building

MIMI TOO: "I'm nervous—I *really* need this job."

IVY GOTCHUBACH: "You've worked toward this interview since I've known you. You go, girl!"
Ivy gently pushes Mimi toward the receptionist's desk and smiles.

INSERT: A gold lettered sign above the receptionist's desk: "Tarquin-Winthorpe Films."

Executives and actors shoulder Mimi out of the way in their haste as an immaculately dressed man approaches Mimi.

KURT REMARK: "Those are last season's shoes—I'm just saying."
Kurt clucks his tongue at Mimi and walks away.

RECEPTIONIST: "Hello, may I help you?"

MIMI: "Yes, I'm supposed to see Mr. Jonathan Perennial about the assistant's position?"

RECEPTIONIST: "He's expecting you. It's the last office at the end of the hall."
Men notice as Mimi walks down the hallway and knocks on Jonathan's door.
Jonathan whisks the door open which takes Mimi's breath away.

JOHNNY PERENNIAL: "Come in, come in. Have a seat." (smiles and checks Mimi over)
Mimi is star-struck by Jonathan's good looks and snappy suit. She sits primly on the seat opposite his mammoth power desk.

JOHNNY PERENNIAL: "Now what do you bring to the table that can help Tarquin Films?"

MIMI: "I'm quite a good listener. I can type 125 words per minute, I've taken several administrative courses at junior college and I'm fascinated by filmmaking."

JOHNNY PERENNIAL: "Let's see your resume. I'll look this over and if we're interested, I'll schedule a dinner interview—say tonight at six?"

MIMI: "You said "if" you were interested—you haven't looked at my resume yet."

JOHNNY PERENNIAL: "Yes—You know what? I've just made up my mind. You have a great attitude. I'll pick you up at five-thirty."
(Checks out her legs from across the desk)

MIMI: "You mean the dinner is someplace else? Oh, I could just meet you there."

JOHNNY PERENNIAL: "Nonsense. What's your address?"

(LATER)
The door closes behind Mimi as she walks down the hall toward the lobby. Two women gossip as she approaches.

LIBBY DOE: "So I see you have a date with Jonathan Perennial? We call him Johnny Forever."

LEIGH MEDOWN: "We call him that because he's the perfect man. Any girl who gets a date with him could land herself one heck of a husband."

MIMI TOO: "You ladies have the wrong idea. I'm here for a job interview."

LIBBY DOE: "So were we. We both ended up on dates with Jonathan. Only we didn't play it right. This is your big chance: if you become Mrs. Perennial you'll be set for life."

MIMI TOO: "Excuse me, but I am a professional. I'm looking for a professional position here nothing else."

LIBBY DOE: "Just get the ring first, Honey."

MIMI TOO: "It's a *job interview!*"

INT. "CURRY IN A HURRY RESTAURANT" - NIGHT
Mimi Too and Jonathan Perennial talk over gourmet cuisine.

MIMI TOO: "You're welcome to contact my references. I helped my former employers with some challenging clients which resulted in my saving them a couple of large accounts."

JOHNNY PERENNIAL: "The job is yours. You start Monday. By the way, that Indian waitress nearly spilled curry on me and she didn't say she was sari. Get it? Sari?" (laughs)

MIMI TOO: "Did you say the job is mine? I'll be a great asset to your firm and that's very funny."

JOHNNY PERENNIAL: "At least she's not one to curry favors. Get it? Curry? If she has kids I wonder if it's hard for her to find a baby sitar? Get it? Sitar?"

MIMI TOO: "You have a wonderful sense of humor Mr. Perennial. Stop, my sides are splitting."

JOHNNY PERENNIAL: "Call me Johnny. So, since you got the job and you think I'm so funny would you like to come back to my place?"

MIMI TOO: "Thank you for the job and dinner, Johnny. But I would prefer to keep things professional."

JOHNNY PERENNIAL: "You must think I'm too old for you. Are you trying to crush my ego? I recently tried a new hair product to Rogaine my confidence. Get it? Rogaine?"

MIMI TOO: "No, I don't think you're too old. You are very funny though."

JOHNNY PERENNIAL: "Well if you do think I'm old then maybe you could grandfather me in. Get it? Grandfather? At least let me buy you a couple more drinks, my gorgeous new assistant, to celebrate your position?"

MIMI TOO: "Alright, I guess one drink won't hurt since I don't start work until Monday."

(LATER)

JOHNNY PERENNIAL'S BEDROOM – DAY

Mimi and Johnny lie beneath the sheets as the sun rises beyond the curtains. Mimi cuddles with Johnny and she kisses him on the cheek. Johnny opens his eyes.

MIMI TOO: "Good morning. I want you to know I don't normally do things like this. I'm terribly embarrassed."

JOHNNY PERENNIAL: "Get out. If I knew you were that kind of girl, I'd never have invited you back here."

MIMI TOO: "But you seduced me. This was all your idea—"

JOHNNY PERENNIAL: "I said get out. I expect you at work by seven o'clock sharp on Monday. Goodbye."

"Okay, let's stop there for today," Jake said. "Feedback?"

"It's pretty goofy," Vera said, "I think you need to be more serious sooner if you don't want everyone to think it's a slapstick."

"I mean, yes, it starts out in a light-hearted way, but then the subject matter sort of sneaks up on you." Jake said, stung.

"Maybe you two could workshop it together," Serena suggested, "since Vera has some ideas and time is short. You need this baby up and running. Soon."

"That's not a bad idea," Jake said. "If you're game, Vera?"

"Sure, Jake, I've got a couple of hours. Besides, we all need this to be a success."

From across the table Jake searched her face for signs of sarcasm or cruelty. *What was that expression she was making? Generosity melting into seriousness, dissolving into compassion?*

All at once chairs slid out and everyone gathered up their coats and belongings. Jake panicked, feeling he was losing the room.

"Great. I mean, not that my screenplay isn't remarkable, but maybe I've been too close to it and I could use some perspective. This is going to be a huge hit, everyone! I'll be in touch. We'll schedule another read-through next week. Vera, let's meet at the Dolly Shot in an hour. Is that good for you?"

"Okay, see you there," Vera said.

Jake watched her leaving in a purple coat, stuffing her shiny black hair under an adorable knit cap with animal ears on top.

"I can't lose her," Jake said quietly.

Naomi and Serena walked up, patting him on the back.

"You've got a really good chance at The Dolly Shot," Naomi said.

"Yeah, you're a good talker, Jake," Serena added. "Go get her, mister."

~

With her status restored as "a star," Vera cruised in the back seat of Barry's limo. She wanted to go home to get something painful out of the way before she met with Jake.

"What a ridiculous screenplay," Vera tittered to herself, and shook her head. *What makes a died-in-the-wool horror writer think he can pen a romance film? Listen to me, such an expert on scriptwriting. All I can really do is scream well. Like a victim—the thing Zaydeh warned me never to become.*

The limo cruised up into Zissell's cracked but well swept driveway. Vera went inside and made her way down the hall and into her bedroom where she closed the door behind her and let out a huff. She gazed around her at the Mandys, their stuffed feet, the flowers in their hair, the red and pink frilly outfits, her only solace throughout the years when nothing had gone her way. "Mandy, Mandy—all of you wonderful Mandys, we've had good times together. I want to thank all of you for your help and all the nights I cried into your blouses. You got me through it. But now, it's time I move on to adulthood," Vera said, stifling a tear. "I'll find you all good homes with someone who will love you."

Vera carefully placed each Mandy Mouse into a box and taped the lid closed. "I'll find you each homes where you'll be loved."

Chapter 30

Reality Check

Vera was already seated as Jake entered The Dolly Shot. She saw him and raised her hand with a non-enthusiastic wave.

It's a start, Jake thought.

"Hi, thanks for coming," he said, sitting and handing Vera a copy of the script. "So, you have some ideas? I thought maybe the pace was a little quick out of the gate—"

"Jake, stop, stop. It's really, really bad."

"Which part? It's meant to have a comedic tone but that's just to offset the heavy sadness of the situation—you know, like in *Life Is Beautiful?*"

"No, I'm sorry, Jake, but it's plain goofy and no one will take it seriously."

"It made Naomi and my therapist—who are women, by the way—both cry when they read it. It works once you get into it."

"Naomi has been emotional ever since coming out of rehab—she cries at those dog commercials on TV—and I can't account for your therapist. Maybe your script does get better later. If it does, I'd recommend getting to the good stuff sooner before you lose your audience. Wait a minute—therapist? Why do you have a therapist?"

The waitress appeared.

"I'll have a cup of coffee and the chicken salad," Jake said. "Vera?"

"I'll have chamomile tea and the chicken salad."

"I know it's bad form," the waitress said, "but can I get an autograph, Ms. Horowitz?"

"Of course," Vera said, signing a napkin and handing it to the girl.

The waitress smiled and disappeared.

"Now why are you seeing a therapist?" Vera asked again.

"I tried to tell you when you drove out of my life," Jake stuttered, looking uncomfortable.

"Tell me what?" Vera leaned in.

"That—that I thought my thinking toward women had become warped from all the years of making these movies."

"Go on."

"I'd objectified them in my mind. When I looked at them I only saw them as victims—dehumanized them." He realized he had bowed his head, and looked up at Vera to gage her reaction: *attentive.* "And I didn't want to be that way. The problem was I wasn't aware of it because it happened slowly over time—the way you can slowly boil a lobster to death if you raise the temperature gradually."

"Gross. So, what else?" Vera said, resting her elbows on the table, resting her pretty face in her small, perfect hands.

"I wanted to change for you, Vera. I worked really hard in therapy, that's why I quit attending the slaughter scene shoots—to get my mind re-channeled to normal, healthy thinking."

"That's why you didn't see Serena's scene when she was attacked by Alex? That's why you weren't at my scenes?"

"Yes, and my therapist had just pronounced me cured, as long as I monitor myself, when you found that old movie mag featuring *Meathooks Some Liberties with the Lady.*"

"*Meat Hooks* for short, right? Disgusting," Vera said.

"I agree. But it got me my start in filmmaking and provided me with a career. The point is, I'm not a sicko, Vera, and I'm still crazy about you. My contract with Barry is over with and this is the new me."

"Well, I like that you're not sick. And—" Vera leaned over and gave Jake a peck on the cheek, "I like that you're still crazy about me, but your script still sucks. What kind of girlfriend would I be if I didn't help you fix it?" She followed that up with a coy smile and a wink.

How damned sexy is that? Jake thought. Warmth flooded into his body. He felt himself smiling back at her. What kind of smile am I smiling? Sadness melting into relief dissolving into joy? Got to stop improvising script!

"I'm so happy, Vera. I feel like I can breathe again!"

~

Doctor Alvarez stood next to Lola's bed. She had been asleep, but she'd heard him and opened her stubby eyelashes, gazed at him with small muddy-grey eyes, set in a pock-marked face.

"I'm sorry to startle you, but I have good news. Your broken arm has healed, so that cast can come off, and the wires can come off your jaws. Let's free your jaws first so we may talk."

Thumbs up.

"Are you ready, Miss Grub?"

Thumbs up.

The doctor snapped on his latex gloves and approached Lola with the surgical pliers. After the wires were removed Lola tried to open her aching jaws, but could barely move them.

"Do not rush it. Your jaw muscles have atrophied. Take your time."

Lola tapped out a text message on her phone and handed it to the doctor.

"You want a toothbrush and toothpaste. Of course, after such a long wait. I'll have the nurse bring them to you. Then we can discuss your options."

The doctor returned to his office where his surgical assistant awaited him.

"Well?" the assistant said.

"Lola Grubb wants to look like Rachel McAdams. That's her number one choice. Of course, she would want to look like her: beautiful, symmetrical features, high cheek bones, flawless smile, radiant skin. The only problem is I see no path from the way Miss Grub looks to the appearance of Miss McAdams."

"But why not?"

"There are too many obstacles: from her tiny buck teeth set crookedly in huge gums, her small eyes too close together and off center, to her non-existent chin; ears without lobes, domed forehead covered with a low hairline closing in on her unibrow, pock-marked, mole-covered face; short, very upturned nose with huge nostrils—"

"Doctor, what do you always tell me? We start with what we can fix. Structure first."

"Yes, you are right. We must back all the way up to her cranial asymmetry. Her orbital sockets can be separated—widened. Of course, her deviated septum is something we can align. A chin implant would certainly help. That low hairline—we can remove and relocate that hair and do a skin graft—give her a forehead. And dental implants with larger, straighter, whiter veneers. The stringy, greasy hair: implants and a regimen of collagen, laser out those moles with the ingrown hairs."

"Yes! You're the *best*, that's why I fought to work with you, Doctor Alvarez."

"Thank you, my friend. Now the only questions are: Does she have the financial resources to afford a year's worth of surgeries, and can she mentally endure a year of near constant procedures?"

"We shall see," said the assistant.

~

Dark Snout re-read the text he'd gotten from Jake L'Hommedieu. A new assignment, not nearly as challenging as the first. Locate a missing person: female, age twenty-three, a Miss Lola Grubb. Occupation: horror film actress. Last known location room 204 Malibu Memorial Hospital, admitted for facial trauma. Jake had texted him a photograph of the unfortunate soul.

Having accepted the contract, he'd gone straight into action—he hated to waste a client's money. He'd gotten his contact to supply him with a hospital security officer's uniform, then strolled into hospital room 204 and confidently removed the camera monitor disk. He took it to one of the staff rooms and inserted it into a computer tower: the dates were only current. The old disk had apparently been replaced.

He went to the lobby and inquired at the check-in desk. The official on duty said the police had confiscated the disk last week and were scheduled to return it today after 1:00 P.M. Dark Snout checked his cell: 11:45. He decided to grab a bite at the hospital cafeteria.

While in the a la carte line, a nurse tried to pick him up. He declined and went to sit by himself at a private table where he called Rhonda.

"Snouty! I love it when you call me during the day. What's going on, honeybunch?"

"Just grabbing some lunch. I was thinking, how would you like to take a vacation when I finish this case? We could tour Cuba while it's still possible."

"I would love that. I haven't been on vacation since I was ten years old and

Daddy took us to see Mount Rushmore. When do you think you'll be finished?"

"A week or two."

"Could we go in three weeks? I've got a cage fight with Damnation Darla in two weeks."

"Sure, Rhonda, just don't get too banged up. I want you looking good on the beach."

Dark Snout took the elevator to the lobby. The disk had been returned. He used his fake credentials to check it out. He drove to the warehouse he rented as a home base and slid the disk into his computer. The digital display was highly pixelated, and he saw what the police had seen. A large orderly had rolled a gurney into Miss Grub's room at 1:34 A.M., lifted her onto the gurney as if she weighed nothing, and transferred her I.V. rack to the stainless-steel rod affixed to the back. He then wheeled her out the door. *Why had no one at the nurses' station stopped him? Why only one orderly? There are usually two to move a patient.*

Dark Snout moved the mouse, backed up, zoomed in, refined, again, until he focused on the facial quadrant. The man had blue eyes; he was bearded under the mask and was quite muscular. As the man pushed the gurney past a laminated anatomical poster on the wall, the top of his head aligned with the top edge of the poster.

Back at the hospital he took the elevator to room 204 where he pulled out a measuring tape. From floor to the top of the poster was six-foot-three inches. This was a big man, muscular, bearded, blue-eyed. He'd be hard to miss around here. But how smart was he? Did he do this for a living? He looked quite at ease in his movements, like he had transported patients a thousand times before. It wouldn't be hard to find him if he worked at this hospital.

Dark Snout texted his contact. This time he needed an ambulance driver's uniform and license. He checked his cell. His billable hours were reasonable so far, the fee only totaled $2,300.00. Still doing right by his client.

Chapter 31

SoCal Stray

Benny sat at a table across from Barry in his trailer discussing murder over a bottle of scotch.

"You want to set a date for this thing before your nephew gets cold feet and backs out?"

"He's on the verge of frostbite now. But he's not going anywhere. Falchion Films is the only life he's ever known."

"Between you pumping him up on his being an 'apex predator' and my discouraging him from making friends because they'd interfere with his acting, I think we're in the clear."

"Let's call it Thursday night," Barry said. He knocked back the rest of his scotch, then leaned forward and refreshed Benny's glass.

"Hmm, three days from now, that's good. We need a couple things from the hardware store, though. First off, a length of strong rope to tie Vera up. I want her tied tight and permanently, so she can't fight back," Benny simulated pulling invisible rope ends tautly. Barry nodded, his face red and on the way to purple from too much alcohol.

"Let's go. I want everything perfect so there are no slip ups," Benny said.

Barry drained his glass and smacked it on the tabletop.

~

The limo arrived at "Hella Hardware" which sat next to an upscale women's makeup and clothing boutique called "Bellisima." Benny and Barry stepped out, wasted and wobbly. They waved off the driver's offer to help them and made their way to the shop. Benny grimaced at the jingling overhead bell as he opened the door.

"Where do you keep the rope?" Benny barked at the cashier.

"Down aisle 7B, next to chains and wire."

Benny waved with a snarl and staggered down the aisle. Barry followed, bumping a display, knocking boxes of lightbulbs onto the floor.

"Careful, fatso," Benny scolded.

"Shut up," Barry managed, low on air and taking on that red-faced basset hound look.

To their left were several large spools of chain, rope and wire. Next to them was a station equipped with appropriate cutting tools for each and a measuring tape.

"Look, you can measure off how much you want and cut it," Barry said.

"Brilliant!" Benny shot back. "Here's what we need." Benny pulled off several feet of white, braided quarter-inch nylon rope. "She won't get out of this."

"Good, good," Barry said, then backed into a rack of hanging shovels, causing them to clang loudly against each other.

"You really can't handle your booze, can you? Go wait in the limo while I pay for this."

Barry muttered and trudged back down the aisle, bumping into shelves as he went, knocking dozens of items onto the floor. Outside, he took in a deep breath as he fell slightly backward, resting his bulk on the brick wall behind him, his heart banging against his ribcage. An attractive, plus-sized woman emerged from the boutique, carrying large, pink wrapped boxes, her three-year-old daughter in tow. Barry was surprised as she approached him.

"Excuse me, sir. Would you mind keeping an eye on my daughter for just a second while I put these boxes in my trunk—just so she doesn't wander into traffic?"

"Sure, babe," Barry said. He watched as she walked several yards away and popped the trunk lid open with her remote key fob.

"You have funny red hair," the little girl said.

She stared up at him with big green eyes as Barry leaned down and whispered in her ear.

"You're gonna be fat one day like your mommy." Barry stood, pleased with his remark.

"'Top it!" the girl said sternly, stomping her foot for emphasis.

"Big and fat," Barry said.

"'Top it!" she said.

"You 'top it,'" Barry retorted, smiling and exhaling scotch fumes.

"'Top it," the girl said, louder.

"Barry!" a woman's voice scolded.

Barry looked up, startled to see Shelley coming out the boutique doorway, strutting toward him, an umbrella above her to shield her skin.

"Leave that child alone," Shelley said.

While Barry was distracted, the girl kicked him in the shin with her hard, little shoe.

"Ouch, dammit! She started it," Barry said, leaning against the wall, holding his shin.

The woman returned from her car.

"Thank you," she said, took her daughter by the hand, and led her away.

"What's the matter with you?" Shelley said.

"Nothin', just jokin' around with the kid."

Benny had witnessed the exchange and shook his head. He grabbed Barry by the upper arm and pulled him toward the limo. Inside, Barry and Benny were pressed back into the cushioned seat as the powerful engine surged forward.

"You're becoming a liability, Barry. Picking on a little girl in public? Are you crazy?"

"She's gonna be a woman one day, ain't she?" Barry slurred. "You do not tell me how to act. I decided to include *you* in my project and don't forget it."

~

Alex Boxwell wandered into The Dolly Shot and sat at the bar. He ordered a mug of beer and sipped it because that's what he always did when he had no plan. He'd had no plan ever since his dad left them when he was just a boy. His mom had fallen apart after that and began her descent into the drug addiction that eventually killed her.

I was so scrawny, Alex recalled, *before I started lifting weights. As my muscles grew so did my confidence. How stupid I was to watch Sly Stallone and Jason Statham movies and imagine I was tough like them. That night, that stupid night, when I entered that downtown bar, got drunk and picked a fight with someone who actually was tough, the guy broke my nose.* A constant visual reminder. *I should have just drunk here at the Dolly Shot on the Falchion lot.*

Barry had told him the nose made him look rugged, and cast him as villains in his films. Alex made more money than he'd ever imagined. Barry suggested he stick to The Dolly Shot where his own people hung out, mostly actors and staff from Falchion Films. But everyone knew Barry was his uncle and Alex had beaten up Serena. So, Alex remained a loner.

He closed his eyes and held his two palms upward, each resting on a knee. He raised his left hand and quietly said:

"A million bucks and I have to kill a person—" He raised his right hand, "—or get out of town, stay poor and look over my shoulder the rest of my life for two guys trying to kill me."

"Hey, you okay, dude?" called an unfamiliar voice from behind the bar.

It wasn't the old man who'd tended bar there forever. The stranger, over six feet tall, tanned, healthy, high-energy, dazzling smile, half his blonde head shaved, the other half long, approached Alex from the kitchen.

"You must be the new bartender. I heard there was a new guy," Alex said, "Yeah, I was just trying to decide something."

"Like what to have for lunch? I have one word for you: tuna-melt. The way the chef makes it it's killer! My name's Pete by the way. What's yours?" He deftly switched his bar towel to his left hand and extended his right across the counter.

Alex took it and shook it. "I'm Alex, and yeah, the tuna-melt sounds good."

"Awesome! And I make a really solid drink to go with that, brau. My own creation, I call it a 'mind-eraser.' Just don't have one if you're about to take your PSAT test, right?"

"Yeah, sure. I'll have one of those, too."

Alex stared at the big screen behind the bar where the Miami Heat was beating the L.A. Lakers in the fourth quarter. He sipped his beer as Pete returned from the kitchen galley. Pete busied himself washing beer mugs in the sink as an eruption of male voices blasted in the doorway behind them.

"There he is. We just came back from Zuma Beach. There was a sig alert and traffic on the 101 was insane, but we heard you worked here and we had to find you, Pete!" the surfer said.

“Pee-eete, hook us up, bro!” the second equally tan surfer said, his blonde hair seeming to float around his head.

Pete smiled, stepped around the bar, gave the men hugs and handshakes, and messed up the frizzy-haired guy’s hair even more.

“Dudes, I want you to meet my new bud, Alex. Alex, this is Otto the Otter and Sammy the Seal.”

Alex shook their hands.

“Tequilla shots?” Pete asked.

“Affirmative,” said Sammy.

Otto and Sammy sat on either side of Alex on bar stools.

“I can move over one if you want to sit by your friend,” Alex offered, slightly unnerved.

“No, I see too much of this dude,” Otto said. “Spend all my time floating on a board next to him out at Malibu. I’d rather meet somebody new. Tell us about yourself, Alex.”

Otto took Alex by the shoulder and gave him a reassuring shake. Alex wasn’t used to anyone’s touching him.

“I’m an actor at Falchion Films. We make horror movies.”

“No way! That pisses me off. I came to L.A. to act but I washed out, ended up chasing waves and working at a skate shop. What’s acting like?”

“It’s not like I’m a great actor. My uncle’s kind of a horror legend, Barry Whitscomb.”

“No freakin’ way. You’re like Hollywood royalty then.”

Pete returned with the shots. “He came in here looking kind of blue. I was all like, no way, not in my bar. Here, Al, have a shot on the house.”

Pete slid three shot glasses onto the bar in front of them. They clinked glasses and tossed the shots back.

“Pete told you our nicknames so here’s his. This is Pukashell Pete. I’ve never seen this dude without a puka shell necklace on,” Otto said, and pulled back Pete’s collar as proof.

“Guilty as charged. Hey, Al, you should come surfing with us tomorrow. We’ll show you how it’s done,” Pete said, patting Alex on the back.

Alex didn’t jump this time. “Thanks, but I can’t. I have a shoot tomorrow. Besides, I’ve never been surfing.”

“Why don’t you play hooky?” Sammy said. “I mean, you are looking at three of the most gnarly surfers you’re ever gonna meet. We’ll show you all you need to know. I mean, I only placed at Mavericks. Limited time offer—tick—tick—tick—”

“I’ve only really been to the beach once in my life when I was a kid. I’ve never even ridden a skateboard.”

Both men grabbed Alex and semi-wrestled him at the bar.

“Rahhh!” Otto yelled.

“We insist. I mean, common decency prohibits you not coming with us, Al.

Skip school, have some fun. We do want something in return, of course."

"What do you want in return?"

"You are a big, buff dude," Otto said." After a day in the surf we have a bonfire. We need you to stand around the fire all hulk-like and draw the ladies in for us. You'd be kind of rare around Topanga Beach. The swells are a little easier to drop into for a beginner."

The tuna melt arrived—toasted tangy aroma, crisp pickle on the side.

"Here you go, Alex. What do you think?" Pete asked, watching for Alex's reaction.

When Alex smiled Pete jumped closer to Alex like he was jumping on a board.

"Ja!" Pete said, laughing, "It's crazy good. I want you to take a big L.A. bite out of that."

Alex took a bite: steaming tuna, near-molten cheddar on his tongue. Delicious.

"Kick ass, ja?" Pete said. "Now pound me out one, brau,"

Pete and Alex pounded fists.

"Here's your 'mind eraser.'"

Alex took a sip: fruity, laced with lots of alcohol.

"That's really good, man," Alex said.

"Now commit. Say you're coming surfing with us tomorrow," Sammy said.

"Say it, c'mon, dude," Otto said, "You'll love it."

Alex looked dubious. It had been years since anyone had been friendly toward him. The three goofy surfers smiled unabashedly at him.

"Okay, I'll go," Alex said, smiling.

"Alright! Best move you could've made," Pete said.

His surfer buddies unloaded a hail of play punches all over Alex's body.

"Hey, whoa!" Alex yelled, but he'd never felt such acceptance.

Chapter 32

Alex is Absent

It was Tuesday morning. Vera called Aaron's phone but had gotten no answer. *Where's my protection?* She rode in the limo, still crunching a bagel and sipping hot tea. Her phone buzzed.

"Aaron, why didn't you pick up?"

"Sorry, I was talking with a buddy on the force. What's up?"

"You're in no position to be smug, mister. Look for my call and pick up when you see it's me. I can still mess up your promotion, you know?"

"Alright already. So, I assume you have a shoot?"

"Yes, meet me at Falchion Films at the staff parking lot, outside the chain-link fence, at 6:45A.M. and I'll walk you into the studio. Oh, and wear your uniform."

"Okay, see you there."

It was a quick ride to Falchion. Since the driver made this drive several times daily he knew which short cuts to take and when. Vera finished the last bite of her bagel and stepped outside. She could already see Aaron on the other side of the fence in his blue uniform. *Oy vey. If I wasn't so repulsed by his personality, or his sexual predator tendencies, I'd think him handsome.*

"Hi," Aaron said.

"Don't you 'hi' me. Why did you tell Shelley I'm a virgin?" Vera paced up to him, all five-foot-nothing of her, and shoved him with all she could muster.

"I don't know, I just—I couldn't believe—I mean, I was so surprised—not that you don't look like you could be—"

"Never mind. Come on," Vera said, and led the way.

A stagehand held the door for a second as he entered. Aaron shot out his arm and caught the door for Vera to enter. Inside, Vera was immediately drawn to Barry's magnificent auburn head of hair which shimmered in the light. She glanced at the two three-sided stages, set up side-by-side. The first stage: a perpetually wet, city street with boarded up tenement windows, overflowing dented trash cans, what Vera knew to be an ever-present poseable, passed out wino dummy, and of course the mildew-covered, refrigerated ice cream tricycle, a front to sell harvested, chilled human organs on the black market. The second set: a small operating room surrounded by counters filled with clear drawers containing cotton balls, gleaming operating instruments, paper masks and latex gloves; and an operating table in the center. This second set was new to Vera, although she had read about it in her copy of the script and she knew her lines.

They were like her lines in the other terrible movies. After she was lured into the operating room for an appointment with her doctor (who had been paid off by Alex's character, The Organ Pedaler, to disappear after letting Vera in), she was to try to reopen the door which had been closed and mysteriously locked from the outside. She was now locked inside the room with the Organ Pedaler. She was to wait a beat, turn around, eyes wide, face Alex's character, and let go with her million-dollar scream. (Wrestle, wrestle) pretend she couldn't get away (in real life she felt she'd have already maced him and kicked the bastard in the balls). Then, overpowered, she was to be tied up (another shriek) and then have her heart cut out. *Whatever.*

Barry noticed Vera and walked over. "Hello, young lady. It's so good to have you back on the set. We missed you."

"Thanks, Barry," Vera said.

Barry looked Aaron over. "I see you brought your friend with you. Welcome, Officer."

"Thanks," Aaron said.

"So, what's on the schedule for today?" Vera asked.

"Let me check with Felix. That's his department," Barry said.

Vera watched Barry go, his beautiful hair bouncing in waves as he went. *I don't love Barry, but I sure love his hair,* Vera thought.

Suddenly, she saw Barry's posture stiffen and heard him bellow at Felix.

"Whaddya' mean he's not here? Get him here now!"

When Felix re-entered and held up his empty hands, it was apparent to everyone that Alex was missing. She watched as Barry conferred with Benny. They spoke in intense, low tones. Benny walked away quickly and exited through the door to the parking lot. Seeing he was on his own, Barry thrust both arms skyward to summon the crowd's attention.

"Okay, everybody, it looks like Alex won't be here today. So, what we're gonna do is have a dress rehearsal *anyway.* Full costumes. I'll stand in for Alex. Felix, we're doin' the operating scene in fifteen minutes. Go!"

Aaron relaxed in one of the folding auditorium seats and watched the chaotic scene unfold. Everyone scrambled in different directions: some to makeup: some to fiddle with the lights, the sound, the cameras: others cleared clutter from the stage. In a few minutes Vera returned from the makeup trailer wearing hip-hugger jeans and a tight yellow tube top, her hair pulled back in pigtails.

"Really?" Vera yelled to Felix. "This is my outfit? Am I supposed to look fifteen?"

"Oh, are you in charge of costumes now, Vera? Just find your mark," Felix snapped.

Everyone became quiet. The actors found their marks as Felix strutted out to center stage.

"Scene sixteen, Virgin Sacrifice, take one!" Felix yelled, snapped the clapperboard together and back-pedaled off stage.

The cameras rolled as there was a knock at the door.

"Yes?" said the doctor, opening it.

"I'm here for my two o'clock appointment," Vera said, in a small, shy voice.

"Yes, come in," the doctor said, swinging the door open, concealing Barry behind it. "I've got to go check on something. I'll be right back," the doctor said, then pulled the door closed behind him. An audible clicking and locking sound came from the other side of the door. After it closed, Vera turned to see Barry.

"W-What? Who are you?" she said, then turned and shook the doorknob violently with both hands as Barry laughed, menacingly.

Barry grabbed her from behind, carried her to the operating table, and tied her wrists behind her back. She appeared terrified and let go with her first scream. Barry looped the rope under the table and pulled so Vera was sprawled across the table face up. He then wrapped the other end of the rope around her ankles and cinched it tightly, so Vera was completely vulnerable. Barry then pulled out a silver spray-painted rubber scalpel and pretended to cut Vera's heart out. She shrieked again, then let her eyes roll back in her head as she pretended to pass out.

For effect, Barry pulled a red scarf meant to simulate Vera's heart from his jacket pocket and held it up for the camera to film, like it was the holy grail.

"Cut! That's a wrap, great take," Felix yelled, as Barry walked off stage.

"Hey!" Vera yelled, "do you have to tie me up so tight? It's cutting off the circulation."

"We're going for realism, sweetheart," Barry said, "They need to be tight for the scene."

"Since when is this scene called 'Virgin Sacrifice'?" Vera yelled after him.

"Since I decided it would. I thought it would play better," Barry said, and left.

"We're the only ones who will see it! Aaron, get up here and untie me!" Vera yelled.

~

Barry climbed into his limo and called Benny. He picked up on the first ring.

"Where are you, man?" Barry asked.

"I'm just leaving The Dolly Shot. One of the extras said he saw Alex chumming it up with the new bartender. So, I rifled through the personnel files and found out his name, address, etcetera, and that it's his day off. We need to pay him a visit. Stay there. I'll come get you."

Five minutes later, Benny slid into the parking lot, tires squealing to a stop, a few feet from Barry's legs.

"Get in!" he yelled.

As soon as Barry closed the door they peeled out.

"I called his number and got his girlfriend," Benny yelled over the raging engine. "She said I could find him and his friends at Topanga Beach, surfing."

Benny entered the beach name into his GPS.

"There's his house," Benny said, as they cruised by, "GPS says the beach is down the street."

He drove into an asphalt parking lot, which was mostly covered with windblown sand, and parked in a space nearest the beach. They stepped out of the limo. Benny pulled a floppy island hat onto his head and pulled out a pair of binoculars.

He could see three surfers about a hundred yards away, lying down on their boards on dry sand, all demonstrating to Alex how to spring up from a prone position and pop up into a crouched standing position on the board. Alex tried, lost his balance and fell over in the sand.

"Your nephew's a clod," Benny said. "We have to get him away from those surfers and get him back on the set."

"How long do you think they're going to stay out there?" Barry asked.

"I don't know. Let's wait a while longer."

"Why can't we let the surfers see us?"

"Because you're too stupid for me to even answer that." Benny pulled off his floppy hat, swatted Barry, then put it back on. "I'll explain it later,"

~

The surfers picked Alex up and put him back on his board. This time he managed to stand up. They clapped him on the back and high-fived him. Then they picked up their boards and got Alex to carry his much larger and wider beginner's board toward the water. They paddled out, crashing through the first set of waves and out deeper, where there were only swells. They all straddled their boards while their legs dangled below them in the water. They rose and fell like buoys in the mammoth, green swells, and it became very quiet—just their voices and the distant crashing surf.

"Hey, you guys? Aren't you afraid of sharks out here?" Alex asked.

"Naah, dude," Otto said. "They don't want us. Sharks need a grippe of calories. Their favorite food are big, fat seals. I mean, the dudes in the gray suits are here, right? Oh yeah. There's probably already been four or five of them cruising around us. But, dude, they can see us. They see that we're just scrawny, bony surfers and they're like, crazy hungry. They don't want to eat *us*."

"But it happens sometimes, right?" Alex asked.

"Just make sure you're not bleeding or acting all spastic in the water like you're injured—you know, like a victim—and those dudes will give you your space," Pete said.

"Okay, if you're sure."

"We've been surfing here for years and nothing like that's happened," Pete said.

"There was that *one* time," Sammy said, "like thirteen years ago. This one dude got wasted and he was wrestling everybody around the bonfire, then he cut his foot on a beer bottle, then he decided to go for a midnight swim and—"

"That's totally bogus, Sammy," Pete said. "Inapropros example. That dude did, like *everything* wrong. Forget you heard that, Al. Just chill. It's hella fun out here and there's not going to be any problem. If we respect them, they respect us," Pete said.

"They *are* going to be out there for a while. Let's go get some lunch and come back," Benny said. He and Barry got into the car and drove.

~

Jake L'Hommedieu arrived exactly at his appointed meeting time with his therapist. He knocked twice, and the door opened.

"Jake, come in. Have a seat," Thelma said.

Jake sat as she closed the door. *Same routine, he thought. Her legs crossed, pen and pad at the ready, leaning forward earnestly peering at me through her cat glasses. I wonder if she really cares?*

"So, what would you like to talk about?" Thelma asked.

"Things have changed yet again, since I spoke with you. Two women talked with Vera on my behalf. Then I met with her and I was able to tell her my side of the story and we patched things up. We're back together again."

"That's excellent news," Thelma said, smiling and sitting upright. "How is your relationship working out?"

"Great. Actually, not great. She thinks my screenplay is no good. She says nobody likes it, and I wonder why you said it was so wonderful? You cried, you said it was so good."

"I was really reacting from a therapist's point of view. Yours was the most rapid and thorough rehabilitation of a chronically misogynistic-adrenaline-addict disorder I had ever witnessed. The fact that you were able to write *any* screenplay that didn't have as its premise the extreme degradation of women, and which involved empathy, redemption and finally portraying that same woman as someone who overcomes obstacles and becomes healthy and thriving at the end, was nothing short of miraculous."

"But what about the screenplay itself? Did you like it?" Jake asked, forehead wrinkling.

"I don't think my opinion of your screenplay is really pertinent. Tell me about your relationship with Vera."

"No, I want your honest opinion of my screenplay. That's *all* I want to talk about."

"I didn't think it was very good. But it was your first attempt at writing a romantic drama. And you said you'd been working on it for five years. That means you were writing it in the middle of your addiction cycle. Even with the much-improved revised draft you still had the original to work from. I'm sure that influenced the final product."

"What am I supposed to do now? I've severed my ties to Falchion Films, not that I wanted to work there anyway, but I've promised a lot of actors this was going to be a big hit. Vera's offered to help me fix it—but what does she know about screenplays? Her previous experience was as a bad waitress."

"You may be surprised. As a woman she is probably in touch with a different spectrum of emotions than you. Why don't you give her a try? Collaborating may net you a better screenplay with the bonus of deepening your relationship."

"I work alone. I've always written alone."

"You've made so many changes through therapy and they've all helped you. I encourage you to trust Vera. She's offered to help you. You wanted a relationship with her. Trust is a big part of that."

"I'll think about it."

"Now, tell me about your relationship with your mother now that you're speaking again."

Oh, wow! I just remembered. I owe her. She helped me get Vera back. I need to talk with her. I promised her I'd start coming to Thanksgiving and Christmas every year."

"Good. Well, I see our time is almost up. Let's schedule another appointment."

~

Dark Snout's efforts to locate Ms. Lola Grubb were well underway, but he had to pick the optimal angle of approach. Would he impersonate a gurney jockey or some other hospital worker, hang out in the hallways and hope for a scoop (the shotgun approach)? Or impersonate an E.M.T. and focus his efforts on one person, his ambulance partner, in hopes he or she would have the right connections (the rifle approach)?

After five hours of surveillance and hacking Malibu Memorial's personnel server, he decided on impersonating an E.M.T. for the private company which serviced Malibu's ambulance needs: R.A.M.P. or Reserve Ambulance Maintenance and Personnel. He located five paramedics who had an open shift, that is, they were for one reason or another driving solo and only showed up on the scene of an emergency as back up.

Of the five, the one with the highest probable social connections to senior hospital staff as well as R.A.M.P. employees, was one Scott Brinker. Scott was a ten-year employee, the president of the labor union, and the one who organized all the company picnics and team sports activities. According to R.A.M.P.'s Facebook account, Scott was quite popular. If he didn't know a bit of insider gossip, Dark Snout would hang up his sleuthing hat and retire.

Dark Snout had no qualms about putting anyone's life in danger should he need to perform in an actual emergency because he had been a superb field medic in the war in Afghanistan, the one the government called "Operation Enduring Freedom."

Per usual, his contact had expertly fitted his E.M.T. uniform. His credentials were perfect: his state E.M.T. card with his photo and name listed and his certificate stating he had passed the national registry test had been sent over electronically both to R.A.M.P. and Malibu Memorial. The only problem was that the daily pairing up of ambulance partners was a moving target and he *had* to be partnered up with Scott Brinker.

By hacking into R.A.M.P.'s digital dispatcher archives, he found the form he wanted: Personnel Change Order form. He downloaded a recent copy and printed it out. He pulled it from his printer and read it closely. It was signed by the Director of Personnel, Henry Tabbs. Perfect. Now all he needed was a couple of actual forms to practice on. He drove to R.A.M.P. while wearing jeans, sandals, a ripped t-shirt and a fake mustache, and brazenly walked down the hallway until he came to a sign that read "Dispatching."

Dark Snout entered and saw two men with their backs to him, both staring at computer monitors. He didn't speak, just took the chance and looked the gunmetal shelving unit over. It was lined with steel trays filled with various triplicate carbon forms. *Old school, I love it!* he thought. He saw the forms he wanted and was about to take a few when one of the men stretched and swiveled around in his chair and saw him.

"Uh, what are you doing in here?" the man asked.

"I was about to ask if you knew where the vending machines are? I've walked, like, five miles and I'm starving."

"Down the hall to your left. It says Break Room," the man said, and faced his computer.

"Thanks," Dark Snout said, and deftly grabbed three Change Order forms on the way out.

He sat in his car, pulled out a notebook and laid one form onto it, and, with the printed copy on his knee, he tried his hand at forging Henry Tabb's signature. He then filled in the rest in the same hand: Simon Anderson, his fake E.M.T. name. "Simon Anderson, E.M.T., partnering with Scott Brinker, paramedic, in unit #13 for the week of May 5th, 2015. Director of Personnel, Henry Tabbs."

Not bad, but I can do better, he thought. He repeated the forgeries two more times, then picked the best one and returned to Dispatching. He stepped inside the door and cleared his throat. This time both men swiveled in their chairs.

"What do you want now?" asked the same man who'd spoken before.

"I found this. It looked kind of important, so I thought I'd bring it to—"

The man stood, crossed the floor and snatched the form from Dark Snout.

"Give me that. You're not supposed to have this. Where did you find this?"

"Look, I don't want any trouble, man, it just looked important, that's all. Bye," Dark Snout said, and he was gone.

He sprinted down the hallway and out into the sunny parking lot. He picked up the pace even more as he closed the space between himself and his car. He reached the door, not even out of breath, got inside and floored it. He took an abrupt left out of the parking lot because he knew his car would be obscured by the row of cars parallel parked there. He knew the man would input the change order data into his desktop without question—to not do so would reflect poorly on his ability to keep track of paperwork.

He checked the time: 10:00 A.M. Plenty of time to have lunch and change into his uniform because Brinker's shift didn't start until noon.

~

It was 11:55A.M. as Dark Snout strolled up to ambulance #13 where a burly older man with a white beard and handlebar mustache leaned against the cab, smoking a cigarette.

"Excuse me, I'm Simon Anderson. I've been assigned to work on this unit for the week." Dark Snout said. He produced his card and handed it to the man.

The man took it and examined it. "Hmm, Simon. Says you're an E.M.T., that still makes me the medical authority on this rig. The name's Scott." He extended his hand. They shook hands and returned his card.

"First thing I need you to do, probie, is clean the rig. Follow me."

Scott walked around the ambulance to the back. Dark Snout could already see blood oozing out the door and over the bumper.

"What happened?" he asked.

"Hit and run. Patient was D.O.A. and the crew had had a hell of a night; they were in no shape to clean the rig out. So, my man, I need you to sanitize everything." He opened the rear door and even more blood flowed over the rubber-coated floor and over the bumper. There was blood splattered onto the shelves, the sides of the interior, even the ceiling.

"Here is a respirator, long-sleeved chemical-resistant gloves, rubber boots, Tyvek suit to protect your uniform and—"

"I know, CaviCide, hardcore disinfectant. This isn't my first rodeo," Dark Snout said.

"Okaaay, I'm duly impressed. Let's see what kind of job you do cleaning. I've got to fill out this paperwork in the office and I'll be back in about twenty minutes."

Dark Snout pulled on the gear and found a squeegee with a three-foot handle and began pulling as much of the blood on the floor toward him as he could. He then found a pump sprayer and the CaviCide, filled it and pumped up the sprayer. He walked to the back of the rig, while wearing rubber boots, and began spraying down the walls, ceiling and cabinets with CaviCide, which sprayed out in a clear fan shape. Once he'd hosed everything down he began again to push the squeegee toward the open doorway. He then Stepped out and pumped up the sprayer again and disinfected the blood on the ground which was rapidly absorbing into the asphalt.

Everything looked much better, so he opened a box of white rags and scrubbed down every square inch of the interior of the rear of the ambulance until it was clean and white again. He stepped outside and looked at his work. There were still traces of blood here and there, which he climbed back in and cleaned.

Outside he hosed down the boots then pulled off the mask, gloves, boots and the Tyvek suit. He disposed of the mask and gloves in a three-millimeter-thick toxic waste bag along with the rags. *That was disgusting, but it was a small price to pay to get close to this guy,* he thought.

"Let's see how you did?" Scott Brinker said from behind him. "Wow! It looks like a brand-new van. Do you need to get cleaned up?"

"No, I was in the suit and gloves the whole time. I only need an antiseptic cloth for my face, just in case."

"Here ya go. I always keep them in this cabinet. You feel like driving? I mean, are you a good driver?"

Dark Snout almost had to laugh as he thought of all the evasive driving he had done under fire which had saved not only his life but his passengers on multiple occasions.

"Yes, I'm an excellent driver," he said.

"Now I'm worried, that sounds like a line from the movie *Rainman*."

"Trust me. It looks like we have some time to kill until our first call. Mind if I ask you a couple of questions?"

"Shoot."

"What's the security protocol like at this hospital—to protect patients in their rooms?"

"Why would you ask a question like that?"

"I have a confession. When my aunt heard I was going to get this position she asked me to ask that question. She has a daughter who was admitted for facial trauma, a Miss Lola Grubb. She was waiting to be cleared for plastic surgery when she went missing. She's been worried sick about her."

"No leads from the police?"

"They say they're still looking into it but that was a couple of weeks ago."

"Well, maybe she was going to be transferred to a hospital which specializes in facial surgery. Have you heard of—"

"Chrysalis? Yes, I've heard they're the best. So, you think maybe she's there?"

"No, but it's possible. If someone wanted to kidnap her, they may have intercepted an encrypted e-mail from the sending doctor, from Malibu Memorial to the receiving doctor at Chrysalis. Then showed up early to claim the body. If they did though the police should have them on video."

"Who could have access to encrypted e-mails between two doctors at different hospitals?"

"Anyone in the loop. E.M.T.s, dispatchers, other doctors, anesthesiologists, radiologists."

"So, you think maybe someone who works at R.A.M.P. may have transported her?"

"If they got the requisition form, sure. But it could also be a lot simpler. Either doctor could have mentioned it to a member of the nursing staff, or a colleague. You know the saying 'loose lips sink ships'?"

"I've heard it. I have another question. I have a cousin who feels like she had a moment with a big, bearded paramedic who works here, tall guy, six two or three. Anyway, she thinks they're soul mates and asked me to ask around."

"Sounds like Ken Adams. At our company basketball games he always gets picked first. He's on rig #18. They start their shift at midnight."

"Thanks. I'm sure my aunt and cousin will appreciate the info."

"Well, saddle up. Here's our first call. Sounds like a myocardial infarction. I'll navigate, you drive."

Scott shut the rear door and rounded the ambulance to the passenger's side.

~

Barry and Benny had been back to the Topanga Beach parking lot and stumbled out onto the dunes with their binoculars twice now, but the surfers and Alex were still out there.

"It's getting dark, Benny. I don't know how you think we're gonna get Alex without those surfers seeing us."

"You just have to be patient. Hey, fat man, they're coming out of the surf right now. Come on, let's get out of sight."

They scrambled back to Benny's car and backed up to the rear of the parking lot, away from the other cars.

~

"Hey, Alex, that wasn't too lame for your first time out," Otto said.

"I am so frickin' sore," Alex said. "I mean everywhere. My hips from pressing against the board, I've got a rash, a sunburn—"

"No worries, Al, it'll get better the more you surf. We're going to change and come back here at 8:00 for a bon fire," Sammy said. "I'll bring my guitar and Puca and Otter here can sing a little, they sound kind of like seals barking, but the ladies don't seem to mind."

Both Pete and Otto punched Sammy in each shoulder simultaneously.

"I'll see how I feel after a shower," Alex said. "I've got to deal with somebody about not showing up at the shoot today."

"Don't sweat it, dude, what's the worst they're going to do to you?" Sammy said.

The three surfers and Alex split up in the parking lot. Sammy, Otto and Pete walked toward their car, carrying all the boards while Alex walked toward the street to call a cab on his cell. Barry and Benny waited until the wood paneled station wagon pulled out of the parking lot to advance on Alex. Suddenly, Alex felt each of his upper arms grabbed and felt himself being turned around.

"Hey, what the hell?" Alex yelled.

"Where do you think you're going?" Benny said, marching Alex back toward his car.

"Why are you here?" Barry said, "You've never missed a shoot, you messed up today."

"I'm sorry, Uncle Barry, Benny, but I don't want to do the thing we talked about with Vera. You guys can have all the money and I'll take your secret to the grave."

"To the grave, Alex?" Benny said.

"Just let me have my life back. I like hanging out with these surfer guys—I feel like I can relax for the first time in years and just, I don't know, be myself. Or find out who I am."

"That's very touching, Alex," Benny said, "but we still need your face in the final scene where you kill Vera for *The Organ Pedaler* so we all get paid. We're doing it tonight."

"Yeah, okay, it's kind of late though," Alex said.

"Let me worry about that," Barry snapped, then picked up his cell phone and called Felix.

"Barry? Hello, is everything okay?" Felix asked.

"No, it certainly ain't. You can make up for losing Alex today by calling everyone to the set right now. We have Alex with us and we're shooting the virgin sacrifice scene tonight at 9:00P.M. The real deal, as many takes as it takes to finish. Got me?"

"Yes, sure, Barry. I'm on it," Felix said.

Felix called the entire staff and threatened everyone with being fired if they were not on the set in full make up in half an hour.

~

Everyone took Felix's call and showed up except a couple of temporary stagehands.

"What's this all about?" Vera said. "I was just getting ready for a date with Jake."

"Oh, boo hoo," Felix said. "The show must go on. Now go change!"

Vera called Aaron and he picked up on the first ring this time. He was sitting across the table from Shelley undressing her with his eyes, already on his second cocktail. Shelley suddenly picked up her phone while Aaron picked up his.

"Hello?" Aaron said.

"Aaron, we're shooting in just a few minutes. Get your ass in here," Vera said.

"I'm kind of busy," he said, but at that minute Shelley stood up and mouthed "Sorry" to him "got to go. Call you later." Shelley pretended to wipe away invisible tears while frowning.

"What?" Aaron said. "Oh, what the hell, Vera, I'll be right there." Then he yelled, "Waiter, check!"

~

Benny got Alex into his dirty organ pedaler outfit and shoved him toward the stage just as Shelley walked in the doorway.

"Shelley, we found our boy out catching rays," Barry said. "We need the organ pedaler looking pale and waxy for the final shoot, can you arrange that?"

"Sure thing, Barry. Alex, come with me, hon," Shelley said.

The stage lighting was adjusted, the camera positioned, the doctor was up on stage and sound was cued up as Vera took her position, just outside the door in the teeny bopper costume.

"Here's Alex," Barry said. "Now you look like the killer I envisioned."

Alex walked by Vera on the way through the doorway. "I just want to say I'm sorry about Serena, Vera. This is my last horror movie," he said.

Vera was so stunned she couldn't speak. Alex stood behind the door as the doctor closed it and waited for the clapperboard to snap.

~

After Alex wrenched the fake heart from the chest cavity of the fake Vera dummy, and after the little motor inside the fake heart had pumped enough fake blood, and after the camera man had filmed the dripping "blood" for a few seconds, and after the close up of Alex, maniacally laughing for the final shot, the clapperboard snapped shut for the last time.

Everyone shut down the equipment, cleaned up, and Aaron once again climbed up on stage to untie Vera.

"Would it kill you people to untie me once?" Vera yelled. "Do I really have to bring my own guy?"

"Okay, thanks, Aaron," Vera said, "You're free to go."

"I thought this would take a lot longer," Aaron said, "So, now I'm not indebted to you?"

"That's right. Go get your promotion and live your life. Goodbye," Vera said.

"But you're going to miss me a little, right?"

"I guess we can leave as friends, sure. Bye, Aaron."

Aaron saw Shelley watch him from across the room as he winked at Vera.

"Hey, Alex," Benny said, "why don't you join me and Barry for a drink?"

As Alex entered the men's room, Benny cornered Barry and hissed in his ear.

"We have to wax Alex tonight. He does not live another day with what he knows."

"I wish we didn't have to do that. I mean, the kid *is* my nephew."

"We're doing it. Too many people around right now," Benny said, "Watch that door while I get a cup of espresso from the machine in Shelley's office. I need to be alert for this."

Barry sat down as Aaron and Shelley walked up to him.

"You know, Mr. Whitscomb, that was really an interesting experience," Aaron said, "I think I'm going to go see this movie when it comes out."

"It's good for a nightmare or two," Barry said, "We make rather good horror movies."

Alex peeked out the men's room door, saw Barry engaged in conversation, no Benny. Alex quickly walked out the exit. He was going to call a cab, but saw the sound man just pulling out and ran across the parking lot to intercept him.

"It's me, Alex. I don't care where you're going but can you drive me a few blocks?"

"Sure, I guess, hop in," the sound man said.

Alex got in and checked the time on his cell as they drove through the gates, it was 10:44P.M. They drove a mile, pulled over and Alex got out. He hailed a cab and returned to Topanga Beach.

When Benny returned, hopped up on caffeine, he looked at Barry and got a funny feeling. On instinct he charged into the men's room and looked in every stall—empty. He ran out the door, up to Barry, who was alone. Benny grabbed him by his collar and wrenched it upward.

"You let him get away, bonehead! Now, come on. Let's go to his apartment."

~

The taxi dropped Alex off at Topanga Beach. He was alone in the cold, dark parking lot. He slowly turned in a circle. Suddenly, he spotted the bonfire 300 yards away, heard a distant guitar playing, saw people drinking, and dancing. He pulled off his socks and shoes and jogged toward the fire. Cold, dry sand gushed between his toes with every step. He approached the party from downwind, a warm breeze and a vortex of swirling sparks from the fire surrounded him. Friendly people at the party knew him and welcomed him. It all felt so right.

~

Barry and Benny checked Alex's apartment, then The Dolly Shot. No Alex.

"He's got to be back with those surfers," Benny said. "I don't trust him. We need him dead before he tells someone."

Benny checked the time. It was 1:30 A.M.

"He's probably not going to be out on the beach right now," Barry said.

"We have to check anyway," Benny said, and stomped the accelerator.

They reached the parking lot and saw the bonfire.

"Stay here," Benny said. "I'll see if he's one of the fools out there dancing."

Benny got out and, and crouching low, jogged over the dunes toward the fire. Once he got within 50 yards he pulled out his binoculars and saw Alex's face, lit up by firelight, deliriously drinking and dancing around the bonfire with a nubile, bikini-clad girl, her arm around him, dancing and laughing too.

"Crap!' Benny said to himself. Then turned and ran back to Barry.

"Well, how does it feel to be completely wrong, fat man? Alex is out there. We can't get him right now—too many people. They're just getting wound up. I know an all-night breakfast place where we can get some grub. I have a plan. I'll fill you in on the way."

~

They finished their meal and Benny checked his cell: 2:45 A.M. They drove back to the beach. Benny got out, ran into the sand, pulled out his binoculars and stared. There was nobody at the bonfire! Benny ran back, got inside the car and sat there, fuming in silence.

"What now?" Barry asked.

"Unless they come back down here I can only conclude they're all inside that bartender's house. I do not see a good outcome if we charge in there and kill all of them just to get to your stupid nephew. We may be screwed."

~

Barry and Benny had commiserated over a bottle of peppermint schnapps and by 4:00 A.M., with the accompaniment of an oldies station on the radio, they had killed off the entire bottle.

"I'm pretty sure we blew it, Benny," Barry said, exhaling schnapps fumes,

"Those kids won't be back for hours and there's no guarantee Alex will be with them."

"We'll get him. Got to be patient, like the apex predators you always talk about. We're crocodiles waiting for wildebeests to enter the water. Let me tell you my plan," Benny said.

Over the next hour Benny had laid out his plan. Barry just stared at him.

"I think I'm gonna' need another bottle of schnapps to swallow that plan," Barry said.

"Look, we've got no choice. We can't afford to let any more time pass with what Alex knows. We've got to kill him, and it's got to happen now, today, at this beach."

Just then the woody pulled into the parking lot and parked near the beach. Benny and Barry slunk down in their seats. Alex and the other surfers got out, grabbed the surfboards from the back and headed toward the beach, their voices laughing, still drunk.

"What a break!" Benny said, "but don't they ever get sick of surfing?"

Benny grabbed a tube of zinc oxide from his glove compartment, smeared it all over his face, then pulled his floppy hat down low above his eyes and pulled on a bulky beige jacket with lots of pockets, the kind photographers wear and stared at the surfers through his binoculars.

After a few minutes he saw what he expected to see. The three experienced surfers were carving up the waves, catching air, cutting back, then expertly riding them in, while Alex flailed out in the swells, missing opportunities to catch wave after wave. Benny took the chance, grabbed the large shoulder camera and strolled down toward the beach.

He jogged up to the closest surfer just coming in for a break.

"Hey, could I talk with you for a minute?" Benny yelled.

"Sure, dude," Otto yelled. He jammed his board into the sand and approached Benny.

As they got within talking distance Benny launched right into his speech.

"I've been watching you three—you're real artists."

"Thanks, bro, we've been at it a while," Otto said.

"Let me cut to the chase. I'm shooting the opening scene for an indie picture. I want it to be you three guys carving up waves from behind—it'll be beautiful. Your names will appear in the credits and you'll all receive at least one thousand dollars stipends. How does that sound?"

"That sounds awesome, dude. But why do you want to shoot us from behind? You won't be able to see us that well."

"Look, that's my vision. It's the shot I want. I'll be out there in small watercraft in about an hour. When you see me out there with my camera, paddle out, turn around and show me your best moves, okay? Oh, and bring that big oafy dude too, bring him way out with you—I can use him for contrast. It will make the scene that much better. I'll pay him the same as you."

"Deal! We'll keep an eye out for you," Otto said, then turned and ran to tell the others.

On the way to the car Benny spoke into his smart phone: "Nearest boat rental." The G.P.S. came back with "Wave Masters," a phone number and directions. Benny dialed.

"Do you have small boats available to rent. Now?"

"'We do. What size do you want? We have sixteen foot, twenty—"

"I'll take twenty foot. Does it have a good-sized engine to handle the surf waves?"

"Oh, yeah, 300 horsepower. Fiberglass skiff. That'll get you out there."

"Great. Do I need a license to rent one?"

"A valid driver's license, you have to a wear life jacket at all times and sign a waiver."

"See you in a few," Benny said.

At Wave Masters, Benny rented the boat, bought a towing hitch and hooked the boat up. He then purchased a top-of-the-line spear gun and seven spears, drove to the pier and backed the boat down to the water.

Once they parked the car and got into the boat, Benny turned it around and sped for the section of ocean across from Topanga Beach. They slowed down as they saw the surfers—500 yards in, standing in the surf, looking out at them. Otto waved, and Benny waved back.

"Great, here they come. Can you drive the boat?" Benny asked.

"Sure, as long as it's nothing fancy," Barry said.

"Here, pull this stocking cap on," Benny said, pulling it over Barry's head, "and put these sunglasses on too."

As they chugged closer, the surfers paddled toward them. After ten minutes they were close enough to shout. Benny held the camera up on his shoulder to hide himself better.

"Okay, that's good enough. Turn around and let me see your stuff!" Benny yelled.

"Okay, dude!" Otto yelled.

The surfers turned and began paddling like mad for one of the swells, leaving Alex behind to clumsily paddle and kick on the larger board.

"Go, fat man," Benny said.

Barry turned the throttle and moved a few feet closer to Alex, now 20 yards away. Benny put down the camera and picked up the spear gun, loaded a spear into it and pulled back and locked the mechanism.

"Closer, closer," Benny said.

The skiff pulled up within ten yards of Alex as Benny took aim. Alex heard the motor and looked behind him. He saw two men standing in a skiff, one aiming a speargun at him.

"Hey, what's going on?" Alex yelled, in terror.

"You failed at being an apex predator, let's see how you do at being a meal for one!" Benny yelled, and let the first spear go. It sunk into Alex's hamstring and punched through the bottom of the surfboard.

"Aagh! No! I wasn't going to tell anybody!" Alex yelled.

Benny locked and loaded another spear. "Can't take that chance, Alex," Benny said and let another spear go. This one stuck in Alex's mid back.

"Aagh! I can't believe you're doing this. Uncle Barry, don't I mean anything to you?"

"We had a good run, Alex. We gotta' do this. I hope you understand," Barry said.

Benny shot another spear. This one hit Alex in the upper arm. There was now blood flowing onto the board as Alex kicked and paddled with his good arm toward the beach.

"Now, we wait for nature to take its course," Benny said. "It shouldn't be long."

They sat, the motor rumbling bubbles underwater. The surfers in the distance had ridden the waves all the way to the beach and were looking back out to sea.

"Aaaannnd, there we go," Benny said, as a black fin emerged from the water and began circling Alex's board from ten yards away.

"Benny, Barry, don't do this!" Alex yelled.

"You want to stick around and watch your nephew get eaten by a shark?" Benny asked.

"I think maybe you're the stupid one this time, those surfers are starting to look out here. We better scram," Barry said.

"I guess you're right. Let's go." Benny took the helm and powered back in the direction from which they had come.

All alone, Alex kicked and paddled toward the beach with all he had. He caught a big swell, which never became a wave, only moved him a couple yards closer to the beach. He saw the surfers, in the distance, paddling out towards him, just as something nudged his board. He looked up to see a dorsal fin cruising away from him and dip under the water. He had no idea where the shark had gone. Suddenly, he saw it emerge ten yards to his right and circle him.

Chapter 33

Man Versus Nature

Dark Snout drove back to Malibu Memorial while Scott attended to the myocardial infarction patient in the back of the ambulance. They parked in the Emergency Loading Zone and together they wheeled the patient into the hospital. Scott took the lead while giving technical information to the nursing staff, who wheeled the man into the examination room.

Afterward, Scott grabbed a cup of coffee on the way back to the ambulance.

"I think we saved him," Dark Snout said, "I think we got to him in time."

"Yeah, he'll be okay. You don't drink coffee?" Scott said. "How do you keep going?"

"I'd rather eat organic blueberries or almonds, they're more healthful," Dark Snout said.

"Don't tell me you're one of those goody-goodies."

'No, I have coffee or alcohol sometimes, I just don't make a habit of it."

Scott tossed back the rest of his lukewarm coffee. They climbed into the ambulance, with Dark Snout behind the wheel again.

"So, do you know Ken Adams pretty well?" Dark Snout asked. "I mean, if he's potentially going to date my cousin I'd like to know what kind of guy he is."

"He pays his union dues on time. He pays his taxes. He has a habit of not showing up for his shift sometimes on short notice. He's a good paramedic when he's here, and he's an impressive athlete. I don't know much more."

Scott switched on the news and lowered the volume while they waited for the next call.

~

Alex pulled his arm and leg, the ones not pinned to the board with spears, to the center of the surfboard and waited for the expected impact from the big shark. He turned his head as far as he could see to his left, then to his right. He mostly feared the shark would attack him from behind.

A big swell lifted his board then fell beneath him as the green mound of water rolled toward shore—trailing white foam, temporarily blocking his view of the beach. As it receded he saw his friends paddling out toward him, but they were hundreds of yards away and they would never get here in time. Besides, what could they do against a shark of this size?

Alex did a quick side-to-side glance and decided to make an all-out attempt to get to shore. He let his good leg hang off the side of the board and he kicked, he held on with the one with the spear through it, and stroked with the other arm. The stroking and kicking caused sharp pains and nerves twinges where his muscles rubbed against the imbedded spears.

God, the one in my back is excruciating!

Suddenly, Alex and the board were knocked a couple feet above the water as a great weight exploded below him, and just as quickly, pull him and the board down sideways, causing Alex to slide off the board. At that awkward angle, just before he was submerged, he saw that the spear protruding from his leg and through the bottom of the board, was now lodged in the shark's mouth. Underwater, surrounded by bloody bubbles, Alex felt himself shaken back and forth by the spear through his leg, as the shark fought against it—and suddenly freed itself.

Alex grabbed the board, and realized that, although still impaled by the spear, his leg was free of the board. He rose to the surface, along with the board, and climbed on top again. He couldn't stand the pain of the spear in his leg any longer. He pulled the barbed end of the spear hard forward and the whole length of the rod came free in his hand. He was not prepared for the agony. Blood flowed freely from his wound into the water. Wasting no time, Alex gripped the spear with the same hand which held the board.

Where is that shark?

Free of the spear, Alex let his legs hang off the end of the board and kicked for shore with all he had. The exertion made the board slick with his blood and Alex feared that, despite its injury, the big predator would return any second. He saw it circling ten yards to his left, its dorsal fin cleaving the water, its tail slapping at the surface as it submerged.

"Help!" he yelled, but his voice sounded small, so far from shore. Alex caught a swell that he wanted to be a wave, but it only carried him a couple of yards. His nerves were on high alert as the shark unexpectedly bumped the back of his board. Despite the pain Alex instantly lifted both legs high into the air.

Two seals and a school of fish leaped above the surface, as if fleeing a predator. Another dorsal fin, much bigger than the first, broke the surface and hissed in a circle a few yards away. He had inadvertently injured the first shark but the second seemed fresh and hungry.

He kicked and stroked for shore. He could hear the distant yells of his friends now.

"—lex!" the "Al" lost in the wind.

The swells occasionally developed foam on top, washing away with the effervescence. That last swell carried him farther than all the rest combined. *The current's in my favor, swells turning into waves, maybe—* Alex glanced side-to-side, preparing for a kicking assault toward shore, when his heart sank. The tall dorsal fin cleaving the water was heading straight for him. Now, he saw the tail, what? Fifteen feet behind, propelling it toward him. *One big ass shark.* The dark gray back rose higher in the water.

"I'm not going out like this," Alex said, grabbing the spear in both his fists, raising it above his head and arching his back just as the conical snout broke the water, open jaws lunging for him. Alex brought the spear down with all his power, stabbing it down and through the fish's snout. He was knocked into the water, the large rough body punching him sideways as it swam away, the tail whopping him in the head for good measure.

Alex, stunned, opened his eyes underwater. Clear and green everywhere, except for his blood, now clouding his view. He swam for the surface, spun in a circle, saw the board a few yards away and swam for it. He reached it, slipped, grabbed again and hauled himself up on top.

Alex's thoughts ran away. He was losing consciousness, and maybe his mind.

"Shark number one's spear-shy," he laughed. "Second one, chew on that spear, bitch." Alex was sure he had gone insane now because he heard voices. "*Stupid sounding angels,*" was his last thought as the darkness closed around him.

~

Benny backed the rented boat into an empty space at Wave Masters. He glanced at Barry who looked back at him with a furrowed brow.

"If Alex survives somehow—you blew it," Barry said. "We're going down for this."

Benny ignored him and got out, his face still heavily smeared with zinc oxide. He hand-cranked the bow into the air with the attached handle, then disconnected it from his trailer hitch. The bow of the boat was now elevated and balanced on the stand in the parking space—just the way he had found it. He adjusted his hat, put on his dark sunglasses, and entered the shop. He showed his fake I.D., reclaimed his security deposit, signed a fake name, and returned to his car.

"We're rid of the boat," Barry said, "but what about the spear gun and extra spears?"

"I'll get rid of them in my own time," Benny said, "We've got to revise our plan."

"Because you completely screwed up the original plan? *Also* your idea by the way."

"I know, but when I knew Alex was too chickenshit to kill Vera I had to take action."

"I used to think you were so freakin' smart, Benny. Why didn't you just shoot Alex in the heart or the head? There's a chance he's not dead."

"Nah, when I shot him full of shish kabob skewers it was like ringing a dinner bell. Then that shark showed up right on cue. I only wish we could have stayed to watch."

"I gotta level with you," Barry said, "I think there's a good chance we're goin' down for this. You can bounce your new plan off me over dinner. It's probably my last meal so take me to the best seafood place in L.A. I need to get my food-on."

"I know just the place. We need to go home, shower and get dressed up because it's a nice place. We'll hide in plain sight," Benny said, and stepped on the accelerator.

~

Otto, Pete and Sammy all had their hands on Alex, or his board, as they kicked their flotilla of surfboards toward shore. Sammy kept his hand tightly over the open wound on Alex's hamstring as they paddled and kept their eyes on the circling shark.

"Kick, dudes!" Pete growled.

"Right on," Otto and Sammy replied in unison.

They were on the downside of a wave when the big shark bumped Alex's board.

"I think it's trying to knock Alex overboard," Sammy said.

"Am-scray, ark-shay!" Otto yelled at the rolling ocean.

"We're pressing our luck, dudes. Now, kick!" Pete yelled.

As the swell ahead of them curled away, a sliver of white foam appeared across the top, then vanished. The surfers exerted a concerted effort: kicking, stroking with their arms until they felt themselves lifted by a wave and propelled forward several yards. Otto glanced behind them at the tall dorsal fin cruising toward them.

"Big dude's comin'," Otto said.

Kick!" Pete yelled.

The water frothed with their kicking, moving them into position for the next wave—a big one, which pushed them within a hundred yards of the shore. The large fin followed, cutting vicious arcs left and right, and finally turning out to sea with an angry splash.

"Oh, my freakin' god, dudes, that was so close!" Otto said.

"No shit, my friend," Pete said. "Now, kick! Al's still in trouble."

~

Dark Snout had been meditating to quietly streaming news, white noise, as the channel erupted inside the still ambulance.

"Unit thirteen, are you currently engaged?" the voice said.

"Negative," Scott responded.

"Deploy immediately to the 400 block of Topanga Beach. Swimmer with multiple puncture wounds, significant blood loss, just pulled from surf."

"Ten four, en-route," Scott said, turning to Dark Snout. "Go."

Dark Snout revved the engine and a look of calm swept over his face as he punched the accelerator, switched on the siren and lights, and slid sideways into moving traffic.

"Holy shit, Simon!" Scott said, and gripped the safety bar as he was jostled sideways. "Get us there alive, okay?"

The ambulance passed cars in both lanes, careened in and out of traffic and accelerated. Scott stole a peek over at the dashboard, which vibrated slightly, the speedometer read 75 mph.

"Hey, you're going kind of fast, Simon," Scott said.

"How many more miles?" Dark Snout said, ignoring his comment.

"Four more, but it's a beach town, for god's sake, slow down!"

"A man's bleeding out and we're the ones who can help. Gotta' get there, right?"

"Yeah, but—"

The siren blared, lights flashed, and cars slid to a stop as the ambulance bounced through an intersection, rocked side to side on its suspension and almost clipped a car.

"You're still not allowed to exceed the speed limit," Scott yelled over the engine.

They picked up speed in the straightaway. Ninety miles per hour. Then came the smaller streets. Dark Snout had no problem driving up onto lawns, across people's driveways and curbs, unfazed by pedestrians—one with a dog on a leash scrambled out of his way.

"Jesus, Simon. You're going to get arrested or sued or something!" Scott yelled.

"Directions, please," Dark Snout replied.

"Turn right at the next corner, then it's straight to the surf, about five blocks."

Scott gripped the safety bar with one hand and the arm rest with the other. Dark Snout pressed the accelerator to the floor. The beach road was in dire need of maintenance and riddled with pot holes. The ambulance bounced and shook as the vehicle climbed upward of sixty-five miles per hour, the tires bouncing crazily into the air.

"Damn it! You're going too fast here! Slow down, Simon!"

Dark Snout *did* slow down, just as they skidded into the sandy beach parking lot. They both climbed out, lights still flashing, engine clicking and pinging from the punishing ride.

Dark Snout ripped the rear doors open and pulled on the body board. Scott shouldered him out of the way and grabbed a zippered backpack and slipped it onto his back. Dark Snout, irritated, yanked the body board out into mid-air. Scott grabbed the back end before it fell to the parking lot and double-stepped to match Dark Snout's pace toward the beach.

"Let's hope you risking lots of peoples' lives was worth saving this one," Scott muttered.

"Let's not waste the time we gained," Dark Snout said, and picked up the pace. He could hear Scott back there huffing. *Cigarettes*, he thought.

As they crested a sand dune and saw three men in swim suits carrying a fourth up toward them. The carried man hung limply in their arms and appeared unconscious. Dark Snout jogged. *Scott can join me or get dragged*, his choice, he thought.

"Damn, man!" Scott protested, but caught up and jogged in step with Dark Snout.

"Lay him down on this board," Dark Snout called to the men.

They obliged him. Scott took inventory of the spears, one in mid-back, the other through an upper arm, and applied a tourniquet to the third—open wound on left leg, apparently all the way through. Scott taped that one. Seeing Alex was unconscious, Dark Snout administered mouth-to-mouth resuscitation.

Alex gasped, but his eyes rolled back in his head. Dark Snout snapped open an ammonium carbonate capsule under Alex's nose and watched as his eyes flew open and his nostrils flared.

"God, what!?" Alex exclaimed.

"You're okay," Dark Snout said, and clipped an oxygen tube into Alex's nostrils.

"We're ready. Let's go!" Scott said.

Together, they carried Alex toward the ambulance.

~

Vera had returned to her grandmother's house. She was caked with fake dried blood, but too tired and troubled to shower. She had gone to her bedroom and fallen into a distressed sleep, and dreamt that someone was trying to kill her. She awoke several times with chills and couldn't sleep. Finally, exhausted, she slept until well past noon the next day. She looked at herself in the mirror.

"Yuck!" she exclaimed. She called Jake from her cell.

"This is Jake."

"Jake, it's me. I'm really hungry. I fell asleep after the shoot last night, but I'm so in the mood for seafood. I can be ready in about an hour if you want to go. If you don't, I understand. I'll catch a cab."

"No, no, I'd love to take you. There's a new place, let me see if I can get a reservation." Jake checked his watch: 3:30 P.M. "I have to hang up, Vera, this place is really popular. I'll pick you up in an hour. Bye."

The limo arrived, and Vera was already out-front waiting. Although the chauffer got out to open the door for Vera, Jake raced around and beat him to it.

"What a gentleman," Vera said. "I guess I was right to take you back after all."

"Yes, you were," Jake said, with a smile. "We got lucky, they had a cancellation."

A half an hour later they pulled up in front of Wah-Sabi? Seafood restaurant and Sushi Bar. There was a short wait while the maître d' found their names on the list. Their waiter seated them at a table with a distant ocean view and just a few feet from two women, dressed to the nines. Jake and Vera ordered. There was a lull in the conversation, and they overheard the women talking.

"That man over there with the smaller man, do you see him?" asked the statuesque blonde, dripping with diamonds.

"Yes," her friend with brunette hair and cheek implants, said, "he's quite overweight."

"Right, but have you ever seen such gorgeous hair?"

"It is amazing. I've noticed that he's had several plates of shrimp and lots of booze."

Vera turned to see Barry and Benny sitting in the corner. Both dressed nicely, two bottles of champagne chilling tableside.

"Oh my god, Jake," Vera whispered, "we've got to get out of here."

"Why? I mean, really, why? They're down there, we've already ordered. Let them have their night and we'll have ours."

"I'll try, but I'm going to be uncomfortable if they see us and want to talk."

"They've got to go soon. Do you see all those plates on their table? Nobody can continue to eat at that pace."

Just then a waiter cleared the plates at Benny's and Barry's table and another waiter brought two more platters heaped full of steaming shrimp.

"No way," the blonde said, smiling, "he's ordered more food. He has quite an appetite."

"Why do you say that as if you might be interested in that barbarian?" her friend asked.

"I know, he's grotesque, but that hair. And the unashamed way he just keeps ordering and gorging himself. It's so brazen."

"He's a pig, honey."

"Maybe, but he's a piggy with a head of beautiful, fluffy hair. I'd kind of like to make him a homecooked meal just so I could run my fingers through his hair for dessert."

"What's wrong with you?" the brunette asked.

"Jake, this is really beginning to bother me," Vera whispered. "I mean the thought of anyone cuddling with Barry is just gross!"

"Do you want me to try to get us another table farther away?" Jake asked.

"No, it's like watching a dog juggle or something," Vera said, "I can't look away."

"He can't see me," the blonde said, "I'll walk by and give him a smile."

"Oh, that wouldn't be obvious at all," her friend said, rolling her eyes.

"I want to warn that woman off," Vera whispered.

"The heart wants what the heart wants," Jake replied, smiling.

"Oh my god! He's almost finished both platters," Vera said.

"Is Benny eating anything?"

"Benny's noshing a little, talking a lot, while Barry's shoveling down food and nodding."

At this, Jake turned behind him for a look. The waiter had opened and poured another bottle of champagne. Jake's and Vera's food arrived.

As the waiter carried the empty bottle, the tall blonde watched. "Those are bottles of Dom Perignon. He must be wealthy," she said.

"You'd better rein it in, honey," her friend said, "that man is disgusting."

"I'll be right back." The blonde stood and smoothed her skirt. She strutted down past Barry and Benny and gazed out at the ocean, then turned and smiled at Barry.

"That looks like a good meal you're having," she said.

Barry looked up, a shrimp hanging out of his mouth. "Hi, yeah, it is."

"I'm Sharon," the blonde said, and extended her hand.

Barry stood, his belly caught the underside of the table and almost toppled it. He wiped his hand with a napkin and shook her elegant, manicured hand with his beefy paw.

"Barry. Nice to meet you."

"My friend and I are down at the end. Why not stop on the way out and say goodbye?"

"Will do," Barry said and lowered his head to resume feeding.

As the tall woman sat down at her table and began to speak, her friend interrupted her.

"Shh! Just shut up. We did not put ourselves through those daily torture sessions at the gym with that expensive personal trainer for *this*. I remember your words. You said: 'I want my ass to look like a nineteen-year-old girl's,' you told him. He worked you like a sled dog, and I couldn't believe it was possible, but you killed yourself and you got your perfect ass. And for what? So you can go out with a disgusting, overweight cretin? I thought this would be fun, we could both meet nice men, all go out together. I am not going *anywhere* with you and *that man*."

"Okay, suit yourself. He's like some magnificent pagan beast and I must tame him."

"Ugh," her friend said, crossing her arms and looking away.

Benny, into his third glass of champagne, gestured emphatically as he spoke. "So, we've got to do the job ourselves, fat man. You want the honors since Vera was your discovery?"

Barry nodded, scooped and shoveled large spoonsful of shrimp scampi into his maw.

"You're kind of making me queasy, Barry."

"Don't care," he said, chewing, "last meal."

Barry washed it all down with more champagne. Suddenly, he looked uncomfortable. He sat very still and gripped the edge of the table with both hands.

"Okay," Benny said. "We tell Vera we need a re-shoot. Tell her the old set is needed for another film and get her in the new one. You wear a mask, we strap her down we do the real sacrifice scene. I'll handle the filming. Hey, Bare, you don't look so good—"

Barry stood, turned and moved like a horse, not running but covering ground fast, like he was returning to the barn. Barry's face had turned waxy green and Benny could tell he was in quest of the men's room. Barry had just passed the women and Jake and Vera's tables as he grabbed his stomach with one hand and his forehead with the other.

"Here come those shrimp!" he announced in a guttural roar.

He bent over at the waist and emitted a colorful wave of shrimp and champagne across the room, as patrons and waiters scattered like a terrified flock of sheep.

Barry stood, panting, and looked at the room full of staring people.

"Sorry about that, everybody," he said, drool dribbling down his $500.00 suit.

There was a moment of silence as waiters moved in, moved tables, and returned with brooms, dust pans, mops, rags, disinfectant spray and a vacuum. The diners stepped back, far away, as the cleaning frenzy ensued.

"We're so sorry about this," one waiter said.

The manager appeared and liberally handed out vouchers for free drinks. The waitstaff set tables up with new tablecloths and silverware. They pulled out chairs for the guests and offered further apologies, as Barry, having witnessed enough, trudged to the men's room to get cleaned up.

"What do you think of your Prince Charming now?" the brunette asked.

"I want him more than ever. I'm equally attracted and repulsed by him. He probably needs someone to wash that hair for him now."

Chapter 34

Freeze Frame

As Barry returned from the men's room, Vera and Jake faced the other way in hopes he wouldn't see them. Barry paused a few feet from their table and wiped his waxy face with a cloth napkin he'd grabbed from another couple's table.

"Barry?" said the statuesque blonde, handing him her number on a cocktail napkin. "Call me when you're feeling better."

Barry nodded, too ill to speak.

Benny walked up to Barry, having just settled the bill, and Jake and Vera ducked down under their table. Benny helped Barry maneuver toward the exit and out the door. Jake peeked out and said, "It's okay, they're gone." He and Vera sat up and faced each other.

"Every time I think that man can't get any more disgusting, he ups his game," Vera said.

"He's quite the glutton," Jake responded. "I'm still hungry, how about you?"

"I need a few minutes to get over Barry's technicolor yawn," Vera said, "but yes, I haven't eaten anything since lunch yesterday."

"Let's change the subject, do you have any ideas to improve my screenplay?"

"I do. You need to change all those ridiculous names. Secondly, the puns must go. Third, the whole cheeky mood has to go if you want women to have an emotional response."

"Jeez, Vera. Anything else?"

"I think that's enough for now. Later, we can get into what your heroine's boss's motivation is for objectifying women. Women aren't stupid, they know when someone isn't being sincere. Why do you have all the female characters act so stupid?"

"I'm used to writing for victims, who are traditionally stupid. I tried to think like a dramatic author. It took all I had to bend my mind that way."

"We'll get your script shaped up, then you'll need a rom-dram scriptwriter. I've heard there's no lack of talent in L.A., just a lot of talented people without the right connections. But you're famous. You have a following." Vera cocked an eyebrow.

"Yes, a following of horror fans," Jake said.

"True, but a lot of people who aren't horror fans have heard of you. They'll say 'Hmm? What kind of romance film would a famous horror director put out?'"

"I get it, like a novelty. And then— "

"And then—surprise! If it's any good, you'll get a lot more people interested."

"I love you!" Jake reached to hug her across the table.

"Don't play around with such serious words," Vera said, pulling away.

"I meant for your insight," Jake said, trying to save face.

~

At Malibu Memorial critical care wing, the surgical team had cut away the ragged tissue where the spear had impaled Alex's leg. They had cut through the case-hardened metal rod just below the barbed spearhead and carefully extracted the spear from the patient's back where it had narrowly missed his liver. They executed the same procedure to remove the second spear from the patient's upper arm where it had grazed his humerus bone.

They had irrigated the puncture sites with distilled water and continued to flush them for fifteen minutes, followed by heavy doses of antiseptic to combat the bacteria-laden seawater.

Although the staff had administered six liters of blood, the patient's heart rate and respiration had dipped into the danger zone four times, prompting the staff to put him into a medically-induced coma for the next 24 hours. The head surgeon would then evaluate the patient's condition. There were to be no visitors until then.

~

Dark Snout had returned to the emergency loading zone and driven the ambulance back to the R.A.M.P. parking lot because his and Scott's shift ended in 15 minutes. He parked as Scott went into the office to fill out the paperwork from their day. Dark Snout sat there and thought for a moment. He'd recognized Alex Boxwell as the man Rhonda had roughed up a few months ago. Dark Snout used his badge number to call the critical care wing administrator to check on the man's condition.

"Medically-induced coma?" Dark Snout repeated into the microphone.

"That's right. Your response time was remarkable," the voice over the microphone said. "He'd have bled out for sure if you hadn't arrived when you did."

Dark Snout cleaned the rig. He checked his cell: 10:00 A.M. He had time to go to Rhonda's trailer to rest and change clothes before confronting that big dude, Ken, when he arrived for his midnight shift. The man who, in all probability, had abducted Lola Grubb.

Scott returned from the office.

"Pleasure working with you, Scott," Dark Snout said, hi-fiving Scott's raised hand.

"You're the damndest paramedic I've ever seen. You drive like Mario Andretti."

"You're dating yourself. How about Nigel Mansell?"

"Don't care. You're a great medic, clean like Martha Stewart—let me buy you a beer."

"Thanks. Catch you next time. I've got to get some sack time."

"I hear you," Scott said, waving goodbye.

~

When he unlocked the door to the trailer, Dark Snout found Rhonda on the couch, reading Double Crunch, a women's wrestling magazine.

"Snouty!" Rhonda said. Her eyes lit up and she ran up to him, surprisingly light on her feet for such a large woman. She hugged him tightly and kissed him.

"I'm going to tell you something against my better judgement," Dark Snout said.

Rhonda looked up at him, her eyes wide, her forehead creased with concern.

"Is it something bad?" she asked.

"I'm telling you this in the strictest confidence. That man who beat up Serena Miles with the rubber-coated cleaver, the one whose bones you broke and put in the hospital—"

"Yes, I know. I pray for him all the time. I feel bad sometimes, but he wasn't going to learn his lesson about not hitting women otherwise."

"Well, he's back in the hospital. Somebody shot him full of harpoon gun spears and left him for dead."

"Goodness! He's been through enough. I want to go see him."

"No. Whoever did this might be coming back to finish the job. Besides, you wore a mask before. Now, you're just going to walk in there? Under what pretense? Besides, he may recognize your voice."

"I don't know, I could say I'm from the church, which isn't a lie. I do attend church regularly. We could pray together. Just one prayer, Snouty, please?"

"Only if I go with you. I'll watch you from a distance. The soonest you can go will be in about 20 hours from now. Even then I don't know how soon he'll be allowed visitors. But I've got business to take care of between now and then. So, don't visit Alex without me."

"Okay, Snouty. I promise," Rhonda said, snuggling up to him and closing her eyes.

~

Benny and the driver helped to shore up Barry's bulk as they walked him up the driveway, guiding him toward Benny's front door.

"Keep him going straight!" Benny grunted at the driver, as Barry oscillated from driveway to lawn.

They thrust him toward the door, Benny released him, leaving the driver to support Barry while he unlocked the door. Benny scrambled back as Barry listed toward the flower bed.

"Come on, get him in there," Benny said.

Barry was stuck in the doorway. Benny and the driver stepped back to catch their breath.

"Really?" Benny said. "You're wedged in my doorway? Shove him through."

He and the driver pushed on Barry's back and he slid through six inches, and hung there. Benny let out a huff and shoved again. The driver crawled between Barry's legs inside the foyer and pulled on Barry's arms. All at once he fell into the driver's arms.

"Good lord help me!" the driver yelled.

Benny helped to right the behemoth in the extra, extra-large suit.

"Get him on the couch," Benny said.

Together they tried to ease him onto it, but he slipped away and fell onto the couch with a crack. Benny knew from the tilt of the couch that the left rear wooden leg had broken.

"Damn you, fat man!" Benny yelled.

He handed the driver a $50.00 bill and told him to see himself out. Benny locked the door behind him and snarled at the snoring blob.

"Sleep it off, you big tub of crap," Benny mumbled.

He wiped the sweat from his forehead and sat at his writing desk. He pulled out a fresh sheet of paper and drafted a timeline for their alibis.

~

It was 9:00 A.M. in Lola's room. The sun shone through her window along with a light breeze which caused the blue and white curtains to flutter, carrying with it the scent of Spanish jasmine. It was another beautiful 78-degree day in Tijuana as Doctor Alvarez and his surgical assistant knocked once, then entered her room.

"Good morning, Miss Grubb," the doctor said. "Today is the day we make you beautiful. We just need to check your vital signs first. How do you feel?"

Lola sneezed. It was a loud sputtering sneeze.

"I'm freezing. I have the worst headache," she said, and blew her nose into a tissue.

The doctor nodded to his assistant who checked her heartrate with a stethoscope.

"Her breathing is ragged, Doctor, and she has an elevated heartrate." He placed a thermometer under her tongue and reported the bad news to the doctor. "She's also running a fever of 102. I'm afraid it's a case of the flu, Doctor."

"We must get you well before we can proceed with the surgery," Doctor Alvarez said.

"You're kidding!" Lola said. "Come on, I've spent a lot of money to make this happen."

"Regrettably, it is not an option. It simply isn't safe until you're well. Tend to her, I have calls to return," Doctor Alvarez said. He turned to Lola.

"You will have the look you want. You will have the face of the lovely Rachel McAdams. Just concentrate on getting well and I'll check on you tomorrow."

The doctor left Lola to snuffle and pout.

~

Dark Snout was looking for rig #18, the one Ken was scheduled to drive on his midnight shift. He had initially had some ethical concerns about taking out a paramedic just before starting his life-saving shift, but he'd seen the number of available paramedics on stand-by and felt confident Ken's spot would soon be occupied.

His next concern was his own anonymity. His disguise was adequate: a bearded, stooped-over elderly man with a cane. He only had to spot Ken and get close enough before he got within sight of his partner or other ambulance personnel.

Dark Snout knew Ken drove a blue Range Rover with an extended cab. That shouldn't be hard to spot. He checked his cell phone: 11:49 P.M. He glanced to his left: the ambulances were 20 yards away. A couple of the staff occasionally carried a piece of equipment out to a rig, but they weren't looking in his direction.

Suddenly, a big blue Range Rover bounced up into the R.A.M.P. parking lot and parked slightly askew. A big, bearded man stepped out and started ambling toward the ambulances. Dark Snout moved into position, stumbling in the general direction of the man—he looked like a typical derelict. The man saw him and altered his path slightly on the way to the rigs. *Nobody likes to get too close to the crazies.* Dark Snout staggered toward the big man.

"God wants you to do better, sinner!" Dark Snout yelled, pointing the cane at him.

As the man diverted his eyes, Dark Snout targeted the man's chest and squeezed a small trigger in the handle. A tiny dart flew soundlessly and impacted Ken's shirt. Ken gasped, lurched sideways and grasped at his throat. Dark Snout was there to catch him as the tranquilizer took effect. He gently lowered him to the ground, down low beside the other parked cars and out of sight of the paramedics.

He then sprinted for his own car, half a block away. Five minutes later he cruised up and, with the engine idling, lifted the big man up and shoved him headfirst into the back seats, then ran around to the other back door, leaned over and pulled him up so he lay across the rear bench seat. He pulled a sheet over him, shut the door, and drove away.

He had used this type of tranquilizer before. His quarry would remain unconscious for about 30 minutes and awake with a headache. This would give him time to prepare.

Inside, he removed the man's clothing, except his underwear, positioned him faceup on a mattress on the floor, and tied his arms and legs to four heavy pieces of furniture. He then walked into the back room and returned, carrying a metal crate of five mewing kittens which he had picked out and paid for days earlier. He had intentionally not fed them for the last four hours.

Dark Snout set the crate down near the unconscious man and entered the kitchen. He returned momentarily with a pitcher of cream. He pulled up a chair, checked his cell, and sat and waited for the man to awake. When there was about five minutes remaining, he pulled on the black furry wolf's mask and waited, aware of his heavy breathing from within the mask.

In short order, the man awoke.

"What—! Damn, where am I? Why am I bound? Oh, shit. Who the hell are you?"

"I am somebody who is going to get some information from you. You can save us time and just answer all my questions, or I will make you tell me."

"What questions?"

"Tell me where Lola Grubb is. The woman you abducted from Malibu Memorial over a week ago. Tell me now."

"I don't know any Lola Grubb," Ken said.

"Alright, we'll do this the hard way."

Dark Snout stood and drizzled cream onto the man's nipples. He set the pitcher down and carried the crate closer, opening the door and withdrawing all five kittens and setting them down on the man's chest. The kittens immediately licked at the cream with their rough little tongues. Dark Snout chuckled behind his mask as Ken squirmed at his ropes.

"Oh my god! Stop them!" Ken cried.

"Are you going to answer my questions?"

"No, Hell no!"

"Then you should know there are other places, more delicate places, where I could pour cream. You see, the kittens are merciless. They only want the cream."

Ken's eyes grew even wider as Dark Snout approached and reached for the elastic band of his underwear.

"Okay, okay! You sick bastard, get these kittens off me and I'll tell you."

Dark Snout picked up the kittens and put them back into the metal crate and closed and latched it shut, then turned to the panting man, whose nipples were red and raw looking.

"Where is Lola Grubb?"

"I drove her out Route 805, through Santa Ana, into Tijuana to a medical facility. She's supposed to get her face done."

"How long has she been there?"

"About a week."

"Why didn't anyone stop or question you when you wheeled Miss Grubb out of the hospital?"

"Because I'm dating the head nurse at the admin desk on that floor," Ken said.

"Give me the directions, the address and the name of the hospital."

"No, I do business with these people. You have to do some of the leg work—"

"Cream and kittens in your underwear, do you understand?"

"Goddammit!"

"In fact, you're going to come with me and show me the hospital personally."

"Why do you care so much about her in the first place? That's the ugliest woman I've ever laid eyes on. Does she have a great personality or something?"

"Hmm, insubordination? Either change your attitude or I'm giving those kittens two minutes inside your shorts."

"No, don't! I'm sorry. I'm sure she's a great person."

"Good, because I didn't want to have to do that" Dark Snout said.

Chapter 35

Cross Cutting

Jake and Vera had finished dinner. Jake held the door for her and, as she passed under his arm, he admired the outfit she wore, the one he'd bought her before their break-up. It was a pale pink number which snugly hugged her curves. *She's so pretty and so graceful,* Jake thought, *I'm lucky to have her back.*

As they walked to his limo, Jake realized he'd had an incredibly lucky life. He'd been brash enough at 19 to sell himself to a heavy-hitter in the B-horror business; he'd made a name for himself, made his money, bought an expensive condo, hired an impeccable driver, James, who'd been loyal to him all these years; met the girl of his dreams, realized he'd become a misogynistic derelict, entered therapy, mostly cured himself, lost the girl of his dreams, escaped those sickos, Barry and Benny, reunited with his mother. And reclaimed the girl of his dreams.

He didn't know how he kept avoiding disaster, but he didn't think he should push his luck. *Better slow down, almost scared Vera away when I told her I loved her at dinner.*

"I'm just offering," Jake said, "you're welcome to stay at my place if you want."

"Great," Vera said. "I think Bubbe's house is in the same direction as your place, so it won't be too out of the way if we stop to get my things."

"Of course," Jake said. "Whatever you want." He couldn't believe it.

It's like, no big deal. Yeah, Jake, I'll move back in with you. She's even being polite.

It was only a five minute drive to Vera's grandmother's home. Jake waited in the limo and watched Vera effortlessly jog up the drive in her high heels, her black shiny hair waving back and forth as she did. She used her key to get inside.

"Bubbe, I'm here," Vera called.

"Vera! What, you go out and don't tell me nothing?" Zissell said.

"Yeah, I'm almost twenty-four years old, Bubbe. I'm moving back in with Jake. I just need to get my things."

She entered her bedroom. Zissell followed.

"I think you get smart. You break up with no good garbage movie man. Now, what? I call Aaron. Or do you want to make your mother cry?"

"I got the wrong idea about Jake before, Bubbe. He's a good man," Vera said, putting the last of her clothes in her suitcase and snapping the clasps shut. "He's helped a lot of the women who worked at Falchion Films get back on their feet."

"Jah, I bet he helps dem off their feet and into bed."

"You're wrong, and you're being gross. he's a good man. I'll call you tomorrow."

~

Dark Snout had donned his wolf mask and loaded the bound and blindfolded Ken into a deep wheelbarrow, rolled him down the hall into his spacious garage and into the passenger's seat of his car. He then leaned over and replaced Ken's blindfold with wraparound dark glasses with the lenses completely blacked out.

"There, can you see anything?" he asked, buckling Ken's seatbelt.

"Nothing."

"Good, we're ready for our trip to Tijuana."

"You think you're going to get me all the way to Tijuana like this? They'll never let you across the border."

"Let me worry about that," Dark Snout said, pulling off his wolf mask, clicking the remote garage door opener, and backing out.

"Could you roll my window down a few inches? I feel sick, need some air."

"Yes. I've got to stop for gas, so be good or I'll buy some hungry chihuahua pups and gravy and turn them loose on you."

"That won't be necessary." Ken said, and slumped in his seat.

Dark Snout pulled into the gas station, got out and started filling the tank. Ken leaned to his right and found that by leveraging the back edge of his right sunglass lens against the molded window frame he could pry the glasses an inch off his face. They clung there, askew on his face, wedged against his nose. He looked to the right and he could see everything out his window.

As Ken heard the driver's door open, he quickly pressed his face against the padded window frame and the glasses popped back into place on his face.

"I'm just getting us some snacks and drinks for the road. Don't do anything stupid or—chihuahuas."

"Got it," Ken said.

He heard the door close and he counted to 15 because he guessed it would take his captor about 15 seconds to get inside the convenience store. Once he reached 15, Ken desperately pried his glasses backward against the window frame. This time he managed to get them three inches off his face and he could see much more to his right. He saw two teenaged boys walking by.

"Hey, kid," Ken hissed.

"What do you want?" one of the boys replied.

"I'm tied up. Get me out of this car and I'll give you and your buddy five hundred dollars apiece." Ken watched as the boys looked at each other and smiled.

"C'mon," Ken yelled, "before that psycho comes back!"

The boys approached and took a moment to assess the tall muscular man, his dark glasses on crooked.

"C'mon, reach in and unlock the door!" Ken said.

The boy reached his thin arm in the lowered window, unlocked the door, and opened it. Ken jostled so much he almost fell out.

"Quick, get me away from this car!"

The boys pulled Ken to his feet—each of them had him by the upper arms—and walked him across the parking lot, his feet only able to take short steps with the length of rope restraining them.

"This your car? Get me into the back seat and drive me out of here. Go!"

The boys got him in and drove a few blocks north on Sutter Street. Without any warning, the driver pulled over and parked on the shoulder. The boy turned around and looked at Ken.

"We got you away from that dude. Now, you said five hundred each," the boy said.

"Untie me and I'll get my wallet. And take off these glasses!" Ken said.

The boys complied. Ken rubbed his wrists and ankles, pulled his wallet out and leafed through it. There were only five hundred-dollar bills. Ken pulled out four and separated them into two folds of two hundreds, then folded them each in half again.

"Here you go, boys," Ken said, handing them each the folded hundreds. Then he jogged across a ditch and toward a strip mall.

From behind him, Ken heard the boys yelling. Ken held his hands up in a helpless gesture and smiled.

"Beats nothing, right?" he yelled, then turned and sprinted for the cover of the stores.

Dark Snout emerged from the convenience store, a cardboard tray of drinks and snacks in his hands. He saw his car from across the lot—passenger's side door open, empty. He calmly walked to his car, got in, set the tray down on the padded console, reached across and pulled the passenger's door closed.

"Time for plan B," he said to himself.

He withdrew a remote from his pocket and turned it on. A green LED grid of Sutter Street appeared. A red dot moved northward across the screen.

"Ken, Ken, Ken—why must we play these games?" Dark Snout chuckled and drove north down Sutter Street.

~

Alex stared at a landscape of red, a network of tiny veins running through it. I must be dead, he thought, *and this is where I get to live. Hell, for how I lived my life.*

He moved his wrist an inch and it touched something metallic—Alex yanked his hand back. *What's this? Must be the Devil's pitchfork, he'll be back to torture me soon.*

But no devil came. Alex couldn't figure out where he was. Fluffy white floaters drifted by the red landscape. Soon more appeared until the landscape was mostly fuzzy, gauzy clouds. A couple of seconds elapsed as the landscape morphed into what looked like either clouds or an ocean of undulating gauze. Suddenly, Alex saw a two-foot-tall dorsal fin wrapped in gauze cruising straight for him, the end of a harpoon spear leading it like a periscope. He felt his heart pounding. Alex fought against metal framework.

That was when Alex realized that this was to be his form of torture in Hell. *I'm staked out here like Naomi Watts in King Kong except in my case: staked out for a great white shark to feast on—the one I injured with the harpoon. That Devil's a funny guy. Knew I had a background in horror film. I'm about to be eaten alive!*

Alex thrashed at the sides of the metal bed frame. He heard rapid beeping coming from somewhere, followed by running footsteps. *That's weird. How can there be footsteps in all this gauzy ocean?*

"Mr. Boxwell, it's alright. Just relax, you're safe," said a disembodied voice.

Alex heard other voices as well.

"The patient has regained consciousness, doctor."

"Vitals?"

"Everything's elevated."

"Administer ten cc's Diazepam."

"Yes, Doctor."

"That's better, heartrate stabilizing. Breathing slowing. Can you speak, Mr. Boxwell?"

"Shark! Shark! Shar—" he trailed off.

"There's no shark. You're safe. You're in a hospital. We're going to take care of you."

"I'm in a—hosp—I can't see."

"His eyes have crusted over. Get some sterile swabs with warm distilled water. Swab his eyelids, *gently*, this patient has endured a lot of trauma."

"No sharks?" Alex mumbled.

"Monitor him constantly. I want you to bring him back, slowly. Notify me when he's able to speak."

"Yes, doctor."

Chapter 36

Alex

Alex lay in his hospital bed in a twilight state, eyes fluttering. His life's history played out, not unpleasantly, like a warm tide lapping over his bare feet. An imagined hospital administrator explained his life's review in third person, where Alex was both spectator and participant. Alex sensed it was both therapeutic and necessary.

Alex Boxwell lived at his mother's ratty Section 8 housing apartment. He had never met his father, and at 16 years old, he felt uncomfortable coming home after school. The place had an unpleasant odor and often unfamiliar men sat next to his mother smoking from a crack pipe. His mother rarely grocery shopped and never cooked, leaving Alex to scrounge for loose change or occasional dollar bills he found on the floor to buy his breakfast from a fast food restaurant on the way to school. For dinner he hoped for a dried-up pizza slice the addicts had abandoned in favor of another hit. He frequently went to bed hungry.

Big for his age, clumsy and unpopular, Alex was lonely and easily distracted. He began hanging out at his Uncle Barry's studio, Falchion Films. Alex was intrigued by his uncle, the famous producer of horror movies. The mammoth, barrel-chested man was also good for a $20.00 bill, which he delighted in giving Alex as he shook hands with him. "A twenty-dollar-handshake" his uncle had called it, followed by his big, booming laugh. *Smooth.*

As he became more of a fixture around Falchion, Alex met the acting coach, the surly Benny Edwards. Benny didn't speak with Alex as they passed in the corridors. He just checked his gold Rolex, impatiently paced into C Studio, and slammed the door behind him.

Alex's mother, increasingly paranoid, asked him where he went in the afternoons. When he said, "Uncle Barry's," she called her brother to ask him to take Alex in permanently. Alex heard his mother argue with Barry on the kitchen phone.

"I got no time for a kid, and I wouldn't know what to do with him," Barry yelled.

"Well, neither do I!" his mother shot back. She finally wore him down and Barry signed the papers to legally adopt Alex.

At 17, Alex dropped out of school altogether in favor of pushing a broom and mopping up fake blood from the movie sets. He was certainly eating and sleeping better at Falchion, where Barry gave him an unlimited food card for the cafeteria, and a small trailer of his own with a bed and a television. When Alex wasn't cleaning or hauling set pieces to and from storage, Barry said he could work out in the weight room. Benny saw him throwing weights around and approached him.

"You stupid punk!" Benny said, "you break those weights you'll pay for them. You have no clue what you're doing."

"I don't, Mr. Edwards," Alex said. "Nobody ever showed me."

Benny turned away with disgust, but the next time he saw Alex he shouted out a few pointers. "No, you still don't get it. Like this," Benny said, then picked up the weights and demonstrated how to bench press, curl, squat and dead-lift.

"There, now you do those exercises like I showed you and pretty soon you're going to look like somebody," Benny said, and marched out of the room.

Most of the actors and staff avoided Alex, too preoccupied with their own ambitions and schedules. Alex was shy and awkward, and he sometimes saw the women staffers laugh at him. He had no social outlet, but Alex was encouraged that Barry and Benny noticed his filled-out frame, and how he energetically cleaned the sets. They didn't seem to care if Alex overheard them, even when they talked about him directly.

"Look how he kind of goes into a trance as he works out," Barry mumbled to Benny.

"Kid's getting big, "Benny said. "The big dork reminds me of Quasimodo from *The Hunchback of Notre-Dame.*"

"I wonder if we could shape him into a cheap villain for some of our movies."

"Maybe, maybe—" Benny rubbed his chin, "—then maybe we can groom him for something that will make us some real money."

"Get him up to speed," Barry said.

Barry tried Alex as a sidekick in *No Anesthetic for Annie.* In make-up, the kid's bulky body and shy demeanor made him a creepy character on film. Barry paid Alex $200.00 per picture—but then started charging him rent, so Alex never accumulated much money. A steady paycheck, and a place to sleep kept Alex close. He'd felt both empowered and dominated.

"How do you feel, Mr. Movie Star?" Barry said, slapping Alex on the back.

"I feel great, Uncle Barry. This is more money than I've ever had all at once."

"Good, good, "Benny said. "You know, everybody who sees this movie is going see you too. You're going to be famous."

"Wow, that's awesome, Benny," Alex said.

"That's a lot better than livin' with that no-good woman," Barry said.

"You mean, my mother? Your sister, Uncle Barry?" Alex said, confused.

"You want to know the sad truth about life, Alex? Can you handle it?"

"I guess," Alex said, feeling uneasy.

"Women are no good. Truth is women don't care nothin' about nobody but themselves. They'll take the shirt right off your back, take your last dollar, eat all your food, let you kill yourself workin' for all the things they want, and never do nothin' that doesn't help them. Believe that, boy."

"There must be some good women in the world. My mom's just got a drug problem—"

"No, the truth is none of them are any good. They just take up space on the planet, breathe our air and take all the good stuff for themselves. If they had their way there wouldn't be no men on earth and those that survived would be slaves."

"You don't really believe that, Uncle Barry," Alex said, fighting the lump in his throat.

"Don't you tell me what I know is true. Thing is, nobody talks about it. It ain't socially polite. But deep down all men know it's true. Your mom hates you. She never wanted you. Me and Benny are your only real family now." Benny had been listening.

"Listen to your uncle, he's right," Benny said, reaching out and grasping Alex's shoulder.

"She didn't want to be that way," Alex said, swallowing and fighting back tears.

"It's tough to hear, kid, but Barry's telling you the truth. Women are scum."

Alex looked back and forth between the men, hardly comprehending the words.

"You both had mothers—there are girls at my school—who seem nice. There are girls who work on your movies who—"

"All scum," Benny said. "I'd rather have been born from a test tube than have come from the witch who birthed me."

"Any of those girls at your school would as soon step on your throat if you weren't helpin' them get somethin' they wanted. If you're not helpin' I'll bet they ignore you, right? Later, in the work world, they'll use all their feminine wiles to get ahead at your expense. If they marry you, you can be sure they're just countin' the days until you kick off, so they can get your life insurance money. Women are no good, Alex. The sooner you learn that the more successful you'll be and the better your life will be," Barry said.

"Bring it in here, boy," Barry said, as both men hugged Alex.

"You gotta' learn who to love and who to hate. Love your family, me and Benny. Get used to hatin' women," Barry said.

Alex slowly extracted himself from the Barry/Benny group hug. He then turned his head, and walked unsteadily to the far corner of the weight room, so the men wouldn't see him cry.

~

Benny was awakened by Barry's cell phone out in the living room. He got out of bed, walked down the hall, and saw Barry lying on his broken couch, Barry's cell phone glowing through the pocket of his suit jacket. Benny reached in and pulled it out. The caller's name: Malibu Memorial Hospital. Barry snored loudly.

"Barry Whitscomb's phone," Benny answered.

"Hello, may I speak with Barry Whitscomb?"

"What is this regarding?"

"I need to speak with Mr. Whitscomb. It's a private matter," the voice said.

Benny kicked Barry several times in the ribcage.

"Whu? What's goin' on?" Barry yelled.

"Phone, for you. Hospital," Benny said, thrusting the phone into Barry's face.

"This is Barry."

"Mr. Whitscomb. I have some shocking news, so you may want to sit down. Your nephew, Alex Boxwell-Whitscomb, was admitted two nights ago at Malibu Memorial for surgery. He had been hauled out of the surf at Topanga Beach with harpoon spears in him. We had to put him into a medically induced coma for his own safety. He's come out of it. We tried to reach you last night since you're listed as his legal guardian, but there was no answer."

"Is my nephew going to be alright?"

"It's too soon to say. He survived the night, and his vitals are stabilizing. We can't rule out the possibility of an infection, but he's out of the critical zone."

"Can I see him?" Barry asked.

"You're welcome to come down, but I wouldn't rush down here. The doctor needs to check him over first. Sometime in the next two hours he may be able to talk with you."

"Thank you for the call," Barry said and hung up.

"Well?" Benny said.

"Alex is alive, you jackass! Get us some coffee. Gotta wake our asses up and figure out what to do. You stupid bastard, Benny!"

"You want some breakfast, fatso?"

"Yeah. We gotta' figure out how. to smoke Alex, now," Barry said.

~

Jake ate breakfast with Vera at his kitchen table.

"Bubbe's such a drama queen," Vera said, "she objects to everything that isn't her idea."

"I hope she grows to accept me one day," Jake said.

"Don't take it personally, Jake, she doesn't like many people."

Jake's cell phone pinged. He saw it was a text from Dark Snout, giving him a status report.

Five thousand, five hundred dollars so far, whew, a little pricey, but it sounds like he's on Lola's trail, Jake thought, noticing a second text.

"Holy crap!" Jake said to Vera, "Alex is in Malibu Memorial hospital in critical condition with three harpoon wounds. He's in the trauma wing. What's going on?"

"What? I have to call Serena," Vera said, "her therapist thought it would be good for her to go to the hospital and forgive Alex, or maybe hoping he would apologize to her or whatever. Give me a second." Vera pushed "Serena" on her cell contacts.

"Hey, Serena, it's me, Vera. I know you were down about Alex's not being in the hospital anymore. I get it that he wouldn't be a threat to you in that condition. Well, he's back in the hospital and still not a threat. Yes. Trauma center, he had harpoon spears in him. He's recovering if you want to go chat him up."

"I can't go deal with this right now," Serena said. "maybe tomorrow?"

"Okay. Think about it," Vera said, "Goodnight, girlfriend."

~

Serena paced back and forth at the little café wringing her hands together. Suddenly, she wasn't hungry for the meal she had just ordered.

How can I face the man who beat me so badly he put me in the hospital? I can't alone. Vera isn't even the right person. I need that big wrestler woman in case Alex gets any ideas. How can I really trust he won't ever attack me again? I don't think I have it in my heart to forgive him. He beat me on purpose, in front of everyone, on camera and they kept the footage and they're going to make money from it! Those sickos!

She texted Jake for Rhonda Roundhouse's number.

~

Dark Snout cruised north up Sutter Street. The little red dot was moving slowly, diagonally across the screen. Ken was on foot. On foot, in a vehicle, it didn't really matter as long as he kept wearing the same button-down shirt, the one in which Dark Snout had stuck the tracking device. It was about the size of the end of a Q-tip swab and adhered to the underside of the shirt collar via a Velcro pad. Even if Ken went home to change that would be okay, provided he could get a visual on him first.

Dark Snout cruised a few blocks behind the red dot that was Ken. He turned the wheel slowly, stair-stepping a few streets over as Ken continued to cut through alleys, probably thinking he was being evasive. When the dot came to a stop Dark Snout realized he'd better try to get in close for a visual. He drove slowly. According to the remote grid he was within a block of Ken. The red dot still wasn't moving. Maybe he was just sitting down after his escape, to rest. He pursued Ken on foot.

He parked at the curb and walked briskly, glancing down at the tracking device every couple of steps. The red dot didn't move. He was now just 75 yards from the dot on the screen. He kept walking, more slowly now. Forty yards. Thirty. The dot moved just a bit. Good, he hadn't been detected. Twenty yards away. The dot was located inside The Beverly, a short-term stay apartment building. Dark Snout paused, then entered the double glass doors to the lobby. The dot on the screen was now only ten yards away.

Dark Snout turned the corner and glanced into the bar area with four big screen TVs. There was Ken, drinking deeply from a mug of beer. Ken had never seen Dark Snout's actual face, so he approached the far end of the bar and ordered a beer himself. It had been a long day and he could afford to unwind a bit, with his mark safely in sight.

Dark Snout sipped at his beer while he pretended to watch the Clippers playing the Mavericks. Suddenly, his cell phone vibrated. It was Rhonda.

"Hello?"

"Hi, Snouty. Can you to talk or are you on a secret assignment right now?"

"It's alright, Rhonda. Are you okay?"

"I am. It's just that I think there's some sort of divine intervention happening right now. That lady who Alex Boxwell beat up and, you know, then those folks hired me to—"

"Yes, I know, go on."

"Well, that lady, Ms. Serena Miles, just called me and she wants me to go with her tomorrow to visit Alex because she's scared to go alone. You see, her therapist thought it would be healing for her to forgive him, and I want to go and pray with him anyway. So, do you think it would be okay if I went with her?"

"No, for the same reasons I was concerned before. Someone is trying to murder Alex Boxwell. If you are with him you could be caught in a crossfire, or maybe they just won't care and kill everyone in the vicinity provided they get him. If you and Ms. Miles must go, I need to be there so if something happens, I can intervene."

"Okay. I do want everybody to be safe. When should we plan on going?"

"I can't say just yet. I have a little bit of a situation here tonight. Let me get squared away on my business then I can give you a definite time. Alright?"

"Okay, Snouty. Will you be home for supper?"

"I don't think so. Go ahead and eat without me. Good night, Rhonda."

"Nighty night, Snouty."

Chapter 37

Everybody Wants You

The attending physician checked Alex's wounds, his vitals, his vision, his ability to follow the doctor's finger with his eyes and to answer questions about time, date, name and relatives. The diagnosis: Alex Boxwell was sane and stable. Now the long process of healing could begin. The team would bring in a PTSD nurse to check him over, too.

"We've contacted your uncle, Alex. Are you up to a visit from him?" the doctor asked.

Alex sat up as straight as possible in his bed, his neck and back stiffened.

"No! Keep him away!" Alex yelled, his strained voice echoed into the hallway.

The doctor was so shaken by the outburst he almost dropped his stethoscope. "Why is that so upsetting to you?"

Alex collected his thoughts before answering, knowing his next words could bring turmoil and the police and he couldn't deal with that. He just wanted peace. There had been enough violence.

"I don't want him coming here. We've had a fight and I'm not ready to see him."

"But under the circumstances, your injuries, I think you'll find him sympathetic—"

"I don't want to see him. I don't want him in this room. Period! If I have to crawl out of here to get away I will."

"Alright, calm down. I'll let him know it's too early for visitors."

"Just *him* though. I have other people I'd like to see, like my *friends.*"

"I'll tell him if he calls," the doctor said.

"No. Call him so he doesn't think he can just drive down here. I don't want him just showing up here. Do it!" Alex yelled.

"Alright, I'll make the call," the doctor agreed. "Before you see your friends, however, I need to inform the sheriff's department of your condition when you were admitted."

"You don't have to do that. They're just going to ask a bunch of questions."

"It's procedure. If I don't, I'm guilty of a first-degree misdemeanor, punishable by a year in jail or one thousand dollars."

"I guess, if you have to," Alex sighed.

"What happened?" the doctor asked. "It did look suspicious, you have to admit."

"I don't want to talk about it."

~

Aaron Finklestein had left Shelley Arcongioli's condo two nights ago and he was already lusting for her again. He called her number and waited.

"Hi, it's me. I was wondering if I could come over after work?" Aaron said.

"You came over a couple of nights ago and had marathon sex with me. You stared off in the distance like a sex-crazed jackhammer. I felt like I didn't really need to be there for the whole thing. You kept me awake until one o'clock A.M. I was worn out and late for work."

"But you liked it, right? So, can I take that for a 'yes'?"

"No. I think you need to find some young bimbo to date, with an endless sex drive and nothing between the ears. Or better yet, you should get one of those blow-up dolls. You could pound away on one of those for hours and you wouldn't have to talk or be mentally present."

"Aw, come on, Shelley. I could bring a bottle of wine and—"

"—and take out? Like before? No, two days without a call and now you just want to come over and have more sex. Forget it! Don't bother calling me anymore!"

The line went dead.

"Well, that sucks," Aaron said to himself.

But he knew what she had said was true. The whole time he'd been with her he had fantasized about Vera. He'd almost slipped once and called Shelley by Vera's name. Vera had been on his radar since day one. He had to have her—

Aaron's phone rang. He eagerly picked it up, sure it was Shelley coming to her senses. Then he saw the screen: Dispatch.

"Lieutenant Finklestein?"

"Yeah?"

"Your vacation ended yesterday. Report to Malibu Memorial. You need to question a patient, one Alex Boxwell. Admitted there yesterday with multiple harpoon wounds."

"Ten four, I'm on it," Aaron said and walked out to his cruiser.

~

Dark Snout sipped his beer while looking past two other patrons at the bar. He kept an eye on Ken, absorbed in a pro hockey match on cable at the far end of the curved polished mahogany surface they all shared. The time would come when he would have to drag Ken outside of this bar, several blocks down the street and into his car. Not an easy prospect with a smaller man, but Ken was practically big enough to be a pro wrestler. Maybe it wasn't a coincidence that Ken had ducked into The Beverly. Maybe he lived in one of the short-stay apartments upstairs. Either way he could track him. Time was on his side and Dark Snout could park his car in front, thereby drastically cutting the distance. He decided to risk it. He laid a dollar on the bar and strolled outside. Once out the door he broke into an all-out sprint in the direction of his car.

With the tracker in one hand and his car remote in the other, Dark Snout continued his dash up the sidewalk, dodging in and out of pedestrian traffic. Although it was becoming dark outside, he recognized a couple of landmarks along the way: a jewelry store, a chained-off tree growing up through the sidewalk. He clicked his key fob and, voila: the yellow flashers lit up on his car. He jumped inside and accelerated into the sparse flow of traffic.

As he approached The Beverly, he saw the red dot that was Ken, in motion—back on the street and moving fast.

He's in a car. Another minute and he would have been out of range.

The engine raged as Dark Snout closed the gap between his car and one with Ken inside.

Twenty yards away, left lane, must be that yellow cab ahead.

He slowed down and fell in behind the cab, cruising at 30 miles per hour.

~

Rhonda had put the leftovers from dinner away, and she was almost finished vacuuming the carpeting of her double-wide trailer when her phone rang.

"Hi, Rhonda, it's me, Serena Miles."

"How are you, you poor dear?" Rhonda said.

"I'm not well." Serena sniffed. "I don't want to see that monster by myself. My therapist thinks I should, but if I don't do it soon, I'll lose my nerve. Will you please meet me in the lobby of Malibu Memorial in the morning?"

"I see your dilemma. Well, I have one too, a dilemma, that is. I promised my boyfriend I wouldn't go with you unless he could come along to keep an eye on me. I can't break my word so I'm going to call him and tell him he needs to meet us there, okay?"

"Okay, I'll be there at eight in the morning. I'm counting on you, Rhonda."

"Don't fret, darlin', I'll be there."

~

Aaron arrived in the lobby at 8:30 P.M. and flashed his badge at the admin clerk at the desk.

"Which room is Alex Boxwell's? Harpoon victim—admitted last night."

"Let's see—he's in room 415," the clerk said.

~

Alex sat up straight in bed, startled by the man in the blue uniform.

"Hi there. Do you remember me?" Aaron asked, smiling. "I interviewed you the last time you ended up in the hospital. Multiple broken bones, I think it was."

"I don't remember you," Alex said.

"Right, anesthesia does that, wipes out short-term memory. Anyway, trust me, we've met. I'm going to go out on a limb here and say somebody doesn't like you. Care to tell me what happened?"

Alex looked away. His mind raced. *Yes, tell him Benny and Barry did this. Simple self-preservation. Do it!*

But some weird, wounded part of Alex wouldn't let him. *Uncle Barry—Benny are my only real family—who cared about me. They helped me before all the talk about killing Vera.*

"I was surfing with friends. These dudes pulled up in a boat and shot me full of spears."

"You know who they are, but you're afraid to say. That about right?"

"I need protection!" Alex blurted out.

"If you want really good protection, you'll tell me who did this to you."

"I want a guard posted outside my room."

"Tell me who did this, and we'll issue an APB, pick these guys up and get you a guard."

"Look, I just want a guard for now. Let me think!"

"I'll make it simple. You did say 'dudes.' That's men, right? How many?"

"Two," Alex relented.

Aaron stepped into the hallway and called the station.

"Dispatch."

"This is Lieutenant Finklestein. Be advised I've taken Alex Boxwell's statement. He's acknowledged that two men pulled up in a boat while he and some friends were surfing and fired on him with a spear gun. I suspect he knows the perpetrators, but he won't ID them because he fears for his safety. He's requesting police protection."

"Copy that. Just a minute," the dispatcher said.

Aaron stepped into the room and smirked at the cowering Alex. He loved to dominate.

"Okay, Finklestein," the dispatcher said, "you're his protection for now. We'll assign someone to relieve you in four hours' time. Get him to fill out the proper form and check in at the end of your shift."

"Ten four," Aaron said, and pulled out the police protection form from his satchel.

~

Barry slapped Benny in the chest with the back of his hand.

"Get this, the hospital says Alex requested I not come and visit him. Things may change, but under his fragile condition it's too upsetting for me to visit. You believe that?"

"That's it? We've got to get down there, pronto," Benny said.

"And do what, Einstein? Kill him in his hospital room?"

"Hell yes. Before he tells everybody," Benny said.

"How you think you're gonna do that?"

"I've got some chloroform and a rag. That'll be quiet."

"Okay, and costumes. That's not the worst idea you've ever had," Barry said.

"Come on, I'll drive," Benny said.

"You wanna' know what the worst idea you ever had was?" Barry said.

"Shut up." Benny said, snatched up his keys and headed for the door.

~

The cab continued through the night. Dark Snout dropped back a bit and even let another car merge in between him and the cab. When the cab let Ken out, he would have to move with great stealth. He would use the tranquilizer gun disguised as a cane again, unless things changed, and he had to think on the fly. His cell phone vibrated, and he picked up.

"Hello?"

"Hi, Snouty?" Rhonda said, "I have a big favor to ask you."

"Okay."

"Oh, honey you are not fixin' to move over into my lane," Rhonda said.

"Rhonda, are you driving?" Dark Snout said. "I hope you're wearing a headset."

"Yes, sorry. Anyway, that poor Serena Miles has mustered up her courage to go meet with Alex Boxwell in the hospital and she needs me to go with her. I told her I would, but I had to call you first. We're meeting at eight o'clock in the hospital lobby. Can you meet us there?"

"I can't guarantee that, Rhonda. I've got a delicate situation in progress. It's not safe. Don't go without me."

"Don't be upset with me, Snouty, but I can't let that woman down. She's been through too much. At least I'm telling you where I'll be. Hopefully, you'll find a way to meet us."

"Rhonda, seriously, don't go. Someone is trying to kill Alex."

"I have to. I just didn't want to go behind your back. Now you know where I'll be. Please don't be upset with me."

The cab pulled over near some high rises and parked. Ken got out and handed some money through the window to the cabbie, who made change. He turned and walked up the sidewalk. It came to a T and Ken turned right and moved into a thin crowd of tourists.

"Rhonda, I have to go. I'll be there as soon as I can. Bye."

Dark Snout spotted a car just leaving from a parking spot and he raced for it just as another car tried to back in. Dark Snout got there first and carefully maneuvered his car into the spot, indifferent to the driver in the other car flipping him the bird. He grabbed the cane gun and tracker and ran into the crowd of slowly strolling people.

The red dot that represented Ken was two blocks ahead, moving slowly. Dark Snout picked up the pace, but a quick walk was all he could manage with the volume of humanity.

~

Doctor Alvarez had just finished a brilliant rhinoplasty operation. He had gone to extremes few other plastic surgeons would dare. He had shaved down the nose bone and maxilla to the point that they would never again support the nose tissue that had once been there. He had then applied the third skin graft so the woman with the once bulbus nose would now have one tiny and thin enough to complement the high, plump cheek bones he had installed earlier that year. He washed up and changed into his designer office wear. His assistant entered as Doctor Alvarez read the local paper.

"Doctor, Miss Grubb has no more trace of the flu. She is healthy and getting a good night's rest. She is ready for the extensive facial surgery in the morning if you are up for it."

"Excellent! Let's schedule it for tomorrow at one o'clock. I need to sleep in just a bit myself because tomorrow I shall do what the old adage says cannot be done."

He looked at his assistant and smiled. They nodded their heads and then said in unison:

"Turn a sow's ear into a silk purse!" They then chuckled at the well-worn joke.

~

Benny pulled out two pairs of reading glasses and a mid-length brown wig for himself, reminiscent of Peggy Fleming, and a long blonde one for Barry, from the props he'd taken from the set.

"Here, fatso, try these on," he said, shoving the wig and glasses at Barry.

Barry stretched the wig over his lustrous auburn hair until it was all tucked underneath, then he slid the readers behind his ears.

"You look adorable. Now, put on this poncho."

Barry lowered the hole in the baby-blue poncho over his head and adjusted it.

"These things don't go together at all," Barry said.

"That doesn't matter at all. What matters is that what you're wearing is something Barry Whitscomb would never, ever wear. Anybody who knows you knows that."

"You'd better look as dumb as I do, so we look like dorks who'd hang out together then."

Benny buttoned up a blousy, silk multi-colored shirt, lots of love beads around his neck, pulled up a pair of tan bellbottoms, and stepped into a pair of sandals.

"Okay, but our faces are still showing," Barry said.

"I've got a box of temporary tattoos. I'm going to put them all over your face and then you do me." Benny checked his Rolex. "We'd better hurry, it's two thirty A.M. already."

The tattoos took a lot longer than they thought. Some of them smeared and had to be washed off and new ones applied.

"I'm hungry," Benny said. "I'll make us some breakfast then we need to get going." Benny convinced Barry they needed to arrive at the hospital by 5:30 A.M. His logic had been that everybody would be settled in for the night, even security guards. Barry would have to chat up the guard, while Benny flanked the guard and chloroformed him first. Then they would advance on Alex. Cameras be damned, they'd see two crazy old hippies—and good luck finding them. The other reason to get there early would be to park a couple blocks away because he was pretty sure there would be cameras in the parking lots, too. They'd find the car, even though Benny had switched the plates.

Then, about two miles down the road, Benny got a flat. He cursed for five minutes as he pulled the spare, and the jack, from the trunk. It was pitch dark and it was

7:00 A.M. before they got it changed and got back on the road.

~

Serena sat in the back of Jake's limo, holding a steaming cup of coffee in both hands, occasionally stealing a too-hot sip, as the driver cruised toward the hospital.

She didn't have any career goals or even have herself anymore. That was the first thing. Get herself back. She'd willingly walked up onto that stage even after she'd let Benny belittle her, and even after she'd let Barry sleep with her all those times, promising her she'd be a star again, she'd stood there and let Alex beat her with that weapon again and again, without a peep, and put her in the hospital. The nurses told her that she'd almost died. And for what? This not okay at all. She had to be strong enough to confront that man, Alex.

~

Dark Snout tailed Ken to his apartment building, but Ken got inside before he could catch him. Dark Snout still had the advantage of knowing what Ken looked like, but Ken had never seen Dark Snout's real face. He entered the building, followed the red dot, which was accompanied by a small exponential number for each floor he ascended. *He's in the elevator,* Dark Snout thought. The red dot stopped on the fifth floor. Dark Snout glanced at his cell phone: 7:45 A.M. Decision time: abandon the chase and let down his client, or endanger the woman he loved? Dark Snout took the elevator to the fifth floor and got out. He'd give Ken a few more minutes, then he had to go.

Chapter 38

Wide-Angle Shot

Twenty-two minutes had passed since Ken entered his apartment. Dark Snout saw that the red dot was thirty feet away. *Ken's apartment, just around the corner from the elevators. If Ken steps outside his apartment and sees me standing there he can quickly duck back inside.* Dark Snout rounded the corner of the hallway with the tranquilizer cane gun at the ready. Yes, from here he could drag Ken back inside and devise a way to get him into the trunk of his car. Then he would be free to go check on Rhonda.

Dark Snout stepped around the corner where the hallway widened to allow for visitors to access the elevators. He'd hoped for a large convex mirror so he could see Ken approaching—*denied. I'll have to rely on Ken's noises to detect him.* He checked his watch: 7:59 A.M.

Rhonda and Serena will be at the hospital in one minute. I'm gambling with both women's lives. I'll have to abandon the chase, a two-day pursuit and a waste of my client's money. I won't charge him to catch Ken again. The clock restarts en route to Tijuana.

Ken rounded the corner in his Bellflower blue EMT scrubs and nearly silent sneakers—catching Dark Snout completely off guard. Then, three people exited the elevator and Ken stepped on. Exasperated, Dark Snout had no choice but to hobble in using the cane, as if he were disabled, and stand in the back of the elevator as they both descended to the lobby.

The doors opened and Dark Snout followed several feet behind Ken as he walked out onto the crowded sidewalk. Bright daylight. He saw his car ahead and decided he'd better move ahead of Ken since he wouldn't have time to catch up once Ken hailed a cab. He dashed in and out of pedestrians, until he reached his car.

No way to track Ken now—he's changed clothes. Must keep him within sight. Impossible to dart him now—too many witnesses. Only hope: get Ken alone once he reaches destination— either R.A.M.P. ambulance service or Malibu Memorial.

~

Barry and Benny arrived at Malibu Memorial in their hippies-of-questionable-gender-outfits and inquired at the front desk about which room was Alex's. They emerged from the elevator on the fourth floor and saw the sign with the arrows: "400-430" left; "401-429" right. They turned right and followed the ascending room numbers until, in the distance, they saw the big muscular cop guarding the doorway. Benny grabbed Barry's arm just as the cop noticed them.

"Hey, that's gotta be—"

"I know," Barry hissed, then said, "I need some water," loudly enough to be heard up and down the hallway.

Barry and Benny turned around and retreated down the hallway.

~

Dark Snout backed out of his parking space and double parked with his flashers on. He strained his neck to look behind him where Ken stood, his blue scrubs brilliant in the morning sunshine, his arm outstretched for a cab. One appeared, Ken got in, and sped into traffic.

Dark Snout glanced left then raced out there—too close but trusting his fellow motorists to have good brakes. Horns blared and skidding tires shrieked as he caught up to Ken's cab. He noted the exit the cab took and realized with a sigh that Ken would be reporting directly to Malibu Memorial. Just a five-minute drive and they'd be on hospital grounds. He's just have to get Ken into his trunk then he could check on Rhonda.

Must see this assignment through, then take a small vacation with Rhonda. Promised her I'd retire in five years—when that time arrives, I'll be ready. Ready to let my guard down, ready to tell her my real name and to hear her say it.

The cabbie had rounded an enormous curve and put on his turn signal for the hospital exit where the Santa Monica Freeway connected with the Harbor Freeway which soared overhead in a ponderous loop of concrete and asphalt that plunged the traffic into deep shade.

~

Rhonda and Serena had arrived and gotten the room number, but then Serena stalled.

"Come on, darlin'," Rhonda said, taking Serena by the elbow. "We need to go see Alex."

"I need a minute before I confront him," Serena said, entering the ladies' room.

Rhonda patiently waited outside. After five minutes she entered and found Serena staring at her reflection in the mirror, as if frozen.

"This won't get any easier by avoiding it. Let's go, honeybunch," Rhonda said, putting her hand around Serena's shoulder, coaxing her into motion.

"Alright, alright, I'm coming."

Serena and Rhonda slowly made their way across the lobby. Rhonda pushed the "up" arrow and waited for the elevator.

~

Ken's cab pulled over next to the curb. Dark Snout saw him pay the cabbie, get out and approach a side door, an electronic key card in his hand. With no time to park in a proper space, Dark Snout pulled over by the egress lines a couple of yards from the emergency loading zone and put on his flashers. He ran across the lawn; he had to catch Ken. Ken, who had already gained entry to the private EMT door; Ken who had disappeared behind the door, which was slowly being pulled closed behind him by a pneumatic device.

Dark Snout sprinted, so unlike his assumed character—the man with a cane—but it no longer mattered. He couldn't run any harder, the door opening was only six inches wide and narrowing by the second. With two yards to go, Dark Snout lunged forward and jammed his cane in the door opening, which abruptly closed on it. He pulled the door open and entered.

He saw Ken just rounding the hallway corner where he waved his ID card over a lighted monitor then walked toward a door at the end of the hall labeled "Lobby".

"Ken, just the person I wanted to see," said an authoritative older woman in a navy-blue uniform. "Bring me a blood panel from the second floor lab marked 'Joyner', please."

"I'm just starting my shift, Katy," Ken said. "Where's your assistant?"

"She's late. Come on, I'm swamped. I'll owe you."

"Sorry, no time," Ken said, and entered the lobby.

Dark Snout followed just feet behind. Ken jogged for the elevator doors, too late, they were already closing, with the faces of two women staring straight ahead. The larger of the two reacted to something behind Ken.

"Alex is in room 415, Snouty!" the woman yelled, her hand held up in a wave.

Cool in a crisis, Dark Snout didn't answer.

Ken turned around, a smirk on his face and said to the man behind him "Snouty"?

"Strange, right?" Dark Snout replied.

Ken's whole body went stiff for a second. That voice. The man who had emitted the sound: the voice of the psychopath who had tormented him the night before—*right here!*

"It's you!" Ken yelled, then lunged at the man holding the cane, but Dark Snout used an aikido move which sent Ken stumbling. "You're the freak from last night!"

"You're flipping out, dude," Dark Snout said.

"How'd you find me? Get away from me, you twisted bastard!"

Ken ran for the stairway. Dark Snout gave chase, up the first flight of steps, pivoted at the landing and chased Ken up the next flight.

"If I'm flipping out, then why are you chasing me? Get away or I'll kill you," Ken yelled down the stairwell, his voice sounding desperate.

Dark Snout paused to aim his dart gun, but his chest was heaving from sprinting and he couldn't get a clear shot up through the metal railings anyway. He continued the pursuit as Ken took another flight of steps.

~

"What are we going to do about that big cop?" Barry whispered.

"You talk him up while I flank him and grab him around the nose and mouth with that chloroform rag. He's probably going to try to hit you, maybe he'll succeed," Benny said. "I need your guarantee that you won't let him use his gun or nightstick on me, even if he hits you. You've got to grab his hands."

Barry looked dubious. "Okay, I can take a hit for the team," he said. "And then? Go chloroform Alex, right? He should be a lot easier."

"You betcha," Benny said.

The elevator "dinged" and the doors spread open revealing Serena and Rhonda. They looked right at Benny and Barry. They took in their colorful outfits, the hair, the beads, the bell-bottoms, and the girth of them, but didn't recognize them and went on their way.

"That was a good idea you had about the disguises," Barry whispered.

"Holy shit. You've got that right," Benny said.

"Looks like we've got to wait."

The cop stepped forward at the women's approach, like the aggressive rottweiler he was. He checked their IDs and asked that they leave their handbags and purses in a basket sitting outside the doorway at his feet. They complied. He then frisked them both, lingering on Serena until Rhonda sternly cleared her throat. The women were about to enter Alex's room when a stairway door burst open and loud running footsteps and shouting filled the hallway.

A large man ran past Barry and Benny, followed a second later by a smaller man with a cane. At the sight of the smaller man, something clicked in Benny's mind. *That face!*

Rhonda and Serena paused in the doorway as Aaron assumed an aggressive stance, his hand on his night stick, ready. The men ran by the doorway in a blur, but long enough for Rhonda to recognize her man.

"We'll be right here when you're finished," she yelled.

Dark Snout glanced at her for a second and nodded. The nod was not lost on Benny.

"Get this guy away from me! Help!" Ken yelled at the cop.

"I'm on duty here," Aaron called back. "I'll call security."

The men continued running.

"Just stop him!" Ken yelled behind him, hitting the exit door at the end of the hallway.

Dark Snout followed. Ken dropped through space, down the stairway, four steps at a time, hit the landing, spun and leaped down the next four. Dark Snout leaped the entire flight of steps and landed in a crouch, stood, leaned over the railing and steadied his aim. Ken, in mid-leap was an easy target—huge, V-shaped back. It was extremely satisfying for Dark Snout to see the little, red-feathered dart appear near the back of Ken's neck. Ken landed, then tried to stand before collapsing on the second-floor landing near the exit door.

"Thank you," Dark Snout said, as he tried to slow his breathing. He took his time, descending to deal with Ken's hulking, unconscious body.

~

Benny looked at Barry, his mouth open in silent protest.

"That's the guy —I know him! Change of plan, change of plan," Benny said, holding his temples, his eyes squinted shut.

Benny crept back into his memories, like slowly moving ratchets covered in cobwebs, to that day in The Grove. *Everything had been going so well, dappled sunlight, nice hot espresso, just worked over the barista kid—then he showed up and everything went to Hell in a handcart! That handsome face, that confident laugh. He said he was an insurance salesman, but I don't think so. Next thing I knew I thought I was a mouse. He made me feel so scared. I can never forgive that.*

"What the hell you talkin' about, Benny?" Barry asked.

"I'm *talking* about that's the guy who apparently drugged me and put me in the state you found me in at my house!"

"You mean when you thought you was a rodent, and everything wanted to eat you?"

"Yes! That's what. And I want that son-of-a-bitch dead. And that big woman knows who he is and where to find him. So, we postpone doing Alex until we find out who he is."

"Too risky. We can't keep pushing our luck; Alex is bound to spill the beans soon."

"No, if Alex was going to rat us out, we'd already be in jail. We just have to wait until those chicks come out then we'll get that big one when she goes outside."

~

Aaron walked ahead of the ladies up to Alex's bed.

"Mr. Boxwell, you have visitors: Serena Miles and Rhonda Franklin," Aaron said.

"I know Serena, but who is the other woman?" Alex asked. But the size of her body, overweight and so musculature, reminded him of something.

"She's my friend, "Serena said. "She's here for emotional support."

"You look like you've been through the mill, hon," Rhonda said.

"Yeah, I'm really sore," Alex said, "How do you two know each other?"

"Rhonda worked for Jake for a while, moving set pieces," Serena said, finding her voice.

"Don't you have something you'd like to say to Serena?" Rhonda asked.

"Thanks for coming to see me?" Alex asked, face flushed red, unable to face Serena.

"No, that's not what I meant," Rhonda said.

"I'm sorry I hurt you. You didn't deserve it," Alex stammered.

"Why did you do it?" Serena said, shaking uncontrollably.

Rhonda put her heavy arm around Serena's shoulder.

"Uncle Barry and Benny told me to do it."

"Oh no, that isn't going to cut it, Alex," Rhonda said. "They told you to do it—and you listened? Whose fault does that make it?"

"It's okay," Serena said, stepping forward, "I've got this."

"Mine," Alex said. "It's all my fault. I'm sorry I hurt you so bad, Serena. I wish I could take it back."

"Well, you can't," Serena said.

"I suffered too. Had my bones broken, got harpooned, almost got eaten by sharks—"

"Good. I don't feel sorry for you, Alex. How did you think it was okay to hit me?"

"My head was so messed up back then. Barry and Benny convinced me I was an apex predator, top of the food chain. That it was the natural order of things."

"Wow, and you believed that bullshit?" Serena said.

"I know. Looking back, it was stupid."

"That's an understatement. What if I died? I almost did, by the way. You'd be in jail, Alex. That's where you should be."

"I know. You're right. But I've been punished a lot," Alex said, "What can I do to prove how sorry I am?"

"I don't know. Your apology is a start, I guess. I can't forgive you, though."

Alex looked Rhonda up and down and frowned. "You're the lady who put me in the hospital, aren't you?"

"Why do you say that?" Rhonda asked, gulping.

"Because you're built like The Hulk and you're here with Serena."

"Yes, I am. You needed to be taught a lesson."

"You're right. I deserved it. You're not going to beat me anymore, are you?"

"No, I'm here to pray for you. Is that alright?"

"Yeah, sure."

"Everybody close your eyes. Heavenly Father, guide this young man, a stray from your flock, to see that this wonderful woman is more than just a punching bag to be beaten. Help him to see that she has a divine soul. Help him to see, Father, that he is better than to have a job where Satan's minions whisper sinful ideas in his ear. Help him to have a stronger mind, oh Heavenly Father, so he doesn't listen to foolish ideas in the future. And, Father, help poor sister Serena heal from this injustice and one day, through your guidance, to find peace. Thank you, Father, for your blessings and help brother Alex to find the way to serve you and seek your forgiveness too. For he has gravely sinned. Amen."

As Rhonda and Serena opened their eyes, they were surprised to see Alex sobbing. He made two attempts to speak but couldn't.

"I'm sorry!" he wailed, as anesthetic-fueled tears and saliva streamed.

~

Benny and Barry watched as Serena and the big woman picked up their purses and Aaron noted the time of their departure on his note pad. The women walked in Barry's and Benny's direction, apparently to take the elevator down to the lobby. Barry and Benny took the stairs.

~

Dark Snout had left Ken's body in the stairway. He opened the door and chanced a casual stroll down the hallway until he came to the dull gray/blue service elevator. He stepped inside. He scanned the buttons on the control panel but found the floors weren't labelled, only numbered. He assumed the laundry room would be in the basement. B1, doors opened: Strike out. B2, doors opened: Bingo.

He entered a room of enormous industrial washers and dryers and mostly

Latino faces. Dark Snout helped himself to one of the hanging uniforms everyone wore. Then brazenly took a twenty-bushel capacity vinyl laundry cart with heavy-duty caster wheels. He pushed it past the staring eyes toward the service elevator, grabbing two dirty bedsheets on the way.

Once inside, he dressed in the uniform and pushed 2. By the time he finished dressing, the doors opened. He wheeled the cart down the hall to the exit door. The cart was too wide to fit through the stairway door opening, apparently so no one would try what he was about to do. He propped the door open with the cart corner jammed in there, so it stayed open.

Now the tough part: getting Ken into that cart. Fortunately, the flexible vinyl sides folded down so he would only have to lift dead-weight-Ken a few inches off the floor.

"Jeez, this guy's heavy," Dark Snout said under his breath, as he lifted and shoved Ken's bulk into the far side of the cart. He stretched the vinyl side back up and clipped the spring-loaded snap hooks into place in the large grommets, so the vinyl held. He covered Ken with the dirty sheets, then wheeled the cart back toward the service elevator.

~

Benny and Barry stood on the sidewalk outside the glassed-in lobby. Once they saw Serena and Rhonda had arrived in the lobby, Benny grabbed Barry's arm.

"I'll be right back, gotta get something from the car. Don't you lose her!"

"Okay," Barry said, rubbing his arm as Benny took off running.

Rhonda had asked Serena if she wanted to talk or have dinner, but Serena had declined, saying she just needed to have some alone time. They hugged and Serena walked in the direction of the parking lot as she called Jake's limo driver on her cell.

Rhonda wasn't sure which way to go. She hoped Snouty would find her. Or maybe she should call him, but she'd been calling him a lot lately and it was clear he was busy chasing that big old dude. On the other hand, she didn't know how soon he would be back. She decided to go sit in her car and wait. She had had enough of this hospital.

Barry saw the big woman walking across the parking lot. He looked behind him to see Benny running with something big and angular held under his blousy silk, multi-colored shirt—his Peggy Fleming wig blowing, his tan bell-bottomed legs churning to close the distance. Seconds later, Benny stopped, leaned over, his hands planted on his knees, his chest heaving.

"Where is she?" Benny panted.

"She's right there, see?" Barry pointed to the distant silhouette walking away from them. She walked beside a brick wall covered with English Ivy, near an alley.

"Come on, we've got to jog," Benny said, gripping the things inside his shirt.

Soon they caught up to Rhonda. She heard their footsteps and turned around. Barry and Benny spread out and Benny circled around behind her.

"Hold it right there, lady," Barry said.

"Hey now, what do y'all want?" Rhonda said, turning from side to side, trying to keep them both in her field of vision. "I don't know you ladies—I mean, fellas. What's that smell?"

"We need some information," Barry said stepping toward her.

Rhonda advanced on him, accustomed to confronting aggression in the wrestling ring. Just then, Benny sprung up onto Rhonda's back, his legs wrapped around her neck, he held the chloroform rag tightly over her nose and mouth. She reached upward to grab the rag, but Barry beat her to it, holding her wrists down to her sides. She stumbled in circles while Benny rode her like a bronco. Gradually, the chloroform took effect as Rhonda collapsed on the parking lot. Benny looked up, saw the alley was a few yards away and pulled Rhonda into a sitting position.

"Come on, fatso, help me get her into that alley."

They carried her into the alleyway by her hands and feet, her body sagging between them, and leaned her into a sitting position against the wooden siding. Benny reached into his shirt and pulled out a length of twine, his crossbow, and three harpoon spears. He tied her hands behind her back then cut the twine and tied her ankles together. Benny and Barry were both huffing from exertion and were content to admire their handiwork and catch their breath while Rhonda gradually came to.

"Ugh, what's this all about?" she said.

"Who's that good-looking guy you were talking to in the hallway? The one who ran by," Benny asked.

"Just some guy," Rhonda said.

"Well, let me see if I can jog your memory," Benny said, locking a spear into the crossbow and aiming it at the siding next to Rhonda's head.

He fired and the spear was instantly deeply imbedded in the siding only inches from Rhonda's face. It stuck there, slightly vibrating.

"Next one goes right in your face, bitch, unless you tell me his name," Benny said, locking another spear into position.

"I don't know!" Rhonda said. "I only know he goes by the name Dark Snout."

"I'm not playing around here, sweetheart. Last chance." Benny aimed the spear directly at Rhonda's face.

"I'm telling the truth! I call him Dark Snout. That's the only way I know him. Please don't kill me. Oh, Lord, help me!"

Benny released the safety and took aim.

"Wait," Barry said, pushing the crossbow aside. "She really thinks you're gonna kill her. I think she's telling the truth. We don't need no more trouble."

Benny seemed to consider this. He lowered the crossbow and took the spear out.

"Okay, chicky-baby. It's your lucky day. You stay here, somebody will find you."

"Uh, we need to be smart for once," Barry said, stomping on the spear in the siding.

He kicked it from both sides, pulled and finally wrenched it from the siding, chunks of wood and pink insulation coming out along with the barbed head. Barry wrapped the spear in a piece of newspaper lying in the alley and tucked it under his arm.

"Fingerprints," he said.

They left the alley. Rhonda watched the two cross-dressing men leave. As they got out of hearing distance from Rhonda, Barry spoke.

"What good did that do? You didn't get any information, we don't know nothin' and now there's another reason the law might be comin' down on us?"

"We just watch her. She'll get loose or call somebody to help her. I'll bet that dude that messed with me will come help her. I meant it when I said I want him dead. Nobody treats Benny Edwards that way and lives."

"We're just supposed to stand around here and wait?"

"No, I'll get the car. We can wait in it and watch from a distance with my binoculars. When that dude shows, we follow him. Stand over there and keep watch until I get back."

Barry walked to the far side of the parking lot and waited.

~

Dark Snout pushed the laundry cart out the side loading bay. He avoided looking behind him so as not to appear suspicious. He had already seen a security guard running past him on the second floor, earlier.

No need to panic. I still have the cane dart gun, all my martial arts skills and god knows I can run fast. But I have no plausible excuse to wheel this cartload of laundry out to my car. If confronted and I run, I'll lose Ken and fail my client and Miss Lola Grubb. Not an option. Bottom line: I'll have to fight if I'm stopped.

He pushed the cart to the rear of his car. He popped the trunk lid and lowered the vinyl siding. In one huge, swooping move he reached his arms under Ken's body and dead-lifted him, then spun around and lowered him into the trunk and closed the lid. He looked around, no security guards in sight yet.

He parked, got out and shrugged out of the laundry worker's uniform, then stuffed it under his seat. He locked up and jogged back toward the hospital. He didn't yet have a plan, but he had to check on Rhonda. He felt confident the guards would never suspect him to come back on their turf so soon.

He came up behind the hospital parking lot—alert for security guards in the distance. As he got closer, he could swear he heard a familiar voice.

Must be my imagination. That sounds like Rhonda.

"Snouty! Snouty, help me!" the voice cried. It seemed to be nearby.

Dark Snout walked more slowly now, cautiously checking out his surroundings. He walked closer to an ivy-covered wall, an alley in the distance, the hospital about a block away.

"Snouty! Snouty! Help!"

That is Rhonda. Down that alley!

He ran, rounding the corner and dashing to her side.

"Oh, Snouty! You came for me. I knew you would!"

"Rhonda, what happened?"

"Oh my gosh, honey, you were right. They were going to kill me if I didn't tell them your name. And it was just like you said: I didn't know it so I couldn't tell them then, and they didn't kill me. You were right. When you made me call you that name, I thought it was the dumbest thing in the world, but you saved my life!"

"How were they trying to kill you?"

"With a harpoon gun. They were going to shoot me in the face! That's where they shot one spear into the wall!"

"I'm glad you're safe, I love you, Rhonda," Dark Snout said, untying her.

"I love you too, Snouty."

"Come on, let's get you out of here. If they wanted me that badly they're probably coming back. Is Serena alright?"

"Oh, yes, she left an hour ago."

"It's not safe to go in your car. We can come back for it later. I need you to catch a cab and meet me at that little delicatessen we like. Order something and pay for it. Call me after you've ordered, and I'll pick you up."

"Okay, Snouty," Rhonda said, and gave him a kiss.

~

Benny and Barry sat in the car, watching.

"Benny, there's your boy. You gonna kill him now, or what?" Barry said.

"Where he's going?" Benny said, the car slowly creeping from the parking lot.

Dark Snout sensed the distant creeping car. *Why so slow? Why so obvious?* He walked back the way he came, stair-stepped over a city block, then cut through a dark alley, filled with trash cans and homeless folks, and out to the street on the other side. No car would be able to follow. He turned left, sprinted to his car, and drove away.

Benny saw the man duck down the alley. He gunned his car and rounded the block. The man was gone.

"There are nearly four million people living in L.A," Benny said, "I'll never find him."

Chapter 39
Fisheye Shot

Benny sat in Barry's office—Barry at his desk and Benny, in an overstuffed maroon leather chair, reading the latest issue of Slasher, THE horror movie review magazine in the industry. Barry had already read it. It featured a glowing review of his most reviled competitor, You'd Better Run Girl Films, and their smash hit, *Sharpest Tool in the Shed,* rated R.

The maroon chair had been Barry's first piece of furniture—paid for from the proceeds of his 1984 blockbuster hit from 1984, *I'll Give You Something to Cry About.* He'd bought it because it was the color of blood. Fresh blood, before it dries and darkens. It was nice reminiscing, but Barry had a serious problem. He cleared his mind and thought of nothing, said nothing, just stared at Benny. Finally, Barry cleared his throat.

"Benny, let me ask you something'. What's the advantage of going to all the trouble of having a cast party, pullin' Vera away from it to kill her, only for her not to come back? Seems to me that just leaves a party full of witnesses with questions."

"You ever go to a party and bug out half-way through?" Benny asked.

"No, I usually close the place down if there's eats and booze."

"Yeah, that's because you're a legendary eating machine. Most folks make a cameo appearance, get revved up, meet someone hot and then say, 'You want to get out of here?'"

"Sounds right. But Jake and Vera are an item now. He'll get suspicious."

"So, we'll spike his drink. In fact, we'll put out lots of top shelf liquor, so nobody's memory is too sharp. They won't be witness to anything—they'll be suspects. In the meantime, you and I will get rid of the body, get cleaned up and get the remaining partiers out into the street. So it looks like just a normal party, the hosts shutting the doors to clean up. Make sure Jake leaves, we can even act concerned, help him into the limo."

"That's the kind of thinkin' the Benny I knew used to do—smart."

"That's what I'm known for," Benny said, "smart thinking."

~

Ken awoke staked out spread eagle wearing only his boxer shorts. He recognized the room—Dark Snout's lair. He heard muted mewing, growing closer from somewhere behind and above his head. The man who wore the black, furry wolf's mask, stooped down and gently set the cardboard box of kittens on the floor next to Ken's head. Dark Snout left and returned with a pitcher of cream.

"You can't imagine how much I hate you, man," Ken snarled.

"What did I say I would do if you gave me any trouble? If you had simply followed the rules we would have already gone to Tijuana and been back by now and you would be free and on your way." Dark Snout started to tilt the pitcher of cream toward Ken's bare chest.

"Wait! Wait, you son of a bitch."

Dark Snout paused, the pitcher in mid-air.

"How did you even find me? Never mind. You know, there's really something wrong with you. Have you ever considered getting professional help? Like from a shrink? You're a grown man—dressing up in a wolf mask, chasing people around the city and doing sick shit like this to them just because they want to make a few extra bucks. I didn't hurt that girl. She sought out the plastic surgeon. All I did was transport her there."

"I'm a professional, I dress to fit the occasion. Shall we proceed so we can hit the road?"

"Just—just don't do this! Let's just go to Tijuana! Don't, man!"

Dark Snout drizzled the cream over Ken's nipples, set the pitcher down and withdrew the first of the kittens from the box.

"You remember this cute little gray one, don't you?" Dark Snout lowered the kitten, all its paws splaying, trying to find solid ground. "And how about this adorable little white one?" Dark Snout set the hungry kittens on Ken's chest.

"I hate you! I hate you! Aughhhh!" Ken screamed, as the rough little tongues made first contact with the cream covering his nipples.

"Duly noted," Dark Snout said and chuckled from inside the mask.

~

Lola lay beneath freshly laundered sheets and breathed the familiar fragrant scent of desert flowers drifting through the open window as gauzy window curtains lightly rippled. She stared at the same Mexican painting on the wall, same ceramic blue water pitcher on the table.

How long have I been here? God, I'm so bored!

"Miss Grubb, I am happy to say all traces of the flu have left your system and we are clear to begin surgery."

It was the doctor. Lola was so out of it she hadn't noticed him there. She looked up from her bed and tilted her head as if to affirm she had heard correctly.

"If you agree, we can proceed tomorrow at one o'clock," Doctor Alvarez said.

"I am so damned ready. Tomorrow at one. It's a date," Lola said.

Lola watched his white lab coat flutter out the doorway.

Alone again, Lola's thoughts drifted to Brian. She and Brian had spent a lot of time together leading up to her accident, and she was afraid to think that he really cared about her. It must have been a sort of fascination with the novelty of seeing the ugliest girl around. But to go as far as to propose to her? She wondered how he'd react after her surgery.

I'm sick of thinking about Brian, and waiting for this doctor to carve up my face is nerve-racking. It's supposed to be an impulse thing—like getting a tattoo. Quick, then if I regret it it's too late. Lola thought, and switched on the radio news channel.

"Numerous sightings reported off Topanga Bay, by the swimmers and surfers, of a metal rod, sticking about two feet above the water, and cruising vertically through it," said the newscaster.

"A local fisherman says, 'It moves like a very thin periscope, and appears to be the end of a harpoon spear.' Both the coast guard and a local marine biologist have announced they will investigate. We'll keep you posted as the story develops."

"That's freaking weird," Lola said.

Chapter 40

Save Yourself

So, this is surgery day, Lola thought, *the day and time I agreed to let them carve up my face, so I resemble Rachel McAdams. Why? Oh, because she's the best-looking movie star from the brochure the doctor's assistant gave me. Pretty random way to choose my new face.*

Lola sat on the edge of her bed and gazed into the small desk mirror. Doctor Alvarez had discouraged her from having a mirror in her room; he'd said it might cause her trauma due to her accident or to obsess over her appearance. She'd laughed on both counts. Face-planting through a mirror while aboard a speeding moped was traumatic, but she didn't fear this stationary mirror on its stand, and *please,* she'd had a lifetime of comments about her face.

Since it might be the last time she saw her face she decided to say good bye. She gazed at the image of her muddy grey eyes, recessed in their sockets, raisin-like, too close together, off-center and shadowed by her unibrow. Her stubby eyelashes blinked; she studied the rest of her pock-marked face. The trace of fine, branch-lightning scars now spread across much of her face, one of the more prominent ones crossed above her lips—and appeared again across her cheek.

She smiled, revealing tiny buck teeth set crookedly in large gums. Her short, upturned nose and huge nostrils were intact, as was her low hairline, which still appeared to close in on her remaining forehead. Thank god her full lips were okay. They were more prominent because her buck teeth pushed them outward, and how Brian had loved kissing them. She reflected on that for a moment.

I'd loved kissing him too, but what the hell was that? The time I spent, at first fending off his advances, then surrendering to them? It made no sense. He could have any girl he wanted. But he'd kept coming back to me. Why? By this time, he's probably with one of those L.A. models or little hottie actresses.

Part of the reason she'd wanted the plastic surgery was so she could become a better match for him. Then, she reasoned, she would be more comfortable with his affections. The other part was that she'd been on a rough path so long she wondered what it would be like to be so beautiful that everybody loved her on sight. She'd had weeks to ponder the subject without the cloudiness of drugs or pain. She now wondered…

What was I thinking? Hells no! I'm not doing it.

There was a knock at the door. Lola jolted out of her musings.

"Miss Grubb? It's Dr. Alvarez. May I come in?"

"Sure," she answered.

He approached her, a twinkle in his eye, white lab coat aflutter, his assistant in tow.

"Are you ready to become beautiful?" the doctor asked.

"I'm not having the surgery," Lola said.

The doctor's jaw dropped open. "But, but why? We've planned this surgery for weeks. You've chosen the look you want. You've already paid a considerable sum—"

"This face is who I am. It's this face and this brain that are responsible for my success so far. We've been through a lot together. I can't turn my back on them now, it would be disloyal."

"But this is the opportunity of a lifetime. You've made the effort to be brought here. You can be a beautiful woman going forward."

"I'm already who I want to be and I'm doing it on my terms. So, how do I get out of here? How ever you were going to get me back to the States I want to go now."

"This is so unexpected. I suppose we can have a truck here in a week or two. You can wait in your room until dinner and I'll make some calls."

"Seriously? Wait in my room? Why does it take a week or two?"

"It is not such an easy thing to transport someone across the border without a passport and birth certificate. I will check the docket to see when our next patient will arrive and to make arrangements for you to be on the return trip."

"You've put me in a real dungeon of distress, doctor."

"Because you changed your mind. I will do my best. Try to relax."

~

While wearing his black wolf mask, Dark Snout walked Ken, in chains and handcuffs, into his garage. He opened the passenger side door of his car, guided hand- and ankle-cuffed Ken in, then seat-belted him.

"I'll be right back," Dark Snout said, as he disappeared through the doorway.

He entered the hall bathroom, removed his mask and expertly applied heavy eyebrows and a thick adhesive mustache. Back in the garage, he slid into the driver's seat, pressed the garage door remote and backed into the driveway.

"I know what you look like, man!" Ken threatened.

"Really?" Dark Snout said, guarding his expression as he drove. "Every time you've seen me—I've worn a different disguise. The truth is you have no idea what I look like."

A lie. It was a risk to show my face in the hospital, but time didn't permit a ruse.

"Look, I'll give you directions to the doctor's practice," Ken said. "That's what you want, right?"

"Yes, but I can't trust that you'll tell me the truth."

"You already have my cell; you can see the last GPS directions I used in Tijuana, so you'll know I'm telling the truth."

"That's true, Ken. Do you make it a habit to travel to Mexico?"

"Only when I deliver a new patient to the clinic. I'm sick of this! I'm missing work."

"Let me set you straight on something. If you lie, I'll catch you. Like I did before, and you'll be punished, this time by hungry chihuahua puppies with teeth. Then we're still going to Tijuana, you and me. Do we have a deal?" Dark Snout said.

"Yes," Ken said, huffing in misery.

Dark Snout pulled over. He parked and scrolled through Ken's travel routes. He found the one in Tijuana and pushed the phone in front of Ken's eyes.

"Is this the location?"

"Yes. Now let me go, please."

"I'll drop you off a couple of blocks from your condo."

They drove into a vacant lot and wheeled the car around, so it faced the street. Dark Snout leaned over and unlocked Ken.

"I've got this dart gun on you. Don't look at me, or my car, keep your head down."

"Okay," Ken said.

Ken got out, his head down. He heard the engine rage, heard and felt a hail of dust and gravel pelt him from the tires spinning out. And suddenly, the stranger was gone.

~

Dark Snout had driven for about an hour when he checked the GPS and pulled off on an exit which led to a smaller two-lane road. He followed the signs for Rodriquez Airstrip. He pulled up next to a hangar and got out. He walked toward the trailer office, bounced up the steps, knocked once and entered. He peeled off his bushy, adhesive mustache.

"Hello, Bill," Dark Snout said to the man behind the desk.

"Well, if it's not the medic who saved my life. What the hell are you doing here?" the man said, rounding the desk. They hugged each other, ending with two hearty back slaps.

"I need a favor. A small plane for a few hours," Dark Snout said. "I've got to make an extraction, a woman being held captive in Tijuana, a U.S. citizen."

"I assume she doesn't have her credentials?"

"No, otherwise I'd just drive her out."

"I have a twin-piston Cessna 402," Bill said, picking up a clipboard with a chart on it, "but a client needs it by five o'clock. That gives you five hours to do what you have to do and get it back here. Make that four hours—I need a cushion to get it fueled up and ready. I have to charge you for fuel too."

"Of course, I'll pay your regular fee and all related costs. I just have to go incognito," Dark Snout said, pressing his fake mustache back into place.

"Understood. Anything for you. At which airstrip are you planning to land?"

"I don't have time for that. I need to touch down, free the woman and beat it back here."

"Oh, that's not going to be so easy. The F.A.A.'s watching, so is ATC. The ATC is going to contact you on a discreet squawk code as soon as you enter Mexico's airspace."

"No problem."

"They'll want your flight-plan."

"Bill, I can tell them whatever I need to say, fill me in. Then I need to go, that four-hour window is closing in on me."

"Okay, if you're not landing at an affiliated airstrip your story is you needed to turn back—medical emergency. A family member. I'll write down the rest for you on this form. Give me a minute," the man said.

"Fill this out and I need a payment method."

Dark Snout pulled a debit card out, which had $20,000 on it, and an alias designation, complete with address, phone number, the works. He filled out the form with the same alias information. The man ran the charge and handed the card back.

"I had to put a $5,000 deposit fee on hold, I'll refund it as soon as you return the plane."

"Understood. Keys now, please."

"Here ya' go," Bill said, handing them over. "Hey, you think we did any good over there in Afghanistan?"

"We did what we had to. Seems like a long time ago now."

"Nineteen years."

"See you in four hours, Bill," Dark Snout said, as he walked out the door.

Once seated and buckled up, Dark Snout started the engine. A loud droning resounded as Dark Snout pulled on his headset and slid on his dark glasses.

Seconds later he was airborne, leaving the land below, the Pacific Ocean to the west glittered with a million sparkles.

Dark Snout responded to the person who contacted him over the intercom, jabbering in aeronautic jargon over the radio. Afterward, he gazed down at the landscape of Mexico. Thousands of small homes spread out to the horizon, punctuated by strip malls and industrial plants, followed by hundreds of miles of brown grasses and cactus, scrub brush crisscrossed by animal trails, and distant mountains.

Dark Snout consulted Ken's GPS and began his descent. He looked down, aiming to land right on the street, on a single strip of blacktop which led in front of the surgical building.

Dark Snout lowered the landing gear. The wind caused the small plane's wings to waver up and down, pulled it sideways, then abruptly released it. The wheels touched down, bounced, chirped and the air brakes roared in his ears. He stopped two blocks from the medical building.

Dark Snout set the brake but kept the engine running. He ran toward the surgical building, the cane-gun in his hand. Tumbleweeds rolled and bounced as he ran onward.

Dark Snout slowed to a walk and approached the double glass doors. He entered and surveyed the interior. A waiting room, Talavera tile floor, a couch where one man read a magazine, a receptionist behind a glass window, and a security guard stood beside a metal door to the hallway beyond.

"I need to see Dr. Alvarez," he said.

"He's in surgery right now," the receptionist said. "If you'll have a seat—"

"Where is the surgery taking place?"

"Just down the hallway," she said.

Dark Snout advanced.

"You can't go in there, Señor!" she yelled, but Dark Snout was already on the move.

The security guard held out one arm and reached for his night stick with the other, as Dark Snout raised his cane and pulled the trigger. The guard looked surprised as the red-feathered dart sank into his chest. His eyes rolled back in his head and he collapsed in a heap.

Dark Snout was already inside the hallway, ripping open doors, looking for someone in surgical scrubs. Beyond the third door he found two men in button-down dress shirts and white lab coats, looking at a chart together. They turned around at the door's banging open.

"Who are you? Get out!" Dr. Alvarez said.

"Where is Lola Grubb?" Dark Snout said, pointing the cane-gun. "Tell me now or I'll shoot you both with tranquilizer darts and you'll wake up with nasty headaches."

"She is a patient in our care. Who are you, Señor?" the assistant said.

"Someone who means business," Dark Snout said and darted him in the chest. "Do you want the same, doctor?"

"Why are you doing this?" the doctor asked, watching his assistant crumble to the floor.

"Take me to her or I'm darting you."

"You don't know what you're doing. Who are you to Miss Grubb?"

The receptionist peered through the opened door and called to the doctor.

"Our security guard is unconscious. I've called the police, Dr. Alvarez."

The receptionist noticed the surgical assistant on the floor.

"Take me to Lola Grubb, now," Dark Snout said.

He followed Dr. Alvarez two doors down.

"This is her room," the doctor said, knocking once and entering.

"What the hell?" Lola said.

"Miss Grubb, this man demands to see you."

"Who are you?" Lola said.

"I'm here to extract you and return you to some people who are very worried about you."

"Extract me? Like I'm a pimple? How did you find me?"

"It's what I do. I find lost people and return them to loved ones," Dark Snout said.

"What loved ones? What worried people?" Lola said.

"Jake L'Hommedieu and your fiancé, Brian.

"He's not my fiancé!" Lola said. "And how do you know Brian?"

"Mr. L'Hommedieu informed me. Regardless, I know you are not exactly here of your own free will, so I am here to take you home."

"She contacted us," Doctor Alvarez said. "Can you believe she does not want to look better? It's her decision, of course."

"I'm here to take you home," Dark Snout said. "Would you like to go home?"

"So, you're basically like a taxi? Sure, I'll take a ride back to the States."

"We have to go immediately," Dark Snout said, "Get your things, now."

"Are you trying to tell me what to do, dude?"

"My plane leaves in two minutes. Come on if you want to be on it."

"There is just the matter of signing her out," Doctor Alvarez stammered, "and settling her final bill."

"I think you've gotten enough of my money," Lola said. "See ya." She grabbed her cell phone and ran for the door. Dark Snout followed.

She raced down the hallway, through the door, past the unconscious guard and out the front doorway. On open ground Dark Snout easily caught up to her and took the lead.

They reached the plane, but suddenly he and Lola stopped and faced the road behind the plane. Their expressions turned serious. The Federales' cars approached, lights and sirens wailing toward them in the distance.

"Get in the plane, now!" Dark Snout shouted.

Lola boarded as Dark Snout scrambled into the cockpit.

"If you get us arrested, I'm going to kill you," Lola said.

"Take your seat, we're taking off."

Dark Snout manned the controls, wound out the engine and eased the throttle forward. The plane's wheels raced toward the surgical building. Soon the engine was up to speed and they taxied to 75 miles per hour, 100...Dark Snout eased the throttle forward an inch and they raced along the street to 120...130 and they were airborne.

Lola heard several distant popping noises. "What's that cracking noise?" she asked.

"The cops are shooting at us," Dark Snout said.

"Holy shit! You idiot, you're going to get us killed!"

"We're out of range. Sit back and relax."

At an altitude of 300 feet, they banked right and reversed course for San Diego.

~

At 4:00 P.M. Dark Snout and Lola had deplaned.

"I'll be right back, then we'll get you home. You can wait in the car, see you in a couple," Dark Snout said, pointing his key fob at his car.

He jogged up the steps to the taxi trailer, as Lola stared after him.

"Okay, Bill, here's your plane, right on time."

"Okay, sign here. Let me run your card again. Your deposit will show up as a credit in a few hours. Don't be a stranger," the man said.

"Unfortunately, that's exactly what I'll be until I retire."

"And I'll bet that's on a need-to-know-basis, right?"

"That's right, Bill. Thanks again," Dark Snout said, as he exited the trailer.

~

Even after driving for half an hour, Lola kept up a constant barrage of complaining.

"Where the fuck are we?" she said.

"Ms. Grubb, we're about an hour from L.A.," Dark Snout said. "I'm taking you home to your friends,"

"Who the hell are you? Who said I wanted to be 'extracted'?"

"We've been over this, Miss. My mission is to extract you from your captors and return you to Jake L'Hommedieu. He tells me Brian is heart-sick for your company."

"I don't like this. I never asked anyone to search for me, and I asked who you are?"

"It's not important who I am. Isn't it enough that I rescued you?"

"Rescued me? Excuse me? You didn't rescue me, Mr. Eighties Mustache. I already had things under control."

"Miss Grubb, people are worried about you, they've paid so much money for your safe return—"

"They've paid? I paid thousands of dollars for that surgery! It's not up to them what I do. It doesn't concern you either. Stop this car and let me out!" Lola said.

"You're probably hungry or thirsty, right?" he said.

"Yeah, I am. They wouldn't let me eat before surgery."

"Do you like Mexican?" he said. "Tacos? Burritos? My treat."

"Yeah, I could eat something."

Half an hour later, Dark Snout and Lola sat at a shaded picnic table outside a Mexican restaurant. Lola had just finished her third taco and a large soda.

"That was really good," she said, with a burp.

"I agree. I'm not really such a bad person," Dark Snout said.

"Let's go, "Lola said.

"Absolutely," Dark Snout said, "let's hit the road."

"You said Jake is the one who wants me to come back?"

"Jake is financing your extraction, but I understand it's only because he was so moved by how heart-broken Brian is for you."

"Brian's not the boss of me either," Lola said.

"You are a spirited one," Dark Snout said with a smile. Lola smiled back, which on her, appeared to be a frown. Dark Snout quickly looked away.

~

At 7:00 P.M., Dark Snout and Lola were back in L.A.

Dark Snout texted Jake that he had Lola and would drop her off near his condo as soon as he received his final payment of $17,500.00. Dark Snout's cell pinged. The money had arrived. He texted Jake that Lola was at the park near his condo, and he could pick her up at his leisure.

Ten minutes later, Jake's limo pulled up, with Jake and Brian in the back. They got out and ran to Lola. She stood, one hand on her hip, not moving, a scowl on her face.

"Lola, Lola, are you okay?" Brian said. He hugged her and kissed her neck and cheeks, then held her out at arm's length.

Lola had not kissed Brian even once as she assessed the situation.

"Let me look at you. They didn't do anything to your face did they?" Brian said.

Lola smiled at the worried look on his face.

"No," Brian said. "That adorable wart that disappeared into the crease when you smiled—it's gone!"

"I lost it in the accident. You remembered, a stupid little thing like that about me?" Lola said, a tear nearly escaping her piggy eye.

"Yes, I loved that wart. But it's okay, it's okay. You're alright and I love you. I'm so glad you didn't mess yourself up with that surgery."

"Look, I'm still butt-ugly and you're so handsome. I was going to look like Rachel McAdams, so we'd be a better match."

"Girls like her are a dime a dozen around here. If I'd wanted someone like her I'd be with someone like her. I only want you, Lola. You're special."

"You're crazy, Brian. But I think you really do love me," she said and kissed him. "Thanks for getting me, Jake."

"I'm just glad you're alright. This guy was so depressed I couldn't even look at him."

"Really? I was sure you'd be off the market by now," Lola said.

"No way," Brian said

Lola and Brian walked with their arms tightly around each other all the way to the limo. Jake sat opposite Lola and Brian in the large passenger seating of the limo. He just smiled on the ride back to his place as they kissed.

After Lola showered and changed into some of Naomi's clothes, and after everyone had hugged Lola, Brian walked to the center of the room. He stood in front of Lola, who sat in a chair, and he pulled out a gray, velvet box.

"Oh my god, you're really going to do this again," Lola said, and laughed, as Brian got down on one knee.

"Stop," Lola said. "Get up. I'm not going to freakin' marry you. It's okay if we let everyone know we're an item though. That's going to have to hold you for a while."

"Okay, but I'm still coming for you," Brian said. "I'll hold this ring until you're ready."

"Okay, whatever, Brian."

~

Jake and Vera sat at his dining room table, Jake with a cup of coffee, Vera with her mug of chamomile tea, revising Jake's rom-dram.

"*Angel in Sea of Sharks?*" Vera said. "Why 'angel'? Why not 'smart girl'?"

"Because if she's so smart she has no obstacles to overcome. Where's the conflict? Besides, *Smart Girl in a Sea of Sharks* doesn't have a ring to it."

"Did I ever tell you my grandfather was a prisoner in Auschwitz? He told me whatever I do in life I should never allow myself to become a victim? What do I do but get a job where I portray one? I can't help someone who wants to write *another* screenplay about a victim."

"But that's not what this film is about. It's actually very empowering for women. The heroine does initially get taken advantage of, but later she turns the tables on the bad guys and even winds up in a romance."

"And let me guess, does this love interest somehow save the poor girl?"

"Yes, how did you know?" Jake asked.

Just then the doorbell rang, and Jake stood to answer it. He peeked through the eye hole and saw Felix and Andy standing there.

"Oh, jeez," he said under his breath, then whisked open the door.

"Ja-a-a-aake, it's been so long since we've seen you! Andy and I thought we'd just stop by and catch up," Felix said.

"We brought wine," Andy said. "I hope we're not interrupting anything."

"Actually, Vera and I were going over a new script and we're running behind schedule."

"Okay, then we'll just stop in for a minute," Felix said, stepping past Jake.

"Um, okay, I guess," Jake said.

"We've missed you at Falchion so much," Felix said. "If you'd been around, you'd see how nice we've both become. We took for granted what a gifted director you really are."

Vera leaned forward in her chair so she could see them through the stucco archway to the kitchen. Felix saw her and waved. Vera wanly waved back.

"Oh Jake, Vera's totes adorbs," Felix said. "It's no wonder you want her all to yourself. Listen, we won't take up much of your time. We just remembered your offer to introduce us to your designer friend, Adriano Moretti, and we wanted you to know that we are very available."

"Any time," Andy chimed in. "Mornings, noons, afternoons, weekends. We'll work around your schedule."

"Okay, I'll think about it. Next time he's in town—he travels a lot, you know."

"Oh, for sure, London, Paris, I can only imagine. We'll be on our way. Hope to see you and Vera at the cast party Friday."

"What cast party?" Jake asked.

"See? You're out of the loop. That's why you need us as friends. Barry is throwing a cast party for *The Organ Pedaler*. It's supposed to be the gala event of the season. At least stop by and say hi to the gang, Jake. Promise?"

"I guess we could stop by for a bit. Now, if you'll excuse me, I've got a script to save."

"We understand, ta-ta for now, Mr. Director. We can't wait to see it on the big screen."

Jake shut the door and returned to the petite creature who sat at his table. Even in her pajamas, with no makeup on, with her brows scrunched in concentration, a pencil in her mouth, even knowing she disapproved of his script, knowing she'd yelled at him, argued with him, stormed out on him, had never had sex with him, challenged him, she couldn't know how pretty she was or how much he loved her.

~

Pete, Otto and Sammy arrived at Alex Boxwell's hospital room and were immediately confronted by Officer Aaron Finklestein.

"I need to frisk you all individually. You, step forward, you other two wait your turn." Aaron had one hand on his night stick, the other patting Pete down, then lightly shoving him toward the wall with his free hand. Once he had frisked all three surfers and had them deposit their keys, wallets and cell phones in the basket at his feet, he faced them head on.

"Now, you all face me, and come in closer, like a huddle," Aaron said.

The men huddled up.

"Closer, come on, get in here," he said.

As the men complied, Aaron grabbed the two outer heads and conked all three heads together. The men staggered back a step, rubbed their skulls and grimaced in pain.

"Bogus!" Otto yelled.

"Hey, man, officer, what did you do that for?" Sammy said.

"You, with the hair, stand against the wall until I say you can go in," Aaron said.

"That's total harassment, dude," Pete said. "It's that kind of uncool behavior that gives cops a bad name. So, why?"

"Because I don't like you guys. Are you high right now? Do you even have jobs?"

"We're pro surfers. Like, on-the-cover-of-surfing-magazines famous. Like we've got sponsors and beaucoup bucks. We just don't dress like it. Free country and all that," Otto said.

"I'll keep that in mind. You can go in now if you want to visit your friend."

"Oh, thanks so much, *your majesty*," Pete said, sliding by Aaron's massive frame.

Alex had heard the commotion and pressed the remote on the tray. The top part of the bed rose as the electric motor whirred, causing the IV attached to his arm to slightly sway. When Alex saw Pete, Otto and Sammy stroll in he had to smile. Because, despite his lousy state of mind and the pain creeping through his body, these guys lit a warm glow inside him.

"Al, dude, it's so awesome to see you," Otto said.

"You okay? They wouldn't reveal your locale," Sammy said, "we had to dig, dude."

Alex couldn't find his voice yet, but he smiled as Pete reached out and gripped fingers with him, Otto gripped Pete's and Alex's fingers, and not to be left out, Sammy gripped the whole pile of knuckles and shook them.

"All for one, dudes, and one for all!" Pete said.

When the fingers released, Alex picked up the glass of ice chips and sucked on one.

"They won't let me have water right now. Thanks for coming, you guys."

"What happened out there? Do you know those dudes who harpooned you?" Otto asked.

"I do—they're family," Alex said.

"No offense, but some family. You've got to turn them in. I cry foul," Otto said.

"I don't think I can do that. Know what else? I'm pretty sure they still want to kill me."

"Dude, you're talkin' cra-cra," Pete said. "Don't be any more of a hero than you already are. Those dudes need to do time."

"Speaking of hero," Sammy said, "we saw sharks, you were bleeding copious amounts."

"Why aren't you being digested by a shark somewhere down below?" Otto said.

"Because when the first shark attacked me from below it got stuck in the mouth by the spear sticking through my leg, through the board and that scared it off."

"Badass!" Sammy said.

"And when another shark, way bigger than the first one, was swimming straight for me, and I'm talkin' down at water level, boys, I thought I was going to die, so I yanked the spear from my leg and took both hands and shoved that spear right into its nose. It was such a big shark, so long, that it still knocked me totally off my board a second later."

"No freakin' way, dude!" said Otto.

"I'd cry bullshit except we saw that shark and here you are—alive," Sammy said.

"I think we finally have your nickname for the beach," Otto said. "Shark-Slayer!"

"Right on, Slayer for short," said Pete. "You know who's really going to dig that? That babe you were dancing with at the bonfire, April. You're the stuff of legends. She loves brave dudes, all the superhero movies. But you're the real deal."

"Thanks for cheering me up, guys, but I have a confession." Alex looked downcast. "I'm not a good person."

"What? How can you say that, Al?" Otto said.

"You guys don't really know me. I grew up with no dad. My mom's a crazy crackhead."

"That doesn't make you bad," Otto said.

"I got mixed up with some bad people who talked me into beating up a nice lady. I put her in the hospital." Alex stopped to take in the gaping-jawed expressions from his friends. "You still think I'm a hero?"

"So, like, you beat up a lady? Is she okay now?" Sammy asked.

"Yeah, she's okay. But another lady, huge lady, broke a lot of my bones: arm, leg, ribs, finger, sprained my back and put me in the hospital as payback. I was in there for months."

"So, okay, you got paid back, right?" Sammy said.

"Yeah, I was paid back. But the lady I beat up was just in here and she doesn't forgive me. She has trauma from what I did, and she had to go through therapy just to face me."

"You mean she was up here, in this hospital room, and she saw how gimped up you are, and she still can't forgive you? Dude, that's like, more than even—cause two beatings for one. Karma-wise that's paid in-full, dude," Pete said.

"But when I beat her up they made a horror film of her really getting beaten up and people made money from her public beating on film," Alex said.

"Wow, that's not cool. Can you get that film off the streets?" Sammy asked.

"If I want to go to prison by admitting to authorities I did it."

"That's heavy. It's not like a dozen roses and a card will fix that," Otto said.

"Know what?" Sammy said. "If you decide you want to go to prison, we've got your back. We'll visit you and bring you munchies and what not. And when you get out you'll have a clear conscience."

"He doesn't want to go to prison, dude!" Pete said, punching Sammy in the shoulder.

"Whoa, hold on. Main thing is you've got to turn those dudes in who harpooned you," Pete said. "Dude, why are you loyal to them?"

"I didn't have any real family, who cared about me. They helped me a lot for a few years before this happened. How can I turn them in now?"

"I know this is hard, Al, but you've got to hear this. Those dudes aren't your family—they're not even your friends. Hell, we're much more your family than any dudes who try to murder your ass. Think about it," Pete said.

"Yeah, we're your true bros, Al," Sammy said. "Turn those dudes in and we'll get you healed up then you can work it out with that lady who won't forgive you. Once that's all behind you you're going to be king of the surf. I guarantee it."

"But it's just so hard turning in your own family" Alex said.

Chapter 41

That's a Wrap

Aaron's phone rang—it was the theme music to Darth Vader's entrance, the tone he'd assigned to calls from the Chief of Police.

"Lieutenant Finklestein."

"Finklestein, this is your make-it-or-break-it moment. You've got some bad press to overcome before you earn your captain's bars. Are you listening?"

"Yes, sir."

"Alright. I need you to solve this little mystery surrounding Alex Boxwell. Normally, a case like Boxwell's fades away either because (A.) he's no one famous or (B.) nobody pressed charges or (C.) he has no family members making a stink about it with the press."

"Yes, Chief."

"But there's a fourth scenario. One where a city desk editor has a history of disliking our department because he feels we've been picking on his reporters: writing them frivolous parking and speeding tickets. arresting drunken family members repeatedly—you get my drift?"

"Yes, sir."

"So, he's written a series of articles: "L.A. Police Detectives Asleep at the Wheel" parts one through three and counting. In short, he's making us look incompetent."

"Excuse me, sir, but I think we have some excellent criminal investigators. Taylor cracked that Valesquez case and Perez solved that—"

"You're right, Finklestein, those guys are good. But their plates are full. I need you to wrap up the Boxwell case. I know you can do it. You're a street cop with your ear to the ground and you've already crossed paths with Boxwell a few times. It should be easy, the reporter from the L.A. Herald Examiner has even connected the dots for you. It all hinges around Falchion Films. I want to know who put Serena Miles in the hospital, who then put Alex Boxwell in the hospital, and then who harpooned him and put him in there again. And why is nobody talking about it? You wrap this up and you'll get your captain's bars. Can you handle it, son?"

"Consider it done."

"Good man, Finklestein. You're relieved of guard duty. Your replacement has already been dispatched."

"Yes, sir," Aaron said. But the chief had already hung up.

~

Aaron already had his confession from Alex Boxwell—months ago. He had spelled it out—he had admitted to beating Miss Miles with the rubber-coated clever. The problem was Boxwell had been under anesthesia at the time, so it was inadmissible in court. Still, he had his man.

By noon Aaron had collected the harpoon spear which the Malibu Memorial surgical team had extracted from Alex's torso. He then did a search to find which manufacturer makes that brand of spear as well as a list of local distributors. His search yielded the brand: Beuchat Espandon and the closest distributor was Wave Masters, boat rentals and fishing supplies.

Fifteen minutes later Aaron entered the store and flashed his badge to the owner behind the counter. He inquired about harpoon sales and boat rentals from the prior week. Sales and rentals had been light: only three spear sales and one boat rental. A couple from Connecticut had purchased three individual spears, a long-time local fisherman bought six, and a man with his face covered with zinc oxide, who wore dark glasses and a hat pulled down low, had rented a boat and bought a complete spear gun and a dozen spears. Aaron asked for and got copies of all three patron's I.D.s.

He walked out to his cruiser and requested background checks on all three, looking for priors. All three came back clean. The I.D. belonging to the man with the zinc oxide mask was a fake. Aaron asked to see the surveillance discs from the prior week. The owner gave him copies of both inside and outside disks. He took them to the station and, with help from the boys in the lab, he found the man wearing face makeup, who kept his head down while inside the store. The only thing Aaron could make out was that he appeared short and stocky.

Outside footage revealed that the vehicle used to tow the boat had stolen plates and there was a second individual inside in the passenger's side who appeared obese. Aaron had the lab boys enhance the pixilated area behind the windshield, but between the tinted glass and the glare on the windshield the best they could get was a more defined outline.

Aaron then visited Falchion Films to look for means, opportunity and motive for the battery on Ms. Miles. He would have to prove Boxwell did it. He was sure the battery on Boxwell and then the harpooning of same would be connected.

The first person he encountered was the woman he had, twice, rolled around in bed with, Shelley Arcongioli, who sat behind the receptionist's desk.

"Well, well, if it's not my big tomcat come back to play," Shelley said. "I do like the way you look in that uniform."

"Shelley. I'm here on business. Do you recognize the car in this photo?"

"*So serious.* Yes, I've seen that banged up car in the parking lot."

"Any idea who this guy is? Or the overweight gentleman in the passenger's side?"

"I can't tell. They're both so hard to see."

"How about body size? Anybody short and stocky or obese who works here?"

"All different size people work here. Some stagehands are short, a couple are overweight. Then of course there's the owner of Falchion Films, Barry Whitscomb. He's on the large size."

Right! Aaron thought back. *Twice I watched Vera on shoots. She'd been afraid of someone. Barry Whitscomb did seem nervous and asked me to leave the set. Huh?*

"Do you know where I can find Barry Whitscomb right now?"

"Let me check. He has a nine o'clock meeting with a bank loan officer, You might be able to find Barry in his office or maybe in the cafeteria. Later, there's going to be a big cast party—biggest ever, Benny told me, they've both been planning it. I think Barry and Benny will be running all over until the party tonight. I'm going to be too, so many details to—"

"Thanks," Aaron interrupted, "Now, what can you tell me about Alex Boxwell? Does anyone have a grudge against him? Is he well-liked here?"

"Alex is Barry's adopted nephew. Barry doesn't like people interacting with Alex unless he's on a shoot. Barry and Benny always keep Alex to themselves—like he's their pet project."

"Who's this Benny? What do you mean 'pet project'?"

"Benny's the acting coach. He's someone who's stocky, like you said. Anyway, Benny encouraged Alex to lift weights and get big muscles, but then when he got them he didn't want Alex to show them off except on a shoot, on set. They don't like him to make friends."

"What's Benny's last name and what's he like?"

"Edwards, Benny Edwards. Tough little guy—intense."

"Thanks, Shelley. Now, what happened to Serena Miles?"

"I really couldn't say."

"You couldn't? Or you won't?"

"That was really sad. Sometimes there are accidents on the set. She got hurt when she and Alex were doing a scene together."

"As I recall it was several well-placed blunt-force trauma 'accidents.'"

"Alex is kind of clumsy. He had to get in close enough with the rubber-coated cleaver—to make it look like he was really hitting her," Shelley said, looking away.

"It's almost like you're trying to protect somebody, Miss Arcongioli?"

"Look, Aaron, you snoop around all you like, but don't you mess with my livelihood." Shelley said, and tapped her fingernail on the desktop.

"Serena Miles was almost killed. If you know something about it and withhold evidence you are an accessory to a crime."

"What's the sudden interest in Serena? That happened months ago."

"I'm leaving now. But I'll be back. Remember, if this goes to trial and you're subpoenaed as a witness I'd think hard about lying under oath. See ya."

~

Aaron drove toward the hospital to question Alex. *One-forty, still early enough to scare Alex into talking. I'll catch up to Whitscomb and Edwards at the cast party. Barry's Alex's uncle?* Right, Whitscomb told me that. Aaron decided to clear his head. He switched on the local news channel on the radio.

"—third report of what some at Topanga Beach are calling a 'thin periscope,'" the newscaster said. "A local fisherman is here in our studio to describe what he saw."

"It was like a thin metal rod, moving vertically through the water, pretty fast."

"Where were you when you saw it?" the newscaster said.

"Out in my boat, fishing. About three-four hundred feet out."

"Thank you. We'll keep you updated as this story unfolds," the newscaster said.

"Huh?" Aaron said aloud as he wheeled into the Malibu Memorial parking lot.

He grabbed his floppy leather satchel and entered the lobby. On the fourth floor, Aaron entered Alex's room without warning.

"Alex, you already told me it was you who put Serena Miles in the hospital a few months back," Aaron said, "Why would you do a thing like that?"

"What are you talking about?" Alex said, sitting up abruptly at Aaron's arrival.

"You told me that the first time you were in the hospital. You also told me some big 'she-beast' beat you up, remember?"

"No, I don't. I never said either of those things."

"Yeah, anesthesia will do that to you. Get you talking—makes it so you say things you don't remember later. Wipes out the short-term memory. The point is, you did it, Alex. Right now—" Aaron reached into the satchel and withdrew a metal spear in a plastic bag, "I'd like to know who shot this into you?"

"Where'd you get that?"

"The surgical staff. It's evidence. Now, who shot you full of harpoon spears?"

"I'm badly injured, almost died. Nurse!" Alex yelled.

"I know you put Ms. Miles in the hospital, and I suspect you know who beat you up the first time. Who tried to kill you? Somebody wants you dead. What are you hiding, Boxwell?"

"Nurse!" Alex yelled and pushed the panic button on his bedside console.

The nurse entered, saw Alex's blood pressure on the monitor and faced Aaron.

"You'll have to leave, officer, you're upsetting the patient and he's in a fragile state."

"I'll go. But I'll be back and you're going to tell me everything. Otherwise, your next stop will be jail," Aaron said, and pointed at Alex on the way out the door.

Chapter 42

The Cast Party

By the time Aaron reached Falchion Films the parking lot was nearly full of catering trucks and beverage vehicles. He circled the block twice before finding a parking space, then made the long walk around the chain link fence and across the lot. Moving people and staff members carried boxes and decorations, and pushed crates of liquor on dollies, through the double doorway.

Aaron stopped a security guard by slapping the back of his hand on the guard's chest.

"Hey, bud. What's going on in there?"

"One big-assed party tonight," the guard said.

Aaron stuck his head through the doorway and took it all in: dozens of people stood atop twelve-foot step ladders adjusting mirrored disco balls and hanging gold and black Greek comedy/tragedy masks. Silver "Hollywood" and red "Horror" cut outs were hung from the ceiling by nine-foot lengths of fishing line, just above head-height. He stepped back as the rapidly rolling end of a two-hundred-foot red carpet slapped open. Two young men, out of breath from pushing it along the floor, jogged to a stop.

"This place is huge," Aaron said.

"You got that right," a mover said. "We're supposed to make it feel smaller, 'cozy' if you can believe that."

"What time does it start?"

"All I know is we've got to be done by six-thirty," the mover said, and helped the others position an enormous antique cabinet.

Aaron checked his wristwatch: 1:50 P.M.

He stepped back into the blazing sunlight and followed the sidewalk to the main entrance. He opened the door and stood before Shelley's desk once more.

"Hey, Aaron," Shelley said, "I have a little bone to pick with you."

"Yeah?"

"The way you spoke with me earlier—that tone is not okay with me. I really don't care what you're investigating."

"Okay," Aaron exhaled. "So where can I find Barry Whitscomb or Benny Edwards?"

"I'm not telling you anything. Nobody talks to me that way—cop or otherwise."

"What do you want, Shelley, an apology?"

"Yes. You could also pretend to be a human being. We slept together, remember?"

"I'm sorry, Shelley. Now, could you please tell me where I can find those two?"

"I don't know exactly. Like I said earlier, there's a huge cast party tonight and there are a lot of details to handle. In fact, I've got phone calls to answer. We might have some 'B-list' stars tonight." Shelley leaned toward Aaron with an insider's smile. Her desk phone rang and she waved goodbye to him with her pinky finger.

As Aaron walked away, he overheard her phone conversation.

"Hello, Falchion Films. How may I help you? No, I don't know where you heard that, but Jessica Alba is not attending tonight—"

Aaron wandered the corridors. He paused at each studio door, trying each knob, turning it if it wasn't locked, and peeking inside. Most had the lights off, but occasionally the lights were on and there were a couple of actors up on stage bouncing lines off each other while a small audience sat and listened. During pauses Aaron would call out.

"Has anybody seen Barry Whitscomb or Benny Edwards?"

He got variations of the same response.

"Not today." "Big cast party tonight." "We're trying to practice—do you mind?"

Aaron continued until he found one door that wouldn't open but there was a light coming from underneath. "Set Piece Storage" was engraved into a brushed aluminum sign above it. Aaron knocked on the door but there was no answer. He moved on, checking more doors as he went. Most rooms were empty, dusty sets; lights, projector stands, fuzzy microphones leaning toward the stage on long metal poles, as if a scene was started and then abandoned.

He reached the cafeteria, which had multiple glass windows flanking double glass doors. Inside, hordes of people sat eating, as others waited in line to order. Aaron got in line.

This detective work makes me hungry.

He reached the front of the line and ordered a double helping of beef stroganoff and steamed broccoli, He sat and ate. *Hot and delicious! Mmmm.*

A young woman approached him. "That's the most realistic-looking cop uniform I've ever seen," the woman said, "I could almost believe you're a real cop."

"I am a real cop. I'm looking for Barry Whitscomb—or Benny Edwards. Seen them?"

"I saw both about an hour ago. I tried to schedule an acting class with Benny, but they were in a hurry and just blew me off."

"Which way did they go?"

"Through that door, they turned right," the woman said, and gestured to the entrance.

Aaron tipped his head to her, ate the last bite and stalked out the exit door. Once in the hallway he checked his watch again: 3:15 P.M. He decided to try the doors with the lights on again. This time most were off. When he came to the Set Piece Storage Room the light was still on. He tried to turn the knob, but it was locked. He knocked on the door and thought he heard a noise from inside. Then silence.

Exasperated, he returned to Shelley's desk. Her eyes lit up as he approached.

"Hey, hon," she said, all traces of her being miffed were gone. "It's been a real madhouse in here. Everybody and their dogs are coming to this party tonight."

"Wow," Aaron said, attempting to show interest. "Any sign of Barry or Benny?"

"No, you won't see them for the rest of the day. They've probably gone home to chill until the party. Too bad you don't have an invitation—you're sure to catch them there." Shelley said, winking and running her fingers across her supple neck.

"I don't need an invitation. I'm a cop."

"So you are," Shelley said, her eyes turning flat. "Well, I'll be there tonight. If you get tired of sleuthing, stop by for a drink."

"What time does it start?"

"Eight o'clock."

"Okay, thanks, Shelley."

~

Barry and Benny detailed the fake set of *The Organ Pedaler* in Set Piece Storage.

"I've come up with the perfect distraction to get Vera away from the crowd to get her in here for slaughter," Barry said. "Trust me, you're gonna love it."

"Okay, let's hear it," Benny said.

"Felix and Andy always demand more pay and status, right?" Barry said.

"Yeah?"

"Jake doesn't work here anymore. Felix has always been jealous of Jake. Suppose I let it slip that I'm thinking of retiring, mention how with Jake gone I'll need someone to direct. How I've got this concept I want to be Falchion's next big hit called *Bavarian Scalps.* If Felix can pick Jake's brain about how he would attack the project, keep the same Falchion feel to it, then this will be Felix's big moment."

"I like it. And I'm guessing they discuss this at the cast party?"

"Exactamundo. That Felix is so jealous and competitive that he'll keep Jake tied up for the whole party."

"While we've got Vera tied up to sacrifice on film. Fat man, that's a helluva an idea. Timing is key though. Too early and they'll talk it over before the party."

"I'll drop the bomb in Felix's lap just as Jake arrives and I'll say Monday is not too soon to start pre-production. That'll light a fire under his ass!"

"Well done, fatso. This looks just like the original set. Here are Vera's clothes to die in, a little bathroom to change in so she's comfortable. I think we're good to go. Is the digital camera all set up?

"Check. And *you* are still the one to get rid of the body, right?" Barry said.

"Yes sir. Here are the masks so no one can identify us. I'll send the digital images to our contact on the dark web as soon as we're finished. I have two tickets for Buenos Aires. Once we arrive, I am assured the money will be wired to the numbered account at the Banco Galicia. Four million dollars, fat man. Can you imagine?"

"I'm tryin' not to think about it," Barry said.

"Now, on another note, come with me. I have something to show you."

Benny led the way across the three-sided set toward the door. Barry glanced beyond the set at the industrial-sized glass blender from *Fifty Ways to Cleave Your Lover* which he'd ordered Lola and Brian to scrub out. Seven feet tall, the clear glass gleamed, so thick it appeared green-blue in the curved sections. He'd meant to return it to get his deposit back but there wouldn't be time now. Just before he exited the room, he noticed the wooden crate where he and Benny and Alex had mangled the heart out of the very human-like dummy for practice. He walked over and unlocked the crate.

"What the hell are you doing, fatso? We don't need any screw ups this late in the game."

"Just for laughs, I want to see if this remote still activates this thing now that we've ripped its heart out."

"We don't have time for this bullshit!"

"Humor me," Barry said and pushed the power button on the remote.

There was a beeping, a whirring then a static burst and the dummy sat up in the crate and cleared the paper away from its face with one arm.

"Holy shit, it still moves," Barry laughed.

"Okay, now turn it off," Benny hissed.

"Okay, okay, settle down."

Barry pushed the power button again. The dummy lowered itself back into the crate in slow motion, the paper crinkling almost imperceptibly.

Suddenly, there was the sound of someone turning the doorknob. Then a loud double knock on the door. Benny's eyes locked onto Barry's. He put his finger to his lips and frowned. Barry nodded. Benny slipped off his penny loafers and tip-toed close to the door and listened. After a few seconds he heard heavy footsteps walk away.

"We're the only ones with a key to this room, right?" Benny whispered.

"Of course," Barry said. "I'm not that careless."

Benny looked dubiously, then grabbed Barry by the back of his shoulder and lead him toward the door. They opened the door and looked up and down the corridor. Nobody in sight.

Outside, Barry fished the keys out of his pocket, locked up and followed Benny.

Benny opened the double-doorway to the studio's largest soundstage, usually separated from the huge antiques set, the enormous accordionized partition on caster wheels was opened. The resulting room was cavernous with wall dimensions of 300 feet long by 400 feet deep and a 16-foot-tall ceiling. The antiques had been dispersed throughout by a staging company. There were people moving and adjusting decorations in the distance, but Barry's and Benny's conversation was well out of earshot.

"You think five bars and bartenders are really necessary?" Barry asked.

"Depends how drunk you want all the potential witnesses," Benny countered.

"Blind drunk."

"Exactly. And yes, it was necessary to spend twelve grand on catering, from crab puffs to filet mignon; caviar and crème tartlets and—"

"Just don't say shrimp—bad memory still," Barry interrupted.

"And yes, it's necessary to have a D.J. and fifteen thousand dollars of top-shelf booze, three mirrored disco balls and glitzy Hollywood decorations hanging from the ceiling. Look at this place, red carpets crisscrossing each other—I've told each of the cast members to invite up to ten of their best friends. It's going to be the best damned party blast ever," Benny said.

"It's gonna be amazing, Benny. Nice work."

~

Aaron drove toward Malibu Memorial again. He checked his watch: 3:45 P.M.

This detective stuff is frustrating, I'm beginning to feel like a pinball driving back and forth. I've got to get those Captain's bars, whatever it takes. Then it won't matter about that French dude, L'Hommedieu. Vera will see that she should be with a stand-up guy like me.

At the hospital, Aaron took the elevator up. And walked right into Alex's room.

"Alex Boxwell. I said I'd be back—now I need answers. We can start with why you put Serena Miles in the hospital."

Alex sat up in bed, his eyes widened. "That's three times today! I'm so tired of this. You want to know why? You really want to know?"

"Yeah, kid, I do."

Alex explained everything to Aaron about being brainwashed into beating Serena, being beaten by Rhonda, then being coerced into agreeing to kill Vera, backing out, being hunted at sea, and now fearing for his life again.

"Amazing story," Aaron said, "In my book if any human could be called an apex predator you qualify, pulling spears out of your body to use as weapons! So, because you bailed out of the deal, they called off killing Vera?"

"No, they probably still have everything set up to kill her live on-screen."

"What?! Where? When?" Aaron said, and checked his watch: 4:45.

"They were originally going to do it during the cast party tonight. I heard them say it would be on a fake set, one made up to look like the set of the movie they just wrapped called *The Organ Pedaler.*"

"Son of a bitch! Thanks, kid," Aaron said, and ran out the door. He reached his cruiser, piled in and punched the accelerator to the floor. He knew the route by rote by now, so he turned on the news again for a distraction.

"We have a local news update on what some have called a 'thin periscope sighting,'" the news anchor said. "A team of marine biologists has a specially equipped boat with a hold which lowers and raises. It can be filled with water or flushed out just as quickly. The team identified the means of locomotion of the so called 'periscope' as an 800-pound tiger shark with a harpoon spear driven down through the top of the snout. The crew lured the beast with chum then positioned the boat ahead of the fish, facing it head on, and navigated toward it with the hold in the lowered position. Once the fish was aboard the water was drained out and water-filled hoses were inserted into the shark's mouth to keep water flowing through the gills. It took four biologists to remove the harpoon from the shark. The animal was treated and released. No information yet on the source of the harpoon."

"Holy shit," Aaron said. "I think I can give you a clue."

Aaron felt a sense of dread as traffic slowed to a crawl. He checked his watch: 5:15.

~

It was Friday afternoon at 5:30 P.M. Vera and Jake had a quiet dinner in the dining room of his condo, comfortable with each other without speaking. T*his is the healthiest relationship I've ever had with a woman,* Jake thought.

"Barry's sick," Vera said. "I'm a bit worried about going, but making this film was a team effort and nothing dangerous can happen with all those people there."

"I think you were right, just having a bite before Barry's big soiree tonight," Jake said.

"It's just because if I gain even a half a pound, I'll never fit into this beautiful outfit you bought me. I love it, Jake. Did I thank you for all those amazing clothes you bought me?"

"Yes, repeatedly. You're welcome. I can't wait to see you in it tonight."

"I never apologized for giving you such a hard time about that whole being estranged from your mom thing or making that gross movie when you were nineteen. I guess you had to do what you had to do to break into the biz, right?"

"Yeah. If that gambit hadn't worked, I'd have had nowhere to go. I had to get out of my mom's house or go crazy."

"And if it hadn't worked out you would never have helped me off that dirty street and offered me that movie role," Vera said, wrinkling up her nose with that adorable smile Jake had come to love. She set down her fork, rounded the table and stood next to his chair.

"And I never would have noticed you if you didn't have that amazing scream," Jake said.

"And then you would never have asked me out. And I was so difficult back then," she said, slipping her small hands behind his neck, running her fingers through his hair and leaning over to face him, "but I'm glad you were so persistent, Mr. L'Hommedieu."

Jake scooted his chair out and made room on his lap and Vera settled in.

Look at those warm, brown eyes, that perfect complexion. She's real and she's really my girlfriend, Jake thought.

"I want to ask you something," Vera said. "Your original passion was making horror movies and you were good at it, so why do you want to make romantic dramas?"

"Because a romantic relationship was always missing from my life—I guess I wanted to fill in the gap," Jake said.

"Well, isn't that what we're having now?"

"Yes."

"So that gap filled itself in. I think you're doing great by the way. But until you get more experience I don't think you're ready to make romance films," Vera said. "Not that I'm a romance expert either, Bubbe never let me date all through high school and even afterward—she doesn't trust anyone."

"No," Jake teased, "your Bubbe, not trust anyone?"

Vera smiled, "Right, so anyway, I think you would make a much better living and be much happier if you kept making campy horror films. Just not sick ones."

"I can't believe my ears," Jake said.

"They're fun, as long as there's some humor and who doesn't like a good scare?"

"Wow, you're full of surprises," Jake said.

"A discussion for later," Vera said, "Let's just have fun tonight."

~

It was 8:00 P.M. as the main lights were dimmed, the laser lights were switched on the slowest setting, and the disco balls began their lazy spinning overhead. The main doors were opened and guests, dressed to the nines, were allowed to enter. Funk pulsed over nearby speakers while rap played from the speakers in a distant corner of the room. The crowds gravitated toward their own musical tastes and the roaming waiters followed.

Barry and Benny watched from afar. They saw Jake and Vera enter, soon followed by Naomi and her date, and Brian and Lola. Barry scanned the crowd until he found Felix and Andy with a huge cadre of friends.

"Go get him," Benny barked.

"I'm on it."

Barry reached Felix and grabbed him by the arm.

"Hey, get your grubbers off me. This is crushed velvet, asshole!" Felix yelled. "Oh my god! I didn't know it was you, Barry. Excuse my French."

"It's okay. Listen, I have something urgent to talk with you about," Barry said, and led Felix to the far corner of the room.

"I'm listening," Felix said.

"For years, I've seen you directing people. You get 'em up on stage, you even improve their blocking at the same time. I've seen you step up and look through the camera lens, then make changes in lighting or sets, subtle things, but always somethin' that improves the scene."

"I didn't mean to overstep my position."

"Not at all. Fortune favors the bold in this business. I was impressed, is what I was gettin' at. I'm retiring from directing and I thought rather than auditioning a bunch of outsiders I'd give you a shot. Assuming you're interested, that is."

"Interested in becoming a director? Is that what you're saying?" Felix gushed.

"That I am."

"Yes! Just give me the chance."

"Okay. I've got a real gem that I want to be Falchion's next big hit. The title is

Bavarian Scalps. I want you to get Jake's take on it—to make sure it's got that Falchion feel. My first choice was Jake, but he's got his heart set on makin' those romantic dramas now. So, learn all you can from Jake tonight. Get his blessing on the film and it's yours. Monday is not too soon to start pre-production. The financing is already in place."

"This is incredible, Barry. Thank you so-o-oooo much. I won't let you down."

"Well, go on. Get out of here," Barry said, swatting Felix on the butt.

Felix jogged over to Andy, interrupted him in mid-sentence, and pulled him five feet away to whisper in his ear.

"No way!" Andy screamed.

"Way!" Felix screamed back as they hugged then chest-bumped each other. The two abandoned their friends and shuffled to within ten feet of Jake, Vera and a few other cast members.

"He who hesitates is lost," Andy said, gently pushing Felix toward Jake.

"Annoying partner gets pinched!" Felix said, pinching Andy's arm. "I need a plot to pitch. Let's see—*Bavarian Scalps*—Indians, scalps, Bavarians—Germans, right?"

"Right, Bavaria is in Germany," Andy said. "Just wing it, you'll do fine."

Felix approached Jake. "Hi Jake, Vera!" he said.

"You look radiant, sweetheart," Andy said, admiring Vera's outfit.

"Thanks, you look great, too."

"Jake, I have something important to discuss with you," Felix said. "Andy, you don't mind keeping Vera entertained for a bit, do you?"

"Not at all. Catch up with the bell of the ball? My pleasure. Now, where did you get that dress? It's gorgeous!" Andy stepped away, so Vera had to turn her back to Jake.

"First off, did you get the bugs worked out of your rom-dram?" Felix asked.

"We're getting there."

"Andy and I are so happy for you. Just the other day Andy said, 'That Jake's someone who made his mark in horror and then he had the chutzpa to move into romance films.'"

"I did say that," Andy said, looking over Vera's shoulder.

"You're supposed to be chatting with Vera," Felix said, leading Jake away.

"What can I do for you, Felix?" Jake said.

"Would it be fair to say that you're finished with horror films at Falchion?"

"Yep, that's a safe bet."

"That's great because Barry has offered me a shot at being director."

"Congratulations," Jake said, but he felt a cold shiver emanate from his lower back, snake its way up his neck and across his scalp.

"That's gracious, Jake. I know that position has been a part of your identity."

"That's true. It was a huge part of my life, but that's all behind me now and I'm truly happy for you." Jake drained his half-full flute of Dom Perignon, then held up two fingers to a wandering server.

"So, Jake. Before Barry would green-light me he wanted me to get your take on the first film he wants me to shoot. The title is *Bavarian Scalps*."

Jake burst out laughing. "Not that dog! Barry and I were brainstorming and drinking scotch one night about six years ago when I threw that idea out as a joke."

"Well, Barry doesn't think of it as a joke now," Felix countered.

"Sure, Felix, you've got my blessing on it. Is that's what you wanted to hear."

"Well, snark the herald angels sing. You're going to hear my vision! I was quite a whiz on the subject of American History in high school, so I thought about this: During the 1600's when immigrants were settling in America the Bavarians settled along the Ohio River Valley. One of the most prominent Native American tribes in the area that had skirmishes with German settlers was the Shawnee Tribe—"

"Wait a minute, so this is set in the 1600's?" Jake said.

"No, the twenty-first century. Some of the Shawnee's modern-day ancestors decided that were it not for those German settlers their tribe would be flourishing to this day. Now it's time for revenge." Felix said, and folded his arms across his chest.

"That's ridiculous," Jake said, gulping his new flute of Dom. "You're proposing the Shawnee tribe is pissed off for hundreds of years and they suddenly decide to scalp the descendants of the Germans who stole their land?"

"Exactly, so stay with me here. It's a radical new group of Shawnees. They travel to Bavaria, scale the alps and exact their revenge there. Hanging by ropes—white snowy backdrop—bloody scalps. Dramatic, no?" Felix said, looking hopeful. "Voi-la, *Bavarian Scalps!*"

"You're an idiot," Jake said, looking away. "Is this horror or comedy?"

"Oh, screw you, Jake. Just admit you're jealous!"

While Jake and Felix squared off against each other, Benny whispered in Andy's ear.

"Oh, Benny, you scared me," Andy said.

"You might want to check the parking lot," Benny said. "I heard a rumor that Bradley Cooper is dropping by tonight."

"Excuse me, Vera," Andy said, and scuttled away.

"Vera, something urgent has come up," Benny said, as the crowd pressed in around them.

"What? When did all these people get here?" Vera said out loud, but her voice was drowned out by the music and overlapping conversations.

"You need to come with me now. Falchion Films is in trouble. Our financier was not happy with your death scene. The scene must be re-shot tonight. Now. And in the can before morning or everything's a bust. The distribution is in place, they're waiting on the final copies. If you don't then your commission won't be paid maybe for months, maybe for a year. We're all set up, come on."

"Benny, I'm all dressed up."

"We've got your clothes in back. We even have a private dressing closet and shower for you. Come on, it'll only take a few minutes and you'll be back out here."

"Let me tell Jake."

"No time, minutes count. The courier is waiting outside for us to shoot the digital film."

Vera pulled free and walked up to Jake, who was in a full-scale argument with Felix.

"Excuse me, Jake?" Vera said.

"Not now, Vera." Jake faced Felix again. "Jealous? You jackass! That'll be the day when I'm jealous of a fledgling director like you, wet behind the ears!"

"I was being kind when I said you made your mark in horror movies. *Meat Hooks Some Liberties with the Lady?* What kind of celluloid trash was that?" Felix spewed.

"The kind of trash that grossed four million domestically then sixteen million on post-release rentals and worldwide distributions," Jake said.

"Braggart!"

"You're so insecure to go there, Felix."

"Jake? I have to go for a few—" Vera tried again.

"You're pathetic the way you've clung to Barry's apron strings all these years!" Felix said, then snatched two flutes of champagne from the server's tray. He held one in each hand, sipping from each alternately.

A crowd had gathered, and Vera was gradually bumped to the outskirts.

"I'm sick and tired of your attitude—Hey, are you crying, man?" Jake asked.

"No," Felix said, as a tear escaped and raced down his face.

"Felix," Jake cautiously said, resting a hand on his shoulder, "I'm sorry about what I said. I was just being defensive."

"No, I'm the one who owes you an apology. I'm pathetic. You want to know why I became interested in horror movies?" Felix wiped his face with the back of his sleeve.

"Sure."

"It was because I was at such a low point in my life that I would watch horror movies and see victims get all carved up on screen—lose limbs, lose their lives—and I'd say to myself, 'Well, I'm still better off than those losers.'"

"Okay, that was pathetic," Jake said. "But we all started somewhere. And look at you now, a burgeoning director of Falchion Films. My background is no less flattering."

"Come on, Vera," Benny said. "This is going to go on for a while. We'll be back before you know it."

Benny led Vera through the throngs of partiers and out the rear exit doorway.

"I know!" Felix said, scoffing, "Everybody's heard your story."

"Where did you hear about that?" Jake said.

"Through the grapevine—Shelley," Felix smirked.

"I was just starting to feel some compassion for you, you little weasel. You've been wrong about so many things around here. You were wrong that Vera wouldn't become a success. You were wrong that she and I would never start dating and—hey? Where's Vera?"

~

Aaron pounded the heels of his hands on the steering wheel because he was now actually parked—parked on the Santa Monica Freeway, with endless lanes of vehicles ahead of him, also parked. He glanced at his watch again and ingested the bad news: It was 8:00 P.M. The cast party had begun. He'd been sitting here for two and a half hours, occasionally moving ahead a few feet while the woman who had always been destined to love him—but she just hadn't realized it yet—was possibly being killed on film at this very moment.

I could just radio ahead and have another cop and his partner intercept the murder, but then they would be the heroes and—NO! I have to be the one to save Vera.

Aaron tuned into the police-and-traffic radio frequency. The traffic had been from a four-car pile-up near the Harbor Freeway. Tow trucks had cleared the area now and traffic began to move, but only at ten miles per hour, and he was still four miles from his turn off.

~

Benny unlocked the door to the S.P.S. and held it while Vera entered.

"You can change into your set clothes in there," Benny said, pointing to a bump-out room with a single door.

"What happened to the regular set?" Vera asked.

"It's needed for another shoot. Barry leased it out to some college kids with big dreams."

Vera nodded and entered the small room.

Inside it was really quite nice. Gray carpeted floor, a small bench seat with a full-length mirror on the wall, her set clothes had apparently been dry-cleaned because they were hung inside clear plastic, and there was a small bathroom with a small sink and a second mirror, and even a blow dryer hung next to the shower. Benny had told the truth: She really would be able to just do the shoot then rinse off and get back to the party. Vera changed into her set clothes.

Barry stepped out of the shadows and lumbered over to lock the door to the corridor.

"My god, Ben, we really get to do this!" Barry said in a raspy whisper.

"Yes, now shut up!" Benny whispered, standing behind the camera. "Get ready."

Vera walked out wearing the now-familiar hip-hugger jeans and bright yellow tube top, her hair in the obligatory pig tails.

"Okay, I'm here. Can we get this done quickly?" Vera said, glancing at the plastic sheeting stretched across the floor.

"You look beautiful, sweetheart," Barry said.

"Gee, thanks, Barry. Now, really, I need to get back to the party. I didn't even tell Jake I was leaving."

"Not to worry," Barry said. "Step right over here and let's get you tied down so we can get you back to your friends."

~

Aaron had made it off at his exit and zoomed through traffic with his lights and siren wailing. He honked continuously as he drove much too fast, passing cars on the left, then right. Falchion Films was two miles ahead now.

She needs me. Really needs me and this is my moment to be her knight in shining armor, Aaron thought. Traffic slowed at a red light, but Aaron drove up on the curb and down the sidewalk, forcing pedestrians onto the lawn.

He pulled back into traffic, in front of the car which sat at the stop light, and with not quite enough room, he scraped the side of his cruiser against a blue SUV, trading paint, black and white for blue. As he glanced both ways and accelerated through the light, the well-tuned engine surged forward. The SUV's horn blared behind him. After a couple of seconds, he glanced at the speedometer: 80 mph. The hungry tires gobbled up the asphalt.

I'm really flying now. Hang on, Vera, baby, I'm coming!

~

"Has anyone seen Vera?" Jake asked, looking concerned, "Felix, did you see which way Vera went?"

"No, my days of watching that little prima donna are over," Felix said.

Jake saw Naomi. He made his way through the crowd and grabbed her elbow.

"Hey!" she cried out.

"Sorry, Naomi, have you seen Vera?"

"How could I miss her *dress?* It sauntered toward that exit a minute ago.

"Naomi, she didn't want to come here tonight. She was reluctant because—well, you know what happened."

"Want me to help you look for her?"

"Actually, yes. In case she's in the lady's room, would you mind?"

"For you, even though I have this fabulous date, Ricky, here, of course," Naomi said and double-timed it on her high heels down the corridor to keep up with Jake.

~

Barry pulled the length of sturdy rope from the hardware store and tied Vera's wrists together over her head, then laid her down on the operating table face up, and looped the rope underneath and out the front so her petite body was taught across the table, and finally he tied her ankles and cinched the rope up so Vera was completely stretched out, her tank top pulled slightly up, revealing her tummy.

"Hey, Barry, that's really tight. It's too tight, you have to loosen the rope!"

"Oh, Vera, it's just for a short while," Barry laughed.

"Why aren't there any other people here?" Vera asked, in the still, quiet room.

"We don't really need them. We just need the slaughter scene re-shot."

"But why are you putting that mask on? You didn't wear that in the original shoot?"

"Don't worry about that."

"I am worried about it. This isn't going to be anything like the original scene. This is going to be for nothing—and that looks like a real scalpel—"

"Vera, I have a little secret. The first time I saw you and heard you scream I knew you were meant for something special. You're going to get the chance to make real art. To turn what would be your ordinary little life—of getting married, popping out a few babies, etcetera—into the art of death. And we're going to capture it on film for future horror fans to adore. Isn't that scary? And you are the perfect sacrifice. A virgin." Barry pulled Vera's tube top higher to expose her rib cage. "You've got a beautiful scream, so let's hear it."

Barry pulled on the chef-grade gloves, gripped the knife, and moved toward Vera's exposed abdomen. Vera's eyes flew open wide. Time slowed to a crawl as she craned her neck to stare at the knife approaching her porcelain skin—the point of the knife had already slid a quarter inch under her ribs—her heart pounded hard against her ribcage, echoing in her ears. Her mind raced on instinct—a millisecond later she faced the camera and screamed. *Zaydeh's words, they stood for something—important. His life—my life.*

"Barry Whitscomb is killing me on film with a knife and Benny Edwards is filming it!" Vera screamed.

Barry stopped, the hand holding the knife went limp and he looked at Benny. Benny stopped filming and looked around from the side of the camera and stood to face Barry.

"Can you edit that out?" Barry asked.

"Yeah. Go again," Benny said, ducking behind the camera.

Barry gripped the knife, inserted the point into the same small cut and started to push as Vera faced the camera and screamed again.

"Barry Whitscomb is killing me with a knife and Benny Edwards is filming it!"

Barry stood and held the knife outward, casually, as Vera's blood dripped from the point.

"She's messin' it all up," Barry said. "She's facin' the camera. I mean, even without noise what if somebody out there can read lips? What's the point if we don't get her real dyin' scream? I gotta' know if it's different from a horror film scream."

"Why don't you push her face the other way?" Benny said, "That way nobody will see."

"Then what's the point? I *personally* want to see her expression when she dies."

Vera was stunned, but she couldn't afford the luxury of emotion. She screamed again.

"Help! Barry Whitscomb and Benny Edwards are killing me on film. It's a snuff film!"

Barry withdrew the knife again and strolled around the room.

"Where are you going, fatso? Get back there—let's figure this thing out," Benny scolded.

"I can't believe this. Vera, you're ruining everything," Barry moped, dragging his feet away from the set, over by the open wooden dummy box.

"Vera, you stupid bitch!" Barry said, pounding his thigh with his fist, hitting something hard, in his pocket.

"What are you going to do, Barry, pout?" Benny said. "Get back over there and let's get the shot. Listen, it won't be so bad, you'll get to hear her real dying scream, you can hold her face with your other hand, so she just looks at you, then hold that heart out for the camera so we get paid, then let's get the hell out of here. She'll stop yelling when you really cut her."

Barry turned away, too caught up in his disappointment to notice a beeping, a whirring sound, followed by a static burst behind him.

"Yeah, I guess that'll work. Damn you, Vera, it was gonna' be perfect."

Barry walked back to the operating table and held Vera's face, so she looked straight up, then pointed the knife with his other hand as the camera rolled. She screamed.

~

Aaron drove up on the film studio's lawn at 40 miles per hour, cut the wheels to the right and rammed his cruiser into the square stone pillars which supported the black, overhead gothic letters: Falchion Films.

He got out and ran toward the entrance, in and out of guests donned in their finest eveningwear. He gave up dodging and simply knocked a guest or two over in his sprint for the double doorway. Two security guards abandoned checking to see who was on the guest list in favor of stopping the big man in the blue uniform charging at them.

"Halt! Show us your ID," one guard commanded.

Aaron flipped it out, flashed it and lowered a shoulder in case that didn't do the trick.

"You let that guy go through," the second guard said.

"Looks like a real badge to me, besides, you see the size of that mother?"

Aaron was inside, but he was suddenly enveloped by partiers drinking, bouncing up and down to the music and laughing.

"Hey, you people, listen!" Aaron yelled. "Where is Vera Horowitz? Has anyone seen Vera Horowitz? This is an emergency!"

Several people stopped talking and stared at Aaron.

"How about Jake L'Hommedieu? Barry Whitscomb? Benny Edwards?" he yelled.

"I saw Jake and Vera earlier," Serena said. "Jake went that way just a minute ago."

"Is Jake in trouble, officer?" Felix said, smiling coyly.

Aaron looked at Felix with annoyance then forced his way through the crowd toward the rear exit, upending hands holding champagne flutes and appetizers in his wake. When he burst out into the corridor, he saw Jake walking beside a dazzling redhead with a pixie cut, looking in empty doorways up ahead.

"Jake, have you seen Vera tonight?" Aaron yelled, running toward the couple.

Jake defensively held up an arm, toward the charging hulk.

"Yes, she disappeared a few minutes ago. We're looking for her now."

Suddenly, an ear-piercing scream echoed from further down the corridor.

"That's Vera's scream," Naomi said, rubbing the hairs down on the back of her neck.

Aaron caught up and passed Jake and Naomi. Jake fell in with Aaron, like the beta wolf joining the pack—both sprinting toward the scream. Naomi mustered all the speed she could, tapping along on her high heels, just as the blur of two thin, well-dressed men dashed by, each seemingly pulling the other ahead down the corridor.

"Hurry, Andy, Jake's in trouble!" Felix giggled.

"I love it!" Andy countered.

"Come on, I've got a good idea where that scream came from," Aaron said.

Jake and Aaron came to a sprinting halt in front of the SPS room, a faint light glowing beneath the doorway. Aaron turned the knob. Locked. He hammered on the door, as did Jake.

"Open up. Police!"

"Vera? Are you in there, babe?" Jake yelled.

Aaron looked at Jake with disgust, then hammered on the door again.

~

Vera screamed again as Barry slid the knife into her another quarter inch and tried to cut deeper, but Vera thrashed her head so violently it distracted him for a second.

"Barry Whitscomb is killing me with a knife! Benny Edwards is filming it. It's a snuff film. Help!" Vera screamed.

Benny stood up at the pounding from outside the door, and when he looked toward it he couldn't believe what he was seeing. The naked, disemboweled surgery dummy had gotten out of its crate and walked to the door. He was witnessing a real-life nightmare: the dummy had turned the lock and opened the door.

"What are you doing, dummy?" Benny yelled.

The dummy turned to him and spoke. "There is an officer of the law who wishes to gain entry. I was simply letting—"

"Oh, shut up!" Benny yelled and backed into the shadows with the camera.

Aaron stepped forward and drew his service revolver, aimed and clicked off the safety.

"Barry Whitscomb, step away from the girl. Drop the knife. Now!" Aaron ordered.

Barry turned slowly in Aaron's direction. "Well, ain't this a big crap sandwich? No, no I won't. You know, I've had just about enough of this horse shit, copper.

And all of you lousy actors can kiss my ass too." Barry turned away from the *Organ Pedaler* set and ambled toward the other set pieces.

"Barry, give it up. Halt or I'll shoot," Aaron said.

Jake ran to Vera and untied her ankles while Naomi stepped inside the open door and held her hand to her lips. Barry kept walking past the wooden crate, over to the industrial seven-foot-tall blender. He reached down and grabbed the plug with the extra-long extension cord, calmly walked over to the wall and plugged it in. He then returned to the control panel and pushed the "puree" button. The huge machine whirred into action.

"Lie down on the ground and put your hands behind your back! Aaron roared.

"Or what, cop? Jake, you idiot. I'd created a paradise for us, kid. A place where we could exploit and degrade women all we liked, and nobody could stop us. It was perfect. But you had to burst my balloon, didn't you? You had to make a film where women come out on top. Yes, I *read* your little rom-dram script. Made me sick," Barry said, leaning a ten-foot ladder against the side of the vibrating glass blender and climbing up.

"Get down!" Aaron yelled. "This is your last warning, then I'm going to shoot."

"Now, this little girl here was always supposed to be my little death project. I nursed her along, put her in quality horror films. She was the perfect sacrifice—a virgin," Barry said.

Aaron fired. The bullet struck Barry in the back of the shoulder and flew out the front.

"Dammit! Do you know how much that hurts, cop?"

"Yes, I've been shot," Aaron said.

"Then you know a little about pain, but nothing like this. This was the biggest tease of my life tonight. It's been weeks since we've had a good slaughter scene. I guess it's going to have to be me." Barry said. He reached the top, stepped over the ladder top and sat on the top of the blender with his legs hanging inside.

"No, don't do that, Mr. Whitscomb, please," Naomi called.

"No, don't do that," Barry mocked, in falsetto.

"Get down from there or I'll shoot, Whitscomb," Aaron yelled.

"Screw you," Barry yelled.

Aaron fired, hitting Barry in the other shoulder.

"Stop doing that, cop!" Barry yelled, and dropped into the blender.

Barry spun in a circle at the bottom of the blender. "This pain is insane! Film me, idiots! Benny, get this footage, my, ouch, shit! My legacy—!"

Felix ran toward the blender, grabbing a gaff hook on an eight-foot pole from the wall as he did. He sprinted up the ladder and leaned over the top.

"Are you kidding, Felix, you're like waaaay too late, dear," Andy said.

Felix leaned over and extended the hook into the bloody, whirling slosh below. He retrieved Barry's bloody scalp, lustrous just seconds ago, and pulled it upward as all eyes stared.

Naomi screamed. Vera screamed and completely drowned Naomi out with an extended high note which bristled all neck and arm hairs in the room. Jake, Naomi and Vera stared, their mouths hanging open

"Don't you look like the cat who caught the canary?" Andy said, as Felix strutted by with the bloody scalp hanging from the gaff.

"Art's not always pretty, people," Felix said.

"No, and it looks like Benny's slipped out during all the fracas," Andy said.

Aaron holstered his gun. "What a sick bastard," he muttered, as he walked over and unplugged the cord.

Barry's corpse ground to a halt.

Chapter 43
Curtains

There was a palpable hush in the room after Felix left with Barry's bloody scalp on a pole. Andy ran after him, but Aaron blocked the doorway.

"Okay, everybody, stop!" Aaron yelled. "This is a crime scene now. What was that guy's name who just left with the scalp?"

"That's my partner, Felix Short," Andy said.

"And you?" Aaron said.

"Andy Faull, I'm the second assistant director."

"What's he doing with that scalp? He needs to bring that back here. It's evidence."

"What?" Andy said, his palms held upward, "Does someone doubt Barry just mixed himself up in a giant blender?"

"Look, smart ass, there are procedures and we're going to follow them. Everyone line up here in a row. I need everyone to write down their contact information on this pad."

Aaron holstered his service revolver and picked up a pad and pen from a nearby table.

"Just so you know, you're letting the guy who was filming the snuff film get away. Benny Edwards is his name and he just ran down the hallway," Andy said, pointing.

Aaron scanned the pale faces, pointing his finger at each one as he counted. "Andy Faull, I need you to copy down everyone's name and cell phone. There are six people in this room. I want info on all six, then wait here with it until I come back," he said, bolting from the room.

"That's only five, officer, the last one's just a dummy," Andy called after Aaron.

In the corridor, Aaron saw the short man in the gray suit sprint to a stop at the end of the hall and enter the ballroom. Aaron called the police station as he gave chase. The desk operator picked up.

"Lieutenant Finklestein, reporting a suicide/attempted homicide at Falchion Films, Set Piece Storage room, down the hallway from a huge party. Left citizen, Andy Faull, in charge of witnesses. Request back up. I am in foot pursuit of second party, Benny Edwards, in possession of 'snuff' film. Confirm." Aaron leaned into the corner and jogged into wall-to-wall partiers.

"Affirmative, Lieutenant. Back up on the way."

Aaron couldn't see Benny anywhere, but he barged forward.

"Police! Make way!" he yelled, bumping people, spilling drinks and appetizers in his wake. It was like forging through a wall of clay.

Benny tripped and staggered his way outside. He had just one concern as he reached the curb: the digital film disk in his hand. *Is it safe? All that bumbling through the crowd. Yes!*

Benny sprinted to the street. *I'll catch a cab, so no questions from Barry's driver. Reach my condo, scan the film of Barry's demise, then strike a deal with that guy on the dark web. It's no virgin death but it's still pretty great! Fat man went out with a splash—life imitating art.*

Aaron sprinted out the doorway and jogged to a stop at the curb. He looked rapidly both ways. No sign of the stocky man in the gray suit. Just traffic.

Don't have Benny Edwards but I have a lot of the answers the Chief wanted. Aaron called in a BOLO ("be on the lookout") for Benny Edwards.

~

The witnesses in Set Piece Storage were still shaken. Everyone had turned their backs to the large, bloody blender. Andy had copied down everyone's information except the dummy's, who now stood in front of Andy with his arms crossed.

"Oh, are you giving me attitude now?" Andy said to the dummy.

"I object to your remark 'just a dummy.' I also object to your collecting everyone's information except mine. I've endured a traumatic experience as well."

"Okay, what's your name and number? Wait, first, why are you naked and why are your—yuck—guts hanging out?"

"I identify as an H.P.S., High Fidelity Human Patient Simulator. My serial number is 370280-13Z. I have been disemboweled by Barry Whitscomb and Benny Edwards. They misrepresented themselves in claiming they were doctors."

"Well, don't touch *me,* you dirty boy," Andy said to the dummy. "Okay, I've got everyone's info so you can all go. I'll stick around for a few minutes to talk with the cop."

Jake had untied Vera. She squeezed him tightly, her breathing deep and desperate.

"Come on, Vera, let's get you out of here," Jake said, leading her into the hallway.

Serena left, then Naomi. The dummy caught up to them with a few light steps. As it touched Naomi on the back of her arm—she jumped.

"Excuse me, Miss. I do not wish to stay here alone. Could I possibly go with you?" the dummy asked.

"Where are you from? Why don't you just go there?" Naomi asked.

"I arrived in that crate which was sent from a science manufacturing lab. I just witnessed a disgusting suicide in this room, and I cannot remain here."

Naomi looked the dummy over, naked, barely four feet tall with a handsome boy's face.

"We can't leave with you looking like that. Let's get you cleaned up."

Naomi returned with a bucket of water and some rags. She knelt and wiped away the dried blood. She picked up a roll of gray duct tape from a table and wrapped it around the gaping hole in the dummy's abdomen. He now reeked of duct tape fumes. She nodded with approval and handed the dummy a pair of underwear. He pulled them on as Naomi returned from one of the hanging clothes racks with a petite boy's outfit, socks and shoes. He dressed quickly and seemed more confident.

"Much better. It'll be fun explaining you to my date," Naomi said, linking elbows with him and entering the corridor.

~

Benny had exited the cab half a block early and jogged the rest of the way home. He had to cover his tracks. He grew more nervous every moment. Inside his house, he locked the door and peered out the window blinds. No one in sight.

In his office, he inserted the digital film disk into the scanner. A minute later the film was scanned and available to send to a recipient. He uploaded the digital video file to his cell, took a deep breath and instant-messaged his contact on the dark web:

Benny: Virgin death film a no-go. Authorities intervened. Have unique substitute. Real film of man's death in giant blender. Interested?

Three dots pulsed on Benny's cell screen, as if the contact were considering his offer.

Dark Web: Not on par with earlier offering. Will pay eight hundred thousand if high production value.

Benny: Shot in tungsten lighting with Canon XA11 Professional camcorder.

Dark Web: Do not send film. Physical exchange. Instructions sent once you arrive in Buenos Aires.

Benny: Could you just wire money to original numbered account as before?

Dark Web: No. New film, new arrangements.

Benny broke out in a cold sweat. He felt desperate but this deal was his only way out. He grabbed his coat and called another cab. Time to catch his flight out of LAX.

~

Aaron entered Set Piece Storage and found Andy leaning against a desk, sipping a flute of champagne. He'd hoped he could catch Edwards quickly, drag him back here then deal with all the questions and paperwork.

"Here's your list, officer."

"Great. Okay, do you know Benny Edward's address?"

"Sure, let me check my contacts," Andy said, "It's right here."

Andy handed Aaron his cell. Aaron copied down the address, tossed the cell to Andy and jogged for the door.

"I assume I'm free to go?" Andy called.

"Sure, beat it," Aaron yelled back.

"Oh, you're welcome, Mr. Policeman," Andy called.

Aaron called for backup at Benny's address and to explain his absence from the crime scene.

"Lieutenant Finklestein, who's overseeing the crime scene if you're gone?" the operator said.

"There's no one there, but I've got a list of all the witnesses. I've got to go catch Benny Edwards before he escapes."

"Negative, Lieutenant, stay put."

"But *only* I can ID him. I'll explain everything when I get back. I saw it all."

"Follow protocol, Lieutenant. Get back to the scene."

Aaron ignored the command and floored the accelerator.

~

Benny's cab arrived. He got in and they drove away. As the cab exited Benny's street, three police cars and Aaron's cruiser raced by in the opposite direction, lights and sirens blaring. Benny slouched in his seat and felt his heartbeat pounding in his chest. He waited for the cab to be pulled over—but it didn't happen. Benny risked a glance behind them and just saw the calm of a thousand headlights. Within minutes he and the cabbie spiraled up the on-ramp of CA2/North Santa Monica Freeway. Twenty-nine minutes and he would be home-free.

Aaron skidded to a stop and parked. He ran around to his trunk and grabbed "The Enforcer"—a manual battering ram. He lugged it to Benny's front door and banged the door with his fist.

"Open up. Police!" Aaron yelled.

Before there was time for a response, Aaron swung back and battered the door in, the frame splintering off the jamb. He flipped on the lights and drew his weapon, aiming and checking room after room.

"Benny Edwards, give it up. You're surrounded. Come out!" Aaron yelled, as cops filled Benny's home, weapons drawn.

A female officer entered the office, holstered her weapon and assessed the room.

"Lieutenant Finklestein, could you come in here?" she called.

"Yeah," Aaron said, lumbering in.

"You said the suspect was in possession of a snuff film?"

"Yeah, that's right."

"Well, I think he's sent it to off to a buyer. This is a digital scanner."

"Dust it for fresh prints," Aaron said. "I've got to get back to Falchion Films."

~

Benny was an hour early for his flight. He checked into pre-boarding and sat at the bar to wait. It was a 17 hour, 21 minute flight. He would arrive at 7:06 P.M. Argentina time. Benny sipped his bourbon and reviewed his career in the horror biz.

Since his 20s, when his witch of a mother had died, and he finally had the place to himself, he had buried his feelings. She had never listened to his ideas; told him he was stupid, and he would never amount to anything. His mother had cleaned and put out the best china, she had never trusted Benny to clean it, or help prepare the food in anticipation of the pretty women she invited to the house, whose opinions she'd felt were paramount. If Benny attempted to comment on the conversation, his mother told him to be quiet, that he was a silly boy. *These feelings of resentment had burned inside him like acid.*

Benny—shuffling around Hollywood without work—it had made him sick seeing all the pretty young women, flaunting themselves in those skimpy outfits, making big bucks from their looks. *Who the hell did they think they were?* He hated them—their carefree attitudes, their beauty, their confidence. It was like an itch he could never scratch. He'd wanted to bash their pretty faces in, but he was smart enough to know that would have landed him in jail.

That itch continued to irritate until the day he'd enrolled in that acting class. After several classes and some role-playing, his instructor singled Benny out.

"You have an intensity I haven't seen in years, young man. I'd like to put you in touch with a director I know," the instructor had said.

That director was Barry Whitscomb. With the aid of makeup, Benny had landed the part of the grizzled motorboat captain in *Gator Ate Her.* The acting had been satisfying, especially watching some of the most beautiful, nubile women in Hollywood get mangled on film. He liked being a part of that.

Benny suggested to Naomi Nivens, one day on a shoot, that if she leaned back on the boat deck on one arm, her exposed neck and collarbone made her seem more vulnerable when she screamed from that position. *And she had listened to him. Like what he'd said was important. She took his advice, and the shot was a success.* He had sensed that that position would make her seem so much more the victim. Back in his trailer he had watched that section of the film over and over. Benny realized he could manipulate actress's behavior on screen. But that was nothing compared to the rush he got from manipulating their feelings off screen.

Soon, Benny had all the "scream queens" behaving like victims both in front of the camera and in real life. There was no difference. The itch in his gut disappeared! He had made them feel completely helpless—which in turn had made him feel supremely powerful. Barry had liked the way the films were turning out and hired Benny as the full-time acting coach.

In the years that followed I'd been at the pinnacle of power. Now, my power is gone. The last time I felt this awful was when that good-looking man drugged me—I know that's what he must have done now—and made me watch those home movies of my wretched mother from when I was a boy. He manipulated the witch's voice to say things—terrifying things about me, her, our family. How we were vermin. Weak, scared victims. I was losing my mind until Barry intervened and talked some sense into me. I may earn eight hundred thousand dollars but how will I ever regain my sense of power in the world?

Benny ordered more bourbon on the rocks. His flight was announced over the intercom. He had 15 minutes to get to his gate and board.

~

Aaron had returned to the Set Piece Storage room. He'd spoken with the chief and assured him he was now in charge of the crime scene.

"I don't know what to say, Finklestein," the chief said." I'd like to say congratulations, but why the hell did you leave the scene before everyone else? This should be your shining moment. Instead, you're already blowing it."

"I have a lot of answers for you, Chief. You'll see. All the evidence you could want. Everything you asked me to get. I wanted to catch the final perp, I guess—"

"You got greedy, overreached. Slow down, Lieutenant. One thing at a time. By the book. When you're organized you can tell me what you've got. Now go."

Aaron directed the forensics team. The area was cordoned off with yellow crime scene tape and extensively finger printed, photographed and finally, a Bio Remedial team sanitized the vicinity. The industrial blender was wrapped in black plastic, so the public wouldn't see, and hauled off with a front-end loader. Aaron called the witnesses and scheduled interviews.

~

Benny slept fitfully, for hours, on the flight. Although seat-belted in, he'd squirmed and tried to curl his body into the fetal position. The dreams were awful. He thought those childhood nightmares were gone for good. His mother had traumatized him, but as bad as those dreams were, they had now morphed into something worse: He and his mother and siblings were dirty, grey-furred mice, with fleas. They cohabitated a filthy nest behind a wall. *All because the handsome man had tampered with Benny's home movie memories. Talk about dirty pool!* Benny wrung his hands together and fidgeted to the point that the passenger seated next to him requested another seat. Hours passed, filled with fitful sleep, more horrible dreams. He awoke.

Benny stared across the passengers' heads, his red-ringed eyes stung from all the booze. Just then he heard the pilot's voice over the speakers. They would be landing soon. Benny couldn't wait for this ordeal to end.

After an hour-long wait in immigration, Benny took a taxi to the room he had booked at the five-star hotel, The Recoleta, right across the street from the Patio Bullrich Mall. He wanted to collapse and sleep so he could get his head straight again.

The sheets smelled clean and the pillows were luxuriously soft. Benny felt himself go under. He was jolted awake by a noise. *That wasn't enough sleep, not at all!* He checked his watch: 8:00 P.M. The noise: an unfamiliar chime from his cell phone. He pressed the home button and the instant messaging screen lit up.

Are you in-country?

Yes, Benny typed.

We have unfinished business. Do you have physical film with you?

Yes

Go to Patio Bullrich Mall. Inside, book store with boarded up storefront next to ATM. Follow hallway next to bookstore. Plywood tacked in place. Pry loose and enter doorway. Your money in bag, center room on metal plate. Take money. Replace with film. Our business will then be concluded.

Why do you trust me? You don't know whether film is good.

You would not go to all this trouble. Go now. Mall closes at 9:00. Proceed.

Benny hadn't expected this to happen at night. He was more than a bit scared, alone, in a foreign land, meeting with strangers for an illicit trade. He changed his shirt and splashed some ice water on his face. It was already 8:20, no time for coffee. Fear, adrenaline, had him alert.

Benny took the elevator to the lobby and exited the heavy glass doors. The traffic was crazy, with cars speeding and zig-zagging in both directions on the four lanes in front of the hotel. Benny focused on the sidewalk on the other side. He would have to sprint. He checked his Rolex again: 8:35. There were too many damned speeding cars—he didn't think he could avoid getting hit.

Finally, he decided to run for it. He looked left, right, left, trying to time his take off.

He ran. He was halfway across the first lane and he stopped on his tip-toes, arms out to the sides like windmills, as a car whizzed an inch in front of him, he jolted ahead another lane and turned back on himself—another car nearly hit him—he ran back to the first lane again, twisted his body and ran all the way across this time, a car bumper just clipped his heel, knocking his shoe a few feet away, as he tumbled onto the sidewalk.

Benny looked up at a family, exiting the mall. They laughed at him.

"Corre como un rato'n," a little girl said.

"I do NOT run like a mouse!" Benny yelled, standing to retrieve his penny loafer.

But this just made the family laugh harder.

"Screw all of you!" Benny yelled, as he limped toward the mall. His heel ached and he thought he may have sprained his ankle. Rage engulfed him.

When the heat dies down, I'm going back to finish Vera off. She needs to die on film.

Inside, just a few shoppers milled about. Some store owners had pulled their security chains down halfway across storefronts to discourage patrons from entering. Benny's footsteps echoed as he approached the bookstore sign in the distance.

I'm in the right place—there's the cash machine by the store. Benny peered down the shady hallway. *There's the plywood nailed to the hallway wall.* He limped toward it and pulled. Nothing. He tugged again, harder and it came loose on one side. Benny squeezed through, plywood, scraping his clothes. There was a doorknob. He turned it and entered. The room was dimly lit but a bright light shone beneath a second door. He turned the handle and peeked inside.

The room was large, and the walls and ceiling were painted white. The back wall and two side walls were covered by white curtains. In the center of the room a wooden platform covered most of the floor. In the center of the platform—a metal plate, a canvas sack on top.

Something didn't feel right. Under the metal plate there was a high-tension spring coil surrounding a metal rod, which led both left and right of the metal plate.

"Hello?" Benny called, but there was no response.

It's a trap, I get it. But I'm very quick—I just dodged that insane traffic.

He stepped up onto the wooden platform and walked to the center. He paused, then, in a single motion, reached down and grabbed the canvas sack and set the film in its place. He turned, ran two steps and, still standing on the edge of the platform, turned around to look.

God, I'm quick! I could have been an Olympic athlete. Nothing had happened.

Some trap. I'd feel more confident if Barry was here for me to abuse.

Benny pulled the doorknob. He heard the spring release, and he felt an overhead metal bar snap down across his back, snapping bones and smashing him to the wooden platform.

A mouse trap, he thought. He saw movement behind the curtain to his right. Just before he passed out, the curtain parted and he saw a man behind a camera, filming him.

Chapter 44

Man Versus Man

Following hours of interviewing the witnesses to Barry's death, Aaron had organized the notes and photos, taken by the crime scene specialist, and composed his report. He had it professionally bound, and he now stood in the chief's office.

"Here is the Barry Whitscomb crime scene report," Aaron said. "I can leave it with you—or answer any questions if you'd like me to stay."

The chief took the bound manuscript, with the police seal and "CLASSIFIED" letters across the cover, and jounced it up and down in his hand to feel the heft of it. He then leafed through the report from back to front.

"Very impressive, Finklestein," the chief said. "You have witness interviews, photographs, sketches and closing remarks. No conclusions, just the facts. What, roughly thirty pages? This is not your only copy, right?"

"No, sir. I have a master copy."

"Go grab a cup of coffee. Come back in fifteen minutes and we'll chat."

The chief read the sequence of events which led Lieutenant Finklestein to the crime scene. The fact that a large social event was taking place simultaneously was curious. The number of eyewitnesses on hand, including Finklestein himself, had potential to make this a slam dunk suicide case, but the lieutenant hadn't dropped the ball. No, he had collected information and documented everything objectively, just in case this was somehow a homicide. *Superb.*

The chief marked significant notes and testimony with his squeaking yellow highlighter. On page ten he encountered gruesome photos. An enormous blender, the interior generously coated with human remains, shot from different angles, close ups of the control panel set on "puree," the plug, yanked from the outlet by Finklestein himself, the distances the witnesses stood from the blender, the doorway, the abandoned camera stand, a close up of the empty film compartment—left that way from Benny Edwards' having taken the cartridge—and Benny's fingerprints.

There were photos of the table where Vera Horowitz was tied, the loose length of rope, the scalpel and chef's grade gloves which Barry Whitscomb had dropped on the floor; photos of the double doorway, steel doors, the deadbolt that had initially kept Aaron and the witnesses from entering. Also, headshots of the witnesses: Andy Faull, Felix Short, Naomi Nivens, Serena Miles, Jake L'Hommedieu, Vera Horowitz, and the Human Patient Simulator, whose testimony was the most informative. And finally, headshots of the deceased Barry Whitscomb and the missing Benny Edwards. Besides Felix Short's vanishing with that scalp—No stone unturned.

There was a rap at the door, then Finklestein entered.

"Nice work, Lieutenant," the chief said. "Let's discuss these comments from witnesses."

"Of course, sir."

"From Jake L'Hommedieu's interview: 'I once walked into a room and found Barry grimacing while drilling holes into his thigh with the drill we used in the movie, The Big Drill. He said he wanted to actually endure the kind of pain portrayed onscreen.'

"From Naomi Niven's interview: 'One time Barry cut himself with the edge of a machete we used in *Seven Flays in May*. I stood right there while he just cut himself. I told him to stop but he said he wanted to know what it felt like.'

"From Felix Short's interview: 'We were shooting a movie called Grammar Hammer where an English teacher was so sensitive about anyone's correcting his teaching style that he attacked his critics with a hammer. Barry was excited about the idea and I found him in the editing room smashing his fingertips with a hammer. He said he wanted to savor the pain.'

"I won't hold you to it," the chief said," but you've talked to Whitscomb before this all went down. What was your gut reaction to the man?"

"He was gregarious, kind of like a fun-loving kid. I sat in on a shoot and spoke with him afterward. He seemed proud of the scene they were making, like he really wanted me to enjoy it. I think he became obsessed by the work—like he couldn't separate fantasy from reality, and he wanted to become a part of the experience. I think he killed himself as a sort of *art project*."

"Jesus Christ," the chief said. "Well, nice work. This is the sort of calm, methodical approach I'm looking for in a captain. You get those other reports to me on Serena Miles and Alex Boxwell soon too."

"They're linked to this case. This report took priority, or they'd be here on your desk. I just need to do a little editing, sir."

"Get them to me, that will get the press off my back, then we'll set a date to pin those captain's bars on you."

"Yes, sir," Aaron said, smiling broadly and exiting the chief's doorway.

~

The day after the mass interview, Jake had done his best to comfort Vera, but he could see he was in over his head. He had scheduled an appointment for Vera with his therapist, Thelma Gladstone, Ph.D., who it turned out was also a certified post-traumatic stress disorder therapist. Jake rode with Vera to her appointment in the back seat of his limo and waited for her there.

After an hour, Jake saw her walking toward him. He got out and opened the door for her.

"How was that?" Jake asked, in the privacy of the limo. "Did it help?"

"I mean, it kind of puts things in perspective," Vera said. "It's still hard for me to understand why Barry wanted to kill me. Why me, of all people?"

"What did Thelma say?" Jake asked.

"I told her about Barry's comments during his attempt to kill me. She said his behavior was consistent with those of a psychopath's."

"How so?"

"The fact that I'm a virgin, along with my lightness and innocence was intolerable to him. It was as simple as my traits aligning with his obsession. I had done nothing wrong and this wasn't my fault in any way."

"It sounds like you were in the wrong place at the wrong time."

"Yes, according to Thelma, Barry's worldview of normal women, whom he considered deeply flawed objects to be destroyed, paled in comparison to an 'unspoiled,' to use her word, virgin. From his perspective, I would eventually become flawed too. This would be a special honor for him to kill me while I was still pristine. I was the perfect sacrifice."

"He was a sick man," Jake said. "Did you schedule another appointment?"

"Several."

"So, do you think you're going to be alright?"

"Eventually. I mean, I get it, everything she said makes sense. She says I've got to learn to trust again. It's taken me a while, but I've learned something about being a victim."

"Go on," Jake said.

"That warning from my grandfather helped me when I needed it most. I was so scared—I mean, he was literally going to cut my heart out. I realized something at that second, anybody can get into a bad situation, sometimes a person needs a helping hand, but when it comes down to it—a person has to save themselves. You can't stay a victim for very long—or you just get slaughtered. Being a victim is not, like, a lifestyle. It's pathetic."

"You were so brave to get yourself out of that spot. I don't know if I could have done it."

"Take it from me—if you ever get in a jam like me—you've got to fight."

"I'm sorry you had to go through that," Jake said, "I'm here for you."

"You're the most stable thing in my life," Vera said and hugged him.

~

Aaron cruised back toward his house on cloud nine. He slowed down for traffic—that's when he saw them.

My little Vera, light, perfect, walking toward a silver limousine. What's she doing? There's Jake L'Hommedieu, that schmeckel, getting out from the back seat.

"That's right, L'Hommedieu, you French skunk!" Aaron yelled, filling his squad car with righteous wrath. "Open the door for her, my beautiful, angel, Vera. She should be my girl!"

Aaron stalked back and forth across his front doorstep and clenched his hands into fists.

Who does this L'Hommedieu guy think he is? He's not even Jewish. He doesn't keep the Shabbat; he knows nothing of the kosher laws. He's not worthy to even keep company with someone like Vera Horowitz. I'm not losing to this schlep without a fight. Aaron touched the mezuzah on his front door—his house was built for a higher purpose.

Aaron stepped inside. He set his satchel of notes on the table, a load off his mind, then went to the bathroom and splashed some cold water on his face. He'd agreed to meet his two cop buddies in half an hour for lunch. He needed to chill first—so he didn't go ballistic.

~

Aaron found his buddies, Ira and Levi, at a booth in the diner and joined them.

"Hey, there he is!" Ira called out.

"Hello, Mr. Captain," Levi said, smiling. "Have a seat."

Aaron sat across from his friends, who each high-fived him across the table.

"I think you're actually going to do it, Aaron," Levi said, "get your bars."

"This day's been a long time coming," Ira said, "but you really wanted it."

"I ordered your corned beef sandwich the way you like it," Levi said. "It's on me."

"Thanks, you guys. I appreciate it, the both of you."

"And yet, our man doesn't look happy," Levi said. "What do you think, Ira?"

"I'd say you're right," Ira agreed. "It takes a lot to make some people happy. Me? I'd be over the moon to be in this guy's position."

"You know, Ira, Levi, I've got something that's been eating at me," Aaron said, as he bit into his sandwich.

"What's up?" Levi said.

"I've known you guys for what, ten years or more?" Aaron said around his chewing, "Had your backs all that time, yes?"

"Yeah, Aaron, why?" Ira said.

"Because I need a favor, my chavers. There's a clown interfering with my happiness. You guys know Vera Horowitz, right?"

"Yeah, freakin' adorable," Levi said. "You've got a thing for her as I recall."

"To put it lightly, yes. I need to go mano-a-mano with a civilian and I need you guys to witness it, so everybody sees it's not just a cop taking advantage."

"I've got no problem with that, Aaron. You sure you want to do this though?" Levi said.

"Oh yeah, Vera's the love of my life," Aaron said and stared into the distance.

"Really, Aaron?" Levi said. "You're like a brother to me, okay. But I need you to think about this, really think. You've got a lot on the line."

"You heard him," Ira chimed in. "So, how and when's this supposed to go down?"

"I've been following this guy—I know his routine."

"Aaron," Ira said, "I think you should let this go."

"Like I was saying, he likes to take my girl out for breakfast about eight A.M. I'll give you a call when I'm about to pull him over. It'll be near a field or a park so we can walk him away from the public eye. Can I count on you both?"

"Yeah, Aaron," Ira said, looking at Levi. Levi looked sad but nodded.

~

Aaron had been on stakeouts before. He'd packed dinner, a thermos of coffee and snacks. He'd sat in his cruiser a block from Jake's condo—and waited. It had been a long night, but it was worth it. It was 7:45 A.M. when Jake's front door opened.

There's the skunk walking down the driveway with its filthy paw holding Vera's hand.

They got into the limo and drove away. Aaron followed. He called Ira and Levi.

"It's almost *go time*, Aaron said. "There's a field just before the farmer's market on Vine Street. Be there."

Jake and Vera were a block away from the farmer's market when a police car pulled them over next to a vacant lot, a chilly breeze moved the tall, beige grass. Jake's driver veered to the right and stopped as three policemen parked their cruisers and lumbered up to the limo.

The driver rolled down his window.

"Is there a problem, officer?" the driver said. "I don't think I was speeding."

"No. I just need to have a word with Mr. L'Hommedieu in the back here. Could you step out of the vehicle, Jake?" Aaron said. Jake looked at Vera then stepped outside.

"What's this about, officer?" Jake said.

"It's about you and me, pal. That little lady in the back is supposed to be my life's mate; I've known it since we were in grade school. We're from the same community, same synagogue—it's just supposed to be that way. So, either you can talk some sense into her, or you and I are going to have it out in that field over there, man-to-man."

Vera got out of the back.

"What?! Aaron are you crazy?" Vera said. "I'm with Jake. You have to accept that."

"So, this is the thanks I get after saving your life?" Aaron said.

"You didn't save me!" Vera said. "I saved myself, then it was *the dummy* who opened the door, and Jake was already there for me."

"Wow," Aaron said. "Come on, Frenchie, let's go."

"I don't really fight," Jake said. "I'm more of a creative type. Besides, you've had training—"

"You get going," Aaron said, "We're doing this. Vera's not going to interfere because deep down she wants to see what her man's got in him anyway."

"No, I want to get back in our limo and get out of here," Vera said. "This is stupid."

"I've got two witnesses here to make sure it's a fair fight," Aaron said. "Come on, you two, Vera you can watch but don't get in the way."

Jake felt himself grabbed by the upper arms and lifted, so his feet barely touched the ground. He was marched by the cops into a lot between two vacant buildings. *I'm surrounded by people,* but I feel so alone, Jake thought.

They covered ground quickly and suddenly the hands released him. He fell to his feet, stumbled, regained his balance. He watched Aaron remove his police uniform shirt, so he just wore a t-shirt.

The guy's *huge*, Jake thought, *look at all those muscles. He moves his arm and they all ripple.*

"You can even take the first swing," Aaron said, stepping into Jake's personal space.

"I don't want to hit you," Jake said.

"No problem," Aaron said and smashed Jake in the mouth.

Jake staggered back, his lips and face numb, his teeth ached. Stunned and outraged, he held his hand to his mouth, glanced at his fingers—saw his own blood.

I don't see any way out of this, Jake thought, and charged at Aaron's mid-section. *I'm in a fight with a cop.*

Aaron pushed Jake back and swung at him—Jake ducked and punched Aaron in the ribs.

It felt like my fist hit wood, that did nothing. The guy's like—armor plated!

"Good shot!" Aaron laughed, "Let's see what else you've got."

"Aaron, stop it!" Vera shrieked.

Everyone paused to rub their neck hairs down from Vera's shrill shriek. Aaron punched Jake twice in the stomach and Jake fell to his knees.

Vera broke free from Levi's grip and ran between Aaron and Jake, her arms outstretched. Jake couldn't breathe, but he noticed more people than before in his peripheral vision.

Three—no, five people, walking over from the farmer's market with I-phones.

Jake took in a ragged breath as he watched the other cops move toward the gathering crowd. One cop moved his hand in a downward motion to the I-phones, the other cop approached Aaron and said something in his ear.

"Take a minute to catch your breath," Aaron said and turned to smile at his buddies.

This is my only chance, Jake thought.

Jake sucked in a breath, shook Vera off, and ran toward Aaron. Aaron heard him and spun around, just as Jake drove in an overhand punch, and luckily hit Aaron in the eye. Aaron held his eye with one hand as Jake, shocked that his punch had connected, punched Aaron in the stomach, then in the side, which did little, but looked impressive. Jake slipped in the mud and fell to his knees again.

Aaron, who now noticed the crowd with their cameras, smiled and held out his hand in a halting gesture near the top of Jake's head.

"Personal matter," Aaron said to the crowd. "It's a fair fight. It doesn't concern you."

"You know what?" Aaron said to Jake. "I'll give you your dues, Frenchy. I guess we're done here. I just wanted to know that Vera wasn't going to end up with some spineless punk. You'd have always wondered, Vera."

Jake pressed his hand against his bruised ribs and managed to stand. Despite the cops' efforts to corral them and confiscate their phones, the pedestrians side-stepped them and continued filming.

"Shake?" Aaron said, stretching his hand out to Jake.

Jake readied his fists, then, reluctantly shook hands with Aaron.

"He's alright, Vera," Aaron said.

"Screw you, Aaron, and your macho bullshit," Vera yelled. "You just couldn't stand that I picked Jake over you. It was *never* going to be you. Every time you had the chance to be a decent human you showed your true colors."

"Yeah, whatever, Vera," Aaron yelled.

Aaron pulled his uniform shirt back on. Aaron, Levi, and Ira walked after the pedestrians, who each jogged in different directions, but kept filming while walking backwards.

"Give me that phone, now!" Levi yelled, but the young man with the phone ran through the tall grass and escaped through the gathering crowd. The two other pedestrians with I-phones split apart as Ira tried to pursue one, then the other.

Vera ran to Jake, wrapped an arm around him and helped him into the back of the limo.

"How pointless that was!" Vera yelled towards Aaron. "What a weak man you are!"

She closed the door behind her. The limo was quiet except for Jake's panting. A faint whirring resounded as the driver rolled down the privacy glass and looked back at Jake.

"I hope you'll be alright, sir," the driver said. "That was quite good fighting considering you've never had a lesson."

"Great. Just take me home, James, okay?" Jake said.

"You fought for me. Nobody's ever fought for me before," Vera said and snuggled up close to Jake.

Is that what I did? Jake thought. *I guess that's what it turned into. I'll take that.* Jake smiled, then winced, as the limo pulled a U-turn.

~

"Are you sure you don't need to go to the hospital?" Vera asked, as she and James walked the limping Jake up the driveway to his condo.

"No, just get me inside," Jake said." I just need to rest."

Inside, Vera led Jake to the couch. "I'll run a hot bath for you," she said.

"I need a drink and some aspirin," Jake said.

~

Jake soaked while Vera sat next to him on a little stool.

"Really, a bubble bath, Vera?" Jake said. "Ouch, it hurts to smile."

"It's Naomi's," Vera said. "I put Epsom salts in there too. What else can I get you?"

"More scotch."

"I feel responsible," Vera said, "Aaron only came after you because of me."

"Did you go out with him or something?"

"Don't be mad. When I moved out of your place and into Bubbe's she tricked me. She invited Aaron over for dinner without telling me until the last minute."

"So, you just had dinner with him and Bubbe?"

"Not exactly. I was mad at you and he asked me out for drinks and to hear some jazz after dinner. Bubbe wouldn't leave me alone about it—Aaron's Jewish, *we're* Jewish, go figure."

"It didn't take you long to get over me," Jake said, sitting up taller in the tub.

"No, Jake. It wasn't like that—not in my mind anyway. Aaron had other ideas."

"Now I want to go fight him all over again," Jake said.

"No, that never should have happened in the first place. But you need to press charges."

"Oh, I don't know, I don't like to get involved in things like that," Jake said.

"You are involved! That fonferer punched you in the mouth. He's supposed to protect the public."

"I would take time away from my work. I really couldn't—what's a "fonferer"?"

"Sorry, its Jewish for a person who acts charming, twists his words and lies to get ahead. Jake, Aaron's walking all over your civil rights. If you don't stand up for yourself, I'm going to lose respect for you."

"Well, we can't have that. Okay, I'll call the police station."

"Thank you," Vera said. She handed him his cell phone and kissed him on the forehead.

~

Aaron, Ira and Levi had hit their favorite cop's bar and tied one on. Their mood was semi-festive because of Aaron's upcoming promotion, but Levi seemed to hold back from full-tilt party mode. Ira just felt bad for his part in supporting the roughing up of an innocent civilian.

~

Aaron was jolted awake from a first-rate hangover by his cell phone ringing.

"Finklestein," Aaron said, and read the word "Dispatch" on his phone.

"Lieutenant, you are to report to the chief's office by 0800 hours."

"Ten-four, Dispatch," Aaron said and hung up.

Aaron looked at his cell again: 7:00 A.M. He showered, changed, and drove to the precinct. He knocked on the chief's door five minutes until eight.

"Come in," the chief said.

"Shut the door and listen. You started a fight with another civilian. That civilian pressed assault charges against you. You beat up on a civilian and three people filmed it this time. What do you have to say?" the chief said.

"But, Chief—"

"Shut up. I don't know exactly how this is going to shake out in court. Fines, jail time, not sure. I *do* know I went out on a limb for you and you let me down. Again. The media is going to crucify us because of you. So, here's what's going to happen as far as your being on the force. You get a demotion, a pay cut, and I'm assigning you to Chesterfield Square."

"That's one of the worst sections of South L.A. I'll have a target on my back!"

"Then you'd better make friends and keep your eyes open."

"But I can still be an asset to the force."

"You will be, we need someone with your temperament there."

"Please, give me a way back, Chief."

"Here's a path: Two years of good cop work, then we can talk a return to lieutenant. Understand, *Sergeant* Finklestein?"

"Yes, sir," Finklestein said and sharply saluted.

"And quit saluting me! Now, go. I'll inform the Civilian Review Board that you're suspended without pay for now."

~

Aaron sat in silence in his cruiser, his mouth agape, just staring at other cops coming and going. His cell rang.

"Finklestein."

"Hello, there, handsome. It's me, Shelley."

"Hey."

"It's been a while. Maybe we could get a drink later," Shelley purred.

"You're on," Aaron said.

Epilogue

Naomi & 13Z

Naomi took the dummy, Human Patient Simulator 370280-13Z, or 13-Z as he liked to be called, in as her roommate. 13-Z was now in permanent ethical mode due to Barry's accidentally smashing the remote control in his pocket with his fist. As a result, it corrected Naomi constantly on her self-centered thinking and slipping into addict behavior. It monitored her diet, pointed out that she must become self-sufficient because Jake's generosity would not last forever. 13-Z also downloaded suitable scripts and scheduled several auditions from film companies seeking actors within the victim/women-in-jeopardy genre for Naomi. It then insisted that she practice, and once prepared, made sure she got to her appointments on time. As a result, Naomi was able to carve out a lucrative living for herself as an actress again. This time by making her own money and building a growing sense of pride in her accomplishments.

Alex

Alex recovered from his injuries and went home to decide what to do with his life. One day he was visited by a lawyer from probate court and was informed that he is sole heir to Barry Whitscomb's estate. The court ordered Falchion Films temporarily shut down until all vendors and debtors were paid. After a month of petitioning the court, with the help of his lawyer, Alex became the executor of Barry's estate.

With Power of Attorney, Alex was able to pay off all debtors and turn on the utilities. Alex realized Falchion was able to cashflow more than $20,000 per month in studio rentals. He learned he had a knack for managing, as well as maintaining the property. He opened Falchion Films to the staff, with Jake in charge.

Jake had done so much to help others that he couldn't afford to finance his revenge horror film, *Vittles*, to get even with You'd Better Run Girl Films for their blockbuster *Sharpest Tool in the Shed.* Alex struck a deal with Jake. Jake could use all Falchion Film's facilities provided Serena was the star. Jake agreed, and Serena starred as lead scream queen in Jake's blockbuster Vittles, with Vera in a supporting role and Lola as the villain.

Alex & Serena

Alex apologized to Serena, but she didn't forgive him. She agreed, however, that he had changed and thought he had become a good person. Alex continued in group therapy and volunteering at a homeless shelter.

He also spent a lot of time hanging out at the beach with his surfer friends. They couldn't convince him to surf, but he watched them from shore with April, the girl he danced with at his first bonfire, who was now his biggest fan. Alex considers Sammy, Otto, and Pete his best friends. Alex and April are still dating.

Aaron

Aaron survived his two-year stint in Chesterfield Square with only one bullet wound to the shoulder, which healed. He was sentenced to anger management classes as well as sensitivity classes and community service by the Civilian Review Board, which he completed. He has since been reassigned to a different district and has been promoted to Lieutenant. He visits Levi and Ira in his old district, where Ira now been promoted to Captain. Aaron has paid off his house and, with help from Zissell, hopes to meet a nice Jewish girl some day and settle down.

Dark Snout & Rhonda

Dark Snout and Rhonda took their vacation in Cuba. After five years, Dark Snout kept his promise and retired. He finally told Rhonda his real name: John Smith. Rhonda returned to the ring after her former manager, Charles, had been fired for embezzling funds. After six months, Rhonda became the undisputed champ of Women's Wrestling in L.A. Mr. and Mrs. John and Rhonda Smith tied the knot shortly after, with all of Rhonda's and John's family in attendance.

Brian and Lola

After six months of dating, Lola felt that she could truly trust Brian to be faithful and became accustomed to pretty girls flirting with him, which Brian uniformly ignored, instead going out of his way to focus all his attention on Lola. They had a justice of the peace wedding with both their families and all Falchion Film's staff in attendance.

Benny

In an A.P. news article, the grisly decomposing remains of Benny Edwards, an American tourist, were found in Argentina, in a closed, boarded up copy shop in what police called an enormous mouse trap. The body was found when nearby business owners complained about the smell.

Barry's Funeral

Felix had shampooed and conditioned Barry's scalp and hair, then brushed it. It was showcased at Barry's funeral. There, the shimmering, glowing, long luxurious auburn hair set upon a blank manakin's head on an ivory satin-covered table, and was dramatically lit from below by Brian. The funeral-goers stood in line to pet and admire the gorgeous hair and pay homage to Barry's life. Vera stroked Barry's hair and became entranced. She could not free her hand because the strands of hair had wrapped tightly around her fingers and would not let go.

Vera screamed for help as her fingers turned blue. Jake and the other mourners moved in and eventually pried the shining strands of hair's death grip from Vera's fingers. Some called the hair tantalizing, others called it evil. Vera said she felt Barry was trying to kill her from the grave. Everyone agreed it was a danger to the public.

The wig was auctioned off to Madame Tussaud's Wax Museum, where it sat perched atop the wax figurine of Barry Whitscomb's likeness—behind protective glass—for all eternity.

Felix and Andy

With Barry and Benny gone, tensions at Falchion eased. Felix and Andy no longer felt compelled to pick on Jake and even formed a friendly working relationship. Jake allowed them to make their films under the Falchion name and *Bavarian Scalps* turned a modest profit.

Jake & Vera

After a joyous reunion between Jake and his mother and sisters, it was clear that Vera had everyone's approval. When Jake asked Zissell for Vera's hand in marriage, Zissell was horrified. She grabbed Vera's hands in hers.

Zissell cried, then kicked Jake in the shin, demanding to know where Aaron was. When it became clear that Zissell would never accept him, and seeing how important Vera's relationship to her grandmother was, Jake offered to convert to Judaism.

After two years of courses, his conversion was complete, and he received Zissell's approval. A traditional Jewish wedding was held and all Zissell's Yiddish friends from the neighborhood attended along with Jake's family.

Six months later, Vera gave birth to a baby girl. The new-born baby's high-pitched shrieking was heard all through the halls of Malibu Memorial Hospital. Nurses and doctors held their hands over their ears as all arm and neck hairs bristled to rigid attention.

Acknowledgements

Of the many people who helped bring this book into existence, I must first thank my wife, Kimmy, for her years of tolerating my writing binges and for listening to my ludicrous ideas. My sister, Merrilea, my muse, who invested years of listening, feedback and suggestions for this and many other stories. My sister, Carla, for reading and listening to this story in its many renditions. Eve Goldberg, for having my back, and for her excellent feedback and for organizing my rough draft into an organized manuscript. A special thanks to Nancy Bourne, Jo-Anne Rosen, Linda Saldana and Richard Gustafson for their superb, in-depth critiques. Guy Biederman for providing a safe and magical learning environment in which to explore creative writing techniques and hone my craft. The members of the Iota Writers Group in its many forms. Toby Cowan for designing the cover and interior of the book and introducing me to the world of self-publishing. Sam LaFever for his custom tweaks to the cover art. Alex LaFever, MD, for answering my medical questions. And finally yet importantly, Morgan Stameroff for answering my string of questions about paramedics and EMTs.